A 'rondel' is the type of insignia marked on all RAF planes in WW2... three concentric circles, red, white and blue. The author selected Henry Rondel as a nom-de-plume which would be unrecognisable and allow him to dissociate himself from it to people who know him.

As a boy, Henry had three ambitions: county cricketer, farmer, and millionaire husband with three children; when John Lennon came along, he added 'paperback writer' to the list. It remains to be seen whether he is a good paperback writer.

Henry hopes you enjoy reading it as much as he enjoyed writing it.

Henry Rondel

THE HUNT FOR COLONEL STRASSER

AUSTIN MACAULEY PUBLISHERS
LONDON · CAMBRIDGE · NEW YORK · SHARJAH

Copyright © Henry Rondel 2025

The right of Henry Rondel to be identified as author of this work has been asserted by the author in accordance with sections 77 and 78 of the Copyright, Designs and Patents Act 1988.

All rights reserved. No part of this publication may be reproduced, stored in a retrieval system, or transmitted in any form or by any means, electronic, mechanical, photocopying, recording, or otherwise, without the prior permission of the publishers.

Any person who commits any unauthorised act in relation to this publication may be liable to criminal prosecution and civil claims for damages.

This is a work of fiction. Names, characters, businesses, places, events, locales, and incidents are either the products of the author's imagination or used in a fictitious manner. Any resemblance to actual persons, living or dead, or actual events is purely coincidental.

A CIP catalogue record for this title is available from the British Library.

ISBN 9781528911993 (Paperback)
ISBN 9781528959964 (ePub e-book)

www.austinmacauley.com

First Published 2025
Austin Macauley Publishers Ltd®
1 Canada Square
Canary Wharf
London
E14 5AA

WW2, Pilot Officer Martin Cohen, shot down near Hanover, is "killed" in cold blood by SS Colonel General Strasser following a failed escape attempt from the Menzenschwand Prisoner of War Camp, in Southern Germany.

Escaping to the British Embassy in Berne, Martin discovers Strasser controls a syndicate hoarding looted gold in a Zurich Bank; suspecting that the hoard has been discovered Strasser transfers the gold to a bank in Lucerne.

Acting on Martin's information, the UK, US and Russian Ambassadors unite and open a "Second Front". Embassy staff ambush the gold on its transfer to Lucerne, Swiss civilians are killed; the Swiss President declares war on Great Britain.

Colonel General Hans Strasser (his brother Gregor shot by Hitler) escapes from the ambush: to cover his tracks, he uses his revolver to shoot his batman who had also escaped, dumping the body in a remote forest pool.

Learning that Martin Cohen, his former prisoner, organised the ambush, he lures him to the "Rhine Falls Hotel" where he uses the same revolver to shoot Martin in the bowel; a defective bullet saves Martin's life, and during his recovery he plans revenge.

His chance comes, as Hitler's war grinds towards Germany's defeat, Martin is posted to a British detachment at Bad Ischl, Austria, charged with hunting down Nazi war criminals. Ebensee, slave labour camp, site of a synthetic oil plant set inside a mountain, was part of Colonel Strasser's industrial empire, making him a war criminal, and a target for Martin's obsession: revenge.

Martin Cohen, however, was not the only in Strasser's little black book; as the war belches to its final days, as the Russians close on Berlin, Strasser flies to the Fuhrer bunker determined to avenge his brother Gregor before it is too late.

And so, our tale begins: one dark and stormy night.

Chapter 1
The Alpine Festung

Early 1944, midnight, Martin Bormann, long an admirer, long-standing second-in-command to Adolf Hitler, clears his desk in the office leading off the Fuhrer's apartments in the Berghaus, Hitler's Alpine Home and Retreat, surrounded by mountains at Berchtesgaden, Bavaria. A reading lamp, its beam rebounding off white painted walls, illuminates a solitary desk set square in the middle of the room. Chairs no longer line the bare walls as the furniture has already been taken away.

Russian armies, for he has fully realised where the main threat lies.

Decision taken, orders issued, Hitler's personal staff are moving lock, stock and barrel to the Wolf's Lair, Army Battle HQ, in the Rustenburg Forest, to be closer to his generals and to a Russian front, drawing ever closer, as each river, from the Dnieper to the Don to the Vistula, is crossed.

The final ceremonial train to transport the Fuhrer's entourage had been summoned days earlier, cleaned, guarded and victualled; too long at 15 carriages it overhung the single village platform, like a bratwurst in a finger bun, the long shining engine has been shunted back and forwards to allow easy loading up these carriages, now the engine sits quietly steaming, one hundred metres up the line from Berchtesgaden Station, awaiting what will prove to be its final departure, though this was never intended. The moment the Fuhrer steps up from the platform carpet to the coach painted in the colours of the National Socialist Party is the moment all the signals from Berchtesgaden to Salzburg, 40 km away, clang to green simultaneously.

At the Berghaus, the drop-head Mercedes Tourer, roof down against the cold night air, waits to sweep Adolf Hitler down the mountain to the station and the waiting train; this Mercedes used for all party rallies, is not to be risked near the Russian Front, not to be risked its very presence would advertise an assassination opportunity for a dissident General, not to be risked on autobahns threatened night and day in 1944 by Allied bombers.

On this last night Bormann had excused himself from watching *Bambi*, the Hollywood film supplied by Goebbels Office for Hitler and Eva Braun's pleasure, pleading administrative work arising from the decisions at the afternoon's conference. Always hungry; a plate of beef and pickles, bottles of Bamberg wheat beer and Gertrude, a plump Swabian blonde, at hand meant that cutlery, glasses and contraceptives were unnecessary, power through work came first with Bormann, appetites followed, the desk the only furniture, the best was to be left till last provided the film didn't finish too early and that the Fuhrer did not linger over his farewells.

Bormann, diligent, intelligent, avoiding cut-throat duels with rivals in the hierarchy, had long cemented his role as Hitler's gate master, through loyalty and by implementing his leader's political decisions effectively. Wisely he had never sought military command, unlike Himmler, who cut little ice as an Army Commander, in the field and little ice as a slight diminutive figure amongst tall SS von Prussian Generals. "Army Commands" after Stalingrad were a rhyming mixture of retreat and defeat, with only Field Marshall Erwin Rommel retaining his status as a national war hero and only Goering retaining popular affection.

Out of public gaze, Bormann's family, lived quietly in an Alpine chalet by the lake at Altaussee, beyond commuting distance of the Berghaus, where Bormann stayed and worked so as to be at the Fuhrer's beck and call, rather like Eva Braun, Hitler's long-standing girlfriend.

Rarely crossing swords with drug-dependent Goering; Goebbels acknowledged Bormann's competence, though Bormann privately regarded Goebbels as the "poisoned dwarf", he also privately thought it probable that Goebbels's family (realistic of his own family's talents) might inherit the Reich, by virtue of Goebbels and Magda's six splendid children, but more particularly by virtue of Goebbels control of German cinema, news, press and radio.

Reality had been faced front-on at that afternoon's meeting. Hitler had recognised the deteriorating situation on the Russian and Mediterranean Fronts, the nervousness about the Allied build-up and the Atlantic Wall, without splenetic outbursts of rage. Speer's drive to increase weapons output by increasing food rations and improving conditions in the concentration camps had been approved; Rommel was to take effective command of the Atlantic Wall. Bormann was working into the night, alone in his office, because the Fuhrer had stopped dead further planning and construction of an

Alpine fortress for a fight to the death by SS diehards, should Germany's armies be defeated.

Bormann had had to countermand himself, for it was he who had approved and led the drive for the planning and construction of a "festung", and he himself had drafted the authorising document recommending the Obersalzberg as the location for a fortress, with underground construction to begin within 60 days of final site selection, with completion within 10 months. The festung to be armed and provisioned for a six-month siege, and a nucleus of volunteer "werewolves" identified.

Quietly and rationally Hitler had summarised his position: appreciating his supporters might wish to maintain the honour of the 3rd Reich by fighting on, construction of a "festung", would raise doubts that the war was going to be won and would divert resources away from front-line troops. He forbade outright the planning or construction of a "festung". 'Unnecessary, we are winning and will go on to win this war.' A firm message indeed as Bormann recognised, but he realised as well as the generals in Russia, that after their failure to rescue Paulus's 6th army, the subsequent surrender at Stalingrad, the failure to capture Leningrad and Moscow, that the swift total promised victory in Russia was now impossible. Furthermore, ever heavier and more frequent RAF air raids on German cities had resulted in the people beginning to realise that the constant retreats from Russia signalled disaster and that victory was now years away even if it remained achievable.

Only in the officer's messes of generals fighting on the Ukrainian and Byelorussian fronts was this realisation clearer than with mothers receiving letters from their sons at the front, and wives in lonely apartments, reading letters bordered in black, from officers telling them of the brave death of their husbands. (Black borders were later banned.)

The Fuhrer's cancellation of Bormann's plans for a "festung" dictated that to preserve face these plans must be destroyed, Bormann's name must be removed, references to the plans and from the instructions to prepare those plans, likewise. He burnt the midnight oil to feed paper down to the Berghaus incinerator, messages were sent to the SS both in Russia, Berlin and the West: 'All references to the "Kiel Project" must be destroyed immediately.'

Pressure of work, under-resourced, lack of investment were the excuses British and American Army Intelligence gave after the war for their failure to follow up on both cipher and humint knowledge and pick up what was happening to the German plans for Central Europe. The festung cancellation was not picked up, and the allies subsequently wasted time and resources in efforts to locate a non-existent festung.

Following a tap on the door, an aide entered, 'The train is ready, but we are having to re-route as the tracks around Nuremberg have been damaged, perhaps we should prepare to leave early.' Sighing Bormann got up and reached for his jacket. Eva Braun was nowhere to be seen.

Michael, veteran driver of the Fuhrer's train, cheeks aged and lined, forehead creased, pulling down the control lever, he turned to his young apprentice, 'This may be the last time, Charlie.'

Charlie, poker-faced, had his shovel poised and with a deft flourish scooped up a kilogram of anthracite and threw it into the roar of the fiery furnace. He hadn't heard.

Mick repeated, 'This may be the last time.'

'The last time, Mick?'

'I don't know!'

Six months since their last meeting, Colonel Hans Strasser sat across the Sutherland table from his totally trusted sister, the only light coming from the drawing room window overlooking the village green focal centre of the medieval village of Dillsburg. This house, built into the original fortifications, was linked to the church by an underground tunnel, before plunging under the foundations of the surrounding wall, to emerge in anonymity in a crevice down in the woods.

The only other exit to Dillsburg was the one-track road over the drawbridge before winding down to Heidelberg and the river Neckar, two hiking hours distant.

In or out of uniform Colonel Strasser dressed with class, visiting his sister, his bearing spoke of a wealthy Bavarian gentleman farmer, thus it was a hurt to prestige as painfully, he outlined the serious setback that caused the delay to his regular six-monthly visit.

'Don't know how they managed it, but the British planted a bug at my conference at that herder's village of Psalm, above Luven I told you about.'

We'd decided on the allocation of the funds and assets held in Zurich, and we agreed our alibi, that if the Gestapo or the SS found out that we were holding assets in Switzerland. We'd originally thought we'd say it was a fund to construct a festung for Hitler, but we changed this and decided that rather than claim it was to construct a death-defying festung, it would be more convincing to claim it was to construct a Statue of Adolf Hitler.

Wasserburg owned a site, and we would produce preliminary plans for the statue to be sited at the confluence of the Rhine and Moselle. The Statue was to be bigger than the Statue of Liberty; it would be on the Koblenz bank of the Rhine, opposite Fortress Ehrenbreitstein and the National Archive. Hitler would be in his party uniform; he would face upstream, looking towards the Lorelei Rocks and the castle on the hill. It would be a statement for Europe and a landmark for the world.'

'Never! You wouldn't,' his sister jerked forward in her chair.

'Don't worry […] only a cover story, never going to happen. The money in that fund was for me, Wasserburg and Seydlitz, nobody else, but we needed a cover story if it was traced.'

'Anyhow the three of us had a talk, and as the Syndicate had been breached and Zurich was known, we decided to move everything out, the gold, the icons, the jewellery, everything to Lucerne, I decided to use BBBB. We hired a van, Wasserburg brought one of his men, I took three of mine as escorts, and there were a couple of Swiss with the van, Seydlitz didn't come, he was seeing Goering about more furnishing for Carinhall.'

'Pont Celere, on the road to Lucerne, they ambushed us, English and Russians, they surprised us, they hijacked us, they blew us off the road; we didn't stand a chance, only me, my batman and Corporal Muller lived, the others were all killed. I escaped, but my batman died from injuries, and Muller went to hospital injured. Fifty million of our money gone in a flash.'

'So you've lost some of your money?' Sister didn't sound too concerned.

'More than some, nearly everything, and I need to get some back quick.' He stood up, 'I might have a proposition for you, Sis,' he paused, putting on his most serious face, 'supposing I brought you the Duke and Duchess of Saxe-Coburg-Gotha to stay as paying guests, what would you say?'

'I'd say—why?'

'The duke's head of the German Red Cross, he's born English, if the war ends badly and he is caught, he's afraid he'd be killed. He might be looking quite soon for somewhere safe to lie low; although he's English, he's all but German after 40 years here, he's a decent fellow, but he's getting nervous.'

'Leave it with me,' Sister hadn't said no.

It was time to go, before kissing goodbye, he poured what remained of the Bernkastel and raised his glass.

'To brother Gregor,' he said, 'rest in peace.'

'To brother Otto,' the sister raised her glass, 'wherever in America you are.'

'Certain death,' they spoke in unison, 'Adolf Hitler.' They had done this before, their glasses were much too old, much too fine, much too part of a set, to throw to the floor, not at any rate until they were toasting the real death of Adolph Hitler.

At the door as he was leaving, 'I'm going to get that English prisoner who organised the ambush, Martin Cockburn is his name.'

Colonel General Hans Strasser drove back to Austria alone, none of his staff in Command HQ in Salzburg, not even newly promoted Sergeant Muller, knew where he had been.

Chapter 2
The Shooting of Martin Cohen

Here our story tracks back in time.

1944, Martin Cohen, was working as an "illegal" out of the British Embassy, Berne. He intercepted a wire-tap—the ambushed remains of the German Syndicate whose gold they had taken, were to meet at the Rhine Fall Hotel, Schaffhausen, which lay in Switzerland just over the German border. Needing support Martin took Nigel Buonaparte, an embassy colleague; booking into the hotel, arriving the evening before the meeting, their twin bedroom (the embassy didn't do luxury for spying) was in the middle of a long corridor, lying deep in the heart of the hotel. They had both showered and Martin was drying himself, when a rap on the door had Nigel saying, 'Come in.'

Martin said, 'Who is it?'

The door opened, their visitor stepped over the threshold:

'Colonel General Strasser,' the words were spat out through clenched teeth.

Raising his arm, Strasser pointed the pistol at Martin's stomach and fired.

Martin fell back, Nigel jumped forward, but a bed in his way, before he could grapple with the attacker, Colonel

General Strasser was back in the corridor and hurrying away, leaving the door open. Uncertain, not wanting to be shot himself, Nigel turned back to see to Martin.

Martin was sitting upright on the bed his back against the headboard, his underpants, the loose cotton garment nearest to hand was drenched in blood which had spread as far as his knees; clutching his stomach, Martin was trying to free a bed sheet in an attempt use a corner to press purple-red innards back into his body.

'Help,' gasping, coughing, clutching and pressing his stomach ever more strongly, as blood welled out with each cough. He closed his eyes, still pressing on his stomach. Nigel shoved a pillow under his head before grabbing clean towels from the bathroom to soak up blood, replace the sheet and underpants, and to press over the hole in Martin's stomach.

It is wonderful what ordinary people and Swiss doctors can do in an emergency. No telephone in the room, a naked Nigel ran down the long corridor to get help from the hotel lobby, with the porter they helped a barely conscious Martin into a car, within five minutes they had reached, the Schaffhausen Hospital 900 yards down the road.

The Swiss surgical team had a clean, naked, shaved, unconscious Martin on the operating table within the hour, with the surgeon scrubbed up and the instruments and dressings all checked by the nurses.

Martin had lost so much blood the surgeon wondered aloud whether "he" would "lose him", but "they", the nurses, didn't and Martin lived. So confident were the operating team, as the last stitch was pulled tight, that they had done a good job, that they were all in bed and asleep before the stroke of midnight, leaving the task of looking after Martin through to the light of day to a single nurse—Steffie.

Four hours after lights out, Martin, still naked, was asleep in his own room, under his own steam as it was hooked up to oxygen, a drip, a blood supply with tubes appearing out of different areas of his stomach, and with a regular bleep from three gleaming pieces of apparatus. Staff nurse Steffie parted the curtains surrounding his bed every 10 minutes to check mercury levels in the dials and the levels of drip and blood supply in the glass bottles. It was morning before Martin made out silhouettes drifting around his bed.

His pulse getting stronger and regular as time went on, visitors came and went, nurse Steffie was followed by nurses Jean, Wendy, Yvonne, Margaret and Susan, with Martin none the wiser as to who they were, only Steffie, Steffie—his lifeline.

At the end of the month, on his first "better day", the surgeon who had led the operating team, came to see him, he had the nurses prop him up and between their changing dressings he made an extended full body examination, comparing current measurements with the various charts and reports handed to him by Matron. He sat down on the end of the bed, well away from all the tubes, taking his time he put his glasses back in his case and his case back in his pocket.

'Well, young man, I'd better tell you what you've missed whilst you've been hibernating,' Martin muttered.

'Miss Cowperthwaite has called in every day. Mr Buonaparte, who helped to save your life by getting you to the hospital so swiftly, has been in, and Sir Pelham Sinclair and Lady Sinclair from the embassy sent flowers and visited the day after you were shot, I don't suppose you remember any of that. You're a lucky man and a highly regarded young man.' Martin again muttered and nodded, going through the motions of following, being barely interested until the doctor changed the tone.

'Not only the British, other nations have enquired, Germany I'm told a German-speaking woman rings every day; Chief Inspector Tonneau from Berne City Police was so concerned about your welfare that for five days he had a policeman keep you company in the ward. Whether to make sure no one came in to finish you off, take a statement before you died, or to make certain you didn't do a runner, I don't know, he never told me; not till l assured the Inspector that you'd survive, did the guard leave, but the Inspector hasn't forgotten you. He'll be back on Monday when I've told him you'll be fit to answer questions.' The doctor got up, pulled back the remaining curtain and roamed around the room.

'Obviously, Mr Cohen, is it Cohen, the police have you down as Cockburn, as a Swiss, it's my duty to help the police, obviously, I want you to help the police as well, but there's a war on I know, so don't feel you must talk to the Inspector if you don't feel ready. Anyhow, he'll be here on Monday, and I'll tell him he's only got an hour for questions.' Martin struggled to speak.

'What's wrong with me doctor, what's the…' he struggled again, 'the damage, the prognosis?' The doctor sat down on the bed again.

'First, if we continue to keep peritonitis at bay you'll live. We'll need to suck, I mean clear, heavy waste products out of your body artificially for a period, you're still on gruel as I'm sure you've noticed, you're still weak and passing ordure will be difficult for months, but eventually the passages will strengthen, the tubes will come out and you should be able to live a long life without public embarrassment.'

'No bags and no sex?' Martin wanted to know, speaking with more animation than he had shown for a month.

'Yes, absolutely, no bags, you're patched up, no sex, well, that's up to you,' he paused. 'As far as the actual damage done, you were very lucky, one or both cartridges were faulty. It was only a revolver I understand, their force was weak, one bullet didn't even breach the abdominal wall, so only half the damage your attacker intended, actually happened, also the one bullet that did penetrate finished in the middle of the large intestine, it made a mess but it didn't do too much damage to the fiddly bits. But you lost a large quantity of blood, I've managed to patch you up, and so long as no complications set in, you'll be fine. Your blood pressure and sperm count are already better than mine.'

Cheered by the good news, Martin spoke:

'Two bullets, I know why the bullet was faulty, the Germans use slave labour to make ammunition, I've seen it before, I saw it at Dachau (actually he hadn't); their workers, Poles, Czechs, are always feeding imperfections into the components, they're shot if they're caught. It's not only you who saved my life, Doctor, it's Stefan and Margaretha, Czech workers and thank god after the war I'll have St Stephen's crown to take back to them.' He lay back exhausted. Doctor wandered to the other side of the bed,

'I've done one or two things to the wounds on your body from your plane crash, but there are still bits of a Wellington's petrol tank in your back, but at least the burn markings have all but healed and disappeared.' The doctor wandered back to the other side of the bed.

'You said two bullets, there were three, two in your gut, the third carried away one of your balls—clean as a whistle, that's why you lost so much blood. Mr Cohen, you're the same as Hitler—one ball.'

'One ball, three bullets, why didn't anybody tell me, how did it hit a ball and miss the old man.'

'It was a miracle, the third bullet embedded your ball in the hotel wall, I didn't need to tell you, I waited to tell you were well.'

'Does Hillary know?'

'Don't think so.'

'What do I tell her? I told her there were two bullets.'

'Rest up now,' the doctor made as if to shake hands, but Martin was annoyed and too tired to pull his hand from under the sheet, Martin mumbled something, his eyes following the doctor through the door. *Shouldn't have mentioned St Steven's crown,* he said to himself, *Is it spelt with a 'v' or a 'p'? Is Margaretha a Czech name?*

No sooner had the surgeon disappeared than Hillary came in, before anything else, she drew the curtains, he rallied, they both cried, she wiped his eyes, she held his hands, she leaned across and gave him a kiss, but there were few words except 'love you', 'how are you' and 'love you', 'I'm going to be all right', Martin stroked the skirt, the only thing in reach or on offer, the only target that was within the reach of his tired hand,' before she left Martin low voiced told her the second thing what was on his mind:

'What do I tell Inspector Tonneau, you remember him, he was the Swiss Inspector in charge of investigating the ambush?'

Hillary departed, a handkerchief to her eyes. In the corridor, she burst into tears.

Martin suffered a relapse during the night. His temperature soared, peritonitis was diagnosed, a second operation was necessary and was performed before lunch, then a stitch gave way. Clinging to life a third operation was necessary as nurse Steffie nursed the infection as diligently as before; it had become personal.

'It was another pesky little fragment of petrol tank there from your crash, it was hidden in the abdominal wall, but it's out now,' the doctor told him, as he cheated death for the third time.

Inspector Tonneau could be put off no longer and a day and a time for an interview were agreed, Sir Pelham Sinclair, the British Ambassador, insisting that an embassy official be present as an observer.

Roger Greville, 1st Secretary, Chief Inspector Tonneau and a Police note taker gathered around Martin's bed; it was a sunny Thursday afternoon. Up till this stay in the hospital, Martin's focus had always been on a girl's legs, but flat from his bed the hemline was mostly invisible, and his attention had switched to the upper deck. He smiled at the note takers 36 font, San Serif bold, he estimated.

Greville arrived early, together they discussed the likely questions and prepared possible answers for the Inspector, Tonneau, impatient after waiting many weeks and never a man to beat about the bush, came straight to the point.

'Who shot you, Mr Cockburn?' (Although Martin's surname was Cohen, the fiction of Cockburn, [pronounced Co'burn] had been maintained in documents in both Germany and Switzerland.)

'I don't know, Inspector, I'd never seen him before.'

'You clearly saw him if you can say so definitely you'd never seen him before. Could you recognise him again?'

'I suppose so,' said Martin, knowing Strasser would be a corpse if he ever set eyes on him again and if he had any say in the matter.

'Good, we'll run some pictures past you later, but who would want to kill you? Let me rephrase that, who would want to deliberately inflict horrible life-threatening injuries on you? Mr Buonaparte has told me your gunman deliberately aimed his pistol at your stomach.'

'I was hoping you'd come here to tell me that, Inspector.'

'Well, I can't, perhaps when the police finally establish what happened and who was responsible for the ambush at Pont Celere, we will both know. You were at the ambush at Pont Celere; perhaps it was one of the losers at Pont Celere, who were the losers at Pont Celere, Mr Cockburn?'

Martin paused for a moment, although Sir Pelham Sinclair had, along with the USA and Russia, made a large attributable charitable contribution to a victims' fund, no admission of being involved in the ambush of gold at Pont Celere or responsibility for the deaths of Swiss civilians had been made. The capturing of gold from traitorous Nazis in a hijack of their road convoy was triumphed by the three ambassadors internally as: "The opening of *The Second Front*", but the Swiss Government regarded it as an assault on Switzerland itself. Allied involvement had been difficult to keep a secret, in fact, it was fictional non-involvement, with Foreign Secretaries glorying in the recovery of sterling, dollars and kopeks, and the restoration of icons, porcelain, amber, paintings and gold to their safekeeping. Swiss Civilian deaths, the attitude in London and Washington to Swiss Public Relations was:

'What Swiss public relations? Win the war—we'll look at public relations afterwards.' Whilst Moscow who didn't at that time have words in their vocabulary equivalent to "public relations" merely added an unnoticed six to the millions of deaths already recorded as "casualties".

Martin cautiously admitted:

'Not myself, but I imagine there were losers at Pont Celere in addition to those actually killed.'

'And the nationality of the people losing out at the ambush?' Tonneau had raised his eyebrows.

'Germans I suppose.'

'Not our Swiss farmers then, Germans from their embassy, or Germans coming over our border from units stationed in Bavaria?'

'Can't help there, Chief Inspector.'

'Make an educated guess,' Tonneau was stopped by Greville.

'Mr Cohen may not know, but it is public knowledge that the dead Germans didn't come from their embassy, the Germans at Pont Celere invaded Switzerland illegally and came across the border, it is now public knowledge they had a confrontation with persons unknown; Mr Cockburn has been laid up here for well over a month, he hasn't read the papers, we understand the Germans came into Switzerland by car, their vehicles were wrecked at the scene, they must have entered Switzerland directly from Bavaria. This line of questioning is not appropriate for Mr Cockburn.' Tonneau brushed him aside:

'Were you at Pont Celere?'

The two answers were simultaneous:

Martin said, 'Non.' Greville said he couldn't allow Martin to answer.

Chief Inspector Tonneau turned to a different line of questioning:

'I'm prepared to assume you weren't at the ambush at Point Celere, in a way it doesn't matter, but I wish to ask for helpful hypothetical not attributable answers on some sensitive matters. Let me ask about another interesting point that has arisen.' He looked down at his notes.

'Witnesses have said there was a gunfight between Russians and two Germans travelling in the end car, and that these two Germans escaped and ran back in the forest in the direction of Zurich. One of these men had a false arm, they said. Theoretically, do you agree, Mr Cockburn?'

Martin glanced at Greville, who nodded.

'Yes, I agree,' said Martin, 'theoretically, of course.'

'Thank you; witnesses also observed a dead Russian being carried out of the forest and taken away in a van. Hypothetically could you confirm that this was possible please?'

'That might well be true, Inspector.'

'Now we come to the mystery, those two men from the last car, believed to be Germans fled the scene, over an hour later, single-handedly, one man with a false arm, resembling one of the two who escaped from the ambush at Pont Celere, tall with fair hair, hijacked a car, three miles down the road back in the direction of Zurich. This car was later found abandoned in the station car park at Emmerich Village, at Emmerich, one tall, fair-haired man alone caught the stopping train to Zurich, one man. Why only one man, when we know two escaped together from the ambush?'

Martin shook his head, 'If two men escaped together, I imagine they split up. When I escaped from Menzenschwand prison camp, two of us escaped. We split up.'

The inspector continued: 'Thank you, that's exactly what I thought, Mr Cockburn, exactly what I thought, Mr Greville,' who had been nodding his head, 'until yesterday when I received this astonishing report, this astonishing forensic report.'

Tonneau paused for effect, flourishing a sheet of foolscap, 'I suggest you take time to examine this forensic report, later and in detail. It makes for an interesting reading.'

He went on: 'It states: on the 20th of August, a group of schoolboys rambling in the woods between Pont Celere and Emmerich had a gruesome experience, a nasty experience, a very nasty experience, I would say. Stripped off, naked, swimming in a forest pool, one of the boys, Peter Leach perfecting the crawl, struck with his hand an eyeball, an eyeball in the process of separating from a man's head, an eyeball which he clasped in his hand. After he'd recovered from the shock, the boys searched the pool, as brave as they were successful, they found the body and the head that had held the eyeball, they even had the courage to lift the body out of the pool, brave of them don't you think?'

Following murmurs of agreement, Tonneau continued, 'Who do we think it was, well, we don't have to guess, although much decomposed, it was still recognisable as the body of an SS German soldier, not any SS soldier, it was a private,' he paused, 'I must respect confidentiality here, we know exactly who it was because his army number is tattooed on his arm, I expected the SS to tell us exactly who that number related to, I expected them to ask for the body to be taken back to Germany and for them to mount an enquiry, but they haven't. Invoking a special protocol, a Colonel Strasser requests us to bury the body as an unidentified deserter. What do you think of that, Mr Cockburn? The Germans can't identify him, but I can because his identity paper was in a sealed cellophane bag. Tell me, what do you think?'

'Not very much, what's it got to do with me?' was the reply.

'I don't see the point of bombarding Mr Cockburn with these questions,' Greville remained on the case.

'Bear with me a moment, speculate, who do you expect the body to be, Mr Cockburn?'

'The escaped, wounded soldier from Pont Celere seems probable,' offered Martin.

'Could you identify him, Mr Cockburn?'

'Oh no, I wasn't there of course and if death is recent and an SS man. Like you, Tonneau, I assume it's the injured man who fled from Pont Celere and died from his injuries.' Tonneau moved around the bed to be directly away from Greville's gaze and to stare directly at Martin.

'As did I, until this forensic report landed on my desk, this forensic report which I hope you'll take the trouble to read, states the SS soldier died between three and four months ago, killed by a pistol shot in the head from short range—less than a metre.'

Although Martin hadn't been asked a question, he ventured a reply.

'Perhaps his wounds were so serious it was a mercy killing.' Tonneau composed himself, poised to pull his masterstroke, he looked Martin directly in the eye.

'Yes, I wondered about that as well, but there were no other wounds, then something remarkable happened, this morning three rooms away, in this very hospital,' he gestured with his left hand. 'I compared the bullet taken from behind the eye socket of the dead SS soldier with the two bullets Dr Cocteau pulled out of your crotch here at the hospital and guess what I found,' he paused again.

'A MATCH, we have a match, gentlemen, three bullets, all fired from the same gun, what do you think of that, Mr Cockburn? The gun that shot the SS man, his head fished out of a forest pool, fired the bullets the surgeons fished out of your stomach, it's the same gun that fired the bullets into your stomach in your hotel bedroom at the Rhine Falls Hotel, bullets fired by a complete stranger, so you told me. Now, further forensic is needed, but you can take it from me, as a policeman with 25 years of experience on the murder squad, the bullets match,' he paused.

'When you are back on your feet, I'll show them to you. I might even let you keep one as a memento, but tell me, how am I to explain this to my Chief of Police, explain to my Minister, Mr Greville? Tell me how you explain identical bullets in Mr Cockburn and this dead German soldier?'

It was a bombshell no one had been expecting. The low regular slurp from the blood pump was the only sound to be heard as the men considered whether to simply shrug and plead ignorance. Martin looked towards Greville, who was the first to speak.

'This is all very interesting, but I'm not sure that Mr Cohen has anything to explain, Inspector, assuming you are correct, and a full forensic confirms that the bullets match, then there are either two identical guns, or the same gun fired both sets of bullets; but fired by the same gun doesn't mean the same person pulled the trigger. You don't tell us what sort of gun it was, guns get passed around all the time, as I'm sure you'll agree.'

Tonneau snorted, 'A coincidence, I'm surprised at you, Mr Greville. A gun shuttled 200 miles between two different men to two different shootings at Pont Celere and Schaffhausen, when we know a tall, fair-haired man fired at Mr Cockburn in Room 27, and a tall, fair man boarded a train at the Emmerich Train Halt within an hour of splitting from the dead SS man, enemy action 200 miles apart, months apart in time, I don't think so, Mr Greville. I just ask you to give me the motive.' Tonneau spoke more in sorrow than in anger, turning to Martin.

'Now your companion in the hotel; Mr Buonaparte has described the man who shot at you as tall, blonde and with an artificial hand. Can you confirm that, Mr Cockburn?'

'I suppose so,' Martin hesitated, annoyed that Nigel had mentioned Strasser's loss of a hand, 'I can't say about his hands, but he was tall and fair.'

'Mr Cockburn, when I find who shot this yet unnamed SS soldier and who dragged him down the bank and threw him in the pool, I will have found your assailant. You must want to help, throw me a name, any name.'

Martin shook his head, 'Then at least tell me why you and Mr Buonaparte travelled to Schaffhausen at short notice, booked in at the Rhine Hotel, for just the one night. The night you were shot within an hour of your arrival.'

Once again, Greville intervened.

'Martin and Mr Buonaparte were in Schaffhausen on confidential embassy business, Chief Inspector, as much as we want to help, I cannot allow Mr Cockburn to answer these questions.'

Tonneau hadn't quite finished; he turned again towards Martin:

'Who were you meeting in Schaffhausen? I need a name, and why you and not Mr Buonaparte was shot?'

'And so do I, Inspector Tonneau, and so do I.' Martin still staggered at what Inspector Tonneau had revealed, turning over and over in his mind why on earth Strasser should have shot the SS man and dumped his body in a forest pool.

The questions grumbled on,

'After this time, are you really expecting to find who shot Mr Cockburn?' Greville finally asked, anxious to bring the questioning to an end.

'Frankly—no, Mr Greville, German bullets, Russians at Pont Celere, a dead Henry Vert's body thrown over a wall, the Englishman gentleman falling off the Wetterhorn, now an SS soldier dead in a forest pond, and the common factor in all these deaths—all are linked, Mr Greville, in some way to Mr Cockburn a Mr Cockburn missing from our immigration records, at the same time as we have a dead border guard on a direct line between Menzenschwand Prison Camp and Berne, none of these cases cleared up, the Swiss police are having a bad run, Mr Greville, I am having a bad run, but a frank statement from Mr Cockburn, telling me everything he knows, would help to resolve some of the puzzles rattling around my mind.'

Greville caught up with Chief Inspector Tonneau in the corridor as he left: 'A word off the record if I may, it may help,' he opened, 'the British Government appreciates the competence and confidentiality you have brought to your enquiry, but we wonder why SS Colonel General Hans Strasser should have risked crossing the border to travel to Schaffhausen to shoot a member of my Consulate.'

'Colonel Strasser, why him?' asked Tonneau.

'No reason except I know he only has one hand, and you say he has requested that the dead SS man be treated as an unidentified deserter,' came the reply.

As if speaking to himself Tonneau said, 'Perhaps he came to avenge the dead border guard who we believe Mr Cockburn shot in his escape from a German Prison Camp, or revenge over the theft of the gold, probably only Cockburn and the colonel know the real reason, and neither of them is talking to me.' The men went out to their respective cars.

That night Martin had an erection.

Gleefully he reported the event back to nurse Steffie, 'I've had a stiffie, Steffie,' was how he put it.

Steffie clapped her hands, 'I'm so glad,' she told Hillary. Martin couldn't wait for Hillary's next visit.

Hillary, who had come for the weekend, staying at the Rhine Hotel, hoping to pick up gossip from the staff about the shooting, was delighted, 'Before you show me,' she said, 'I want to know how we're going to get our own back at SS Colonel Hans Strasser, so you'd better start thinking about that, never mind your bodily functions.' The listening device below the mattress stirred into action, installed after the

Minister's call to the hospital's administrator; as well as Greville, Chief Inspector Tonneau had his name direct from the horse's mouth.

Hillary reported that Nigel Buonaparte had drawn a blank on uncovering the source of leakage of information from the Berne Embassy. Only two people knew they had gone to the Schaffhausen Hotel. Martin's investigations into Gustav Holst, banker husband of Brenda Chan, Sir Pelham Sinclair's private secretary, were getting nowhere, progress must wait for his recovery and return to the Berne Embassy.

From his bed, they planned revenge on Strasser, it wasn't easy, the best, the only thing, they came up with, was to send poison pen letters with detail of the Syndicate's activities to SS and Nazi Party officials in Salzburg and Munich.

Hillary's draft detailed how Strasser hid Reich gold and art in secret deposits in Swiss Banks, that the Allies found out and hijacked the gold when the Syndicate transferred it from a Zurich bank to one in Lucerne. Not knowing any names, the letters would have to be sent to the titles of positions like "Director of Personnel", rather than to named individuals. Together they composed a guess list of Regional Officialdom.

Then Martin had an idea. 'Konstanz is German, but half the town is in Switzerland and operates on the Bavarian phone network. The Swiss Constitution doesn't allow calls to and from banks to be monitored. We have two numbers for Strasser's department, go to Konstanz, dial and get transferred to other departments, get some names, put numbers, positions and titles together, you never know what we might find,' Hillary was dubious.

'Could we really do that from outside Germany? What would I say?' She had tumbled that with Martin lying in a

Swiss hospital, he was going to delegate this trip to Konstanz to her, and she wasn't keen.

'Don't know until we try it, are you up for it. No risk?'

Together they worked on a script, Hillary would go to Konstanz, phone German numbers and try to get into their system.

It worked, from the Swiss area of Konstanz town, the German phone network was accessed automatically without raising suspicion. Once accepted into the phone system at back-office level, she found it easy to be transferred up to the hierarchy, within an hour, she had earmarked seven men holding titles and positions where a poison pen letter might harm Strasser. Hillary soon had her own little phone book of numbers with the names of Germans holding specific office positions.

Rain at the hospital, mist fought with rain and spray over the Rhine Falls. At last Martin's red-letter day had arrived: only one valve protruded, draining down to once a night. Intercourse would be easy, if he could match Hillary's enthusiasm. The ambassador's black Rolls Royce drew up at the hospital; the chauffeur tucked the blanket around a wincing Martin wan, sick and uncertain about leaving the cocoon of a warm hospital.

By the end of his second day back at the embassy, Martin had read everything available on Gustav Holst and the BBBB Bank; without phone tap information, without an informer at the bank or the Vatican based insurance company he had come to a dead end. He just "knew" Holst was the source of all the leaked information. In desperation, he picked up the phone and rang Chief Inspector Tonneau, but the call was a waste of time.

Next, he rang the Russian Embassy and arranged a meet with Major Irina, fellow companion at the hijack and a friend who liked him considerably.

The secrecy Irina insisted on was ludicrous, an hour of tracking and back-tracking. When they finally came together, it took less than five minutes for her to agree on the loan of a car and the services of three of the Czechnyans. 'Nothing extreme, I just need to frighten to death the man who set me up to be shot. No "shooting up the tyres".' Irina grinned.

'Just say, "when"—you remember, just like when I poured tea for you from the samovar. I liked that, say "when", I've taught all my men to say "when".

For three days Martin observed Gustav Holst's movement; on Tuesday the following week, Brenda was taken home from work by taxi and warned that her husband would be "late". Phone to the BBBB bank, her husband was told his wife had gone home with a stomach bug.

An empty road, the Czechnyans held up Holst's car a mile from his home, his chateau Le Cygne. The Czechnyans dragged him out of his Lagonda and forced him into the car Irina had provided. Sitting between two Czechnyans, Holst spoke into the back of Martin's head, who had made no attempt to hide his identity.

In the desolate forest location, without so much as a jab in the ribs, Holst admitted share trading with the Grevilles, 'Part of the job,' he said. He admitted extensive official currency transactions with Munich, Berlin and Colonel Strasser, 'I'm a dealer, it's my job, it's what I do.' It was a smooth transition to admitting he passed on gossip picked up from his wife. Yes, he might well have known that Martin and Nigel Buonaparte were going to the Rhine Hotel. Yes, that was the sort of gossip of interest to Colonel Strasser.

It was all an anti-climax, no force was required, shivering Gustav Holst, not a mark on him, was taken back to his car and was home before 10 pm. Disappointed there was no need for rough stuff, the Russians parked up at a late café, wondered why the British had paid them so much money and drank sufficient Italian spirits, vodka not being available, for the proprietor to keep his café open till the streets were empty and even the Berne police had gone home, Berne is a peaceful city.

Holst told the Germans, the prime source of information was his wife, Brenda Chan, the ambassador's secretary; Martin was not surprised, knowing that there would be jealousy, he had neglected to tell Hillary of the exercise involving Irina, instead he went straight to Sir Pelham Sinclair to tell him that his secretary had been the source of the leak of information about the Rhine Falls Hotel, and that her husband had passed the information on to the Germans.

Sir Pelham Sinclair thought long and hard, but it was two days before he chose his moment to tell Brenda, warn her and ban her from taking work from the embassy to type at home. 'Sod your good typewriter,' he told her, 'stay later at the embassy, I know you're prepared to work anti-social hours for the good of the country, we all are, but if you have work to finish, you must do it at the embassy, nothing must be taken home, yes, I know I take papers home, but Lady Sinclair isn't a spy, and she isn't leaking,' the "or else" was not spoken, never spelt out, but it was there.

Chapter 3
Find the Festung

Sir Pelham perused the latest instruction from London, he was to report back any and every item of news or gossip concerning a German Festung. The flimsy was marked MOST URGENT. He had the librarian do a paper search, he rang Russian Ambassador Morov, he spoke to Gorgeous George, the American Ambassador; he arranged a round of golf ahead of his normal Sunday 18 holes and had copies of southern Bavarian and western Austrian newspapers sent in from the Reuters office.

With Martin Cohen clicking his heels around the embassy, he told him that he had arranged for a "golf pal" to fly him on a recce in his Tiger Moth over southern Austria to see if he could spot any sign of the construction of a fortress thing (as he called it.)

Following instructions Martin turned up bright and early at an airstrip running alongside Lake Neuchatel, a long way from the border, Berchtesgaden and Hitler's Berghaus, but when "the pal" arrived, he seemed nervous at the thought of flying across the border into German air space.

'What's our route?' Martin enquired.

'Let's see how we get on.' His pilot climbed after Martin into the open cockpit. No sooner had he dipped his toe into Germany airspace than he saw a plane on the horizon, climbing towards them, the pal pilot banked, opening the throttle to increase speed and get out of German airspace. The flight was an utter waste of time.

'He'd have shot us down, couldn't risk going on,' Martin didn't argue.

Back at the embassy, Sir Pelham was not too surprised. 'Trouble is,' he said, 'I've already told London I've launched an air survey, I'll tell them our plane was buzzed. Grevilles identified several sites in the Berchtesgaden area needing investigation that should keep London off my back.'

First Secretary Roger Greville reported his interim brief to London about the "festung" had mentioned the air survey, he would like to add that already they had men undercover on their way to potential sites to establish facts.

'Peddle back,' offered Martin, 'my air survey was useless, I didn't get near "potential sites".'

'Maybe,' agreed Sir Pelham, 'but it'll report better, and that's what London wants to hear. Anyhow, I'm glad you used the word "peddle", that's exactly what I want to happen next, "peddle", peddle bikes around Berchtesgaden and the Salzkammergut to verify the accuracy of our information, see if you can find anything, and bring out plans and rumours about a festung.' Greville spoke up quickly.

'I've got a bad knee, I can't cycle; it's in your court, Martin, are you up for it? You're as fit as a fiddle after those months with the nurses. Look at it as a cycling holiday on expenses. Take Hillary, both of you on expenses, tax-free,' he added, Sir Pelham nodded vigorously.

Greville and the Ambassador had discussed this plan beforehand and this was a "set-up".

Martin liked the idea of a challenge, the adventure, better than kicking his heels around the Berne Embassy, but was taken aback at being asked to put Hillary at risk; he agreed he would ask Hillary, wondering whether a motorcycle would be quicker and easier. To Martin's surprise, Hillary jumped at the chance of a cycling holiday. Martin emphasised that if they were caught they might be shot.

'But we won't be caught, we'll have perfect passes and perfect papers, a lot of money and we speak German. We'll come back and win a medal!'

'I've already got one, don't need another,' Martin knew when he was beaten, he came to attention and saluted, 'Mein liebchen, would you prefer to go on a motorbike or a cycle?'

Hillary hated motorbikes, so cycles it was.

Feverish preparations, the embassy engine room as the Ambassador called it, provided the papers, the passports, the maps, the back-up support letters, the used currency, clothes with the right labels, in 24 hours everything was prepared, checked by Martin and Greville, checked by Hillary, handshakes from the Ambassador and Brenda, his half cast Malayan Secretary, still brooding from being told off about the leak, quiet "good lucks" from the staff in the know. Evening meal on an island in the River Aare and an early night. Taxis on the embassy, meals with your new best girl, excitement on the morrow.

Another taxi to Berne Station, crossing the border into Konstanz, return tickets to Vienna, getting off at Salzburg, easy; under a wrought iron sign, hung high above a shop in the middle of a row of old gabled emporia, cycles to choose from, nothing flashy, they selected two with black frames, paying the £19 (Martin always converted all currency in his mind to recognisable £'s sterling) with used notes in small denominations; away from traffic, they practised riding their cycles in the peace and solitude of the Mirabel Gardens.

Registering as Martin and Greta Manner, Swiss citizens from Thun, joint owners of a hardware shop, the receptionist in Hotel Klagenfurt hardly raised an eyebrow, business was slow because of the war and double beds were standard.

In the yard behind the hotel, checking no one was watching, Martin taped his pistol to the inside of the pannier, covered it with his spare shirt, leaving shoes and waterproofs in the rucksacks.

Rising early, Hillary stood before the mirror, preening herself.

'How do I look?' Hillary was wholesome and attractive, her skirt, pinafore, a square-cut white blouse revealed a full pink bosom, white ankle socks halfway to the knee, a picture of wholesome Austrian perfection, her hair done up in an ash-blonde hot cross bun.

'Absolutely fine,' Martin gave her a kiss, pulled on lederhosen shorts, with matching gaiter socks, which did nothing to hide the disfigurement and discoloration from calf to thigh caused when his Wellington exploded (*Damn Barnes Wallis, the designer, much too flammable, much too flimsy,* he thought); the wounds he felt certain, were better than any disguise, provided his war wounds were never linked to his false Swiss passport. War burns could hardly be passed off as an Alpine climbing accident.

Corner table, minimum conversation, breakfast at the hotel, ersatz coffee, they cycled out of Salzburg, taking the road to Hallein, an old salt town. Their destination was a salt mine above the town. Hallein lies to the east of a low mountain range separating the Salzkammergut from the Obersalzberg, areas they were to cycle around as both held sites for a fortress, which they categorised as high pitted rocky regions with difficult access.

Early afternoon, exhaustion, even the lowest gear was insufficient for Hillary's attempts to pedal up the mildest of slopes, and it was a long climb and it took a long time, pushing their cycles up the hill to the mine entrance. The café bore the sign "Mine Visits", the word "salt" being unnecessary; boards with curled up bleached photos and diagrams showed that a series of wood slides dropped visitors thousands of feet through many salt levels to ride out in style through underground tunnels in a free-wheeling tram car, right into Hallein Town Square before all the pavement cafés.

Even with a war on, the mining company ran an hourly vehicle service from this Square back up the mountain to the highest entrance to the mine, so taking no risks, although several thousand feet above the town, Hillary locked the bikes together, stuffed the key into the pocket in her bra, and bought two tickets. Before entering they looked long and hard across the valley for any sign of military construction. From the ridge, they could see towards Munich but nothing looked anything like a festung.

Putting overalls over their clothes, clipping on old battered lamps, they joined with a group of eight teenagers, linked each other's waists, and with legs spread apart, make up a train which sped on rails made out of smooth tree trunks, down steep dark tunnels through the different working levels of the old mine.

The girls shrieked and held on fiercely to the boys in front.

'That was fun.'

'That was frightening.'

The reactions differed, but as they blinked out into the daylight of the Town Square, the teenagers animated chatter told passers-by that for boys and girls alike, fast descents locked on to the girl in front, with a girl locked onto a boy, was unbeatable.

Down tunnels, along galleries, across underground lakes, nothing indicated the mine was being prepared for any clandestine activity.

Late afternoon, taking the mine bus back up the mountain, reunited with the cycles. Early evening booked into the Franz Huber Hotel, large black musical notes painted on the smooth dashed wall of the building lying across from the churchyard grave of the 16th-century composer of Silent Night.

'I think the hotel must be named after the composer, Franz Huber,' Martin was good at stating the bleeding obvious. 'Are you going to look at his grave?' he asked, to be met with a shake of the head.

The restaurant was full by early evening, later the bar filled with men; there wasn't talk of a festung, there was a concern at the long retreat back from Stalingrad, which was now an understated topic on radio and in the papers. Sitting at the long pine communal tables. Martin was sufficiently confident in his linguistic ability to join the conversations, Hillary mostly smiling and nodding.

Tired, Martin tossed and turned, he pulled the duvet over him, he was lying on four oblong hard mattresses, nothing seemingly was going to make the ridges between them disappear as they trapped different parts of his anatomy at different times.

'Nothing, absolutely nothing,' he said, 'we've learned nothing about any fortress.'

'We have learned something, in this case, nothing is something, the salt mine still functions as a salt mine and they're not constructing a fortress near Hallein,' Trust Hillary to take the half full rather than the half-empty view.

Even by 1930's standards, the heavy bicycles left much to be desired. Hillary was riding a man's bike, complete with a crossbar. Neither dynamo produced much light and the drag reduced speed and increased fatigue, but as they only travelled by day and as roads were devoid of traffic, light wasn't important. Both bells were loud and though leaky valves meant tyres had to be checked and pumped up every morning, the rubber was thick enough to repel thorns and throughout the journey, they didn't get a single puncture.

But the seats!

'I can't ride anywhere today, my legs are jelly and my bum's sore, you'll have to go without me,' Hillary repeated next morning, 'I'm sore,' what she had been saying all through the night.

Rather than split up they decided to take a train to their next destination, the valley town of Werfen, south down the line towards Villach, which lies towards the southern slopes of Grossglockner, High Tauern, the highest Austrian mountain chain and a prime area for a festung. They overheard that Werfen held the Police HQ and Army Training Unit and was in easy reach of Hitler's Berghof. Gossip from the night before suggested that special units trained in the hilltop castle of Hohenwerfen, built on the top of a volcanic plug, whilst other training units were attached to a nearby airfield.

The train from Salzburg pulled into Hallein, it was full of military personnel, and by the time Martin had located the goods van and got their cycles stored upright and safely, all the seats had been taken and they were forced to stand in the corridor.

Through the open door of a compartment full of police cadets, they listened in to unbuttoned conversations, comparing police training to SS training and to events in Russia. Running along a fast-flowing river of swirls and low waterfalls, the line passed under the looming castle of Werfen, perched on top of a forested peak; the conversations were so interesting, they decided to overrun their tickets and stay on the train to listen in, but as the train slowed down for the Werfen station, the men got up, shouldered their packs, preparing to leave. Hillary and Martin retrieved their bikes and followed the men out of the station.

Not one serviceman had mentioned a festung. Werfen itself was cold and uninteresting, with the Hohenwerfen castle and hill off limits, they walked a mile to the cable car station joining other holiday tourists in the swift ascent to the Tennengebirge ice caves. From this high cave overlooking the river valley and the mountains over to Berchtesgaden, they got an expansive view of the castle, the airfield, the long valley north and south with its rail line, but saw nothing that looked like a festung, no new constructions could be seen.

Their guide lit his acetylene torch, 'Don't worry about the fumes,' he said adding out of nowhere that nothing ever happens on the 10 mountains.

Another nothing is something,' said Hillary just to annoy Martin.

Next morning was damp, misty and still, without enthusiasm they wheeled the cycles out of the shed. Surprisingly cycling was easy, the wind on their backs, they walked when the hills were steep, their objective was the Salzburg Oberland and the area around Hitler's Berghaus. Once over the col, a large undulating area of meadows, woodland dotted with farms and hamlets was a delight. Twice they had to turn back, warned off by roadside signs; looking at the detailed maps Martin concluded that the signs were to keep people away from Hitler's Berghaus estate. Beautiful landscapes with streams, trees and meadows in abundance, but no sign of new roads, major constructions or military installations.

It was late in the afternoon; panic, around a blind bend they came tight upon a check post. They made a mistake, instead of continuing, they stopped and made to turn back, only to be shouted to stop by a policeman, firing his rifle above their heads in emphasis.

They braked to a stop, wheeling their cycles around to face the advancing policeman. Martin feared they might unwittingly have strayed onto the Berghaus Estate. They hadn't, it was a random check for verification of documents. Hillary hurried to pull their papers out the pannier. The constable hardly glanced at them, he had seen Martin's burnt legs.

'Look after yourself, mate,' he said, giving Hillary more than an admiring glance, 'you'll be in town in 20 minutes, the weather's going to be even better tomorrow, have a good holiday.' As they remounted he glanced again at Hillary adding, 'We all drink at the Fatted Calf; it's got the best beer as well as being the cheapest.'

The burnt misshaped, multi-coloured knees had acted better than any identity card, the constable had barely glanced at the travel documents.

Exhausted and saddle-sore Hillary chose a restaurant/hotel half a mile out of Berchtesgaden, on the road down to Lake Königsee, about to say, 'We're full,' the wife of the owner liked what she saw, 'We've just one room left.' Although it was her best room, a room she normally held back, she quoted the standard rate, saying it included breakfast, chatting as she plumped up the pillows, drew back the curtain, lighting up a beautiful bedroom, in the distance Lake Königssee caught a flicker of sunshine as the sun faded behind its necklace of mountain peaks.

'You can just see the lake from here, and Kehlstein and all the mountains when the clouds aren't down. There's plenty of drawer space,' she pointed to a large antique chest.

Drawing back the duvet, 'What happened to you, love?' she asked, pointing to Martin's knees, bringing forth his stock reply.

'My Dornier exploded as we flew back from London over to France, I'm lucky to be here, my crew weren't so lucky, if it hadn't been for the doctors I'd have died as well.' The words rushed out.

'He was unconscious for 10 days,' Hillary added, 'he needed over 6 pints of blood and over 50 stitches.'

'Blood! Now there's a thing, our daughter works at a clinic in town where they make blood… plasma I think she calls it. She always knows in advance when a battle is coming up, the army stock up with really large amounts of plasma so as to be ready. It's awful, Russia, I wish I'd never heard the word, all our fine men shot at in summer, frozen to death in winter. They need so much of this plasma blood that I don't think they tell us everything on the News'

'Your daughter actually helps to make artificial blood!' Hillary was astonished.

'Yes, and over at Ramsau in the next valley they've just opened a factory making artificial limbs, and in a new one, next to it in Ramsau, they're making wheelchairs and zimmers, and they're building another further down the valley to make something else, but that's secret and nobody knows, they can't manufacture up in the Ruhr now because of the bombing, so they build here out of the way. They say that men without limbs may soon be able to drive.'

'I heard that a new airfield was to be built?' Martin was anxious to continue the conversation, but the woman shook her head. 'That would be something, but there's still only the one airstrip for the Berghaus, but it isn't used much, I think the Fuhrer's away a lot these days. He used to be here nearly all the time.'

She turned towards the marble top on the toilet cabinet holding a large jug and a bowl.

'I'm sorry I haven't much soap for you,' plonking down a dark brown mini-brick, 'but there are two good big towels.' She bent down to lift them out of the heavy ill-fitting bottom drawer of a matching tallboy. 'I can manage,' she said as Martin went to help.

'We open the restaurant in an hour, the table in the corner's warmest, I'll save it for you, I'll put a teddy on the chair, and I'll make sure you have a good meal… Mr Sammel will give you our biggest breakfast in the morning, make sure you've got him ready to eat it,' she gave Hillary a nudge.

Hillary took the woman's arm, 'Thank you, you're very kind.'

Frau Sammel burst into tears, 'No, I'm not, I just wish the Fuhrer would end the war.' She went to the door, 'Every night I dream the same dream, Fritz, our son, paddling a dinghy across a river, the Dnieper I think it is, with bullets splashing everywhere, I pray every night and every morning now, I never used to pray when we were really winning.'

There was little to be learned in the restaurant, the diners being civilians on holiday, except that at breakfast coffee beans previously taken for granted, had become scarce and Frau Sammel had substituted them with roasted acorns and beechnuts. Leaving, after saying thank you and goodbye to Herr and Frau Sammel, they free-wheeled down to the lake, watching a launch laden with provisions set off from the jetty for the community at the distant end of Königssee. Hand in hand they walked across the bridge over the river flowing out of the lake.

'It's lovely here, one day we'll come back,' said Hillary, 'and we'll stay again at Frau Sammel, but she must never know who we really are.'

'Such a lovely couple,' Frau Sammel told her friend, 'such terrible burns, one of his legs looked like scarlet charcoal.' As well as including breakfast, she hadn't charged for dinner but felt it was the best thing she'd done for weeks. *Perhaps I'm becoming a Christian and going to heaven, after all,* she thought.

Before completing their circuit of the Obersalzberg, they put Plan B into operation. Seeing a woman outside her cottage, they stopped, wished good day and opening their map asked if she could point the way to Grimsau, too small to show separately on their map. After deciding it was near to Waldkirch, the woman poured over the map and came out with the sort of detail that Hillary and Martin were risking their lives to get. Her thick finger pointed out the road fork, 'Keep left, you'll see a factory down by the river Poldarn on your right, it's more of a stream than a river,' she corrected herself, 'you can't miss it, the railway runs into the site. Further on you'll see a camp, it's not used now, it was for the workers building the factory and the road, in about three miles you'll come to a main road, on one corner there's a big wooden building, it's a prefabricated factory, you can't miss it, it's got a panzer standing guard at the gate, turn left again, it will be signed Waldkirch, when you get there, you'll need to ask again.

In saying thank you, Martin asked if it was a big factory,

'Quite big, it was only finished a year ago, it does spinning and weaving, they make bandages and war dressings, it's been a big boost for us, because it runs 24 hours a day, 7 days a week, there's no factory like it between here and Salzburg. There are trains every day bringing cotton bales and taking stuff away.'

Thanking her once again they rode off.

They found the mill, they rode past the abandoned camp. They made no markings on their map, agreeing that a map with markings might invite suspicion.

'You'll just have to train your memory.'

'OK,' said Martin, 'but that's another no.'

'Another yes,' said Hillary, 'yes, it's not a festung.'

They set off south-east in the direction of Bad Aussee, their second objective, convinced there was nothing of specific interest on the Obersalzberg. The weather improved, just as the policeman had told them.

It was late afternoon, all they had had since frühstück was water and the fruit for lunch provided by kindly Frau Sammel, so four kilometres from Hallstatt, the target for the night, they were happy to stop, prop up their bicycles, and stand by the level-crossing barrier waiting for the long slow goods train to pass. The train was double-headed, slowly pulling 45 wagons, some filled with limestone and aggregate, some with salt, and some stacked with thick tree trunks.

A gleaming black Mercedes Benz drew up alongside, soundless, such was the quality of its engine. Martin looked, then jerked away, sitting in the back was Colonel Strasser, Hans Strasser with two other men. There was no mistake, Strasser tall upright, fair-haired, he even produced in the second Martin watched, his characteristic mannerism of stroking the back of his ear with his opposite hand. Martin moved behind Hillary so that his face was now out of the line of sight.

Leaning over he whispered, 'Don't look now, the man in the car's Strasser, the German who shot me, the German in charge who we ambushed at Pont Celere, the driver's name is Muller, He was a corporal at Menzenschwand camp, he was at the bank in Zurich and at Pont Celere. He was wounded and taken to hospital, but he walked out before he could be questioned. If he sees me, he'll recognise me.'

Martin stayed behind Hillary, pulling his cap down. Two cars and a following cart waited for the train to lumber past in the direction of Stainach. Hillary looked aimlessly towards the car, but avoided eye-contact saying later, 'I recognised Strasser from watching at the Zurich Bank, but I wanted to be able to recognise the others again.'

Not until the railway engine and the clank of the wagon wheels could no longer be heard, did the barrier swing up and the crossing open, the car moved smoothly away, 15 minutes later Martin and Hillary rode abreast on an empty road into Hallstatt: outside the 'Golden Crown' sat the Mercedes Benz, a one-armed porter carrying a suitcase into the hotel.

Further down the narrow one street to village Hillary and Martin, stopped at a café, three tables on the narrow pavement, they ordered sausages, rolls and coffee from a waitress who was so anxious to close and go home, that she swept up around their feet, banged chairs to make her impatience obvious, but it did get them speedy service.

'We must stay here, Strasser's a colonel and he's important, he's more likely than anyone else to lead us to a "festung". Why else would he be spending the night in a one-horse lakeside village like Hallstatt?'

Across from the café, a wall lined with rose bushes was a trim garden, a cottage and a sign saying "Zimmer". Hillary went across, disappearing for five minutes, she returned saying "booked". Finishing his coffee, Martin unhooked the cycle panniers, following Hillary upstairs to the small back room with Lake Hallstatt and the church with bright flowers in its graveyard, brightening the small window.

A shower, a change out of lederhosen to slacks, he looked and felt a different man. Hillary, a shower, a change out of demure cycling slacks to a skirt, looked and felt a different woman. They embraced, fell back on the bed, and tickled and kissed, fatigue forgotten.

'That driver, Corporal Muller, if he sees me, he'll recognise me, we bought seeds together for the allotments at Menzenschwand Camp. He recognised me when I went back down to Pont Celera after our van stopped. I doubt whether Strasser will recognise me even though he shot me at the Rhine Falls Hotel, I was only a boy when he gave our class glider lessons. The small man was at the meeting at Psalm, he's head of the Museum Service, his name's Seydlitz. He's civil, not military.'

Hillary was excited.

'I'll go to the Golden Crown tonight and see what I can find out,' before Martin could object, 'I'll be alright by myself.'

But Martin wasn't having any of it, 'They won't recognise you OK, but that's not the only thing, if Strasser wants a woman, he's SS, that's exactly what he'll take. It's too risky we'll find some other way. Anyhow, your German isn't perfect.'

He would not agree to Hillary going alone, instead of thrills they settled for a walk down the lake. They would try to track Colonel Strasser in the morning.

Up early, Martin grabbed a roll, slipping out of the cottage, the village silent and empty, he found a perch in the branches of a tree on the hill behind the "Golden Crown". It was an hour before the men left the Crown, two carried briefcases, but no suitcases were loaded in the car. Martin took this to mean they would, probably be staying another night. The Mercedes swung out and had no sooner turned onto a small road leading up the hill when to his surprise the car stopped, the driver, Muller, got out, went to the hedge where he took hold of the dedicated hand-painted tourist sign:

'Hallstatt Salzbergwerk,' and wiggled then wrenched the post out of the ground. Getting a screwdriver from the boot, he unscrewed the Salzbergwerk sign, threw the post behind the hedge, and put the sign in the boot. Hurrying, he got back behind the wheel and drove swiftly up the narrow road.

Martin cold and stiff, climbed out of the tree, hungry for hot rolls, jam and coffee, real beans this time. With Hillary he poured over their map, a minor road climbed the mountain, past a marked salt mine, then looped to re-join the main road leading to Bad Ischl. Unless Strasser was sight-seeing, his destination must be the salt mine as nothing else was marked.

Reserving their room, they climbed on their bikes, the official iron county signpost at the junction was still in place; it read: "Gosau", pushing their cycles a full kilometre up the steep bits they peddled to the salt mine.

The Hallstatt Salt Mine is but one of the 50, claiming to be the oldest salt mine in the world. For over five hundred years, it was the financial prop of the village, supplying salt to a hungry and thirsty Europe, then as cheaper salt became available with trains to move it around, business fell away, however, these trains allowed Hallstatt to convert itself into a popular tourist destination. Squeezed into a narrow strip of land between mountains and lake, shortage of space dictated that the graveyard was small, and because the graves were tended by competing living relatives, beautiful; a picture because after 10 years the bodies were dug up and stored in the "bonehouse" for the graves to be "hot-bedded", followed in by the newly dead. The old skeletons then lay alongside the bones of husbands, imbeciles (much intermarriage in Hallstatt) or even Protestants' (no Luther, no Reformation for Hallstatt) bleached bones, neatly and systematically piled together in the medieval "Bone House", names on skulls marked up by the blue butcher's pencil of 83 years old Hubert Rosencrantz.

To reach Hallstatt, visitors had to cross the lake by boat from its railway station, positioned on the far side of the lake. As well as the twisting narrow road the mine was accessed by a rumbling cable car, screened by trees in the centre of the village; which ran straight up the mountainside. Of the three cars parked at the mine entrance, the Mercedes Benz stood out.

'Ride Past,' said Martin. The café, 50 metres past the mine entrance promised: rest, drink, eat, toilet, reminding Martin to tell Hillary that Poles only needed two meals a day, tight pussy and a warm place to... (Martin could never bring himself to complete the sentence... whereas Czechs...

They sat alone facing up the road to the mine entrance. In her own time a girl, the café owner's daughter, came to take their order.

'Quiet today,' Martin observed.

'Quiet every day,' replied the girl, 'war eats holiday-makers and visitors.'

'Does they still mine salt?' Martin followed up.

'A skeleton team, but they do more maintenance than taking visitors through, they only pump out brine one day a week and that's often just to show visitors. But things are changing, it looks as if they're going to be taken over by the Ministry of Works, there's an inspection party in there now. We're making them lunch, a special four course meal. We could make lunch the same for you, Mother's making soup, then there's fat, 10-inch long trout, from our fresh water tarn over there,' she pointed. 'Boiled potatoes, appelstrudel and cream from Daisy,' she pointed again to a white and brown cow munching grass in the meadow. 'You won't eat better even in the residence at Ischl, and I'll charge you less for the wine than the Inspectors, it'll cost you less money, it'll be very good, please stay, we need the custom we're so quiet now.'

'Sounds lovely,' said Hillary, 'but I'm slimming and it would mean changing our plans. By the way, is it still possible to go down the mine?'

'Not while the Inspectors are here, old Fritz might be happy to take you when they've gone. Nothing gives him more pleasure.'

Martin was adamant that Muller would recognise him, even Strasser might recognise him, after all, he'd shot him, they mustn't go near the mine whilst the men remained.

'We might find something out,' Hillary wasn't averse to taking risks.

'Daren't risk it, if Muller sees me, we're as good as dead.'

Martin got up from the table and went to his bicycle, returning with a small, oblong object the size of a sweet tin, laying it on the inside chair, he pulled off the tape covering a recessed switch and flicked it, a small light, barely visible in daylight flickered, showing the recording device was working.

'If this doesn't work, I'll never use British wireless equipment again,' he said.

He looked around, the girl had laid the table for the men's lunch. Martin pulled off further pieces of tape and careful not to touch the exposed surfaces, he sauntered up to the lunch table. Holding the device in both hands, glancing, checking there was no one looking, he put both hands underneath the table and pressed the gadget hard, smoothing the tape so that it was stuck firmly underneath the table top. Satisfied it was firm, he walked unconcernedly to the toilet.

Before returning, he sought out the flirty girl, paid the bill, sorry they couldn't stay, hoped they would all have a good lunch, and gave her a tip.

'Sorry, we couldn't join you.' Making sure he wasn't overheard, 'I'd have loved the trout. Ten inches is so fulfilling. Don't you think?' They both laughed.

Further than expected they cycled downhill into Gosau, past the shops, past the rail station, a sign pointed to Bad Ischl. 'Let's treat ourselves,' said Hillary selecting a late lunch in an elegant café, where even more elegant Austrian ladies, some wearing a local costume, toyed over coffee and cake. After noodles, watching what others were eating, they ordered cream and chocolate gateaux which were so good the ordered second helpings, hang the expense. Uncomfortably full, Martin uncomfortable at the high cost when the bill arrived, guilty at being so far away from the war.

Come afternoon, another push of bikes up a hill, they again approached the entrance to the Hallstatt salt mine. The Mercedes Benz was gone, a further cup of coffee at the café, consternation, the lunch table had been moved up against a wall. Seeking his moment, Martin went over, running his fingers underneath the rim of the table, a sharp tug, he slipped the recorder into the pocket of his lederhosen. Panic over, they walked over to the mine entrance, "old Fritz" was there, not working leaning against a wall, talking to two girls in the office, he brightened up at the prospect of taking a war hero and a bonny girl around the mine he had worked and loved for 50 years.

Taking off their cycle jackets, both drew on a pair of rough overalls, patched and strengthened with leather on the inside of the thighs.

'We slide down on parallel pine trunks,' old Fritz said. Few words passed during the tour, no evidence that the mine was a basis for a fortress. It was only when they were back up and shedding their overalls that "old Fritz" began to talk.

'Do you know that may be my last individual tour, we've only got one party booked for the weekend, then the Ministry takes over for renovations, and the mine is closed for visitors… renovations my eye, they just want it to store things, they've taken down all the directions and the road signs, I'll be dead before we see another visitor. Anyhow, they're going to pay me more as a caretaker than tight old Stuckel ever paid me to dig five trucks of salt, so that's good, I shouldn't grumble. They say they'll pay overtime as well… Stuckel never once paid me overtime the whole of the 51 years I've worked here, all he ever gave me was an eight-pound duck every Christmas, tight arse. An eight-pound duck every year for 50 years.

But only God knows what we'll find when they re-open Level Four, it's been shut for 60 years, I'm going to make sure I'm first in, see if they left any manganese bronze hoses there, worth a fortune since the war started.'

The older of the two office girls piped up:

'Do you two want a fortnight's work by any chance? We've got to make over a thousand direction cards, signs and labels and other things and they've all got to be pasted on board and cellophane stuck over, I'm not expecting to see my bed for weeks.'

'Gretl, you can see my bed any time,' said dirty old Fritz.

Martin and Hillary looked at each other and grinned.

'Sorry,' they said.

It was free-wheel all the way back to Hallstatt and Hillary came off on a bend, fortunately only grazing her knee. Martin "rubbed it better"; the Mercedes stood proud and alone outside the Golden Crown.

Deciding it was better to discuss plans away from the cottage, relaxed after a sauna, a converted wooden shed at the bottom of the narrow garden, they walked away from the Golden Crown, at the Baren saloon they ordered steins of Erdinger beer, bemoaning that the recorder was just that, until they bought more equipment they couldn't listen to the lunchtime conversation. They decided to return to their original plan and cycle to Bad Aussee and its lakes when in walked four men. Martin turned his head away.

'They mustn't see me, that's Muller.'

The men sat down in the remaining empty table, next to the door, directly in the line of sight. Martin became anxious and restless.

Finishing his Erdinger in one belch and a gulp. 'I'll get out through the lavatory, follow me in three minutes, I'll wait outside.' He disappeared, only to return whispering. 'No way out there, we'll have to hang on, the back exit is through the kitchen and I don't want to draw attention to myself.'

Ordering a second Erdinger, they sat in silence. After half an hour Muller and another man got up and headed for the "Gents".

'Drink up,' swallowing the remaining beer, he put notes under his glass to cover the bill, they pushed past the talking men who did not take the slightest notice and entered the narrow, unlit street into a lovely calm moonlit night a stroll along the edge of the Hallstadtersee, arm in arm, hip brushing hip, in harmony. A mile seemed the right distance, they sat on a bench in the shadow of a white lilac bush, whose smell matched Hillary's welcoming bosom.

'There's something I've never told you,' Martin began. Hillary stiffened, instantly alarmed at the tone, she feared a hurtful past love-affair.

'Who is she?' she asked.

'No, nothing like that,' Martin laughed, 'have you heard of King St Stephen's crown, no, why should you, Stephen was boy King of Czechoslovakia hundreds of years ago. A crown was made for him, but he only reigned for nine months before he was killed by a cousin. All very sad. Anyhow after the death of the cousin, this small crown was kept in Prague castle. Hitler stayed in that castle after the occupation of Czechoslovakia, after the Sudetenland was annexed, and the crown disappeared.'

'No, I've never heard of him, but then I'm not a Czech. Don't tell me you've got it,' said Hillary.

'Well, no, but I know where it is.' Neither spoke.

'Martin, don't tell me, I bet I know where it is: Box 21, the box missing after the hijack, the missing box Sir Pelham went on and on about. You hid it when we were at Kiental, I always thought it could only have been you, or Irina, there wasn't anyone else... I'm sure Sir Pelham thought you took it. I could tell... it had to be you.'

'Was I so obvious,' Martin laughed ruefully, 'well, as I'm the only Czech around I guess I'm best entitled, the English and the Russians have no more right to King Stephen's Crown than the Germans.'

'At least the English would have seen that the rightful owners got it back eventually.' Martin laughed out loud.

'Eventually, after five hundred years, you mean, who are you kidding Hillary, just like the Elgin Marbles, and the Hebrides Chess Set, anyway I've got it and I've written to London, to Dr Benes, Czech Government in exile to tell him. Not who I am, or where the crown is. I've just said "it's safe",' Martin hadn't expected Hillary to challenge him.

'I was going to tell you where I hid it in case I'm killed, but perhaps I'd better not,' he said.

'Oh, do go on, tell me, I think it's brilliant, I won't tell a soul.'

She snuggled up to him and gave him a kiss, her fingers pressing his hand against her heaving breasts.

'OK, this is our secret, cross your heart and hope to die. Remember the day at Kiental when you went to buy food, I was the only one left up at the chalet. I burrowed into the woodpile in the woodshed around at the side, it was awkward, but when I'd made a deep enough channel, I hid the crown in its box, right in the middle of the stack. Until someone burns off a huge stack of wood, no one will find it. As soon as this war's over, I'll pull it out and make certain the crown goes back to Czechoslovakia.'

'You're wonderful,' Hillary repeated this time and again on the way back to the cottage.

'If you don't get out of this alive, I'll see it gets back to Prague.' Martin squeezed her waist.

'I've let Dad know,' he said, 'I'm getting out alive, we're both getting out alive, just don't do anything silly like trying to chat up Colonel Strasser.'

Arm in arm in harmony they swung back to their cottage and bed.

Hillary never again rode as many miles as she did the following day, Altaussee, Bad Goisern, Bad Ischl, where a tour of the town shops revealed an electrical shop selling devices that would play back the tape recorded at the Salt Mine. There followed a heated discussion, Martin hated travelling with expensive suspicious devices in case they were stopped. 'Expense,' Hillary mocked his meanness, 'What do you think Greville and the Ambassador spend when they put taxis on their expense sheets, do they actually pay out the backhanders they put down as "grease", what does Buonaparte put down on his expense sheet when he spends a fortune at that Basel nightclub?' Martin didn't argue, they plunged into the shop and bought the only play-back equipment in the shop. He had Hillary promise that as soon as they had played it back, the tape, the player and the recorder would all be burnt.

Arriving at Bad Ischl, holiday town of Austrian Monarchy, pushing cycles up the hill to the chalet hotel, Alte Carinthia, they booked in. Hidden high enclosed by tall trees, close to the station, its timbers the colour of burnt toast, mountains only visible by climbing a rope ladder into high branches.

Alone in their bedroom, they plugged in the playback monitor, inserted the tape, holding breath until it crackled into life, sitting close, no one about, volume low, they played the recording of four men eating trout and appelstrudel, belching and drinking beer. The conversation was earthy and business related.

'If we're caught with this recording, we're as good as dead,' said Martin, 'we must both remember the details, then I'll burn it.'

Martin tested Hillary's memory, and she tested his, then they listened to the more interesting bits for a second and third time boiled down:

'Levels two through five of the Mine were to be fitted out with fully labelled racking to store Museum valuables, racking made from local timber, by labour, brought in from "Mauthausen Concentration Camp", the same labour that had been brought over and were busy converting limestone caverns into a munitions factory at Ebensee, on Lake Traunsee.

Construction of the racking and securing the levels was expected to take about three weeks, when finished, the workers would be shot and buried lower down the hill in the spoilings. Later, when the paintings and artefacts arrived from the north, a different team of men would be brought in to unload, stack and be killed so no witnesses remained. Large paintings would be difficult, they would be left near to the doors of the cages, there would be damage as they were moved through the lower mine levels. Nine thousand artefacts had already been listed for transportation.

Although the men were surveying and planning what had to be done at Hallstatt Salt Mine, they spent time discussing the progress of the excavations underway at Ebensee where the cavern excavations were such a gigantic undertaking that 10,000 men were already involved. Setting up a factory inside a limestone mountain wasn't easy, already over 150 men had died or been killed by rock collapsing. Many thousands extra men were being brought in to excavate and line the caverns, tank manufacturing equipment was already in situ, rocket component manufacture was next, but the largest, most important and most difficult project of all was the installation of a synthetic oil manufacturing plant underground in the largest cavern in eastern Europe. The men weren't entirely sure what was to be used to make the oil, the consensus was that it was lignite, brown coal from east Austria.'

The train line up to connect to the main line between Salzburg and Vienna was being improved with double the number of passing places.

Martin got Hillary to recite parrot fashion what had been recorded:

'Linz Construction Group had the contract to improve the rail spur to the mountain face, designed wide enough to bring large, heavy equipment in and take finished product, particularly petrol tankers away, half the excavated limestone was to be lifted onto covered rail trucks and moved to a cement works north of Gmunden, where another underground facility was being constructed. The other half would be taken by lorry to a cement works north of Munich.'

She remembered that the Ebensee Building Company were building a housing estate for workers, huts for slave labour, and were constructing mock houses over the main cavern entrance to act as camouflage against RAF air raids.

The scale of the excavations had even impressed Albert Speer, the new armaments minister, who congratulated them on his recent visit. The cavern was so secure that further excavations were envisaged even though it was a long way from where finished goods was needed, they guessed that more plant for oil conversion and storage must be envisaged, but none knew for certain with Strasser thinking it might be for the assembly of a new jet engine for a fighter currently being tested near Augsburg.

Martin was impressed with Hillary's memory, squeezing her hand tight, something he did all the time, he gave her a kiss, confident that the information on the tape was now locked in their memories.

Most of the discussion had centred on the Ebensee complex with relatively little consideration of the paintings and sculpture being moved from all over the North and East of Germany. Not one of them was an art-lover, not even Strasser, 'give me a nude every time' was the consensus.

The pair sat back to consider:

'Where is this Ebensee?' Hillary asked.

Meeting a chambermaid in the wide upstairs corridor, 'Which is the way to Ebensee, please?' she asked, to be told it was five stops down the line, halfway to Gmund, with stations for the quarry and a second near the landing stage where a paddle steamer sailed between Traunsee and Gmund.

Finding Ebensee on the map was easy, it was on the River Traun, at the near end of Traunsee Lake. Rather than cycle, they decided to take it easy and see if there were trains running the following day.

After a final check of memory, Martin searched out the drying room, bad Ischl being in the mountains, the stove at the end of its working day, still held hot embers, Martin watched the tape flare up and burn, the recorders destroyed beyond recognition, not leaving till he had raked the ashes. The camera remained rooted in the pocket of the rucksack, no incriminating pictures, only holiday snaps of Hillary and Lake Königssee; what more natural and charming.

Bad Ischl station was built with the Austrian Emperor expressly in mind. Waiting on the platform before the train arrived, was a joy, a gurgling river, wooded low hills, old signals, shiny sets of rails merging into a single track before it went around a hill. A horse and cart trundled past the forecourt towards open meadows.

Near now to the end of their spying mission, they fastened their cycles to a custom-built frame, threw their panniers on the overhead rack, and sank into corner seats, the half-filled train puffed its way out of the station onto on the track following the river Traun down the valley to Lake Traunsee. They followed the schematic of the line painted by hand on the carriage wall; short of Ebensee the line went double track, and the train creaked to a halt, new sidings away to their right held 20 flat roll trucks, each loaded with identical wooden crates. Painted on each crate were the letters P---A. Hillary pointed to the end crate, in letters 12 inches high, just one crate was stencilled "PEENEMUNDE".

Neither knew the significance of Peenemünde, but the name went into their memory bank, along with the significance of P…A.

Grunting, their train slowly moved past a cleared area of flat ground, stout wooden huts lining up against tall pines, reminding Martin of the prison camp at Menzenschwand. To the side of the clearing, a narrow channel stripped of trees had been cleared through arched trees stretching away toward the foot of the mountain; a branch line, a road or both, was under construction, a tree groaned and cracked as they watched it being felled.

A wooden archway with an iron gate hung across the narrow entrance to the site, Martin pointed:

'ARBEIT MACHT FREI'

'"Work makes free", I saw an identical gate at Dachau, it's an indirect quotation from Stalin: "You eat if you work".'

The other passengers were also looking out and talking, one asking what was happening at Ebensee, "thousands of workers", "1,000 trees down", "a hundred new houses", "30 explosions every day", "diverted river", were among the happenings.

They looked at each other, they leaned across and squeezed hands unable to take their eyes on what was passing before them, hundreds of men working everywhere. 'This is all we need,' whispered Martin,

'At last we've got something Sir Pelham can tell London, no point in our getting off, we've seen it, we've heard it, let's stay on till we get to the main line, the junction at Attnang-Puchheim will connect us to trains to Munich and from there we can get to Berne via Konstanz or Stuttgart as fast as you like.'

Stopping had made the train late. Engine gently steaming, it again pulled up to wait at the second Ebensee station hard by the lake steamer pier. They looked away from the boat lying at the Traunsee jetty to watch as an old engine pulling 15 dilapidated cattle trucks emerged from a tunnel down the line where it ran along the side of Lake Traunsee. Slowly it rumbled past their window, so close they could see outstretched arms and faces visible through the gaps in the truck walls. The cattle trucks were full of people, not cattle.

Conversation in the carriage ceased as it trundled past, only the slow clunk of the wheels from the passing train could be heard. No one spoke, Martin and Hillary looked at each other and again raised their eyebrows. 'They're Poles,' someone said.

It was not until a second train heading north with a line of hoppers full of rock had passed them, that the 8.50 am from Bad Ischl to Attnang-Puchheim, resumed its journey along the shore of picturesque Traunsee. Passenger trains clearly didn't have priority over goods trains going to Ebensee.

'That rock's limestone,' said Hillary, 'It'll be stuff they've dug out, it's crushed and turned into cement to make concrete.'

Attnang-Puchheim Junction, 30 minutes' wait. The first thing Martin said, alone at last on the long platform was to seize Hillary's shoulder: 'Did you read what was painted on two of the cattle trucks holding those prisoners?' Hillary shook her head. Martin used his finger to trace the words on an unwashed windowpane:

'POPE ISCARIOT'

'It was written in black bitumen paint.' He rubbed the window clean.

'"Pope Iscariot" what do you make of papal nonsense?'

'I'm a vicar's daughter, you know, and couldn't possibly air my views on Pope Pius Iscariot, the virgin birth, Lazarus, or bitumen paint. Sufficient for the Church of England that Jesus has risen from the Dead, and God save the King.' So ended their first and last religious discussion till the marriage service itself. Born Catholic, Martin was having doubts, Daughter of a C of E vicar, Hillary was not going to allow religion to drive a wedge between her and the man she loved.

'Spoken from the bowels of purgatory like a true bloody pious agnostic Anglican. Tell me, are all Anglicans really agnostics?' replied a pugnacious Martin, 'Viva Galileo Galilei.'

The express to Salzburg and Munich, with connections to Konstanz steamed in.

Buying extended tickets with two bicycles gave the station ticket office at Attnang-Puchheim a problem, but most problems can be solved with money, and eventually via Salzburg and Munich they crossed the border back into Switzerland at Konstanz, where they rang the embassy, locked the cycles together for later return to Salzburg; before nightfall a taxi had dropped them off outside Agincourt, home to the British Embassy in Berne. Lights ablaze, no blackout here, Sir Pelham Sinclair was waiting at the door.

'Need to get my report off to London, tonight,' he said.

'Done it,' Martin handed over the page of foolscap he had written as soon as they had crossed the border into Switzerland, Sir Pelham picked it up.

'One sheet, is that all? Where are the photographs? You'd a camera, why didn't you take any photographs?' his words spoken with exasperation.

'I didn't take any photographs.'

'Why not?'

'Because I didn't take any photographs, I'm not risking Hillary's life or my life taking photographs of a bandage factory or Ebensee Labour Camp. Let the RAF fly a spotter plane if you need photographs.'

'Of course, I need photographs, London will want photographs, a rail line, a camp or something, anything to demonstrate you've actually been there, I'm not looking for the German order of battle.'

'Well, there aren't any.' Martin was not apologetic. Sir Pelham moved on.

'You said you had a tape-recording, where is it?'

'It isn't any more; we destroyed it for safety reasons, like the photographs.' Martin was annoyed with Hillary making approving sounds and felt emboldened to go on. Sir Pelham moved on

'Are you sure there's no fortress under construction in the Obersalzberg or the Kleinwalsertal. Could Ebensee double as a fortress?' Neither Martin nor Hillary spoke.

'Or in other places.' Further silence.

'You've listed first aid manufacture, blood plasma factories.' Nods

'The Hallstatt Salt Mine you say is being modified as a safe store for paintings.'

'We stand by that,' said Hillary, 'but can't you see, the main thing is Ebensee, it is immense, the biggest thing since sliced bread!'

'Sliced bread, there's no such thing,' Sir Pelham and Martin spoke in unison.

'This war factory, Traunsee! Ebensee! Same difference,' said Sir Pelham, then changing tone, 'it so happens my wife and I camped at Traunsee in 1933 and a lovely place it is. It's so beautiful I can't see even Himmler putting up a Concentration Camp or building a factory in such a spot. They must be desperate. You think over 10,000 workers you say,' he paused, 'before I send this to London, I've got to be certain,' he looked up, it was Hillary he looked in the eye: 'Are you sure?' he asked.

'I'm certain sure,' Hillary replied. Sir Pelham breathed a sigh of relief. That "sure" from Hillary coupled to the reputation Martin had established in London, meant he could put his name behind Martin and this Ebensee report and still sleep at night.

'Anyhow, this is really good new stuff and important.' He looked up, 'very well done both of you. I'm sorry, I was cross; there's enough here to keep London well busy, Austrians erecting houses to hide mine entrances from the RAF, what next?'

He picked up the phone and dialled.

'Oh, Brenda, sorry to trouble you at such a late hour, but Hillary and Martin are back, and we have some typing to do, can you come in, we'll have to burn the midnight oil I'm afraid.' Brenda, the half-caste gorgeous Chinese/English Secretary wasn't given an option. Sir Pelham replaced the receiver.

'Martin, I need you here till I get this off, sorry, Hillary,' he picked up his phone again, ordering a taxi for her.

'I'd rather stay here with Martin, if you don't mind, Sir Pelham,' she said primly.

Chapter 4
SS Luftwaffe Colonel General Strasser

Swiss banker Gustav Holst was stocky, dark with thick, black hair rising thickly from a low forehead. Not an immediate match for half cast oriental wife Brenda Chan, intelligent, sexy, lazy, greedy and cruel, characteristics never far, never fully hidden from her lovely delicate face. As you can imagine, Gustav's suits, shirts and ties were day to day immaculate as he entered the bank, only his shoes could cause comment; Gustav never found comfortable black leather shoes, so he chose suede dark grey casuals which he kept in the well of the back seat of the car.

Brenda was the private secretary of Sir Pelham Sinclair, the English Ambassador. Her attachment and loyalty to England had been sealed by the death of her twin brother in a Nazi brawl, and like Sir Pelham Sinclair, the Swiss Ambassador, she had bought the RAF a Spitfire out of her fortune, her family having traded to the four corners of the earth out of Singapore, since the 19th century. Her clothes were the envy of the embassy, men and women.

Gustav Holst, without any deep national commitment, supported Germany, how could he not, conducting extensive business through his bank (BBBB) and insurance businesses operating through Zurich, Rome and the Vatican. His wife's employment as Sir Pelham Sinclair's secretary gave him a window onto English worries and thinking. It was a continuing puzzle to him how his wife had passed UK vetting to work within the Foreign Office.

Suspicious by nature, ultra-cautious running a bank, paranoid in daily insurance dealings with the red-hatted cardinals in the Vatican overvaluations of fragments from Christ's Cross, panels painted by Fra Lippo Lippi and the like, only recently had his staff reported a break-in at his Chateau, Le Cygne, the killing of a guard dog, a different scale from the netting of fish from his lake, and the scrumping of apples. Most recent, without a word to him, Brenda had agreed to store "boxes" at Le Cygne's coach house, 'boxes' which arrived unannounced in the middle of the night, "boxes" he soon associated with the hijack and massacre at Pont Celere, after the ambush and the hijack were widely reported throughout Switzerland. "Boxes", which no sooner arrived than they were immediately moved out from the chateau to destinations unknown.

For several years, part of the bank's trading with Germany had come from Munich Offices controlled by SS Colonel Hans Strasser; in return for this profitable business, he fed share tips to the colonel; passing investment information the world over was an inherent part, parcel and perk of banking, in addition, he passed over such snippets of information he gleaned from Brenda, his wife, who habitually left office early, typed documents at home on a cherished IBM typewriter, and left them lying on her desk. When Brenda told him that an embassy employee had been shot and seriously injured at the Rhine Falls Hotel, he was fearful, having earlier fed through the names of two embassy employees who were attending a secret meeting at this same hotel.

Strasser had profited from Holst's share tips, *No wonder bankers get rich*, he thought, and had reciprocated by channelling an increased volume of work through Holst's bank BBB. From the very beginning, Strasser had asked Holst to confirm that the Swiss end of the phone through which they transacted their secret business, was secure and had not been breached or tampered with, Holst's latest tests revealed that the line had been tampered with and security breached. Strasser had then used this line to transmit the fake message that an urgent meeting between him and Seidlitz, German Chief Museum Curator, was to be held on the morning of the 20th, at the Rhine Falls Hotel, Schaffhausen.

Although still using the rank of colonel, Hans Strasser was a star in the ascendant and had the full rank of colonel General and his staff and contemporaries knew it, no one knew why he still chose to be addressed as colonel. His wider responsibilities had been marked by his having grand offices in both Munich and Salzburg where his new suite, on the ground floor of the Holy Roman Empire's Palace. The Palace, its original construction undisturbed, the gold gilding, the locks, the wooden panelling, maintained in pristine condition by craftsmen who worked diligently at both the Palace and at Strasser's houses (believing it essential to prevent their being called up to the Russian front). Without attacks from Flying Fortresses or Lancasters, old-fashioned craftsmanship allied to quarried building materials, the Palace continues to stand steady and ready firm and true for another 500 years.

'Jed—a nickname (his christened name being Hans)—was the youngest of four Strassers; his two older brothers were contemporaries and joint members of the Freikorps with Hitler from the early Munich days, Otto, in particular, knew about Hitler's lifestyle and sex life}. Gregor, the oldest brother, a with a strong worker power base in northern Germany was, like Ernst Röhm, killed on Hitler's orders, consequent to the Night of the Long Knives. Second brother Otto escaped to publish in Britain and America scurrilous pamphlets detailing the sex life of the unmarried Fuhrer, detailing one particular episode resulting in the death of Hitler's young niece, Geli. The Strasser brothers were so upsetting to Hitler that even of the name Strasser was anathema, and his entourage knew better than to mention the name.

SS Colonel Strasser contrived to meet sister Edda, twice a year, once on the Anniversary of Gregor's killing, reminding each other that revenge was still outstanding. It was his very name that had caused Major Hans Strasser to be interrogated in the cellars on Albrightstrasse despite his ability being widely recognised and without any evidence of personal disloyalty; Were it not for older party members, Wasserburg and Rondel speaking up for him, Strasser believed he would have been dismissed from the Luftwaffe at the very least, but that was a long time ago and Colonel Strasser, via Goering, and Speer had finally received the promotion and recognition his ruthless determination the State needed and his intelligence warranted.

So Strasser held an unusual position, formerly a Luftwaffe Pilot, now an SS Luftwaffe colonel general; having been a pilot accounted for his early responsibility for RAF POW

Camps, along with supervision of many other peripheral establishments, amongst them a home for disabled airmen. His current responsibilities, mainly reporting to Minister Albert Speer, gave him overall control of labour at Mauthausen and its radial labour camps, including the huge installations at Ebensee, where a pre-existing limestone quarry was to be so expanded as to create a hollow mountain, so large that a series of plants could be installed to produce enough petrol, to compensate should the Ploesti fields in Roumania be lost to the war machine.

Alone in his office in the Salzburg Palace, he contemplated his position.

His nickname "Jed", short, warm and friendly, had a hateful origin—"Jesuit", the third form at Tubingen High School. "Jesuit"—cruel—because classmates thought him cruel, righteous and aloof, too ready to rebuke, too quick to point out the righteous way.

Over time, Jesuit, the schoolboy "Jes", which he hated was corrupted to "Jed", a name he liked.'

"Jed", his stately office masked ruthless, self-centred greed within the shell of an Aryan physique and appearance. In his drive for efficiency and advancement, he continued to encourage even lowly colleagues to call him "Jed"; but woe betides any old school mate who used the hated "Jes".

Before his major advancement, his thirst for money and the security going with it had placed him in peril, he became involved in a Museum Syndicate moving illegal gold and treasure seized from Jews and occupied Museums, into Swiss Banks. The Syndicate's original cover story—they were building a reserve to finance a "festung" but that fiction changed to building a fund for a worthy status of their leader—Adolf Hitler. This was now behind him. The thefts, the hijack, the deaths of German soldiers at Pont Celere, had been blanked off by Goering's agreeing a TOP SECRET' fake classification of the gold, as being finance originally for a statue 7 as the war situation deteriorated a fund for construction of a Festung, preventing any enquiry by the Gestapo. The incident was now history, the families of the dead—informed, the file—buried deep in the archives in the tunnels on the cliffs of Ehrenbreitstein by Koblenz, on the heights above the confluence of the Rivers Rhine and Moselle.

He unlocked the bottom drawer of his desk, laid out on the leather surface his "Black Book". It opened itself on page 18, at the top of the page:

18

{1st and 8th letter, position in the alphabet are shorthand for Adolf Hitler}

Below

2 escapees Menzenschwand. bullets to head

1 ' ' Koln ' '

1 ' Rhine Falls ' stomach

1 thief Psalm bullets to head

1 talker Pont Celere '

He entered 1 man posted to Russia '

The only entry on the right hand side was Margarethe

18 *again shorthand for A H,* was printed in regulation at the bottom. Only Colonel Jed Strasser knew why page 18 had been chosen for these entries.

He picked up his phone:

'Bring me Major Johan Pikle's file, please.' It was on his desk within 10 minutes. On a red pad, he signed: "Colonel H Strasser" above his stamp. Tearing the form off, he gave it to the orderly, pointed to a corner table:

'Make it out for Major Pikle—for action, please.' The form authorised a transfer to the Russian front.

He sat back, rolled up his sleeve, rubbing his arm above the amputation, in anticipation. *Revenge delayed is sweet,* he thought, Major Pikle was responsible for Jed Strasser's missing hand. 'Missing page 88' was the message he passed to his sister and brother.

88—(Hail Hitler) like 18 was shorthand.

Major Pikle bought his friends a drink. 'Bye, chaps, don't expect to see you again, I'll be in Lvov tomorrow, Strasser's orders.' Everyone was silent.

'That's a bit quick,' someone remarked.

'I'm the fellow who trapped Strasser's arm,' said Pikle, 'I'm surprised I've lasted so long.'

Strasser's fury at the hijack of the gold had been satisfied by the revenge of shooting Martin Cockburn in the stomach, but his nest egg, his pension, had been wiped out by the hijack, the personal cost of the deaths at Pont Celere and the cover-up to save himself had been huge, with little money left, he needed to rebuild his pension pot. Self-preservation, now that it was clear to him that Germany would lose the war, rather than building a career, SP had become his new priority, but self-preservation in the style he demanded, meant he had to quickly re-establish what he called "a pension pot"… and time was running out.

It was not entirely the surrender of the 6th army at Stalingrad that convinced Strasser that Germany would lose the war, months ago General Halder spoke of a surprise lightning advance by part of his 7th army group that had overrun a portion of the Russian line. The Ukrainian Artillery Regiment had left markings on the ground for air supply drops, lo and behold, an Ilyushin came over and the parachute drop was made shortly after the 7th had taken over the Russian positions; three of the containers dropped were labelled:

"NEW YORK'S GIFT TO 3 REGIMENT Dneiperproposk HAPPY EASTER".

There weren't weapons, petrol or ammunition, just home comforts; pies, biscuits, hamburgers, cake—nicely wrapped, boxed, date coded, everyone had been baked less than one months before the drop, from places as far apart as Houston, Boston and Fort Lauderdale. The container had been consolidated outside New York and shipped to Europe by air.

Halder and Strasser worked out the logistics, concluding that with these US resources devoted to trivialities, allied to the Russian manpower coming ever stronger from east of the Urals, ranged against them, the Axis would surely be defeated. Furthermore, it was increasingly obvious that Ribbentrop's diplomatic attempts to bring Spain and Turkey into the war against the Allies had failed, the promised quick successful wars like 1939 and 1940 were not going to happen, but wild horses wouldn't drag this opinion out into the open, and with his comrades he remained optimistic in public. His dream of a comfortable retirement in a Crimean dacha melted further away with each strategic withdrawal, only ambition now hid a wish to vanish to a remote Alpine cottage, (emigration to South America had little attraction) he shuddered, to survive the war, he needed strong currency under firm control. The gold had been lost at Pont Celere, forget it.

Bormann had ordered 'Get secure storage for National Art—Paintings and Sculpture. Seydlitz, the National Curator had procured thousands upon thousands of artefacts seized from Museums and the aristocracy throughout occupied Europe.

Strasser finally selected the Hallstatt Salt Mine as the main deposit for paintings, and both Minister Speer (an admirer of Strasser's efficiency) and Air Marshall Goering (who had a soft spot for his only senior Luftwaffe Officer who was a member of the SS) had given their approval.

Under his plan prisoners would be taken from the Ebensee Building Program to open up the old mine levels at Hallstatt and make them fit to house priceless works of art in secure storage; to safeguard the location, on completion of the work, these prisoners were to be killed and left hidden in the mine, their names expunged from the Ebensee records.

'Any chance of profit?'—The Mine had been owned for centuries by the Halders, a family of inbred Bavarian Catholics, who watched each other like hawks. A back-hand arrangement with the Managing Director brother, the family looking on, was out of the question.

Curator Seidlitz had taken fright, the death of his protector Gauleiter Wasserberg, the new overwhelming handicap of his very name, "Seydlitz" having been taken over as the description to describe the sprinkling of captured German officers who had agreed to help the Russians. Von Paulus, who had surrendered the 6th army at Stalingrad was a case in point, in other words the name Seydlitz, through no fault of his own, had become synonymous with the word "traitor".

Seydlitz, his art market on the floor, was no longer in a position to engineer a financial coup.

Strasser's responsibilities for RAF POW Camps at Menzenschwand and elsewhere, were now but a fraction of his responsibilities, an important part was his overall control of the construction of a labour camp and the operations of the plant and equipment being installed out of reach of the RAF, at Ebensee where thousands of slave labourers were hollowing out limestone caves, for the installation and operation of a synthetic oil refinery and tank component manufacturing and other special equipment. Minister Albert Speer watched its progress like a hawk as the ability of the Reich to move its army was to depend on oil from the Ebensee refinery.

So, looking for money-making opportunities, when the file came across his desk of the Luftwaffe home for injured airmen Altaussee (a prime mountain village favoured by Nazi Officialdom), which was an extension to a row of old almshouses, he wondered if this could be turned into a "safehouse" and become a money pot.

"Wealthy Construction financiers" had become concerned that disfigured men, loitering, leering and littering "our village of Altaussee" were reducing property values, depressing prices and profit on the projected nearby high-value housing estate. The thought was raised, under his protection, the extension of the chalets in Altaussee should go ahead, but the retirement places for the disabled should be moved to Walserval, a remote "more suitable" location, the apartments at Bad Aussee intended for injured airmen, should then be upgraded to suit affluent married couples.

Walserval this "more suitable" location, was situated in an offshoot valley off an offshoot valley, between Munich and Salzburg, healthy climate, quiet, remote, unspoilt, cheap, where crippled drunken ex-servicemen would not disturb the ambience of Altaussee.

Luftwaffe benevolent fund money was available, Walserval was built as a series of separate small "pentlets" built in two adjacent blocks. These pentlets were easy access apartments for couples, in secluded grounds in a landscaped estate. Paying peppercorn rents, the injured airmen had lifetime occupancy, but their wives could be moved to allocated widows' accommodation on their husband's death.

Colonel Strasser used his position; Walserval was under his control.

Sergeant Muller put his head around the door, he had not waited for his knock to be answered for weeks now. Colonel Strasser looked up, the form before him needed his signature and TODT was committed to a half million spend.

'Something's happening sir, perhaps you should switch on,' he looked towards the wireless.

Before either moved to the wireless, one of the phones rang. The radio must wait, the colonel general picked up the red receiver.

'No.'

'No.'

'I'll switch on now.'

'Yes, I'll stand by,' putting down the receiver he gestured Muller to the wireless set. 'What's happening?' he asked.

Different messages came in on every radio channel, 40 messages came in over the Salzburg Palace's forty telephone lines, just one thing was clear and consistent: a small number of junior officers with grudges had tried to blow up the Fuhrer a bomb had detonated at army HQ.

Until he made his live broadcast, no one was certain whether Hitler had lived or died. Strasser had radios brought to his office; Muller fed office rumours, but after signing the TODT requisition, he did nothing, spoke to no one, stood by musing, waiting for the red phone to ring again.

Stationed In Austria, SS Luftwaffe Colonel General, Strasser was well away from army conspirators in Berlin and army HQs, neither the SS, the Kreigsmarine nor the Luftwaffe were involved in the assassination attempt, it was an army plot. Goering, Speer and their Ministries were in the clear, Strasser was in the clear. The red telephone summoned him to Munich, where Goering waited, considering conflicting objectives. Hitler dead he would need to seize power, Hitler alive he must remain whiter than white, yet stay out of the acrimony which would surely follow the attempt on the Fuhrer's life. He awaited instructions and dossiers from Berlin.

Hours after Strasser arrived Goering passed on instructions, 'Strasser must do some "clearing up", he must, as far as possible keep the Luftwaffe out of the mess, it's an army thing, let's keep it that way.' He mumbled the name of an underachieving suspect fighter squadron commander 'only if you must.' Armament Minister Albert Speer rang, concerned that nothing put back the installation of the prototype synthetic oil plant at Ebensee.

'I want Strasser back at Ebensee at the earliest possible moment.'

The locked file from Berlin, the file Goering was waiting for, arrived, it was not opened until guards were in position in the corridor outside the locked room that the red file taken out of its box. Headed in black capitals:

'Field Marshall Erwin Rommel.'

Strasser was about to be handed the political hot potato.

His remit was to examine the conduct of Field Marshall Rommel and his Staff.

Strasser hated it, fingering a fellow hater of Hitler, he followed an unaccustomed path… Although Sergeant Muller had driven him to Munich, Strasser, was there without his own staff. He never left the office, he interviewed no one, he visited no one; what he did was to spend many hours on the phone, he telephoned everywhere and wrote little, There were advantages, it ate up time because many people were never available to answer his questions, these lack of answers led to lack of clarity, lack of clarity led to lack of certainty, but by the end of day two it did not take the heavy breathing coming from Berlin, for him to conclude, demonstrate and report that Rommel's immediate staff knew there were plotters and plots against the Fuhrer, that Rommel must also have known and that he had been holding himself in reserve behind the plotters, until the time was ripe.

Phone calls, phone calls, little written on the files, Rommel's staff were identified and shot. National hero Erwin Rommel, at home recovering from wounds, received when an RAF plane strafed his staff car, needed finesse. Rommel along with Goering was still popular with the people, for the media now to name him as a traitor to the Fuhrer and the Fatherland could not be contemplated.

Strasser proposed the formula; two armed officers go to Rommel's home where he was recuperating, with orders not to leave without an answer. Their message as short and stark as the time Rommel was given:

'Die this day—from war wounds—and your widow, your family and her pension walk tall behind your draped coffin with full military honours at a State funeral.

Refuse, to be killed miserably, the fate of you and your family undecided.'

Rommel chose a quick lonely bullet:

Whilst this was happening, Goering called for a formal dinner in the mess. Not as sumptuous as his shooting lodge Carinhall, the airfield mess still reflected polished wood bronze and silver, and for the first time for a month four courses were to be served, but these were Bavarian cooks and not until wine flowed did conversation unbutton.

Their weapons program had averted Hitler's displeasure from Goering and the Luftwaffe, the V1, the V2, the jet engine had become the vision of victory following the reverses of the armies in Russia. Goering held that he never had the slightest confidence that the V1 would be effective, 'I told him (no longer did he say 'Adolf, Hitler, or the Fuhrer) they were slow, flew on a fixed course at a fixed height and we couldn't fix their crash point. It was silly for Josef (Goebbels) to make such a public song and dance, the British simply ignored them and gave them no publicity.'

Arter, a rocket scientist at HQ chipped in, although it was thrilling when the first successful V1 trialled at Peenemünde we never thought it a war-winner, the ramps were vulnerable to the RAF, but we thought the jet engine and particularly the V2 would win us the war.' Goering sparkling in the morning, now a drowsy shadow but still the WW! Fighter ace rehearsed his pet subject,

'Speed doesn't win the air war, to see that look at the Ruhr. The RAF bomb at night, the Flying Fortresses bomb Essen and Koln during the day. Our fighters and our pilots are better, faster, but the balance is narrow and the bigger numbers and formation organisation mean we haven't been able to stop or defeat them. Our extra speed is good but by itself, it doesn't win the war.'

Strasser never involved with the tactics of fighting bombing raids on Germany, summoned up courage, 'Is it too late now for the V2 to win the war for us?' Goering took a long drink, wiping his mouth with the back of his hand, his eyes sank even deeper into their sockets, everyone was nervous, the V2 was still highly secret, would he answer the question?

'I'll let Arter answer that.' Everyone looked at Professor Arter, he got to his feet adding emphasis to his low-pitched voice carrying the echoes of doom.

'The V2, it could have won us the war, it just might still help us win, the V2, whoever becomes its owner, will certainly win the war after this one. The V2 can hit your enemy at any time of day or night, it can hit him anywhere and he can't do a damn thing about it. At present, it isn't long range enough; at present, it isn't accurate enough and doesn't carry enough explosive. Colonel General Strasser can't make enough in the time available to us,' he paused, 'The British don't know it, but they saved themselves when they found and destroyed the Krupps Essen factory and of course Peenemünde where three top people died and von Braun was injured.' Murmurs went around the table, Goering coughed and sat forward,

'Thanks Arter. If we, Colonel General Strasser, can build enough quickly, and improve its sense antennae so we could strike at Churchill himself, and if the army can last out until its development is complete, we can win the war.' Goering slumped back in his chair.

Discussion rumbled on till Goering fell asleep and they all said 'good night' and went to bed.

Strasser had never wanted or sought to be the instrument to bring death to officers who hated Hitler; he had made the best of a bad job, not seeking further employment to track down the conspirators, his task over, he ordered Muller to prepare his car for a dawn return to Salzburg.

Dawn had broken, Strasser saw it first, Muller driving fast, focussing on the long open straight stretch of autobahn before him, the speck above the trees quickly changed from a UFO to a low-level plane, a plane flying straight up the autobahn towards them. Strasser reached down and pulled up the Mauser light machine gun he always carried and cradled it and cocked it, one good hand one false hand. 'Look out,' he said.

At that time in the war, at that time in the morning, with only the one car within miles and with only one clear intention for the plane. Strasser, air-craft recognition being a must for all officers of the Luftwaffe, recognised a Mosquito and took aim.

Travelling at a 170 km an hour, manoeuvring of the Mercedes was limited, at the very last moment Muller braked and edged right, edged enough for the cannon to kick up tar rather than mangle metal, 40 seconds later the Mercedes was in the shadow of trees and the Mosquito had vanished.

'Well done, Sergeant,' Strasser highly excited had, at last, fired a weapon in anger, 'I think I might have hit it with a couple,' he rubbed his wrist, burnt by touching the hot barrel.

'I thought we were going over the embankment,' Muller was equally elated at his skilful driving. Between them, they had saved one another.

The Wehrmacht's failure to win the 1943 tank battle at Kursk, resulted in Strasser, along with many Generals, deciding that the war was no longer winnable. With control of the apartments at Altaussee and Walserval, he would get rid of service pensioner tenants and replace with frightened Nazi officials prepared to pay for a safe haven. Ease out the old, bring in the new to pay him to live together in desirable boltholes safe from being named as war criminals.

Kursk was the trigger, income from frightened men would outdo a hundred times income from service pensioners. Income he could divert, "his way".

Below part reposition before assassination section.

The plan; he would need strong full-time supervision of the apartments, with backing from an enforcer. When the time was ripe the service pensioners would have to be moved on, forced out if necessary. His new frightened tenants who had gorged themselves on a conquered Europe. They would pay the earth to save themselves until the war had passed over, for his secure accommodation and a false identity, available on demand.

The pensioners in the almshouses at Altaussee who were to be moved to the new apartments at Walserval, must either die or be persuaded to move again. He knew just the man to be such an enforcer, Ritter, top of any Allied war crime list. A cold killer of errant slave labourers at Ebensee, a man he could rely on to carry out his orders and enforce discipline on pensioners or new tenants alike. Tenants would have to be intensely disciplined, war-crime refugees living in the close-knit apartments, one loose word to family or friends and his safe apartments would be in jeopardy.

Strasser realised that timing was key; to get empty apartments (pentlets, as he liked to call them) the sitting servicemen, most living alone, must be moved out days beforehand. The new tenants were much too scared of the SS to leave their official posts prematurely, if they did they would be at greater risk from the SS than from the Russians, like lemmings they would only rush for safety the day it became clear that the capture of their town by the Allies was imminent, or that Hitler was dead.

Timing crucial, he noted further requirements.

'Deaths of the tenants must be suppressed so that their identities, as well as their accommodation, became available, his staff in Salzburg in central control of the paperwork were well equipped to do that.'

The "war-criminals" wanting a new identity, which again his staff could provide, must pay; cash in hard currency, not DM, in advance, plus cash for maintenance, as he intended to control the supply of food. He would offer new identities, either by transferring the identities of dead pensioners or by using his Salzburg offices to create new identities, where an official scheme was already set up in conjunction with the SS, to issue the SS with fake identities.

Strasser alone, his scheme set up well in advance, would then be in a position to offer wealthy officials and their wives, good isolated secure accommodation away from the mayhem which would inevitably follow the breakdown of society. Foreign troops, whether Allied or Czech, Russian or Pole, every man jack of them would be intent on rape, pillage and revenge. Dark days lay ahead and there were women in Eastern German fringes to vouch for this.

Strasser still couldn't sleep, he turned over, he would start to put this plan into operation the next morning; he already had in mind the perfect "enforcer". Tomas Ritter, who he had promoted into Ebensee from Mauthausen Forced Labour Camp, a natural sadistic bully, was beholden to Strasser, for keeping him out of Ukraine but more than that by saving him from SS's own punishment for an astonishing crime. He visualised Ritter strangling vulnerable pensioners with his bare hands. Before sleep came he had gone on to imagine a stone-faced Ritter drown, run over, decapitate and electrocute pensioners both women and men of all ages, to clear them out of their apartments to make way for paying customers.

But what would the Allies do, it was more and more likely that the Americans would take Southern Germany, ordinary soldiers might well ignore Wehrmacht atrocities in Russia; after all, US marines and British paratroopers were hardly noted for taking prisoners in the jungles in Burma. Would the Jews of New York, their money behind President Roosevelt, allow Nazi officials, Gestapo, SS, even Labour Camp functionaries and there were many such at Mauthausen and Ebensee, escape retribution? He didn't think so, and there were thousands upon thousands of such people, and he, Strasser, was one of them.

His gut feeling was that out there was a market who would prefer to lay up for a year in the backwater of Walserval, than come face to face with occupying troops of whatever nationality.

'I'll really start in the morning.' He went to sleep, dreaming that the path to regaining his lost fortune was opening up in front of him, the opportunity to restore his fortune was there waiting to be grasped.

Next morning, he called for the property transfer files for Walserval and the almshouses at Altaussee files and reread them, noting the legal steps needed for full control, he asked Sergeant Muller to get a full list of residents and staff, then issued an instruction that all admissions must be approved by a new "steering committee", a committee he nominate there and then from his and associated Command Offices, without Colonel General Hans Strasser's name appearing on a single document.

6/8/18 words 130,848

Later in the week, he called Ritter in to see him, Ritter, controller of the forced labour and Russian prisoner work force at Ebensee, ostensibly to report on the progress of the construction of tunnels, caverns, road and rail connections, and (a recurring problem) the quality of the supply of slave labour coming in from Mauthausen. Finished he took Ritter, to dine at Heytorn, a lakeside restaurant on the Gmund road, a thousand miles from the salt water of the Black Sea.

Ritter was everyone's image of a German butcher, thickset, thick neck, thinning blonde waved hair, common but cunning and hard-working, street-wise, that goes without saying, the only other thing it is important to know is that as a known ruthless killer, 10,000 worker slaves at Ebensee would have willingly slashed his body into a hundred strips, such was his reputation.

Strasser sketched out a wealthy future, even with the war as it was if Ritter agreed to work for him, a future requiring secrecy, nerve and skulduggery. He sketched out his plan, Ritter would be the enforcer for Walserval, no regular duties, live out, good pay in hard currency. Ritter knew full well that once the camp labourers were released and ever got hold of him they would kill him outright in the most horrible fashion He knew full well, he would be listed as a major war criminal, if he were to outlive the war his only chance would be to disappear for good and that before the Allies arrived.

'I know the job's a bad "un", Ritter was not an educated man, 'I reckon I'll need three years up on the mountains before I'm likely to be safe… even the,' he shrugged, 'I've got hides ready up on the Dachstein, that's where I'll go when the time comes, I'll be OK,' he told Strasser. Strasser's offer had come out of the blue, a well-paid shadowy enforcer was just the job he needed and was qualified for—non-better, he would live on Dachstein and come down from the mountain, do a job and be back in the mountains in no time at all. He agreed the pay, he agreed to be the enforcer, 'Love it,' he said to himself.

'Unless Hitler dies, the war won't end for months' Strasser said 'but something has to be attended to within six weeks.' He handed Ritter two pieces of paper, each a different colour taken from a different pad, one held a name and an address in Rothstein on Ebbs, the other, a four-figure number.

'By the end of the month,' he said.

'I'll see to it within a fortnight,' Ritter replied.

Corporal Muller, ever loyal, but fully aware of Colonel Strasser's disloyalty to the Reich, promoted as promised to Sergeant, had followed Strasser to the Salzburg Palace HQ and Command Post. With such a high rate of wastage in German Generals, Strasser now a three-star SS Luftwaffe Colonel General was strongly supported by Armaments Minister Albert Speer and Goering, though for reasons of his own, he continued use the simple addressed of colonel.

Muller, working in the offices at the Salzburg palace, had recovered from the bullet wounds received at Pont Celere and was none-the-worse for being sprung, brought back into Germany, still fully-bandaged from the Zurich hospital.

In the car on the journey to Ebensee, he looked back at Strasser through the rear mirror. 'I hear Major Passau's received a poison letter telling him about the ambush, saying you were stealing Germany's gold reserves that you had had packed into boxes made by British airmen, prisoners at Menzenschwand.' Strasser didn't reply, 'I believe the letter came from the prisoner who escaped, "Cockburn" if I remember his name correctly.'

In the mirror he saw a look of worry turn to anger. 'Is that so?' Strasser paused, 'Don't worry about it, Sergeant, it's all over now, the gold was originally to pay for a statue of our leader on the Rhine, then when things took a bad turn to build a "festung" on Dachstein, but the plans have been discarded, a festung is not necessary, we're going to win the war.' Strasser mused aloud,

'So, I'm still bothered by that schweinehund Cockburn, I thought I'd killed him,' it was a minute before he spoke. 'I'll put Major Passau in the picture as soon as we get back,' Strasser mused further, 'Just when I thought that particular

Jack was back in its box,' then speaking to himself, 'I should have killed that Cockburn. The Swiss doctors must have patched him up.'

In the morning he dropped into Major Passau's office, coming to the point straightaway.

'I believe you've had a poison letter about me.'

'Have I?' Passau acted surprised.

'Yes, you have.'

'Yes, so I have,' Passau now on tenterhooks passed the buck and waited on Strasser.

'Well, some of it will be true, there was a failed Swiss operation, finance intended for a secret "festung" was stolen, it was run by Wasserberg, who I think you know, and yes, he was killed, and yes, several men died, including my batman.' Passau murmured sympathetically.

'Operation Kiel, the name of the operation, was blown, all traces were deleted on the instructions of Air Marshall Goering and Martin Bormann, the failure was an embarrassment to the highest echelons of the Reich, it was decided not to allow our enemies to have any chance to publicise the failure. Operation Kiel was made the subject of a "Silent Order" and, as such, even the very name mustn't be divulged, so I can't tell you more, nor can I authorise sight of any file, if you need more, the permission of Seyss Inquart will be needed.

'Oh, Colonel, I don't think that will be necessary,' Passau said hastily; he opened a drawer, pulled out the letter, ostentatiously tore it to shreds and dropped the pieces into his waste bin. 'There's to be no "festung" then.'

So it was a damp squib that ended Martin's poison letter revenge on Colonel Strasser. The stolen loot, the death of five

Germans at Pont Celeste, the gold, the porcelain, the paintings, the artefacts had all been covered by the Silent Order, and the obliteration of Operation Kiel was complete, the hijacked gold was now officially secret funding for a "festung".

In the clear, there was nothing to prevent Strasser from putting his plan into operation.

Chapter 5
Martin Bids Farewell

'So you've nothing to do?' Sir Pelham Sinclair faced Martin across the desk carved out of the trees from the clearances at Glen Borrowdale, a desk which had followed him from Moidart to Istanbul, to Delhi, to Riyadh then on to Berne. 'You haven't told me much of what you think of the state Germany's in. Will they keep on fighting for Hitler with the Russians over the Vistula or will they battle on until the Russians are drinking vodka and dancing in the Unter den Linden?'

'Hillary thinks they'll keep fighting, the innkeeper's wife we told you about at Berchtesgaden, hated the war but she still had faith, but I'm not so sure. I know that I wouldn't.'

'Neither would I ,' Sir Pelham changed the subject: 'What a stint you've put in here at Berne since your escape from Prison Camp, you've fingered my secret Zurich bank account, burnt my secretary's fingers for letting her husband Gustav Holst see our papers and pass them on to the Germans, Vert's been killed, Harris fell off the Wetterhorn, you've had splinters of window glass taken out of your shoulder, you've had three bullets in your stomach and lost a ball, and you've got yourself a fine, busty wench,' he laughed and chortled out loud, 'and lost poor Greville and his wife a fortune.' He beamed, 'But, and I've only ever admitted this to my wife, best of all you've put a big, red star up on my career, Moscow, even the Washington Embassy could be next for me young man, Sir Pelham Sinclair the Swiss Ambassador, opening 'the Second Front,' beating Monty and Patton to it, there's a dinner with brandy from the vaults, at the Bank of England as soon as I'm back in London, with gold cufflinks from the Yanks and the Russians after they melt down the gold teeth and the spectacles,' he paused, 'I don't know whether I told you this, the Russians recovered an icon hung at the college where Stalin studied to be a priest, and he is so pleased he's given Ambassador Morov the order of Tsar Dmitri or somebody, or other, Nicholas the third I think.' He stood up, came around the desk and shook Martin warmly by the hand.

'Your Second Front has made me a star, I'll never be short of a Foreign Office dinner whilst I'm still able to tell the story of how I stole millions from under the noses of the SS, I'm sorry to lose you, but believe me I won't be sorry to see you go.' He smiled benevolently. 'Is your English up to knowing what I mean?'

Martin spoke:

'I know you think the hijack is the hi-light, Sir Pelham, but I think that what Hillary and I did in finding Ebensee was the best, we risked our lives, and I don't understand why the RAF haven't blown it to smithereens.'

'Give them time old boy.' Sir Pelham changed the subject.

'London, want you back. Transport's fixed for next week, you and Hillary go together. No argument.'

He pushed across a stack of documents, 'Translations, before you go I want translations from you, nothing else.

Translations, that's your job now, I don't want you doing any investigating, no more revenge or tying up loose ends for Christ's sake.' It was all spoken happily. Martin picked up the papers and made for the door before turning:

'Boss,' it was the first time he had called Sir Pelham "Boss", 'I've still got to get my own back on Strasser.'

'Of course, you have. Go back to Germany, do it when the war's over, and do it when I'm not there,' said Sir Pelham.

Before the end of the day Sir Pelham called both Martin and Hillary back into the office.

'I know it seems a long time ago but because of the deaths and your shooting we never properly celebrated "the second front", after all, it happened before the Normandy landings, Lady Sinclair's arranged a get together, Le Cygne seems a good place, and Brenda's agreed we can use the chateau. It's time I had a social chat with the US and Russian ambassadors again, anyway.'

Hillary gushed with pleasure, Martin wasn't so sure.

'It's an order, Martin, Saturday, it's fixed, Brenda's chateau, Le Cygne, Brenda's Chateau host Gustav Holst, he's offered to pay, can't think why, feels guilty I suppose. One way or another they all played a part. Neat don't you think?'

Martin's face said he didn't think.

Different guests had different slants on the party, Gorgeous George, the American Ambassador wrote to the chair of New York Republicans:

We celebrated our "second front", I told you about me, Morov and Sinclair finished bottles of whisky, bourbon and vodka. I didn't tell them the value of our cut, didn't want Sir

Pelham to be sick, I gave everybody a Yukon gold tiepin telling them we got a good deal over Alaska… all that gold!

Stalin's concerned that Roosevelt's ill, I told Morov Harry Truman's OK. Stalin's got FDR to agree that they can take Berlin—reward for their millions of casualties. He's giving the main tank divisions to Zhukov for the push, Churchill is furious, but then he dislikes Monty as much as Bradley does.

Germans can't go on, stupid to continue resisting, rape in the east, pillage in the west. Sinclair doesn't believe for a minute that Churchill stayed in Marrakesh from fatigue, he thinks a stroke or DTs or something!

Morov's rock-steady, daren't say who would follow Stalin if there was an accident, but frowns when I say Molotov; my guess Vyshinsky, or Malenkov not Beria.

Lady Irene had asked each embassy to provide a national dish using "wartime" rationing ingredients; her waspish letter to spinster elder sister gushed:

Tour of Brenda's chateau, Brenda disappeared with Martin to the Priest's Hole I've told you about, Martin's partner Hillary was furious. Everybody wanted to see the Priests hole, I squeezed in for a session with Groper George! What a nerve that man's got, how his wife puts up with it!

Food: Martin and Hillary brought cabbage and potato peeling soup, served in billy cans, staple diet at POW and Gulags apparently. My Burns night main course had added testicles and cow's eyes, it didn't get finished (even started really) till we put it on the Czechnyans table. (We kept them separate, disgusting really but fun!)

Gorgeous Georgette turned up trumps with Texas steaks and Maine lobsters, FRESH, god knows how long it took to get them to Swiss. I don't know how they do it, the Yanks seem to beat us at every little thing, even canasta.

No wine, just Russian Champagne and caviar for us, lumpfish and beer for the ORs.

Morov's wife's dress came from an 1890 Bolshoi Swan Lake production, she's a failed ballerina: beautiful, white, fitted like a glove, jewels and sable white calfskin moulded boots half way to the knee, the bottom of the dress swan scalloped. Head dress, from Kirov ballet, Giselle, made especially by Igor Zhdanov for Berisklava. She put even six ft. Brenda Chan in the shade, who was in full fig, a silk Chinese job, tight as a guardsman's breeches, even the part of her bosom which wasn't covered up, Sir Pelham insists on her as his Secretary, just because, like him she bought Churchill a Spitfire, my husband will pay for it if it's the last thing I do.

Gustav Holst, Chan's husband looked terrified the whole time we were there, even though he'd offered us the Chateau, he hardly said a word.

Sir Pelham drank too much so he missed his Balkan romp when we got home and he's sulking… I asked if he'd noticed my recently acquired diamond earrings. Of course he hadn't, he hadn't even noticed Elspeth Greville's sash was secured with a Clasp from an eighteenth century Polish coat of arms, Greville had an identical Clasp on his cummerbund. Shhh, Shhh wonder where they came from.

Morov and his wife wore silver Polish Guards Cap Badges on their chests, shh, shh, Major Irina had bracelets twinkling with more diamonds than ever came out of Siberia, she insisted in pointing to them and telling everybody 'Ambush Job.' Shhh

The US wore a tie clip and dangly earrings, but I don't believe they came from you know where Tryfan's belt buckle looked heavy. I said "have you had it long?" "Since the battle," he said, only Martin Cohen, whose battle it really was, wasn't wearing anything pinched from the "second front".

Must stop if I'm to catch the post.

Irene

PS

Stop Press

When we came out to the cars, lying on the gravel was Gustav Holst. Head bleeding, sprawled out like a Swastika, a dog beside him.

'Get in the cars,' Morov shouted and we were whisked away before the police arrived.

They'll want to question us I'm sure, particularly after all the other shootings and stabbings, I'll let you know how we get on.

Irene.

As their final day in Switzerland loomed, unfinished business, Martin unhappy that Colonel Strasser remained alive, it seemed he would have to wait till the end of the war to get revenge. 'What about a final attempt?' he asked Hillary.

He wasn't optimistic but using Hillary's phone book, he phoned SS HQ, in Salzburg, using the patch that Tony Adams had rigged, allowing him to ring into Germany as if the calls came from Konstanz.

'Sergeant Muller.' Muller wasn't available, he arranged to ring back an hour later; to his surprise Muller himself answered the phone.

'Perhaps you remember me,' he began, 'Martin Cockburn, Menzenschwand camp, buying seeds, the escapee, the ambush, the ambush, surely you remember me.'

All quiet then a hesitant, 'Yes, it's Cockburn, isn't it, where are you speaking from?'

'Doesn't matter, it's just that I have a message you should consider carefully, it may help you. Are you ready?' Another pause.

'Go on, it's Martin Cockburn, isn't it?'

'Yes, I knew you'd remember me, you recognised me when you were lying injured in that ditch at Pont Celere didn't you?'

'Not at first,' Muller replied, 'only later it came back to me, when I'd recovered a bit, 'his voice still uncertain.

'I'll go on then. It's about Hallstatt salt mine. Bodies in Hallstatt graveyard lie 10 years before their skeletons are dug up and piled up with the others, you know.'

'Yes I know.' Muller was now speaking louder, more confident and animated.

'Yes, well if you leave bones in that salt mine when you hide your paintings, well, we'll find them and we'll know who left the bones there. You'll be hunted and the evidence of those bones will kill you, because it was you who put them there, capish! You know what I mean?'

Although Sergeant Muller's reply could hardly be construed as a "yes", Martin kept going.

'Something else, you remember Pont Celere, you know that an SS man escaped into the woods with Strasser?'

'Yes, I remember, he was shot and injured and he didn't make it back.' Muller was now speaking normally.

'I know he didn't make it back, and I know why he didn't make it back, Strasser shot him and dumped his body in a forest pool, but I don't know why Strasser shot him, and I think you should ask Colonel Strasser that question.'

Muller mumbled uncertainly, then: 'How do you know that?'

'Because the bullet that killed him came out of the gun that shot me in the stomach at the Hotel Rhine Falls, and I've seen the match, but leave that aside, I'm enquiring into Strasser, I'm enquiring into Ebensee, and I'm enquiring into that dead soldier shot in the head by Strasser's gun, and Strasser will pay. You're a decent fellow, Muller, tell Strasser I'll get him. I'm coming for him; if I were you, I'd get as far away from SS Colonel Hans Strasser as I could, the war's nearly over, he's on my list and he's on every war criminal list from here to Auschwitz, and he's bad news.'

He replaced the receiver before Sergeant Muller could reply.

Lying in bed he told Hillary what he'd done. She sat up in bed and punched him.

'You idiot, you've actually told Strasser you're alive, you've told him you know where he is, what he's done, and you're going to get him. You know what he'll do now, he'll come after you again, he'll come out of the shadows. Next time he'll kill you. You're a silly billy.'

'I know I am, I know I shouldn't have, I can't help myself, I want that bastard…'

'Go to sleep.'

'I can't sleep now. You're silly, but I love you.' She snuggled down in bed, drawing him towards her.

Martin's orders were to return to England and report to Fowler Bottom, the airfield where he was stationed so many months ago, but the war had moved on, and Fowler Bottom was now too far from the front line and was no longer an operational airfield flying active missions; it had been turned into a fighter training camp, bombing raids on Germany were conducted from airfields in France and Belgium. Fowler Bottom runway wasn't long enough for the latest Lancaster bombers, and to retrain on Lancasters Martin would need to go to the east coast of Scotland. Worried that time and injury might have closed down his career as a pilot, he decided to set his jaw and attack, using his DFC as a weapon.

Two days later, Hillary and Martin were back in England, Lady Irene Sinclair again put pen to paper to her spinster sister.

... last letter... Dear Sis... that evening entertainment. Major Irina brought a huge samovar from Kiental and guarded it as if it were the crown of the Tsars, never stopped poring tea all night.

The Yanks showed a military film unit newsreel showing Hitler opening an autobahn at Rothstein where Martin was a boy. He pointed excitedly at the screen

'That's me,' but he was too small and too far away for it to mean anything, then again when a little girl gave Hitler a posy...'My Friend Gretl, I think,' he said.

Madame Morov changed into a "Giselle costume" and danced it with "Tryfan", she'd danced with the Kirov before her injury and this was her "party piece". We all did a turn, talk about Xmas, sorry Christmas, I know you don't like shortcuts, we did the charade when we were all drunk that Christmas.

Cars at 1 am, the bathroom looked as if a tsumani had hit it. Brenda was furious and so would I have been.

Love Irene

PS

That bit I put in about Gustav Holst being found dead was a tease. I thought the letter wasn't interesting so I spiced it up, Holst is still alive, repeat ALIVE. He looked like a dead man walking however!

Love,

Irene

Back in England, no one at Falmouth, no one at Paddington to meet them, Martin saw Hillary into a taxi to take her straight to her parent's vicarage in North Sussex. Before Martin left Euston Station, he rang Moxon, asking if he would let him know if any traffic came in relating to Hallstatt Salt Mine, which was being adapted by the Nazis to store art treasures.

He rang Fowler's Bottom who told him to take 10 days leave, as they weren't expecting or ready for him.

Two days later with his mother and father, 3d paid for three platform tickets, they met Hillary's train at Piccadilly, hot sunlight beating off the stone sets of Peterloo Square they walked to the LMS Midland Hotel for a banquet November 1944 style; brown Windsor soup, boiled chicken with mashed potatoes and peas, Tetley bitter, apple pie and custard; Father grumbled at being made to shell out for a pot of tea costs less at Schmidts in Berne,' Hillary remarked, turning her saucer over, it was stamped "LMS Goods , Mirfield".

'Where's Mirfield?' she asked.

'I'll make us something nice when we get home.' Martin's mother and father were fully taken with Hillary. Before going to bed his mother caught him alone in the kitchen.

'When are you going to marry her?'

'As soon as the war's over,' he replied after a pause, 'if she'll have me.'

The sleeping arrangements were fluid as his father was to say: 'Ad hoc.'

Chapter 6
Ebensee Mountain Graveyard

Lorries, bellowing tarpaulins stretched over iron frames, converged from museums throughout northern Germany to the wide grounds of Belsen hospital, lying by the river Weser, deep and wide to the south of Hamelin. Under the watchful eyes of SS guards their contents were unloaded, sorted, grouped, ticked off, allocated and reloaded. The lorries left at 20-minute intervals carrying gold, foreign currency, platinum, etc., but the bulk comprised paintings. Two trucks together had a motor cycle escort; petrol tanks and jerrycans full to the brim. No stops, the lorries drove through Frankfurt and Nuremberg to Dachau, where they met up, and where after more checking, they split—gold and currency went towards the deep lakes of the Bavarian Alps, the pictures and the Pergammon sculptures east to Austria and the Hallstatt Salt Mine.

Although Strasser was instrumental in the selection of the salt mine, he did not attend at the unloading, this was left to Seydlitz, German Curator of Reich Museums, who oversaw the unloading and stacking of the paintings Ritter had selected strong men from Ebensee to unload the pictures and statues into re-opened levels 4 and 5 of the Hallstatt mine.

It took a day before the contents of the last lorry were carried manually underground, Seydlitz emerged from the gloom, visibly agitated, he went the 60 metres down the road—to eat, where he was served by the same flirtatious waitress as had annoyed Hillary. Seated next to Ritter and the convoy commander, the waitress had the cake knife in her hand, lifting the home-made apelstrudel off the tray when. 'What's that?' she said. 'Sounds like gun shots.'

'It is exactly that,' said Ritter, 'it's, "gun fire",' wiping his spoon on the tablecloth.

The prisoners did not expect to be killed, the waitress had brought down bottles of beer, said to be rewards for doing a good job well and quickly. They were sat in a circle, the light was dim, the guards fired from behind. Two prisoners weren't shot, their fate was to dig a shallow trench and dump the bodies along with the empty cartridge cases. Before completely covering the bodies, realising this was to be their final task, they made a run for it, a reasonable gamble considering the gloom and the myriad tunnels and niches on the different levels, but the guards were ready, shots echoed around the tunnels and they fell. Dragged back, their bodies were put alongside the others and the last of the loose soil kicked over their corpses.

Unobtrusively, Seydlitz dumped his apelstrudel in the field near to the cows, wiping his plate on the grass before returning it to the table. He was almost sick, but not quite.

On that same day, Colonel General Strasser returned to Salzburg from Berlin. Calling in his section leaders, he announced new priorities and allotted revised responsibilities, the main concern being that the prototype synthetic oil production facility at Ebensee be given an even higher priority.

'The army on the eastern front must be reinforced, Hitler gave at as his main concern after the explosion. The Generals are on to Speer, all the time, "more ammunition, more tanks, more petrol", when infantrymen are limited to 20 bullets a day, tanks to 10 miles a day, when anti-aircraft batteries can only fire 10 shells a night at the Flying Fortesses, which are so difficult for our Focke-Wolfs, when company commanders staff cars are withdrawn and have to cycle to inspect forward units. Petrol is vital, Ebensee must be encouraged to exert every muscle to support the men at the front line. None of you must tolerate any slackness!

'Fuel for our fighters is in such short supply that disputes break out even at HQ because sufficient petrol and planes aren't available to give air support to the battlefield, defend our cities, and to defend our vital manufacturing plants at one and the same time. The Fuhrer of course is magnificent, he has recovered, but he needs all our efforts to deliver him the resources to secure victory, the oil plant must have our total support. I know I can rely on you.'

Strasser reached one arm behind his head, scratching below his ear. Next his artificial hand reached into his pocket, drew out a cigarette holder, extracted a cigarette, lighting it from the lighter on his desk, all with the same maimed hand. It was a show-stopper.

Major Schwartz tabled a summary of progress at Ebensee, remarking that high prisoner death rates were reducing both output and the progress of excavating the caverns. He said Passau had transferred 15 White Russians (White Russians were Ukrainians who supported Germany) to act as guards for the prisoners, these Ukrainians had earlier fought in Vlasov's Army Corps, against the Red Army, regarded as deserters they were as good as dead if the Russians ever caught them. This had caused a problem as some 200 of the forced labour were Russian Prisoners; these prisoners had already killed two of the Ukrainian guards; in retaliation Ritter had ordered the execution of 18 Russian prisoners. 'Quite right,' Strasser remarked, exactly what I would have done, however we must remember that dead prisoners can't make shells. Please bear that in mind.'

Strasser felt the labour being sent from Mauthausen was of poor quality and asked for suggestions,

One strand of what followed was that prisoners were now beginning to believe that Germany were losing the war, some had been shot for shouting at German technicians working on the Plant, that they would all be killed when the Allies arrive, and there had been attempts at sabotage. Strasser rapped out final instructions:

'We stop all work on extending the caverns, our only priority is to get out tank parts and especially oils,' Turning to Ritter, bring in more wood to heat the huts. Increase the bread ration, increase work time by an hour.' Ritter look gloomy,

'Is that each day or per week?'

'Per,' Strasser hesitated, 'per week, we must think of our guards as well as the prisoners. Can't you get more bread?' Strasser questioned.

'I can try,' Ritter replied.

'Schwartz, ask for 300 additional men from Mauthausen to work on the roads and to straighten the line by the castle, iron out the loading bay, extend it, no cavern extensions for now, double up hut occupation, if necessary, don't accept weaklings in this 300, I'll speak to Mauthausen this afternoon.

The work at Hallstatt Salt Mine is finished, unfortunately the detachment working there are no longer be available to us.'

'Go to it, on our work depends the victory.'

The briefing over, the men and both women present, rose, saluted and filed out, leaving only a hovering Muller. 'What is it, Sergeant?' He had picked up the signals.

'Remember the letter that Cockburn sent the Area Commander,'

Strasser nodded. 'When I picked up my phone yesterday, it was Cockburn on the line, I've hesitated mentioning it to you.' Strasser sat back, stubbed out his cigarette.

'Cockburn! He what? He phoned you, saying what?'

'He's going to hunt you down when the war's over.'

'Hunt me down, hunt me down, some chance,' Strasser reached behind his ear with his opposite hand, 'what else did he say?'

'He mentioned Hallstatt and Ebensee, he said that if the Allies find dead bodies at Hallstatt they will hold you responsible, as well as all the guards at Ebensee, every single one of them will be listed, tracked and treated as war-criminals, something like that.'

'What did you tell him?'

'Nothing I just listened, I was trying to figure out how he knew we had been at Hallstatt, how he'd managed to get a phone call through to me, how he knew about the problems. I asked the operator for a trace, the call came from Konstanz, sir.'

'You did well, Muller, if he rings again put him through to me.'

Code word "Watch on the Rhine" Germany's "last hurrah" for the war in the west, the code word's significance missed by both British and American Intelligence: "Battle of the Bulge"; the last significant German tank force in the west crossed their start line in good weather and with surprise on their side scored early successes, initial optimism soon gave way to the realism that Germany losing battles consistently over the previous 18 months wasn't going to change.

Strasser's promotion to more stars and incentive pay as a Lieutenant General had boosted his enthusiasm and effort, but this enthusiasm soon evaporated, and he reverted to his personal and financial preoccupations and survival. He decided upon a visit to Digby, *SBO (Senior British Officer)* at Menzenschwand RAF Prison Camp, an old stamping ground.

Gauleighter Wasserberg and Strasser had provided work for RAF Menzenschwand prisoners. With his death, work ceased. the Allies landing in France, why risk your life in a prison escape, and escape plans remained just that—plans, food shortages were protested, and when the head of the German Red Cross, the Duke of Saxe-Coburg-Gotha, visited the camp, he listened politely to Digby, hid the fact that he was the English born grandson of Queen Victoria, but could do little to improve the circumstances of the prisoners.

New! News! News became the POW camp obsession, news, cards and letters from home, news and food was all they lived for, with sex outside Hut 3, taking a back seat for at least some of the time. Then, Bets! Bets! Bets became the compulsion and order of the day, not so much within the card schools where rivalry was the main driver.

Bets on everything: how many miles would the Russians/ Monty/ Patton/ Clark/ advance per day. What day would Duisburg/ Koln/ Strasburg/ Hannover/ Dusseldorf be captured, what date would the Russians cross the Vistula, the Danube, the Elbe? What cities were to be bombed that night, how many bombers would Goebbels claim were shot down? How many fish would lie in the holding bubble in the stream at 6 o'clock each might. The Berlin nine o'clock news was the basis of settling most bets, the currency for betting—cigarettes, chores, like making beds and IOUs.

Bookies black boards featured in every hut, listing bets and odds; punters busied from one hut to the next, comparing odds and whether bets were based on the BBC nine o'clock or Munich's 6 o'clock news, when Red Cross parcels dried up cigarettes were in even shorter supply, the currency for the bets more and more became IOUs.

Queues formed as POWs wrote out the terms of their IOUs. The bookies met in Hut 2 every night after the nine o'clock news over a single glass of weak cherry wine, discussing the bets for the following day.

Disliking what was happening, in an attempt to bring order to a wild field of play, Digby, Senior British Officer, organised a grand sweepstake, every prisoner entered including the padre, the stake was a day's pay, payable after the war. The guards were invited to enter; none took up the challenge, they had seen the writing on the wall, to enter such a bet invited an SS bullet in the head; the event on which the sweepstake depended was the day and the hour the first Allied soldier came through the Prison gate. The pay-out was to be at the end of the month following repatriation.

A second sweepstake, voluntary this time, was organised by Hut Two on the date of the Japanese surrender and was won by Flight Engineer Tom Margerison who's bet of Christmas Day 1945 was nearest but as he missed it by over five months, and as the treasurer had emigrated to Australia he never received his winnings; such was his intense annoyance, that he wrote to both the Times and the Sydney Times in an attempt to shame the treasurer.

Wireless sets came out into the open and openly broadcast, albeit at a low volume, indeed some English-speaking guards were sufficiently emboldened as to lurch around to overhear news broadcasts. It was in this changed environment Digby, Senior British Officer, was called to the Camp Commander's Office. O/C Major Weissman had given up his chair to SS Lieutenant Colonel General Strasser, who stood up and shook hands with Digby as if greeting an old friend.

'Such a nice morning perhaps a stroll will do us good,' he said. The entire complement of prisoners watched as they circled the perimeter, even the card school in Hut 1 broke off for all of five minutes, speculation was rife and on the mark, 'he wants a deal,' on passing the marked spot where Tom and Dick had been shot dead.

'Looks as if you've won.'

'Looks as if we have,' replied Digby, 'Russians, Zhukov crossed the Vistula, Patton's over the Rhine at Remagen, Elbe next I expect. Montgomerie and Zhukov shaking hands soon.'

'I'm hoping and expecting Uncle Sam to reach Menzenschwand before Ivan, I expect you want that as well.' Digby knew that Strasser was angling for something, conciliation was in the air, stronger than the breath of eau de cologne rising like breath from Strasser's collar, but he didn't know what.

'What about Hitler?' The question could have been asked by either of the men, though it was Digby who asked. 'I expect he will shoot himself,' came the reply, 'but what if he doesn't?'

'He will, no one would be so silly as to leave it to the Russians.' They walked side by side, step by step.

'Our guards have been told to relax, we're supplying as much food as we can get hold of, rationing is severe, you are fortunate, we supply you with as much ration as we feed our own people you know, we're in a difficult situation.'

'Appreciated,' said Digby, 'I believe you're doing your best, but our men are itchy, we're too near the end of the war to allow stupid incidents, neither of us want trouble now whether by guards or prisoners. I try to keep control, after we stopped making the boxes it's difficult to keep the men occupied, and I'm always looking to get something for them to do.' Strasser stiffened, those boxes, his fortune had disappeared along with the boxes,

'Yes, it must be difficult keeping a pot of pilots out of trouble. Well, I'm here, if I can help, say, I can't spend time here, my duties spread far and wide, I'm responsible for 50,000 men in places as far apart as Munich, Augsburg and Salzburg. I have a problem. Ebensee Labour Camp on the Traunsee is a way from here and Mauthausen Camp is still further away to the east; both camps are horrible, and I'm trying to improve them, but there's little I can do. Dysentery, typhus, not enough of even basic food. Any of our people associated with those camps is bound to be in trouble with your War Crimes and Jewish people.' Strasser waited for a response but got no reaction, he went on

'To help you, supposing it was held once a week, if we abandoned "Lights out", minimum camp patrols and tried to get some extra sacks of potatoes, would that help?'

Digby thought it would be a good start, particularly if he would not discipline Guards from listening to the BBC. Strasser pulled a face and continued.

'If you agree, I wondered if you could write a note saying that for three years Menzenschwand has been regulated under my humane command, meeting the Geneva Convention on POWs, Red Cross Parcels and so on, just an informal note signed by you and witnessed by one of your men. The orderly room could prepare it before I left.'

Two hundred yards further down the track, Digby said it could do no harm, and he couldn't see why not, and on this note they returned to the Commandants Office, Strasser produced a bottle of schnapps, after several attempts Major Weissman had an appropriate letter, including both his name and Strasser's, prepared in English and German, Digby signed. As Digby was leaving, Strasser made a mistake:

'Sergeant Muller had a call from Switzerland from your escapee Pilot Cockburn, he sent his regards to Hut 3 and to all his friends at Menzenschwand.' It was a bad error, Digby frowned:

'Cohen, oh yes, a friend of Tom and Dick, they weren't so lucky, they were shot in the perimeter escaping, so long ago I'd forgotten.' From the far side of the door, he turned, 'Best forgotten,' outside, he kicked himself, 'should never have signed that letter,' But he had not asked any of the prisoners to witness it. He was to deny it had ever existed when later challenged.

Strasser returned to his Salzburg HQ: taking the letter from his pocket, he sealed it in an official brown envelope and marked it to be filed under "Contingencies", praying the Americans arrived first; the Russians didn't read English or German, and he daren't let the SS see it, particularly as he had put a German translation alongside.

Next day Seydlitz, curator, self-styled grand master of art, responsible since 1937 for selecting art to be brought back to the Fatherland, came to see Strasser; he was now a diminished figure, with a greatly diminished role, working to a disillusioned Air Marshall Herman Goering. The only art pickings available in 1944, were also ones which hadn't been selected or looted as German troops swept across Europe. There were no territories left for Germany to ransack, Seydlitz came to sign off the schedules for the paintings and art treasures transferred for storage at Hallstatt.

'My job's finished. I'm now nothing but a night watchman,' he told Strasser, who in turn had his own woes reciting the difficulties and bribes he had had to pay to bring back the bodies and cover-up the army deaths, particularly the cost of bringing back the body of Gauleiter Wasserburg after the hijacking and fixing the paperwork afterwards had taken all his savings but, looking on the bright side, he still held (he didn't say owned) two Breugels.

Seydlitz knew what they were, he knew they were famous and recognisable and had come from Rosenbaum's in Berlin before he legged it to New York. 'If they were ever to appear on the art market,' he told Strasser, 'the family would come crawling out of the woodwork, like Formula 1 lice to claim them.'

'I need help, Seydlitz, you're the expert what should I do?' Seydlitz the art master couldn't wait to show his expertise:

'Short term, do what I've done, get a painter to over paint using water colour, that way no one will ever give them a second glance. Keep them dry and safe. In 10, 20 years, who knows, wash off the water colour from just one of them, tell everyone you found it at your aunt's farm, it had been covered with a sack in a barn. The Breugels should be as good as new, or at least as good as it is now, old Rosenbaum will be dead by then and everybody might have forgotten. Keep the other another 10 years. I'll deal for you, I still have contacts.'

'Brilliant,' Strasser beamed, 'Give me a name and I'll get them painted over right away.'

Salzburg was largely undamaged and there were still restaurants in Salzburg trying to maintain a veneer of elegance, over an extended lunch of small boiled potatoes and perch, Strasser outlined his plan, how he was setting up safehouses for SS and other war fugitives, impoverished, he needed funding. Seydlitz, wealthy from the war and a potential fugitive himself, was looking for an outlet for his currency, he quickly agreed to fund Strasser's scheme, using Swedish kroner as collateral.

'I may need one of your apartments for myself, although I've never been near the SS or a labour camp, being linked to Goering for seven years will make me as good as dead, his anti-Jewish diatribes are as good as signing my death warrant.'

He spent time seeking details on the apartments from Strasser,

'Yes, a pentlet might be just the thing, I don't fancy going with the Auschwitz people who're moving to the Argentine, I might try though the church, a year dressed as a monk, A year without a woman though!' He laughed.

'No one's sent me a ticket for a seat on the submarine going to Japan.' He laughed sardonically.

'It's going to Osaka via the Kiel and Panama canals,' laughed Strasser in turn. 'Turn Catholic, get a cloak and a red hat, go and confess, the cardinals have arranged for an escape route through genoa for the panzers.'

'Seriously Colonel, mark me down for an apartment at Altaussee or Walserval, I don't mind which.'

Check position and no duplication

The thousands of officials connected with the transport and administration of Forced Labour and Extermination Camps knew they had no future. Camp Guards were being killed daily by desperate inmates. SS fighting on the Russian front fought to the death rather than face capture by the Russians. They knew full well that after the Ukraine they wouldn't stay captive long enough to say Baba Ya *(Site of a massacre of Jews and others five km from Kiev)*; they would be shot out of hand. Ukrainians, White Russians who had volunteered to work for Germany, would be thankful for a simple bullet to the head.

Strasser's expectation was that the Allies would first give captured war criminals hope, with show trials, before being hanged and that any SS soldier identified to a unit like the Einsatzkommando (Death squads operating in Russia) would face certain death. Throughout Germany, trading in false papers and passports was rife, now he decided was the time to make his safe refuges known and available to the thousands of war wealthy Nazis prepared to pay handsomely for the security and anonymity he could offer them and their wives: a safehouse: with a false identity courtesy of SS Luftwaffe Lieutenant Colonel General Hans Strasser.

Strasser picked up the phone, with Seydlitz finance behind him, he could set in motion the next part of his plan, within five minutes he had more than halved the distressed asking price of the steamship "Queen of St Gilgen", a large pleasure steamer laid up in a hidden creek on Lake Wolfgangsee and had made an offer reducing the price even further. This clinched the purchase. He added this to his other addresses at his sister's at Altaussee, Dilsberg and Walserval, deciding that the "Queen" could be his very own "bolt hole", away from the "rabble". He put in a further derisory bid for a second steamer "Spirit of Vienna" laid up in a hangar at Strobl, but this bid was so low as to be insulting and wasn't accepted. Next, he gave his notary a false name under which to buy a derelict manor house, Schloss Mozart, near Titisee in the Black Forest.

Next day the owner of the "Spirit of Vienna" was in touch,
'About that offer, kroner was it?'

The Way We Were!
FRIDAY'S 1937, as Germany invaded the Sudetenland, the 4.30 pm, Inter Continental Express pulled out of Platform 15, Munchen, stopping at Salzburg, Attnang-Puchheim and Vienna.

Only on Fridays was the 16.30 express to Vienna, carriage A100, plastered with reserved notices, taken out of sequence and linked as a reserved carriage at the end of the train. Carriage A100 was shunted to the nearest end of the sealed in-out, one-way platform 15, thus saving its regular Friday occupants a trek down the 15 coaches lining the formidable length of Platform 15.

Carriage A100 held six tables, Orient Express quality seating, with a catering bar cutting off access from the forward carriages. The next five years to the end of 1943, high ranking party officials, all men, travelled in this coach; linked by wealth and power, they all owned chalets close to the single-track branch, which joined the main line at Attnang-Puchheim and went via Gmund, Bad Ischl, Hallstatt and Bad Aussee to Trautenfels and Stainach. The men in coach A100 were known mockingly by the regulars, jealous travellers seated nearer the engine further up the platform, as the "Brain Trust", not because they were brainy (they weren't) but as only having a single brain between them. One rainy autumn weekend, a landslide blocked the line, trapping A100 for the night and causing a major row; inadvertently Munich Radio called this the "Brain Bust", a name gleefully adopted by the jealous.

The privileged trust were founding Nazis with power, power marked by many receiving Xmas cards from the leader himself, one, Johan Schmidt also receiving birthday cards from Adolf and Rudolph (Hess then Hitler's Deputy).

There was a redeeming feature of the 'Train Bust, however,' they all kept fit, walking and climbing in the mountains, many resuming work on Monday morning more tired than they had been on Friday night.

Up till the tank battle at Kursk, these party leaders, stood on the platform outside the door of Coach A100, greeting and shaking hands with lesser party members, as they trooped along the platform to carriages nearer the engine. A distinctive piercing train whistle signalled when it was time to get on board, deal the cards, snack, drink and catch up with the gossip. So around 8.30 pm, in valley mountain dusk, Traunsee, Bad Ischl, Bad Aussee and small village platforms, absorbed the men of Coach A100, met and welcomed by happy wives, ponies and traps, coach lights twinkling, they were contentedly driven home, glasses of schnapps to hand.

Winter 1945, the residue of this cabal still met on Friday evenings, not in coach A100, but in a reinforced auxiliary building in the grounds of a Munich area hospital, marked conspicuously (and honestly in this instance) with a red cross to show the RAF and Archangel Gabriel that beneath this cross lay a 'Hospital.'

Reflecting his status, Strasser had been taken along by the most senior SS General remaining in situ in Munich. Like Strasser, severely injured, unlike Strasser regarded as useless by the real hierarchy, he needed Strasser more than Strasser needed him. Seventeen men were grouped around the room, half-drinking wine, half beer, half were lately sprung Nazis, half were old men, Nazis from the Munich Putsch. Conversations covered physical infirmities, dirty jokes, air raids, the killed and the war.

SS Major Karl Webermann put it rather well: 'Twelve months ago, I was a hero, now I'm a leper, all because the SS were tasked to solve the Jewish Question.'

In the distance, the sound of exploding bombs as another night raid began. It was early, over by 10 pm perhaps, they might all get a good night's sleep.

'Can't the Luftwaffe do anything?' Although he was a civil administrator, as the only Luftwaffe Officer present they turned to Strasser. Were there no new planes, no wonder rockets to change things, was Germany past the point of no return, without petrol or fuel for civilians, without enough fuel for planes, tanks, not since the Bismarck sinking the pride of the British nave, the Hood, had anyone mentioned the navy; little fuel despite the great efforts in defending Roumanian oilfields and the successes of manufacturing artificial fuel; with decreasing optimism, Strasser outlined the V2 weapon program and offered that if our armies can't win, the best hope was to hold on and for America to turn and fight the Bolsheviks, after all, no one hated communism more than Winston Churchill.

What remained of the bedraggled Brain's Trust considered their options, Hitler's next move, did he really have a next move with the Russians first to Berlin, if troops captured Hitler would they publicly string him up, or take him back to Moscow for show at a gloating people's. "Show Trial". If Hitler opted to leave Berlin for the west and surrendered to the Allies, there would be a lot of photographs, he would be paraded around Europe and America, there would be a show trial to end all show trials, followed by a hanging. They would hang high every high-profile Nazi Party member and a high proportion of the SS, particularly ones who had served in Russia, and this included several of those present. All agreed that Hitler wouldn't let himself be captured, he would either kill himself or he would die fighting alongside his troops in Berlin… the alternatives for him are too awful to contemplate,' Captain Schultz, a Frei Corps Munich veteran summed it all up. 'He's doomed, we're doomed, Germany's doomed,' his voice sounding like his words. The room fell silent, Schultz was a brave silly man, among several who still asserted that the war could be won.

There was a flash, the lights went out; in the ensuing silence, they imagined the faint drone of a disappearing plane could be heard. Matches were struck, half-burnt candles scattered about the room were found and lit.

Among the swearing, a lone voice continued a monologue, as if the lights were still on:

'The Jews will see to it that the SS, the SA and anyone at the "camps" are tried and hanged and their homes seized.'

'That's all of us,' muttered someone.

'We'll all need a disguise to escape and stay alive. I'm burning my files.'

'If the RAF don't burn them first,' came a cynical comment.

'The Concentration Camp men plan to go to Argentina.'

'May I just say something…' Strasser got to his feet, candle in his hand. 'If those of you who need a new identity, or a safe apartment for you and your wife…' it was an unusual setting for a sales pitch, but his pitch was not interrupted; sales talk over, several men passed him contact details which he promised to follow up.

Marketing his safehouses, selling war criminals false identities had begun.

Silas von Homberg from the Ministry of Justice, joined the Party in 1934 and didn't look Aryan; from a wealthy family, he looked more Jewish than the Jews, a worrying fact that caused him to carry identifying papers at all times Working earlier in conjunction with Streicher, his job pursuing Jews, marked him out as a prime target for retribution, identified and arrested his passport was equivalent to his death certificate. He was an obvious customer for both a new identity and a refuge in a safehouse, he was Strasser's target customer.

His door closed and locked, mutual assurances that neither Strasser or his Salvation project or von Homburg's name would be divulged, Strasser set out his plan.

'My team have established apartments in a safe complex in a healthy secure location in open countryside, away from towns. If the unexpected happens, they are ready immediately so your wife could move in advance of our final collapse, in two days from now, if you so wish, false identities and papers for up to 50 pensioner couples in two separate and divided blocks are available. Silas von Homburg requested that his wife make a personal visit she lived near. Arrived Strasser spoke to her to the point:

'Couples live in self-contained flatlets, we call "pentlets"; each pentlet has power, water, heat and sanitation within three rooms. Having up to 50 couples, no children are allowed, as we are designated to the authorities as a pensioner establishment. There is ample space for outdoor activity, including allotments, and in due course tennis courts and other social and sport activities.'

'What about food?' Frau Homburg wanted to know, 'What will we do with our time? Is a town nearby?'

Strasser's thinking had been that the "customers" would be so relieved at being offered safety that detailed questions wouldn't be asked till much later. He had to think quickly or lose a customer.

'Good questions, first of all food, we are assuming that this area of south east Germany and western Austria will be occupied by the American Army, for months the Americans have operated a system through France, of central food supplies to hospital and pensioner establishments of central distribution of food (he paused) I may of course be wrong, but I assume our resistance in Austria and the South against the Americans will be less effective than against the Russians, and that they will move swiftly to occupy Southern Germany and Austria before Ivan can get here. The only safe haven is likely to be in the Yankee zone, so If they follow the precedent of France, Holland and Belgium, every civilian will receive a basic ration, controlled centrally, our apartments will be falsely designated as a Pensioners Hostels and will collect food for all our pensioners' in bulk, rather like a hospital and distribute it to our boarders.

The land surrounding our haven is sparsely inhabited, being in an agricultural area, fertile and sheltered, ideal for intensive allotment horticulture, giving the chance to grow additional food. I foresee no shortage of root crops, potatoes and so on. In addition to growing food we intend to build additional buildings, so your husband can dig, plant, lay bricks, decorate, grow mushrooms whilst you wash his clothes and cook his meals and attend the keep fit class.' He smiled, 'only joking. You look fit enough to dig your own vegetables!'

'How far to the nearest town?' von Homburg asked.

'No town is near, a village at three km, but at this stage I can't give details.' Von Homburg nodded,

'OK, Security and cost. How secure, how much?'

Strasser had prepared for this, even if he had no intention of giving a clear answer.

'Your identity papers; typically, will be those of a blemish free 80-year-old couple, should inspectors visit to verify identities, we have lined up old couples from the village who we will bring on site to act as if they are you and your wife, whilst we hide you out of sight on site,' he smiled at his own joke. 'Neat, don't you think?'

'And the cost?'

'Payment for the minimum 12-month initial period is in advance… we've spent large amounts in setting up our "safe homes". Different apartments have different tariffs, before I give figures and show you both the options, I need you to confirm your intention to proceed and that you hold sufficient funds in an acceptable currency.' He coughed apologetically, 'marks are rather tricky at present as you can imagine.'

Von Homburg got up and paced about the room, 'would you mind if we had a word in private?' Strasser went into the adjoining office where an operator at a small switchboard was already putting a call through. Strasser walked over to the board and flicked a switch.

'Can't have me or anyone listening to what Silas is saying can we?' he smiled at the young woman. When he went back to the main office, von Homburg had several further questions from his wife.

'Running water, electricity, sewage, gas, fires, rubbish disposal?' Strasser smiled, 'you have my assurance that you'll have no problems in that area whatsoever, the apartments carry the Bavarian Tiger Tank Mark.'

'My wife has a cat, a dog and a pony, will they be able to come with us?'

Strasser was prepared: 'Cats, no problem, dogs bark, the pentlets unfortunately aren't soundproof, so I'm afraid dogs aren't allowed. If the pony could be used on the estate, we would allow it otherwise we could turn it into stew for you,' he smiled to take offence out of the comment.

'Would letters and visitors be allowed, Colonel Strasser? My son, for example?'

'Only in exceptional circumstances in the first six months, then the situation would be reviewed, a poste restante address will be available which we would monitor and we will post letters as required, well away from the apartments. Security is key, we must avoid drawing attention to ourselves, visitors would only be allowed in exceptional circumstances, and we offer priority to residents who are child free, all must remain incommunicado until the peace situation is known and has stabilised, and the hunt for party members and the SS is over.'

'How long do you anticipate that will take?' Strasser continued,

'A year is my estimate—in France and Belgium, and this really shows the enemy's resources, their troops were followed in by teams with their own individual transport tasked with the sole job of winkling out people who had cooperated with us. Teams where every investigator is provided with a car, whilst German Generals cycle to view the front line and our soldiers fill the petrol tanks of our panzers one jerry can at a time, that just shows where we are at. Their hunting teams are established and follow in their army's wake within days of them occupying a town.'

Silas von Homburg unlocked his briefcase, drawing out a thin, locked file which he proceeded to unlock.

'Please count us in, I'll give you a deposit now and the balance when we've selected the apartment we want.' He drew out four three-inch high stacks of Swiss and German banknotes.

'I can give you Swiss francs if you prefer.' Strasser preferred, the weakness of the deutschmark was a nightmare, particularly for the Swedes, whose sales of iron ore had been payable in marks, and for months as it became ever clearer that Germany was losing the war, had insisted that gold be substituted for part of the purchase. It was now common currency that the German mark would shortly be worthless. The most recent form of financial protection by the Swedes was to claim that after the crippling of battleship Tirpitz, it was too dangerous for their ships to sail down from Narvik or even to leave Malmo for the short journey across the Baltic.

As the notes were being counted and checked, Silas was told that a Sergeant Muller would identify himself and contact von Homburg's wife and arrange to take her to view and select an apartment.

Strasser kicked himself, making a mental note; in his keenness to sign up his first customer, he should never have agreed to potential tenants being allowed to make a site visit, in future tenants would have to pick their pentlet by photograph and description, visits were time-consuming and risky, furthermore the pentlets were fairly similar.

Six of the potential tenants canvassed during the bombing in the air raid shelter, expressed interest, showed the ability to pay and, handed over a premium. The Bavarian Nazi Party Secretary wasn't interested, he had made his own arrangements and wouldn't hint at what they were. Strasser was annoyed, the Secretary was a wily old bird, and his information would have been useful.

Von Homburg had not asked for a movement date, but Walter Burnow wanted his wife to move in immediately.

'I'll get back on that,' he was told, 'we plan to show her shortly.' This second promised visit required Strasser to advance a key detail of the planned arrangements.

Walserval, the apartment blocks in the countryside of Southwest Germany began at Aussee, a star in the Salzkammergut of Austria.

Bad Aussee, in the bosom of the Salzkammergut was created by a "Big Bang", a thousand stars rocketed to sparkle across a coverlet of meadows and hills. With the effluxion of time each star turned into a flower decked chalet, where a wife, three children a dog and a cow, awaited the arrival of a loving father following his horse in from the pasture!

The "Andromeda" of this galaxy is Altaussee.

For two hundred years Altaussee housed four individual almshouses in central parkland. The charity—ALM— expanded, shortly after Hitler took power, LCC (Lake Construction Company) were engaged to build further good apartments for worthy old servicemen. Price was low because LCC were simultaneously building an identical country apartment complex at Walserval, two hours distant using identical plans.

Old soldiers were earmarked as tenants, an opening date had been set, when LCC with planning permission for a high value chalet estate on land adjacent to these new Almshouses, asked the Council whether they really wanted dirty old men in dirty old cardigans, overlooking the children's playground, whether they really wanted a bus shelter covered in spit, rude drawings, chewing gum, fag ends and broken bottles, at Altaussee. Would this draw wealthy purchasers into buying high-class, high rated chalets?

LCC put forward their own solution; move the charitable accommodation for great war pensioners out into the country side at Walserval and let LCC upgrade the standards of the Altaussee Apartments so as to be suitable for affluent couples in private occupation. Field trips for council officials to similar apartments in the Italian and French Riviera were arranged, hospitality was lavish. Altaussee, planning permission with regard to ownership was transferred to LCC with the council taking control of the similar facility at Walserval, which would now be used exclusively for the old soldiers and their wives.

LCC made a financial killing, they more than tripled the rents for Altaussee apartments, asking prices for the detached chalets on the lakeside view estate, were similarly increased, the road construction for Walserval was taken over by the Council. The Charity didn't lose either, company gifts, a rates holiday for Walserval, together with a new connecting road, all became part of the arrangement, everybody gained except the pensioners.

The new Walserval Estate, shaped like a crescent moon balancing on its points, was cradled below low hills. The road came in through the left horn of the moon, the river the crescent moon's shape and flowed out through the right horn, small hills and woods masked the apartments from view from the road, likewise a nursery wood masked the view from the hills, it was pleasant, it was almost invisible, it was secure and Strasser through his Office in Salzburg was in control.

Manipulation of the Charity Trustees deep within his offices in the palace, Strasser was effectively in command of Walserval before the close of 1944, without his name appearing. It was the world of nominees, committees, bonds, opaque ownership and mist. Strasser knew how the system worked and how to work the system. From a low base his instructions to officials was law.

Strasser's sister, Edda Strasser, owned Number 33, Dilsberg, the rear of the house, like its neighbours, built into the wall of the medieval walled village, set on the ridge overlooking the Neckar River. Ten miles from her flat in Heidelburg, she tripped out regularly to check "it was all right" and cook herself a meal. Held under her married name, she'd agreed to allow brother Hans (Jed was never a name used by the family) to use it as a safehouse for endangered Germans.

The house held a secret, a stone lined tunnel ran below the cellar to connect to the tunnel running from behind the altar of the church, to trees beyond the graveyard. The exit from the tunnel was in the wood. This exit was covered by a rocking stone slab, invisible to all but prying eyes.

Dilsberg village sole entrance is through a gate in the wall on the side away from the river Neckar, its portcullis being closed every night on the stroke of midnight. Perfect, number 33 was big enough to accommodate families, Strasser could charge what he liked.

Strasser reviewed his team:

Private, then Corporal, then Sergeant, now Colour Sergeant Tomas Muller, he had promoted, recognising his loyalty and competence. Muller knew most of his secrets, shot and injured when the treasure was hijacked at Pont Celere; it was poverty with its associated curse of limited education that had held Muller back from the commission his talents warranted. Now Muller was privy to how Strasser organised, financed, manipulated, planned and cajoled, how he kept a low profile, Muller was Strasser's quiet man in the administration.

Ritter, the enforcer, was a different kettle of fish, again dependent on Strasser for his advancement, even dependent on him for his life, following a most unpleasant incident which Strasser fielded, labour controller/organiser at Ebensee he was Strasser's "enforcer" who would carry out unpleasant orders, unpleasantly, but Ritter wasn't document savvy, customer smooth, or sales driven and needed to be kept away from safe-house customers until they were "signed up", but Muller could, and Muller had a wife who was pretty, ambitious and competent. The three would make the sort of unit Strasser was looking for to run Walserval. Muller, a lukewarm Nazi at best, had little stomach for war, as well as promoting him Strasser had kept him from being posted to the Russian Front, would he and his wife take on the risks and rewards of the job of looking after Walserval, a melting pot shortly to be filled with frightened men and women?

Strasser called Muller to his office, putting the best first; he could de-mob Muller out of the forces, he could wipe his name from Labour and Extermination Camp records, it would be as if he had never worked for the Reich, he would follow this up by give him a bonus and give him and his wife an interesting well-paid job with more responsibility and independence. He paused to let the carrot sink in before he came to the tricky bit.

'We all know that the war is lost, and it's only a matter of time before we are over run. The Jews, the Czechs and the Poles are so bitter that all officials dealing with labour camps will be killed, killed quickly if caught by the Russians. You've seen that hatred yourself in the animals at Ebensee,' Muller nodded. 'Even fighting units of the SS are likely to be rounded up by the Allies and put through de-Nazification show trials, this is already happening in France and the Ardennes,' again Muller nodded.

'We can't afford to wait till the enemy arrive, a short time ago I decided to do something, as you may have guessed, I've set up safe accommodation where the SS and others at war risk can lay up until the hunt for war criminals is over. I want you and your wife to run a safehouse, Walserval, a safehouse for pensioners, run it for me.'

With Muller's immediate answer being neither a 'no' or a 'yes', he continued, outlining the planning for Walserval, emphasising that in addition to safety from arrest, food and false identities would be provided as standard, adding to an already attractive proposition. If Sergeant Muller agreed to run Walserval, he repeated Muller's connection with Ebensee would be taken off—erased—from the files, only by this could he avoid the attention of Allied war crime hunters.

Pay would be double what he was paid, with an opening bonus of 1,000 Swiss francs, his living would be free at the apartments, his wife would be appointed as live-in manageress of the complex. Together they would be in charge, supervising the site, resolve disputes, maintain security, draw and distribute the ration entitlements for the 'nominally old residents' from a central warehouse over which Strasser exerted a degree of control. Muller would be given command, working directly to him at Walserval, he would have four "Vaclov Volunteers", Ukranians, who had thrown in their lot with Germany and who were terrified of being found and handed over to a Red Army, who if they found them would simply butcher them.

Muller asked if he would be discharged from the Luftwaffe, what would be his title, and what would be the extent of his responsibilities, 'You yourself nominate titles for yourself and Frau Muller, you install any extra staff, be the contact point for residents, maintain discipline, you run it. Regarding security, Ritter, you know of him, will handle serious discipline matters, you refer to Ritter all disciplinary matters you can't handle. He'll be paid to deal with them. He won't live at Walserval, you will see little of him, nothing at all if no problems arise, he won't be under your feet, and neither shall I.' was the answer,

'Talk it over with your wife, it's a great deal for the pair of you.'

Muller did just that, taking Ingrid next morning to the Palace Office, for Strasser to go through the offer again. Frau Muller was more enthusiastic than her husband, she accepted, they accepted, all shook hands, Strasser produced glasses and a bottle of Jeigermeister, handing an envelope containing 1,000 thousand Swiss francs to Frau Muller.

Muller's first job was to drive Strasser's staff car to pick up the wives of Homburg and Burnow, intended customers, and drive them to Walserval. Before turning off the autobahn Muller slowed down, telling his passengers, that until everything is settled he must ask them to put on masks, handing them two face masks, to further confuse, quite enjoying this little charade Muller took a circuitous route to the complex.

'You can take them off now.' Sun shining, the apartment blocks set in newly planted gardens, shining after rain, reflected with credit the efforts the recently installed elderly residents had put in, despite initial disappointment that their new home not being at quite as convenient or as prestigious an address as the salubrious Altaussee.

The "pentlets", received an "OK" seal of approval; the address "Walserval" being mentioned inadvertently, they got back into the car. Muller opened up:

'No need for your masks now, Walserval, what can I tell you, you probably noticed the church spire as we went through that little village, the garage repair shop sells local vegetables, there are two buses a day to Rothstein on Ebbs from the village, but they only run twice a week, Tuesday and Saturday, and that's before the Americans arrive. Rothstein has trains to Ulm and Tubingen,' he paused, 'of course no one knows what will happen when the Americans arrive.' He turned the car onto the main road, Frau Burnow spoke up:

'She wanted to know why the sign off to Walserval said Barn Croft, Muller congratulated her on splendid observation, saying this was just one aspect of their attention to security, all the road signs out of Rothstein say "Barn Croft" with one exception, just one narrow track two km away is labelled "Walserval", at the bottom of that dead-end track is a cottage. Should an American take it into his head to visit Walserval, our plan is that he would see the sign "Walserval" and go down this track, before he could turn his car round, Frau

Wormser, who lives there would have phoned us to say that the enemy was at the door, allowing us to take precautions in good time.' The women murmured their appreciation.

On the other side of the hump bridge leading into Rothstein Centre was a café with tables outside, he bought his passengers coffee and a biscuit—ersatz ground coffee substitute, beechnuts ground on the premises, hard tack biscuits which they dunked, to avoid breaking a tooth. Reporting back, he was reprimanded, Strasser's staff car must never go near Walserval again, Strasser was never to be linked with Walserval.

Muller changed duties and was given his own office in the Palace, no one there, apart from Strasser knew what he did, under Strasser's direction, he organised the transfer of ownership and management authority to himself of both the occupied and empty pentlets at Walserval which had passed smoothly from the builders LCC into the charity ALM. ALM appointed Tomas Muller, Muller chose his own title—Chief Executive and Financial Controller. He became aware that LCC had exchanged Walserval for the apartment blocks at Altaussee. He had never before felt so important, he had been lifted into a different sphere, conspiracy, duplicity , fraud survival, exhilarating, a whole new world lay before him and Ingrid.

Strasser insisted, nothing was to be pinned on the office wall, never more than three documents on his desk at any time, special security steel drawers and cupboards were requisitioned, drawers which must be locked when not in use, names of 'pensioners' must be kept at Walserval, never at the Palace. First day of the month, Tomas Muller, he no longer called himself sergeant, had hardly unlocked his desk, when Strasser entered with instructions and a problem.

'Did you hear the radio this morning?' he asked, an unnecessary question, knowing every living German age 9 to 90, listened to every breakfast bulletin with bated breath, as if their lives depended on it. Muller nodded.

'Germany can't go on much longer, I need to set a date for our 'pensioners' to move in. We need genuine pensioner names transferred and registered by next week ready to be allocated.

'Could we simply enter fictitious names?' Sergeant Muller offered.

'I've a better idea.' Said Strasser, pleased that Muller had recognised the problem. 'Last night the Herman Goering Geriatric Institute at Ulm was struck and half the residents killed. Look at this, Muller moved around the desk, Strasser wrote a series of instructions; Muller was to take control of the procedures concerning these deaths, get hold of and transfer the files of some of those pensioners, who instead of being registered as dead would be registered as residents at Walserval; as well as the internal documentation you'll have to get them registered with Schmidt and Schmidt and Co, for ration books. If Schmidt raises objections refer him to me, he's made tens of thousands of marks out of us; for years he's supplied all the food for the prison camps, he owes me a favour.' Thus Strasser demonstrated his strengths, he knew the system, he knew how to make it work for him.

'How do we know the Americans will use Schmidt to distribute?' again Muller had asked the right question.

'We don't, but who else is there for the Americans to use, there isn't anybody else, unless of course they handle the detail of the distribution themselves.'

'What does my wife do with the food before our pensioners arrive?' Muller was unhappy.

'Save it, any that won't keep, she gets rid of discretely in the village, that that won't keep.'

Muller was still troubled, 'the lists of the dead will be on a separate list showing them transferred to Walserval.'

'Yes Sergeant, but you're in a position to see the lists from the dead at Ulm, are never able to be brought together to compare them with Walserval, death lists, bad for morale, pay the man at Ulm to destroy their copies.' Muller moved back to the other side of the desk. 'How much do I pay?'

'That's for you to decide, pay whatever's necessary, if she's too greedy, tell Ritter and ask him to have a word, he'll know how to fix her.' He went on:

'Two jobs for Frau Muller, please ask her to write out and give Ritter a list of the 12 oldest residents currently living in the pentlets, and tell her that the Vaclov Russians will arrive next week, they can live in one of the empty rooms for the time being… nothing elaborate, they may have to move to the boot room when we're full.'

Strasser was leaving on a friendly note, Muller had a query of his own—who were LCC the builders, and why had LCC exchanged ALM at Altaussee for Walserval. Strasser came back into the office and sat down. 'Business,' he said, CC had built an estate of expensive chalets at Altaussee, army veterans or not, an old peoples' home in the centre of the village would have reduced their price and their value. So LCC did a swop, the Altaussee pensioner apartments would be converted and changed into high class flats, LCC then exchanged the Altaussee complex for similar apartments they built, the ones you will manage at Walserval, in the country nine miles from Rothstein, the nearest town. Where better for old soldiers to live, particularly as they are backed by the Charity ALM; ALM the charity where your nomination as Chief Executive Officer, has been approved by the Council. Everyone benefits.

LCC gain with higher prices for the high-class chalets on the new estate and with higher rents for the apartments at Altaussee. The pensioners gained, getting the same class of accommodation, albeit in a different place, at a cheaper price and a quiet location, and the trustees of ALM got a cash settlement and a free access road to Walserval, or Barn Croft as we've put up on the road signs; it was win, win, win all the way. Muller mulled this over before enquiring: 'Who's LCC?'

To receive the answer, 'LCC is LCC, they do the construction work for BMW, they're a subsidiary of BMW.'

'But who owns LCC?'

Impatiently Strasser replied, 'BMW owns it.'

'But who's running LCC, somebody agreed to swop a multi-million DM asset with the charity, somebody set that up, I know shareholders own it but who runs it?'

'BMW.'

Muller followed on, 'Then who runs BMW? Who calls the shots?'

Strasser sank into thought, then he spoke, 'Do you remember the pantomime the prisoners did the one about Goering and von Richthofen?'

Muller nodded, 'Well, those prisoners were smarter than they knew, remember they said Goebbels family would succeed Hitler because Josef Goebbels controls the Media, well, who do think controls BMW?'

'Porsche,' Muller made a one-word reply.

'Porsche years ago, BMW now, Not Porsche, BMW isn't owned by Porsche any more, think "G".'

'Not Goering…!'

'No,' Strasser waited for more.

'Goebbels, surely not Goebbels.' Muller had stumbled on the answer.

'Yes, Goebbels' family call the shots at BMW, Josef Goebbels' cousin masterminded swopping Walserval for Altaussee Apartments. With the war as it is, BMW shares are at rock bottom, they aren't worth anything, but I think they are, not all the money they've stashed in the banks is in deutchmarks, not all of it is in Frankfurt, some of it will be in Zurich, some might even be in New York. I'm holding on to my few shares. Inside BMW's bombed out factories and offices hides a coiled genius, a spring, and controlling that spring is Harold Goebbels. Let me give you a tip, if you ever have any money, find out where Harold is working and buy their shares, he's still young, Germany's future will be in the hands of people like Harold Goebbels, survivors and they won't sit back and take crap from the rest of the world for long.'

Leaving Muller, Colonel Strasser felt his plans falling into place, with the list of the oldest and most vulnerable residents, he would instruct Ritter to get rid of the existing Luftwaffe paraplegics from Walserval. Time was now of the essence, he needed pentlets empty, with the wives of potential war criminals asking to move in, with the Russian advances they would move in ahead of their husbands, who weren't yet prepared to leave their posts and risk the wrath of a still functioning vengeful SS.

When Ingrid Muller listed the 12 dodderiest Walserval residents, she was not expecting Ritter to sit down beside her to plan how best to get them out of Walserval within a week. She imagined they would be persuaded and cajoled to move into other Old People's Homes nearer to their relatives or where they were born, and true Ritter did examine those details, but this was mock-interest, a smokescreen, it wasn't how Ritter was going to do it.

She was horrified, that same afternoon, before Ritter had left the premises, Herman Flack fell down steps, broke his neck and before help arrived, bled to death at the foot of the steps. Going into Rothstein to register the death, upon return six of the original residents were waiting by her desk, old Herr Rheingold had not come out for his usual drink and had been found dead in bed, although he'd been ill for some time, he had eaten lunch. Two days later the daughter of Herr and Frau Bilmarck turned up to collect her parents, she was suddenly a widow, her husband had been killed by a delayed bomb explosion, and she came to take her parents back to live with her.

Although there wasn't a standard pattern, there was a sinister pattern, after 10 days, 10 "pentlets" had become available, none of the 12 on the original list were still living at Walserval, and Ritter had drawn up a second list. Ingrid watched anxiously. Next to go was "Ganger".

Ganger was a former military air policeman who out of the blue, announced he was leaving; a cousin had found him a widow, and a small cottage outside Stuttgart next to a brewery, who would give him two pints every day for looking after its guardian geese, now Ganger was well known as a heavy drinker, who never had any money left after Tuesday each week, this new arrangement came about because Ganger had promised the cousin that she would inherit his entire estate. It was unbelievable, Ganger didn't even have funds to cover his funeral which took place four weeks later. The cousin was furious, when confronted with the bill for funeral expenses.

The next vacancy was even more sinister, Boney Inquart was infirm and rarely went out, so it was unusual to see him stagger to the village with Bea to wait for the bus into Rothstein. He didn't return, killed two hundred yards from the Central Post Office where he was to cash the small bearer order found in his pocket. The hit and run driver was never traced, 'It was almost as if he'd been waiting for Boney,' Bea told Ingrid. Ingrid retold all these deaths to her husband. 'I'll have a word,' was all he said. He never did.

As each "pentlets" became empty, the Ukranians, big grand lads only needing to be told once, quickly became expert in repairing malfunctioning water, heating and electrical systems, refurbishing inside and out, rubbing down before applying one coat of undercoat before two coats of top paint. Walserval wasn't under-resourced.

With the departure of the Herr and Frau Bilmark, Johan Franck who had depended on them for dinner and friendship, decided he would return home to Munich. Now Ingrid had a reserve of empty apartments, Dr Henri Shipster, registered as Walserval's doctor, a quiver full of unasked questions and

Ritter had received his bonuses. Anxious wives could move in whenever they wished.

Chapter 7
Martin's Proposition

Two expresses and a stopper, Martin changed trains twice to reach his old Unit at Fowler Bottom Airfield. Unlike his first posting direct from Burtonwood, no one met him. Getting the two miles to camp was a struggle with an awkward heavy bag, a painful shoulder before a taxi arrived. Not expected, reporting to a busy Adjutant was a cold impatient affair.

'The CO would see him in the morning.' A 24-hour scheme was in progress, few officers were in the Mess, he'd been three years away, it was hardly surprising he didn't know anybody and that several fitters remembered, he could hardly claim to know them. *All the old squadron have been shot down, have moved on, or invalided out,* he thought dismally, only the bar steward remembered his name, remembered him because he had been both a non-drinker and a non-tipper, but he warmly shook his hand recalling how proud they were when Martin Cohen's DFC became the squadron's first decoration, he also spoke that an Air Marshall had come to Fowler Bottom bought drinks all round and told everybody in the mess that the raid on Cuxhaven was the first time the RAF could demonstrate to the Prime Minister, photographs proving that a specific target had been hit and destroyed.

The picture of Malmsley Chivers, the former CO's stately pile, no longer hung on the wall above the CO's chair, it had been replaced by a picture of a wan looking King George VI. There was not a photo of a Wellington.

'What are we to do with you?' the CO wanted to know next morning, 'I've a note here telling me you're special,' it was hardly welcoming.

'Refresher course for Lancaster bombers, sir, obvious, isn't it?' Martin had prepared in advance how to put the CO on the back foot. The CO frowned:

'Not on, Cohen, I'm afraid, the RAF have bomber pilots coming out of my ears, we've no bombers here now, bomber pilots now have all passed intelligence tests, aptitude tests, bombing courses, they've all got degrees, all as fit as fiddles. Times have changed since you last flew out of Fowler Bottom. Bombing Squadrons fly higher, have long range fighter protection, component inspection and certification are now so thorough that when engines start they don't stop, undercarriages don't collapse on damaged runways, self-sealing fuel tanks, sirens telling us long before we run out of fuel, so we don't run out of fuel… well, not often. We bomb at night, the Americans by day, thankfully Gerry doesn't shoot as many down now, the days when we lost 30% aircrew are over, I've got more spare pilots than Marlene Dietrich has had hard dicks' Martin had to stop this.

'OK, OK, but none of them has got my experience of flying Northern Germany at low altitude, I know every chimney, every church tower, every power station, every bend in every river from Lubeck to Hanover.' Martin tapped the desk at the mention of every landmark; the CO looked for an easy exit to the conversation.

'I'll send you to Ely for a medical,' knowing exactly what the result would be. Martin went to Ely, passing every exercise and examination to his own satisfaction at least.

'Failed, sorry son.' The headman gave his verdict.

'Failed, can't have, I'm as fit as a flea, what's on?' Martin wasn't going to let it go at that. 'I passed all the tests.'

The doctor showed him an X-ray, 'Those dark bits—shrapnel.' Another X-ray, he pointed. 'Cavities, son, you've got bits of metal in your back and all over your body, and a hole in your gut; who's going to volunteer as tail end Charlie in a plane with a metal hollow ghost like you sitting up top. You've got to face it laddie, we'll never let you fly an RAF kite again; not if I've anything to do with it, never, never, never.'

Martin was indignant, 'I'm as fit as a fiddle.'

'Come with me, I'll surprise you.' Martin followed the doctor, the small room housed a truckle bed.

'Swallow these, drink this, take you shirt off and lie on the bed.' Stiffly, he did so.

'Your flying helmet saved your head and your neck, I'm going to take a bit out of your back.' The doctor sprayed an area beneath a shoulder blade. 'You'll only feel a pull.' A minute later Martin was holding a bloody wadding bandage to the wound, with the doctor holding up a minute fragment of fuselage.

'That was just under your skin, son, but there are deeper bits lurking around, nothing moves, no problem, move about and seven men and half a million sods, goes for a Burton, and I get kicked out of my job. No medical certificate, no flying Lancasters, sorry soldier, you'll never get a certificate out of me, DFC or no DFC, you'll have to buy a plane of your own if you want to play with a joy stick. Up to me, I wouldn't even give you a licence to drive a 9 horse Flying Standard.'

'Sod it, half a million sods, you're a sod.' Martin's English was as good as the doctors and he needed to get the anger out of his system.

Back at Fowler Bottom, the Adjutant was sympathetic and in awe. Just heard you got the first DFC flying from my airfield, I didn't know, nothing on file. Well done indeed. Anyhow, I've had a message from London, you are to report to Site Ops at Verney Maison, Hants, tomorrow. I'll have a travel warrant ready. Cheer up, somebody's really looking after you, Verney Maison is the Savoy for pilots.' Martin brooded, he rang home, he rang Hillary.

On the way to Verney Maison he bought five Woodbine, in an open paper pack, cost 3d. He half smoked two on the train out of Waterloo, throwing the stubs out of the window. *Wouldn't have dared throw butts out of the window back in hygienic Berne, much too clean there,* he thought. Waiting at Verney Maison Country House was Moxon, greeting him like a long-lost son. They went for a stroll around the gardens, Martin offered a cigarette. Moxon looked at the crumpled ciggy and shook his head. 'I smoke Senior Service, not that rubbish,' he said. Martin threw what remained of the pack into an ash tray when back in the Country Mansion.

'I've got just the job for you,' Moxon sounded more enthusiastic than he felt. 'The war, it doesn't need me to tell you that the end is only a matter of time. Somebody puts a bullet into Hitler and it's over; even if no body kills him and the Germans keep fighting, it's weeks rather than months, and we have to plan for it. I can't understand why they keep fighting us in the west, they surely can't want the Russians occupying the whole of Germany. Anyway, the Politics have decided to send in groups to follow the army with the aim of arresting Nazis before they can disappear into the woodwork, many will try to get to South America so I hear. It's the bad ones we're after, the top bosses, the men who sanctioned the atrocities, the ones running foul camps like Belsen and those that ran the massive labour projects, like the one at Ebensee you told us about.'

'I told you but you never bombed it' Martin was fierce, 'Does that mean my leaving the air force?' Moxon nodded.

'You'd become a sort of Civil Servant, senior for your age, you'd have a contract for a year, good pay as an HEO or a SEO, a firearms certificate, clothes an overseas allowance and expenses, a car would be made available, you'd have to live in Germany, travel all over to investigate and arrest the people we're after; might be quite dangerous. We believe it'll take years, there are a lot of them, and after we catch them there'll be trials, proper trials I should add, we're not just going to hang them.' Martin had questions,

'Do I arrest these people, shoot them, hand them over to the army, hand them over to the Americans, the Russians?' Moxon was relieved that Martin hadn't rejected the proposition out of hand.

'There hasn't been time yet to sort out all the details with the Yanks, you'd be in there right at the beginning. Any one resisting, you'd be cleared to shoot them, saves time, probably get you another medal; until a proper peace's signed we're still at war, an armistice doesn't really count. We're not after officers who've been doing the fighting, fighting's their job, after all, it's a war, it's what the Russians call the "apparatchiks" we're after, those, the SS and the hands-on murderers running the camps. Well, Martin, are you up for it?'

'It's clear the RAF won't let me near a Lancaster, and at my age I'm too young for an admin job.'

'Something else, nearly forgot, I'll backdate your pension to the day you joined up.'

Martin had realised immediately, that living in Germany, this job presented an unrepeatable opportunity to track down Strasser, he would never get a better opportunity, but he didn't want Moxon to know about that and he put on a poker face, determined not to be a pushover and to get the best deal possible, he led on,

'It would have to be Southern Germany, with Hillary, you know Hillary helped me find Ebensee, we both know the area well, we both speak German, she knows the ropes, she would be an enormous help.' A little bit of blackmail seemed appropriate. 'If she'll come I'll go, if she won't go, I won't come, but she's good and she'll need you to give her a job.'

'You're twisting my arm.' Moxon frowned, he hesitated, not pleased.

'OK, Hillary then, we'll find a slot for her with you.' The words were hardly out of Moxon's mouth when Martin spoke again, 'the posting has to be Bavaria or Austria.' Moxon wasn't used to his arm being twisted, usually it was him calling the shots, but he needed people for Austria, so he smiled and amplified the position.

'You'll be working independently in the American Zone, we're slotted to have a team in that area, following in behind Patton's, army, the Americans will have an investigating team there as well, you'll need to liaise and know what they're doing. There will be German's we want and the Yanks aren't interested in and vice versa. I'll give you an example, just prior to the war Ribbontrop and Canaris tried to set up a 3rd column in the Home Counties, they called it the "White Club" or some such name, it's possible that this was run from Augsburg, we'd like to know, then a fellow called Amery, son of a Tory MP, friend of Churchill, broadcast German propaganda, we want him, and Lord Haw Haw, a fellow called William Joyce, he's been broadcasting to England for years, at one time he had more listeners than ITMA, the Yanks aren't interested in civilian British traitors, but we are.'

'I know about Joyce, a chap in our hut at Menzenschwand used to go about saying "Gairmany calling" in a silly accent.'

'That's him,' Moxon continued, 'Another thing, we know the Yanks aim to ship the best German technical people back to the States, the rocket people particularly, we'd like to know who they're taking because we're not too keen on them mopping up all the best scientists, and you'll need to keep a look out for scientists we can use in England, tank designers, radar, jet engines, nuclear, people like that. We know Messeschmidt had a big engine development factory near Ulm, and keep this quiet, some of us think German engineers are better than the bunch of bolshies we have in Birmingham.' They shook hands.

'Ask Hillary to get here to Andover at once, I'll get you both onto the course at Verney Maison, started yesterday, it's fronted as a course for army Chaplains, so Hillary should be at home... But the name's just a cover, join it tomorrow; you'll catch up, you've got to be in Stuttgart inside a fortnight.'

Martin, now ranked as an SEO (Senior Executive Officer) was the youngest, fittest and the only fluent German speaker of the 16 men and two women on this closed course being instructed on the resources, aims and conduct expected from a small team identifying war criminals. They were to follow US troops as they cleared the final pockets of resistance in southern Germany and Austria, areas which had suffered little bombing being south and distant from where the main line of battles directed at berlin and the heart of Germany.

Martin was to be second in command to Trapper Travers. Their brief was to identify, search out and arrest Nazi war criminals, before passing them over to the military until a trial could be arranged.

Sons and daughters from public schools, who had travelled on the continent before the war and who could claim a smattering of German had been identified and it was from this pool of doubtful linguists that Moxon had selected his Nazi hunters plus Martin and down-to-earth, experienced sergeant Partridge, with an older university don:- chief "Trapper Travis".

Rough spoken Partridge said the team selected wasn't even good enough for the Quorn and would have been more at home with the Bakewell Hunt on Boxing Day, fuelled with alcohol and bonhomie, than hunting Nazis.

Martin kept to himself his vendetta with Colonel Hans Strasser, his reason d'etre for joining, as he repeated and repeated to himself

'Herebegineth the Hunt for Colonel Strasser.'

The course was an enjoyable swan, firing a pistol, memorising profiles of Nazi leaders, learning of Katyn, Auschwitz, Dachau (where Martin had briefly stopped when transported from Hamelin on a prison train—to drop off Jews) and other atrocities, the Ghettos in Poland; he could sit and dream some of the time as he already knew by heart the divisions between Blackshirts, Brownshirts, Gestapo, SS Waffen, SA, Hitler Youth and the Gauleighters.

They spent half a day at the US Army Training Base near Farnborough to meet their American counterparts.

'We pool all our information with you guys.'

'Like us,' said Trapper.

Like hell, thought Martin.

Political diktat from London and Washington determined that the hunt for war criminals should begin the moment an area was liberated, so high was the confidence that the war was as good as won.

On the final day Travers and Martin were told to report for a secret meeting in number ten, Northumberland Ave, No one with lower rank than brigadier was at the meeting, Martin only admitted because Moxon insisted. The Conservative under-secretary to the Foreign Office, who like Moxon was privy to coded messages (viper) intercepted by Bletchley Park without (so they naively believed) the CIA knowing that it wasn't only the German Enigma Code that had been cracked, locked the door and closed the windows before starting the next section of his briefing.

'Of course, the government wanted Nazi criminals caught and punished, if anyone needed to be roughed up to give information—go ahead, the Queensbury Rules were in abeyance, no publicity you understand.'

With guns held high above its head, financially Britain was on its knees, a major political aim was that every ounce of blood extractable from the corpse of the Hun was to be squeezed out and where most value lay was in German engineering expertise, like the UK Germany was beyond bankruptcy, gold lying in bank vaults was illusory. Artefacts salted away in salt mines were to be sought, but as they couldn't be turned into hard cash they were a lower priority, furthermore pictures might have to be given back to the original owners. The man on the rostrum intoned:

'Gold in the hand is worth two war criminals for us to feed, only sheer fortune and your sharp eyes will bring us gold.' *What the hell does that mean?* thought Martin.

'Pillage, not in our vocabulary, British troops merely provide accommodation until property can be returned to the rightful owners.

HM Government are aware that the Americans have teams sieving out the best German brains and are even prepared to overlook their crimes and relocate the best to the USA. Sir Anthony has decided we must know what the Americans are doing and if we can't get the best men, we must get the next best and the men who know what their best men were researching. You must find where German engineering expertise lies and to do that you may quietly keep an eye on our friends and report back.

The German's will undoubtedly have dispersed the wealth kept in the banks, but gold and paintings aren't always easy to hide or dispose of, so keep your nose to the ground, your ears in the air, and stay one step ahead.' Everyone chuckled. Separate teams will be examining German banks and financial operations particularly those with Swiss and Swedish firms.'

Bus from Verney Maison, each carrying their own pistol, money, ration card, identification papers and letters of authority. Fifteen out of a listed sixteen men, all men, lined up at 4 pm under the massive clock on Platform 4, Liverpool St Station. Waiting for them, a harassed clerk, with a tray full of sandwich packs, individual travel documents and vouchers for three cups of tea, to be given out by their leader… but there wasn't a leader present. Anyhow, the clerk called the roll and loaded them into their reserved compartment. He handed the tea vouchers to Partridge. The train full of soldiery, travelled non-stop to a bleak windy Parkestone Quay at Harwich, at the foot of the gangway stood a sailor with a gun and a bayonet,

'Gentlemen, your carriage awaits.'

'Fuck off, who said the army wasn't full of wits.'

The carriage was hammocks, a rough sea, unpleasant washrooms, next morning they grouped on the equally grey cold quay of the Hook of Holland. Carrying kitbags, nine men straggled over to the "Green train", taking them to Maastrict on the Dutch/German/Belgian border. Martin and the others were told to stay where they were, 'Someone will come.' An hour later, thoroughly annoyed, cold, tired and bored, they were led to an outlying platform where the "White Train", still warm from its journey from Rotterdam, was waiting to take them non-stop, war permitting, to Augsburg in Southern Germany.

The climb on board was a mood changer, the carriage carried the number "1", upholstered banquette seats, white table cloths, three course meals with beer and wine, pull down bunks with starched clean cotton sheets, nothing was too good for conquering heroes travelling across an almost vanquished country, waited on by the fearful. The two days it took to reach Augsburg, damaged rail tracks, notwithstanding, was bliss to all but Martin, who had become used to living in the luxury of the Berne Embassy in peaceful Switzerland.

Evening came, warm, fed and watered, Martin and others chatted. 'What brings you here?' a burly friendly Manchester man asked.

'De Nazification job; I speak German and I was a POW in Bavaria.'

'He escaped,' Partridge butted in.

Martin continued, 'How come you're here, you don't speak German?'

'No,' the man replied, 'I'm with him,' he pointed to the neatly dressed man asleep in the corner.

'You know who he is?' Martin shook his head. 'That's Pierpoint, Albert Pierpoint.' Seeing that Martin was no wiser. 'Albert Pierpoint, he's famous he's the public hangman.'

'I've been out of England for the last three years,' Martin said apologetically, 'are you a hangman as well?'

'Not really, I'm Bert, I'm his assistant, I'm a carpenter by trade, I do the preparation, the odd jobs and tidy up after he's finished.' Bert was keen to talk.

'I make sure the trap's working and everything is as it should be. After the job's done I wheel the cart into the pit, Albert sees to the rope, I unfasten our client's hands and feet and drop them on the cart. It's dead easy, Albert has the rope the right length so I never have to pick them off the floor, I just push them over and they fall onto the cart, I'm supposed to clean up as well, but I usually give Tom, the undertaker, a couple of quid and he does it. It's no skin off his nose, he's used to it, he cleans dead bodies up all the time.'

'Pay good?' Martin asked.

'Not really, if it wasn't for the perks, Albert only does "bespoke jobs", new equipment every job, he keeps the rope, he uses a different skein of rope for every job and sells the used ones to a chap in Liverpool, half the ships leaving the Mersey have one of Albert's ropes on the yardarm. Albert lets me keep the straps, you'd be surprised if I told you how much I can get for them, especially from some of the big jobs.'

'Albert collects the hoods separate, he folds them and stuffs them into rovers he gets from Folly Hall Mill in Huddersfield, marks whose name he used it for and stores them in a tallboy at home, calls them his pension, reckon when he's finished all the jobs lined up over here, he'll need another tallboy.'

'Are you here for a job now then?' someone asked.

'No, not initially, Albert's inspecting the equipment in the towns, I've got my carpenter tools, Albert likes a wide trap; he's a stickler for a good job is Albert. He won't be having hooks on beams like an abattoir, nothing like that. They may have a dozen jobs ready for us at Belsen before we go back to Manchester, depends how quick they get through the paperwork, we're expecting a lot of jobs at Belsen.'

The train didn't move for three hours, Albert, Martin and two others played "penny knocks", a pub game, a form of dominoes. Albert had brought his own set of ivories, said little and won 3/11d. As he stood up to put the heavy brown coins in his purse, Martin asked, 'Theoretically, Albert, if you were hanging a war criminal, would it be possible for me to be there?'

'Have you anyone in mind?' Albert lifted his eyes.

'As it happens I have, when two of us escaped early in the war, we separated and I later heard that my mate was captured and shot out of hand by a particular SS Officer, if I manage to nail the bastard, I wouldn't mind seeing him hang so that he knew that it was me who caught him.'

'No chance, not allowed, you couldn't be there.' Albert's reply didn't allow discussion.

Next day, standing beside Bert in the corridor watching the River Rhine flow quicker than their train, Martin asked.

'Does Albert do private jobs?' Bert looked sideways.

'Albert's as straight as they come, I must say that. Now me, I'm always on the look-out.'

'Just supposing I was writing a book, Bert, and just supposing I wrote that a couple of Jews wanting revenge, broke into a Prison Camp holding Nazis waiting to be put on trial and hanged one of them, would this be a possibility?'

'That would certainly be a different twist,' it had taken Bert 20 seconds to come up with his reply.

'Perhaps we could exchange phone numbers Bert, in a month or two I might be able to put something your way.'

'It'll cost,' were the last words on the matter.

Martin, Bert's telephone number in his wallet, walked from under the damaged canopy of Augsburg Hautbahnhof, unbelievably a long black Hudson complete with GI, stood waiting on the empty square to take the "Trackers", as the handful of investigating officers were beginning to be called, to offices and accommodation in the Fuggerie, buildings built centuries earlier by the banking family "the Fuggers", buildings little undamaged by a Lancaster block-buster bombing raid of 1942, Down the road, the Americans had commandeered Schaezlerpalais as their HQ and had already begun on a makeover.

In 1945 Britain missed an opportunity, the US transferred the best engineers and scientists to the USA; East Germany's newest manufacturing plant, was moved lock stock and barrel to an expanded Magnetobirsk. British troops occupied the Ruhr, heartland of German engineering know-how, the total Volkswagen Beetle manufacture, tools and designs, was considered and spurned.

Major Humphrey Travers, hence "Tracker" arrived two days later, to take command, Major Travers, partly disengaged, partly 'semi-detached, never useless, after all, he had come up with the title of "Trackers", overruling Martin's suggestion of "OMSK". Humphrey Travers (born "de Travers" the "De" dropped 10 years earlier by deed poll) was more interested in German Castles, Culture and booty than arresting War Criminals. The first thing he did was to arrange a visit to King Ludwig's Bavarian Castle at Neuschwanstein, along with a US general he had made a friend.

With this hollow at the top, Martin became organiser in chief, making the arrangements for US prison transport to be available, for the supply of food, the arrival of funds for the budget, passes for access to the PX Store at the near-by US Air Base (previously a Messerschmitt diesel engine facility). They began the sorting of German records, without seeking permission (which he knew was unlikely to be given), he engaged German women for this and to clean and make the tea. He realised they were there in Germany and Austria for the long haul, hunting down the thousands of people involved in the Holocaust was like a quickie (a turn of phrase that was quickly dropped).

Amidst this frantic setting-up activity, Martin never lost sight of his secret objective—find Strasser.

Investigating the Labour Camp at Dachau was expected to be the "Trackers" first target, Martin remembered Dachau, his train turning down the branch line, the gates opening, the shunting of the stinking goods wagons with their cargo of inhumanity, the angry shouts of 'Raus Raus'.

Dachau was much too big a task for a small team, and "Trapper Travers" was glad to agree with Hank Marvel, another US General friend that the British would concentrate on the nearer smaller Augsburg camp, whilst the Americans tackled the major site at Dachau, on the Munchen Road.

Upon his return from sight-seeing at Neuschwanstein, Travers decided that "as time is of the essence", all of the "Trackers" would go to a subsidiary camp outside Augsburg, where several hundred labourers had serviced the Messerschmitt Engine works. Although the camp had been captured by the Americans days earlier, many Czechs and Poles remained on site as travel was almost impossible for them, resting, building up their strength as food slowly became available. The decent accommodation had been taken over by the ex-prisoners so Travers set up tables in a former hut occupied by slave labour. Although the huts had been empty for over a week, the stench proved so awful that after 20 minutes, with the day warming up, Travers had the tables moved outside.

The prison labourers still conditioned to obedience, sat down in a line, nibbling away at Hershey Bars. Martin spoke briefly in Czech, German and English, separating them into three lines, Russian, Czech and Polish, the Dutch, French, Serb and men from the Baltic States falling in as they chose.

Two 'Trackers' behind each table, two ex-prisoners sitting in pairs on chairs in front of them, Martin had drawn up a standard form, for a signature, personal detail and an original address. Details of brutal conduct they had witnessed, were written on separate sheets and double stapled.

The Augsburg camp had been a model camp, small and attached to an important high-tech works employing first class German engineers using state of the art latest equipment. Workers were weeded and brought in as needed from the huge concentration camp of Dachau, as a result the worst atrocities stapled together, occurred months, sometimes years earlier, at camps distant from Augsburg.

It was late morning before Martin got a sniff of his quarry. It was a slow process. They had nowhere to go or anything to do, Russians slowly filed up to his table. Stanislaus, last man in the line, was a motor mechanic, he listed the camps he had worked; Mauthausen he described as an extermination camp, Ebensee where the stronger people from Mauthausen were sent, was a work not an extermination camp. Ebensee Mountain had been gutted and the original limestone works expanded beyond recognition. He joined the tips of his thumbs to the tips of his middle fingers to illustrate the size of these immense caverns before drawing down an index finger to show the number of separate manufacturing lines installed,

Dachau, like Mauthaausen was a mixture of labour and extermination, he had been signalled out and brought to the Messerschmitt works because he was a skilled motor mechanic who could turn his hand to many types of complicated equipment, he had arrived just a few weeks earlier. Stanislaus seemed to be the strongest and most intelligent of the Russians, and although making no complaint about the guards at Augsburg, he was most anxious that Martin recorded in Russian on his file that he was not a Nazi collaborator, 'I'm not a Vlasov, or a White Russian he said over and over again. Write down; if you don't, my people will shoot me.'

'Ebensee, tell me about Ebensee,' Martin had picked up on Ebensee, 'What happened there?'

Stanislaus had been lucky, he had mended one of the excavators and thereafter had been assigned to the motor pool to service the vehicles, he had even acted as chauffeur, once driving top people up to the salt mines. 'Yes' he said, 'the mines were at Hallstatt.'

'No,' he said, he never saw other vehicles going there. 'Yes, there were labourers from Ebensee at the salt mine.' He didn't know what they did because he never mingled or went into the mine.

He confirmed that inside Ebensee caverns, the Austrians constructed a synthetic petrol plant believed to be safe from bombing,

'No, he didn't know where the raw material came from, other than it came in hoppers by train and lorry.' Ebensee also made thick steel components for tanks. Although Ebensee wasn't used for mass killings, food was scarce, conditions awful and men died like flies. He didn't know the names of many Nazis there, "they don't go in for publicity", certainly not since they started losing the war… oh we knew they were losing, we heard things and they knew they were losing, they started to become really anxious by January and gave us more potatoes and more fuel for heating.

Martin didn't smoke, but he had a pack of cigarettes, Stanislaus didn't smoke either, but he carefully put the proffered cigarette into his top pocket, equally carefully he buttoned the pocket up, saying, 'Currency, don't know any names, never knew the bosses—hardly ever got to see them.'

Ritter was the one name he remembered, Ritter was the man in charge of labour at Ebensee, but he wasn't the boss. The Engineers and the Petrol Superintendents, and the Machine Line Managers all told Ritter the men they wanted and Ritter jumped, but Ritter did control the forced labour and he was a bastard. The weekend we heard that the Russians had crossed the River Vistula, some shouted over the fence, 'Five-nil, five-nil, you're going to lose!' and pretended to slit their own throats; Ritter emptied his machine gun into the group, bodies everywhere.

'Was Ritter's Office on the top floor?' Martin asked. 'Do you know the names of anyone on the top floor?'

'There wasn't a top floor as such,' Stan replied, 'There was an office in the railway station, but direct control was from a line of offices built inside the cavern, near where the trains came in through imitation houses. No, I didn't know names. Ritter's was the only name I knew, his office was at the far end, bigger than the others. The doors didn't have names only stars.' Martin persisted:

'Did you ever hear of SS Colonel Strasser, of SS Colonel Hans Strasser?'

'No, never heard of him.'

'He was a boss man, tall, with fair hair and a metal hand?'

'Yes metal hand, him, yes I did, definite, it was his car that broke down, I was sent specially out to the mine to repair it, lovely job a Mercedes Benz.' This news didn't take Martin much further.

Major Travers called a break and his staff all gathered round.

The three tables reported similar dismal events, the same names recurring. Martin wanted away from the long lines of men still waiting to give their stories, he knew a better use of his time, but before he left, he asked for the most knowledgeable man interviewed so far to be pointed out.

He took Pietr Fletch over to his car, sat him in the front seat, gave him a cigarette and opened the window. Establishing that Pietr had been at Augsburg Messerschmidt Works for over two years, and that he had moved around in different areas, he came to the point jotting the answers in his notebook:

'Top man?'

'Main project?'

'Most successful?'

By the time Pietr got out of the car, Martin knew the names of the six best engineers, the four jet engine projects absorbing the most money and effort, and that the most successful involved the miniaturisation of engine components for strength, lightness and fuel efficiency, thereby increasing range, pay load, speed. He knew the Americans had transferred several jet engine scientists to California.

Going back to Travers, his chief, 'I've got details now, I'll go into the offices and trawl the files for the camp hierarchy rather than the guards.'

Travers agreed, moaning, 'We've got lists of war criminals as long as your arm.'

No fraternisation, Augsburg town centre dark and ruined, whilst away their quarters in the Fuggerie broken into and food and the coffee stolen, Major Travers decided to run a vehicle to the US PX Store, hoping their passes would enable them to buy American goods, all American goods counting as luxury at that time in Southern Germany. Six officers piled into their car, the main roads had been cleared of debris, on empty roads Partridge drove the five miles to the PX in less than five minutes flat.

Battle-hardened Partridge knew the ropes, having spent two months directing disembarkation as an Artillery Sergeant at Zeebrugge on the Belgian coast. Transferred to the "Tracker" unit because he spoke German, and his job had moved up the coast, he was a mine of information. In those five miles he put flesh onto the fiddles telling of a nightmarish situation where mayhem ruled, where rootless men ran wild, taking whatever they could.

'The Germans want coffee, cigarettes, perfume and food; cars are beyond them at present, anyone caught stealing petrol is shot, they want the treats they remember and haven't had for years. They want gramophone records that aren't cracked or chipped, but nothing beats silk stockings and ciggies, and I don't understand that because there are 10 women standing for every dick,' he went on:

'There's food about, potatoes, cabbage, beans, they're not starving; the more citizens the Russians and the RAF killed, the more food was left for the rest, cos they hardly fed the fucking Poles and didn't feed the Jews at all. Every frau's been hoarding food since the Wehrmacht lost 1,000 Tigers at Kursk, she's got enough pickled eggs and cabbage to give Goering constipation for a year, but they've got no luxuries and with currency 20,000 lire to the dollar and marks as bad, the troops aren't interested in their currency so they can't buy from us, they can only barter.

'They barter everything; remember that everybody, bartered, means swopped, like at school, three alleys for the

Beano. I once swopped five Player's Capstan cigarette cards with Traffic Signs for one Senior Service cigarette card of Jack Hobbs.'

'What's favourite left to swop?' Travers asked.

'Men or women?' Partridge was cheeky, everybody laughed, Travers a second after the others.

'To us, war stuff, Nazi badges, flags, banners, medals, then there's jewellery, typewriters, dictaphones, that sort of stuff, but most of it is too heavy unless you're going back to Blighty with a lorry.'

'Wouldn't mind a camera,' somebody spoke up at the back.

'Germans had good binoculars.' somebody followed, 'and hand guns and holsters, leather. Good pans.'

'You can stuff pans, my missus would brain me if I pulled a pan out of my kitbag.'

'Luftwaffe had good watches, Swiss made and small,' Martin added, 'small items mean there's no need to tip half a crown to red caps at the ports.' The man in the back seat spoke again.

'The NAAFI's useless, and they don't stock coffee or stockings, it's tea, chips and marrowfat peas or nothing.'

'No, but the PX has,' said Partridge. 'The PX have.'

Everybody fell silent, the significance sank in.

'They'll not take BACs; even I won't take British Army Currency,' the pessimist in the back seat spoke for the last time. 'Filler fountain pens are OK, Waterman have gold nibs.'

They piled out of the car and piled into the bright lights of the PX.

Martin always carried cash, with over two month's pay and expenses in his back pocket, he decided to speculate. He bought sachets of coffee, lipsticks and multipacks of seamed stockings, his colleagues were astounded at the cash he pulled from his wallet and the volume of goodies he stowed into the two strong canvas hold-alls he had brought with him, hold-alls, he said, made from Nile reeds fitted to ride on a camel's hump a thousand miles across the Sahara, not tourist trash made from straw.

Later he got Partridge alone in the bar, drink driving being de rigueur, Partridge volunteered some delightful information. 'The Yanks are mad on HLI tartan trews, and Stewart kilts, they've got money, you're doing them a favour if you sell them a pair at 10 times the price we pay for losses at RASC stores. To get them out of stores, you must tell them the old ones got ripped on bolts sticking out of Matilda tanks.'

In the middle of the night three gunshots wakened the Trackers, loud and ominous, Martin grabbed a weapon and pointing it forward went downstairs, nerves on edge; Paul Newby was in the lobby standing over a body, chattering to himself and waving his gun about. Turning the body over Martin knew the youth was dead, he covered the face with his handkerchief. Newby was still chattering, walking nervously up and down the lobby, eventually they calmed him down and got him to talk sensibly about what had happened. Waking up during the night, he'd remembered he'd left the keys in the ignition of the jeep. Fearing if the jeep were stolen he'd be blamed, he got up to get them. He'd picked up his revolver, afraid of the unknown. Downstairs, before he'd had time to go out to the jeep, he'd been startled by a figure appearing out of the gloom, scared stiff, without stopping to challenge or even think, he'd just fired in the general direction of the threat. 'No, he hadn't seen anyone else, but he thought he heard a door slam. Martin looked more closely at the intruder lying dead in the hall, young, fair-haired, a look alike for a member of the Hitler Youth Movement he thought. Paul continued to shake uncontrollably, he was a wreck.

Dealing with shock hadn't been taught on the training course, shooting an intruder hadn't been covered either, disposing of corpses had been covered—get the Pioneer Corps, Travers brought down a bottle of scotch, he poured out a full glass before drinking a good gulp from the neck of the bottle.

'Get some Johnnie Walker down you,' he handed the glass to Newby and stood over him till it was drunk. 'I've got to be at US HQ at 10 o'clock, you handle it,' thus Travers handed over the situation to Martin and returned to bed.

'I know what to do,' Partridge had warmed to Martin as "the man", 'leave it to me.' Turning to Newby, 'Pick up his feet.' Together they carried the body out and put it in the back of the jeep. Finding paper and pencil he wrote out:

Thief shot, attempted escape.

Martin got their new stamp from the office, dated the message, signed and stamped it. '

'For Christ's sake, don't give anybody our bloody address,' Partridge's voice carried a pained note. Martin tore it up and wrote a plain note out again.

'Leave it to me,' Partridge repeated, 'I know what to do.'

'You drive,' Partridge threw the car keys to Newby. 'Not be long, lads.'

They returned the jeep empty, Martin, who had by now cleaned up the blood and who was annoyed with himself at not going with Partridge, wanted to know what he'd done with the body.

'If you must know we laid it reverently in front of Augsburg Police Station, let them sort it out, you get back in the office and make out Newby's travel documents that guarantee he'll be in Osnabruck by tomorrow night, and Harwich the day after, he's packing right now.' Newby didn't eat fruhstuck, they all shook hands telling him he'd done the right thing, not to worry, as he was driven off to Stuttgart, where the one line of the railway north had been repaired.

Neither Newby nor the event was ever mentioned again. The police paid a visit, but Travers was away, Martin was out, and Partridge had no idea what the police were talking about. They didn't return and Partridge saw no reason to mention the fact.

On his return, Travers was very "matter of fact"; Martin and Partridge had wiped his face clean. Newby was back in the UK, his "cards marked" and sent off to Shepton Mallett.

11 am the following morning, there was a knock on Martin's office door, before it was pushed open.

'Guess who it is?' Hillary had arrived. They charged at each other, he swung her around. Swinging her legs, she sat on the desk, 'I had a fantastic journey, they flew me to Berne where everybody at the embassy wanted to know about you, then they got me a taxi would you believe, taxi from Berne to Augsburg and here I am. You can tell we're winning the war all right!'

Before farming turned into an office job, tracking war criminals was knocking on doors in the open air, just like farming once was, but then Hillary arrived and took over the office organisation and the filing, the tracing of war criminals went indoors and changed from stalking men in bars into being a paper tracking system, largely an office job.

Next day, Travers tired of listening to the repeated stories of camp guard brutality and murder called a meeting. Martin, Partridge, and Hillary kept hammering at Travers that this was a long-term operation. He simply must keep records, he must have a proper agreed budget, and if the War Office won't provide bodies to do the filing, they must do the job themselves and employ German civilians to open files, keep and cross check the entries, after all, German pay was at an all-time low and there was no shortage of intelligent women begging for a paid safe job that didn't entail shovelling and carrying bricks and mortar. 'It's a big job, and it'll tell us where to go to find and identify the real nasties, at the moment we're like a navy press gang, raiding the pubs on Saturday night. We've got the riff raff, but we haven't even caught a bos'n or a mate yet.'

Travers wasn't available to interview the woman with "private information", he was fourth rod in an American Party on a fishing trip to Chiemsee, a lake south of Munich holding one of King Ludwig's palaces. The trip's code word: "Catch Himmler". 'Pathetic,' said Hillary, fast becoming more forthright than Martin, 'they'll only catch dabs and flounders, what they should have called is "CATCH TROUT", they'll be calling the Christmas party, "Operation Nazi Sleigh", next.'

Travers left Martin in charge.

Next morning, Earnshaw, candidate for the Protestant Ministry when the war was properly over, was waiting in the office. Earnshaw taken his turn and had been in charge of last night's town patrol. A drunken German had been knocking a woman about and he'd brought him in. Not sure what to do, he was taken aback when the now sober drunkard spoke good

English and he would only talk to American Major Frank Wayne. Wilhelm Gunter was sitting in a high-backed chair in front of Martin's desk. Without a word Partridge grabbed the knobs on the back of the chair and pulled back so it was resting on the two rear legs. Then kicking out he made Herr Gunter put his feet up on Martin's desk.

'Wider,' Gunter spread his legs, his balls tight against the seam of his gusset, he both looked and felt vulnerable.

'Imagine that's Major Wayne behind the desk, imagine I have a baseball bat in my hand, and the Major wishes to hear all of what you have to say,' barked Partridge, 'Speak.'

Gunter spoke, he was an aero engineer, a scientist. In two days, the Americans were to fly him from Stuttgart, to Shannon, to Reykavik, then Philadelphia, before going on to California. Last night was to be his final night in Augsburg; he was sorry, he got drunk but he must speak to the real Major Frank Wayne, but Hillary had already rung an anxious Major Wayne who confirmed that a Gunter was to be shipped over to the States, willing or not.

All four feet of the chair back on the floor, questions took a more sympathetic turn, 'why would the Americans send a pathetic worm like you to California?' Partridge demanded.

'Let Herr Gunter explain in his own time,' soothed Martin.

Gunter was now on home ground, proud to explain his knowledge. 'Aero Engines, BMW and Porsche engines lead the world, better than Rolls Royce, Pratt and Whitney, better than any of the engines in Spitfires or Flying Fortresses; it's just that we can't build as many as the Allies. A key is fuel handling. I'm telling no secrets, just something every engineer knows.' Martin adopted a posture of disbelief.

'Engineers know the smaller the droplets in a spray of petrol, the more controlled the formation of these droplets, the better the explosion, more and bigger explosions inside the engine, whether it's a car, a plane or a lawn-mower, the faster goes the ME110 *(Messerschmidt fighter)*. Reduce by 10% the size of each droplet, improve the spray geometry, you can make the ME110 go 10 per cent faster, super explosions drive pistons and spin propellers quicker. But there's more, you've all seen water splashes sizzle on Grandmas hot greasy stove, mix an ultra-fine spray of water with an ultra-fine spray of petrol, if explosions stay the same or better, just think of the petrol, but you've got to use a metal which doesn't corrode or you don't save.' Martin would have liked to have listened longer, but Hillary came In, Major Frank Wayne had arrived to take Gunter back to base. Martin reported the conversation in Tracker's next London Report.

Hillary picked up the phone, she spoke to the Editor of the Augsburg daily, or more accurately every second day daily.

'Place this advert, please.' As there were only four pages, the ad couldn't be missed as it took up half a page.

'Give in confidence, the location of Nazi officials wanted for questioning by the Allied War Crimes Unit. 30 Fuggerei, Augsburg, Tel. 77 99 66 55. Reward of cigarettes.'

Not a single communication arrived, then four days later, news of an Austrian holiday village being eliminated by a celebratory Russians Mongolian unit and the telephone line became hot, Partridge made an urgent visit to the PX for more camels and Lucky Strike.

The roads to Munich, Salzburg and Bavaria and beyond were now clear of resisting troops. The war was petering out, the population had new priorities.

The information from the Messerschmidt Augsburg Camp inmates was to be cross-referenced and collated with the information picked out of the town record files and the camp's own records, from banking records Martin selected Tomas Elke, Minute Secretary between the Council, Nazi Party HQ and the Camp, the main reason being that they were showing an address in Rothstein on Ebbs, Martin's home town till into his teens, although Tomas Elke was low on their wanted list, a single man, he should be a straightforward target to start with.

He consulted Partridge: 'Go early in the morning, go in force, waken everybody up who lives in the street, go hard, threaten his family, make him sweat, offer a carrot for cooperation, he'll know where some of the bastards are hiding.' Partridge spoke in summaries. 'Standard police procedure.'

Although it was outside the "Trackers" area, six am, four men forced their way into Elke's flat, half-dressed, blindfolded, they threw him in the car, threw him out of the car, force marched him to cells in the Messerschmidt camp.

Still hooded, hungry and thirsty, in a pattern which was to be repeated a thousand times, Elke admitted he worked at Messerschmidt's, admitted to knowing what happened in the camp, he knew nothing about Dachau or what he called "the Eastern Camps", he had never been there. Yes, people died at Augsburg, but that was to be expected as some men arrived in a low physical condition, yes, the work could be arduous for some, yes, he knew what the standard food allowance was, but there were additions, the airfield was plagued with rabbits which the prisoners hunted and which they cooked, yes, burial arrangements were primitive but there were no families to grieve, they were at war and these were enemies of the Reich.

He simply obeyed orders, if he hadn't he would have been shot or sent to the Russian Front. Yes, of course he supported Hitler, a great man at first. Yes, Speer controlled the recruitment of civilians and the forced Labour at the Camps, but this was at the National level, what Speer ordered was outside the control of the Augsburg bosses, never mind being outside his control.

Elke had left Augsburg some nine days before the Americans arrived and had gone to stay with people he knew in Rothstein, there was more food in a small town, his job was over, he hadn't gone to hide, what had he got to hide?

Martin lit a cigarette, holding it in his fingers a few seconds, he passed it over, pushing a new full PX packet half way down the table, on top of a handwritten list of 10 names.

'Where can I find these people?' he asked, 'Tell me and no one will ever know, and you can leave here today, don't help and we'll tell everyone how helpful you've been,' he paused to let his words sink in, 'you wouldn't like that would you?'

Elke scanned the list.

'I only know of three.'

'Write down what you know,' Martin pushed a pen and the cigarette pack across the table.

Elke wrote slowly, 'Don't know anything about Elder,' he said.

Martin looked at the list. He wrote down at the bottom, then pushed the list back.

'SS Colonel Hans Strasser.'

'Yes, I know of him, he's Lieutenant General Strasser now, he's in charge of all the camps, Mauthausen, Ebensee and some further east, was in charge,' he corrected himself. 'He came to Augsburg, but I never met him.'

'When Strasser's not in Augsburg, where would he be?' Elke frowned.

'His offices are in the Salzburg Palaces, but for month's now he's been in control of much of the area from Stuttgart to Linz I imagine. Although he was Luftwaffe SS, he'd become almost an assistant to Arms Minister Speer.' Martin realised that Elke was something of a gatherer of gossip and he encouraged him.

'Strasser goes climbing with friends, I'm told he has a farm in Dachstein Austria, where friends go for weekends.'

'Don't know Dachstein, is that a salt mine near Hallein?'

'No, it's a mountain area, away from Bad Aussee, its salt mine's at Hallstatt.'

'What did you mean "friends", what friends?' Martin had seized on the word "friends".

'A lot of us spend weekends at Bad Aussee, some at a Health Farm, some own chalets, I was told he takes women to his farm.'

'Does he own other property?' Elke didn't really know.

'How many Nazis have chalets at Bad Aussee?' There was an increase in ferocity, the question demanded an immediate answer.

'Yes! A lot, it's like a private holiday spot, but I don't know how many.' Martin wanted to know about the Health Farm.

'It's a clinic on the lake at Altaussee, it's expensive, they have water treatments, diets, a gymnasium and gym walk in the woods, I did it once, it's about 4 km, you climb up, then drop down finishing with a short swim across an inlet, but every 300 km there's rough gym equipment, climbing frames, tunnels with stalagmites, waterfalls, balance tests. It's very interesting, but very expensive.'

'If only rich people can afford to be members, the clinic will have details of some very important VIPs, won't they?' Martin demanded.

'I suppose so.' Elke was troubled at giving so much away.

Martin changed the subject, 'The American's believe Himmler set up "werewolf groups" to fight on after the war, is that right?'

'No, don't think so, nobody ever asked at Messerschmidt, there may have been a few volunteers, but the Fuhrer always insisted we would win and demanded total concentration on defeating the Jewish-Bolshevik menace.' Martin eagerly responded.

'Exactly what I've always claimed, both Hitler and I were wise, don't you think,' said Martin, sitting back in his chair.

'That's all for now, go away and have a think, tomorrow, we'll tell you what's going to happen, but I expect you to be going home for a period.'

Allied forces meeting, shaking hands and drinking together, the whole world knew the war was over, except Hitler stuck in a beleaguered bunker believing Steiner's army without petrol, shells or desire would come to his rescue, just like the US Army in the cowboy pictures he watched, believing the spirit of the German people ought to be as unbreakable as his, it wasn't.

Throughout Germany the fog of rumour was thicker than the fog of war. Alan Dulles was intent on negotiating a surrender from his Switzerland base, Air Marshall Albert Kesselring, commander of German forces in Italy, thought that distance apart. Sharing a birthday with St Andrew and Winston Churchill qualified him to negotiate surrender behind Hitler's back. No one knew what to surrender, how to surrender nor to whom they should surrender. It was open season and there were a lot of contenders with the common goal of making themselves appear important.

The Americans were still advancing, enough of the Fuggerie and the Augsburg model camp, Tracker Travers wanted to move on behind the front line and set up permanent headquarters in pleasant, historic peaceful Austria.

The American Control Zone in Southern Germany extended into Austria. With London's backing, Travers pulled off a coup, sealed with a bottle of Dimple, that his team of "Trackers" have prompt control within a 30km radius of his new HQ, the Imperial Hunting Lodge at Bad Ischl, Austria, generously allocated, sight unseen by General Walker. From there the Trackers would work, cooperate and exchange information, with access to the far larger US military back up and support services at Gmunden, far enough away to not get under their feet. .

Incidental to this, Albert Pierpoint, Britain's Public Hangman would hang convicted War Criminals in both British and American Zones of Occupation.

Travers was delighted at getting the Imperial Lodge as his HQ and moved the "Trackers" to Bad Ischl the very next day. General Walker loved his HLI trews, a further gift from Travers, provided by Martin on the advice of Partridge, Travers, interesting and pleasant company with 500 years of family anecdotes behind him, subsequently figured on every

Walker hospitality list till 1963, when the General died in Memphis of cancer, with an invitation to the remote, wet and cold Travers's Estate on the Island of Mull still to be taken up.

Although the 30 km area around Bad Ischl excluded Hitler's Berghaus and Berchesgarten, it did include Bad Aussee, and it was here, the Hallstatt salt mine and the valley holiday resorts, and Altaussee, the exclusive lakeside mountain village, that Martin aimed to concentrate "the Trackers" efforts, not only because thousands of Nazis bought holiday houses in the area, but also because the bosses of the huge forced labour complex at Ebensee, commuted daily along on the single track railway that ran along the valleys to Ebensee.

The Imperial Hunting Lodge
Bad Ischll,
Salzkammergut.
Austria

Ran the heading on the notepaper of Martin's letter home, accompanied by a pencil sketch of and from his own office, once a minor drawing room at the rear of the Imperial Hunting Lodge. A panorama of leaded light windows looked down on the Imperial town of Bad Ischl, holiday retreat to the Emperors of Austria.

Instructions had been issued instantly for Ischl phones to be monitored, but as German operators, daughters and friends of the guilty, were engaged to do the monitoring, dramatic results were hardly expected. Records at the Town Halls had been seized and moved into an empty school building, but Travers was not yet willing to demand from an impoverished British Exchequer the money required to make a thorough analysis.

Martin was delighted, away from interviewing camp survivors, haunting gaunt emaciated refugees, unable as yet to shake off their legacy of hunger and squalor, he could now concentrate on getting after the real war criminals and their hideouts. (There had been Jews fed to bad Ischl, but they were nowhere to be seen and Travers ignored them.) His staff drew up a list of the buyers and holiday makers and renters of property in Bad Aussee since Hitler came to power, this was proving to be a long a list, so he ended it after 5 years at 1938, except for Altaussee a nearby village whose population had dramatically soared. A second scan of the records brought out the former addresses of the buyers. Four out of five had previously lived in property in Berlin or Munich, prominently the Salzbergerland apartments were owned by men born in Munich. Travers not being there, he consulted a rampant Hillary who gave her opinion;

'Get the ration registrations for Altaussee, look out the voting register, mount surveillance, concentrate on men, what work do they do, have you got hold of their tax files yet?

'Come on, stir yourself, Martin.'

Stung, Martin retaliated: 'Who's a pretty bird then?' Whatever he was, Martin wasn't lazy; he was a thinking idle.

After a brief consult (not long enough to warrant being called a consultation), Hillary announced that before long they'd decided they should return to England, get married and decide where to settle, Martin had no intention of returning to England until he had caught Strasser, accepted that his wishes would always be largely brushed aside, quite liked the idea of getting married, afraid of being left on the shelf, but unlike Hillary, shied away from telling his mother.

All agreed that Altaussee was a prime site to target important Nazis, the pair decided on a day-out, a Sunday "recce". Filling the car with petrol, locking the security attachment, they drove on the main road along the Wolfgangsee to St Gilgen, returning by the chocolate box route through meadowlands, then on over the low pass towards Bad Aussee.

Petrol being unavailable made any car conspicuous, so they hid off road, two miles short of their target in trees. Sitting on the running board, tying stiff hiking boots with bows, they walked past a house advertised as a doctor's surgery, up the hill to Altaussee.

A Tyrolian steeple, tall and elegant, a few old houses, a lake, a shop next to a workshop and a bus stop; further on, off one side of the road stood a new extensive estate of family houses, lawns in front, vegetable patches to the side and rear. Set back 100 yards opposite the bus shelter were the expensive renovated Salzbergerland apartments, the apartments Strasser had exchanged with similar at Walsertal, a quarter acre of cultivated lawn, hedges in front, vegetable plots behind. Over a low cropped grass hill lay a lake, a chalet hotel, a single man fishing from a row boat. On the far side of the lake, partly masked by reeds stood the Hydro Clinic.

'That's our first job,' said Martin, pointing.

The raid some days later, was a disappointment, membership lists, appointment books had disappeared; the accounts, the books and the records were at the auditors in Freudenstadt, but the auditor's offices like Freudenstadt's instrument workshops had been burnt to the ground by the RAF, only a housekeeper and gardeners were at the Clinic to answer questions.

'Altaussee's idyllic?' asked Hillary, 'How do we get behind the idyll?'

Wooden seats across from the bus terminal backed onto the lawns and down they sat, sprawling at opposite ends: apart from children playing, no one was about. Hillary undid then slackened the laces, she kicked off her boots, she swung her legs onto the seat for Martin to dig his fingers in and massage one foot then the other, two women approached, level they stopped and exchanged greetings.

'Walked up from Bad Aussee?' one asked.

'Up the hill, we'll just about make it to the lake, is it suitable for swimming?' Hillary decided she should ask the questions, not answer them, she followed up asking if the church was worth the detour, was the clinic still functioning. Then she stood up and fiddled with her socks. Impolite to stay, showing that the conversation was premeditated, the women turned back the way they had come, disappearing around the rear of the apartments.

'What do you make of that?'

'Praetorian Guard,' replied Hillary. 'Sniffing us out.' Boots back on, hand in hand they walked over the meadow to the boathouse, Martin skimmed stones. They detoured to the church, shortly they returned to the garden, sitting down on the same seat watching the houses. The same women followed them, 200 yards back, for a mile down the road. 'Walk past the car,' said Martin, 'I'll come back and pick you up.' Satisfied they were no longer followed, after a further half mile Martin returned to the car, collecting Hillary for the drive back to the hunting lodge.

Both agreed, their research, the women's questions pointed to Bad Aussee being a nest of Nazis, but what to do next—tell Travers. Observation would be possible from a mile up the mountain, but surveillance from an empty house would be impossible. Next port of call, Martin turned the car onto the Hallstatt road, half way up the hill to the Salt Mine he had second thoughts, stopping, as he turned the car.

'Better stay away, London passed on our information about the Art storage, the Yanks are planning a full-scale raid, and I may be going with them as an observer, they're sending in everything except tanks, Tuesday morning I believe.'

Tuesday, alarm clocks at 4 am, a car took Travers and Martin to the rendezvous. 6 am: the heavy mob broke down the ancient double door that the Curators hadn't replaced when the racking and lighting were installed. A surprise raid indeed, except there was no one there to be surprised.

A US colonel and five majors each had a map of the mine workings. Doubtless all six were masters of fighting their brigades down the valleys leading to bridges on the Moselle, but without red arrows pointing "Painting's this way", they were soon at a loss, if not actually lost, in the darkness, the offshoots and the adits of the different working levels of the old mine.

Everyone was ordered to spread out, save their batteries, keep in touch with each other, not get lost and look for traces of recent activity, GI's soon found one, a foul smell, a broken panel blocked a short passage way, at the end were the bodies of the Ebensee labourers. Their tasks finished they had been shot, bodies dumped against a rock face, little attempt at burial. A wooden cross, had fallen over, it was broken.

The GIs didn't hang about, they replaced the panel, keeping the bodies out of sight, 'Bury them later,' Major Downing wanted to find the paintings before anyone else, and before anyone else could pick up anything small and interesting and certainly before his men dealt with the rotting corpses.

The break into the key workings coincided with soldiers bringing down to the workings, the old guide who had shown Martin and Hillary around months earlier.

'You've found the bodies I see,' he said, 'It wasn't me and it wasn't necessary that.'

A metal grill could be seen above the pile of stone blocking a tunnel. Major Gibbs put (he didn't want his rivals to hear) his finger to his lips,' Sush everybody.' The two shovels were enthusiastically applied by the men taking turns until a gap wide enough for a man to go through was excavated. The Major went up to the grill and shone his torch.

'This is it,' not allowing anyone to see, he pointed to where he wanted digging to continue. They cleared up to where the grill was attached to rock, a heavy hammer shattered the holding rock pillar, and the grill was forced back to enable one man at a time to go through. "Oohs" and "Aahs" filtered back down the passage. It wasn't until more digging had enabled the grill to be lifted out, that Travis and Martin entered the tunnel feeding into a long wide passage, as wide as the St Bede's Abbey cloister at Runcorn, thought Martin. The larger paintings stood vertically, the biggest near the entrance, the paintings getting smaller and smaller as Martin walked a kilometre down the gallery, then he came to the racks, the artefacts and paintings neatly stacked with the racks jutting out into the cloister. Not a stalagmite or a stalactite in sight.

Major Gibbs put a guard at the entrance as he went back to announce the discovery to Colonel Skinner. Skinner had pretensions to scholarship, but knew his advancement would be ruined if his men were found to have looted "this lot". He doubled the guard, had the grill re-erected, and planned how to present his find to his wife, the General Staff, the Press and the Literati.

Major Gibbs was sent back up to his jeep to radio through, despite being over three thousand feet high in the mountain he didn't get a signal: 'The guy who gets a gizmo to work from here is on a winner,' he said, driving down the mountain to Hallstatt and a working phone connection.

It was not till the following week they began to move the paintings and artefacts to the rail sidings at Bad Ischl. It took four weeks for four agreed copies of the inventory to be signed, no signature was above the rank of captain. Only the large paintings inventory tallied with the one Seydlitz had lodged with the German National Archive in Koblenz, small artefacts from jewellery to porcelain to sculpture had been misdescribed and wrongly attributed, some spirited away by German soldiers, by GIs—who knows, off Broadway, sales mean nothing. Damage sheets listed the broken items. Souvenir trinkets (priceless miniatures) from Meissen and Dresden were wrapped in dustsheets and misfiled in the corners of the departing vehicles braving the bumps and corners of the Dachstein Mountains.

Martin didn't hang around, there was nothing there to help him catch Strasser. He had taken Partridge into his confidence, that Strasser was his main target. How to get a line on him? 'Raid a vehicle leaving Bad Aussee, you know your man owns a house in the area,' was his advice, 'No buses are running, sooner or later a vehicle will go down to Bad Aussee's shops, stop it and scare the passengers stiff.'

Travers for whom the phrase 'laissez faire' was invented, reluctantly agreed that Martin should take two vehicles for the job. Out of view, overseeing the corkscrew mountain road descending from Altaussee, they waited. At half past nine a farm truck full of passengers appeared. No sooner had the truck stopped in the town square, they surrounded it back and front, anticipating a thousand war films by shouting 'Raus, Raus' pushing the six passengers and driver into their vehicles marked with an unobtrusive Union Jack, they drove a mile out of town onto the isolated station car park. There they separated the man from the women and drove them to the Royal Hunting Lodge in Bad Ischl.

Hard cop, soft cop, Martin chose to be sympathetic, Partridge acted in character, Hillary just made sympathetic noises. The first woman questioned lived in one of the estate chalets. They brought her down to the cellar, sat with a light trained on her face, staring, opposite the bare wall.

Martin had decided on kindness and reassurance for this, his first ever rea-l time interrogation. Hillary took down the family details of Frau Ilse Kogel, details of the house and of adjoining houses, her view of Hitler and the war. The men took up the questioning. The answer to Martin's very first innocent question could have told him how to find his enemy Colonel Strasser, but he missed the clue. The question asked:

'Why did you select Altaussee to buy a chalet?' No hesitation for an answer…

'We first looked at houses in Bad Goisau, but when the Salzbergerland Military Pension Apartments moved to Walserval and the Altaussee Apartments changed to high class accommodation, we decided to live close to our friends.'

'By friends do you mean Nazi Party members?'

'I suppose so.' (It was much later that Martin realised the significance of the Altaussee Pensioner Apartments exchange, with the apartments at Walserval.)

'Was your husband ever in Frei Corps?' *(Frei Corps were the original Nazis guards for protest meetings who targeted Jews, Bolsheviks and the like.)*

'That was before we were married,' the woman replied.

'Where is your husband now?' Partridge had jumped in, thrusting his face right in front of the woman. She started to cry.

'I don't know, he hasn't returned, he was defending Berlin, I've not heard a thing.'

If the woman spoke truly, half the houses were now occupied by widows, she did however name seven men who had returned, two were living in the apartments. She knew nothing of what they had done in the war, only that they had recently returned home to Altaussee. Hillary led the woman away.

Interviewed next, named by Frau Kogel as having just returned from the war, despite a fair amount of shouting, Jon Sellen stuck to giving his number, rank and name and that was that.

The second woman interrogated lived in the apartments, she was nervous and was expected to be the woman most likely to give Partridge all her information without threats or offered cigarettes. Hillary drew a diagram of the apartments and asked Frau Evangeline Brodinck for that was her name, to fill in the details of who lived where. She wrote down the names of two men as tenants, neither being on Frau Kogel's list. Evangeline's husband was still in Norway, he had never been in the Frei Corps and wasn't a Party Member, 'as far as I know.'

'You're lying,' Partridge spat in her face, 'the blanks you've given us are the spaces we're going to fill, nil information is the good information, stupid whore.' Partridge's promise to behave hadn't lasted very long. Evangeline sobbed and sobbed.

Those interrogated were kept separate, the following morning as they were climbing into a jeep for return to Altaussee, Partridge approached, shaking the "number, rank and name" man by the hand he thanked Herr Sellen profusely for his cooperation.

'Nothing, I told them nothing,' Sellen insisted again and again to the women on the journey back to Bad Aussee. 'Nothing, I told them nothing,' he sobbed. No one spoke to him.

Evangeline sobbed, 'What are they going to do with us?' The question on all their minds.

Back in the hunting lodge they played the tape recordings recorded secretly in the stables where their "guests" had been quartered overnight, the tape recorder in the jeep gave the names of three men hiding in the apartments.

Searches were conducted at the town halls and Nazi party offices at Ebensee; Bad Ischl and Bad Aussee followed a similar pattern. Little was left, records had been burnt or sent to Munich weeks earlier. Hillary had an idea.

'Some of the people we want most, worked at the Ebensee complex, the railway line was never put out of action, I don't believe it was ever bombed, it's fully intact between Altnang Putnang and Stainach, hundreds travelled each day by train, Ebensee was working a three shift system, 24/7, every commuter means season ticket, every season ticket means a cheque and a record.'

Travers climbed aboard that train of thought.

'Great idea Hillary, tomorrow we'll raid the stations, Traunsee, Gmund, Bad Ischl, Bad Aussee, they won't be expecting that, let's turn them all over at the same time, see what we can come up with.

Later, 'oh Partridge, I forgot, there was a message earlier, Ten, repeat ten, service women arrive tomorrow, I want you to sort out their accommodation please.' Partridge didn't know whether to laugh or cry.

'I'm very pleased with the way our German girls work,' he said, 'Must I get rid of them?' Travers didn't want to lose blonde Trudy either.

'These girls from home are coming as staff, office staff to help us catch Nazis, they're WAAFs and ATS, no WRENs, I'm told, and no NAAFI girls, so that's a relief. The big wigs are trying to keep in line with the Yanks and are insisting our men are kept pure and out of reach of the frauleins, keep the frauleins on, don't raise questions, just make sure you put up all the, "no fraternisation",' notices he grinned and winked.

The conjunction of unattached soldiers and impoverished German women who had lost husbands and boy-friends, was addressed by Allied soldiers being forbidden to have social contact with the enemy. NO FRATERNISATION signs were posted in every NAAF, Orderly Office and rail station throughout Germany. They were even distributed in London, presumably to reassure their English girlfriends, opposite perhaps to the German propaganda with emphasis on wealthy GIs taking English soldiers' girlfriends,

There were six working locomotives serving forty miles of rail line running from Altnang Puchheim to Stainach; two were held in the sidings at Bad Ischl. 9 am: Travers, Martin and a team descended on Ischl ticket office, although no trains were running, the full complement of female staff were at their posts, platforms and buildings immaculate, the restaurant preparing to serve drinks, crumbs from yesterday's buns swept out from under inverted clean glass covers. Underneath the booking desk, cabinet trays held lists of season ticket holders, with renewal dates and telephone numbers, but no addresses,

'The telephone exchange, it's opposite the Baths,' said Martin. Taking three with him he rushed off, to get hold of directories so they could put names and numbers against addresses, before they could be destroyed.

Travers put on the Station Master's hat, had his photo taken under the station sign and ordered steam to be raised into locomotive: 'Use wood if you have to.' On Martin's return, ignoring unmanned signal boxes and signals set at red, Travers went north stopping at Ebensee, Traunsee turning back at Gmunden; Martin travelled on the footplate, south to Goisau, Bad Aussee and Trautenfels, having been careful not to mention to Travers, that there was a medieval castle at Trautenfels, otherwise he'd have exchanged areas.

Evening, the engines met up facing each other on Platform 1, Bad Ischl. Eschewing the delights of the Station Restaurant, a lorry zipped everyone back up the hill to the hunting lodge, they tore into the soup, steaming in an antique Delft tureen, complete with Delft soup bowls on matching plates, a matching ladle lay alongside. Later came the preparation of a "Most Wanted List" using the records brought from the stations and the Telephone Exchanges, Travers wanting to impress the "New Girls" that evening working was necessary—they were there to do a job of work.

It was immediately clear, none of the new arrivals rivalled Trudy; Travers assigned her as his PA. Hillary (from the Home Counties) immediately classified the seven ATS (Auxiliary Territorial Service) as "scrubbers", although unimpressed by the intelligence of the three WAAFs

(Women's Auxiliary Air Force). Travers assigned them to work on intelligence.

Together Travers and Martin scrutinised the season ticket holder lists, surprised there were as many as 910 season ticket holders going by train each day to Ebensee, between 5 am to midnight, Travers was further surprised, as they were going through the lists Martin told him of how he came to know about Ebensee:

'I came past Ebensee on the train with Hillary about a year ago. We'd been sent undercover from the embassy in Berne, where we were working, to locate Hitler's Alpine Fortress which the Americans suspected was being constructed to carry on fighting, after the war was lost. We overheard that Ebensee was a huge underground construction, and we thought it might be the festung we were looking for. As the train trundled past, we saw wagons holding machine components, long trains: 50 trucks long, full of limestone. Further on we were passed by a train load of slave labourers in fish wagons. There was a lot of talk in the compartment, we listened and learned that Ebensee employed thousands of workers to excavate and enlarge caverns inside the mountain, where they were installing an underground factory with component lines for tank parts and a synthetic petrol refinery. No one knew at the time what the components were for, only that they were using thick, stainless steel. We only saw a couple of petrol tankers in the sidings, they were scattered among coal and coke carriers.

We saw wagons marked Peenamunde with material shipped from Peenamunde after the RAF bombed it, but we don't think they ever built V2s. Actually we still don't know for certain what they made. Even the men making components often don't know what they're going to be used for.' Trapper was interested to know more about the limestone as his uncle's Yorkshire estate at Giggleswick was full of limestone, but the council won't let him mine it as it was in an area waiting to be classified as a place of natural beauty. Then thinking aloud, 'Silly question, Adolf needed millions of tons of cement for the Atlantic Wall, millions for his unfinished autobahn into Russia and his silos.'

'How many experts would be needed at Ebensee?' came next.

'Experts! Don't annoy me,' said Martin, 'just call them criminals, you've been to Dachau, you've seen bodies at Hallstatt Salt Mine, Ebensee Camp is on a different scale, thousands are dead and thousands of men dying on their feet are still living there. The people on our lists did that; stuff them all telling us "following orders". That fellow Ritter, for instance, how many more times do we have to be told he just shot people out of hand, to believe it. Then the big boss, Colonel General Strasser away in Salzburg, I know personally of a very good reason why he should die.'

'Well, you know,' Travers shuffled, 'I don't like you using insulting language, most Germans my father knew before the war he thought were decent men, and we're going to have to live with them for a long time after the war's finally over, whether we like it or not. They're hard workers. Hitler put a spell on them.'

'Don't let him put a spell on you.' Martin could be rude.

They began to talk future arrangements. Travers suggesting they split the area into two, he'd take the north, Martin could take south of Ischl, Martin liked the idea preferring the southern area, away from Ebensee—believing the bosses lived and commuted from the Aussee and St Wolfgang areas, which were in the south, and having scrutinised the season ticket list knew that Ritter, controller of the Labour Camp, lived there. They agreed the split, with Martin taking the south, 'You know that as well as Ebensee the Nazis bought homes in the Salzkammergut to be near their Fuhrer, all in beautiful locations, all excellent hiding places.' Tracker wanted to be near historic towns with libraries intact and castles built before the 30 Years war, and with good communications to Salzburg and Linz, and grand hotels like the White Horse Inn at St Wolfgang, as a centre to explore his pursuits in comfort and at leisure.

Strasser wasn't shown as holding a train season ticket, but appeared on the telephone directory at an address "Back Lane Farm", confirmation of what the terrified Elke from Augsburg Messerschmidt works had said. "Back Lane Farm" lay on a track, off the road linking Alt and Bad Aussee. That same evening Martin drove Hillary past the track lane end. Up the road, he stopped the car, leaving Hillary on watch, he walked onto the mountain pasture, looking down at the isolated farm, no animals, nothing moving, no sign of life.

Next morning Martin came down to his office, curled up by his chair was a large Alsatian dog. On enquiry, the house keeper told him it had belonged to Fritz Neumann, a previous administrator whose office it had been, and that the dog's name was "Adolf". As "Adolf" never answered to his new name of "Winston", Adolf didn't last long.

Travers gave the season ticket detail to newly arrived Yvonne de la Hay, calling her into his office he gave instructions. Yvonne could have sat at a table, she could have stood at the far side of the desk; instead she stood by Travis's right hand, a hand which swiftly trembled to her thigh. Trudy wasn't the only mare who had found a stall in the hunting lodge.

Walter, the former groom at the lodge, had nowhere else to go, currently unpaid, Trapper allowing him food and a bed, he brought out a pony and trap, Yvonne and WAAF Jean Fisher proudly sat tall as they trotted down the hill, past the church to the station. Yvonne made herself known to the station master and together they copied down more ticket details. As the central station on the line, it held the details in a separate drawer, of every season ticket holder at every station between Stainach and Altnang, a detail missed on the earlier raid. Copy book stuff, cross referenced with telephone data, copperplate, Hillary was surprised at how good a job Jean and Yvonne had done when they brought it back.

Martin examined the lists of the season tickets for stations south of Ischl, he had questions. He drove down to the station, Helmut, the women said, was the man with the answers. Helmut senior guard on the silent line, was sat by the brightly burning stove in the signal box, wood was not a problem, Martin chatted, sharing a slice of potato and turnip pie he produced a bottle of beer from his coat pocket. Helmut was 65 and had worked at Bad Ischl for over 40 years. Helmut, a proud guard, proudest that "his train" was only more than 30 minutes late twice ignoring as he said, 'Delays when trees fell across the line, when rivers burst their banks and avalanches of snow or rock, and anything beyond his control, we weren't even delayed when my fireman young Oscar Rudenthal died stoking the boiler, I took over, we were only 10 minutes late at Trautenfels Castle.'

'What did you do with the body?' Martin wanted to know.

'We put it with the bicycles.

'Apparently the first proper delay was 28 November 1933, a woman got flustered, trapped in a carriage with a dozen soldiers from the Brandenburg's 2nd Regiment, she panicked and there was a hell of a fight. Helmut looked back on the fight with pleasure, six men had to be taken to Traunsee Hospital, where the nurse who had been molested, helped to treat them as she was worked there.

'He did not find pleasure in the other long delay, 50 minutes and only a few weeks ago. He remembered every detail, the 10.30 is timed to meet the Grand Continental Express at Altnang Puchheim, no matter that the express has not always run because of air raids and had not always run to time because of the lazy Hungarians. An extra van had been booked and Gert Muller turns up at Dachstein Halt with two carts full of furniture, and although he had foreign labourers to help him it took 35 minutes to load up, they had paid for the van, but they didn't pay for the delay. I couldn't refuse, they'd booked; it made us an extra 35 minutes late. Karl tries to make up time, he ran straight through every platform from Goisau to Ischl without stopping, but we're still forty minutes late through Ischl.

'Gert Mailler stops us at Kleine Schwartzel, it's an optional request stop, even though it has a fine long station, then one of the foreign workers drops a box and shatters some glass, a venetian chandelier, the thing that hangs off the ceiling, the guard shoots him, then a worker attacks the guard and Mailler shoots him. They wanted to put the bodies back on the train, then they wanted to put them in my guard's van, but I wouldn't let them. I made Mailler just leave everything on the platform. We finished up over an hour late, it didn't matter as it happened, the through line had been bombed and the connecting express train had been stopped at Linz.'

Martin asked about Bad Schwartzel. 'It's a nothing anymore,' he was told, 'Sixty years ago, they opened it up as a spa hotel in a fairy-tale valley, a hung valley they call it, when it was nearly finished they found the water was poisonous so eventually they abandoned the hotel.'

'Was Gert Mailler going to the hotel?' Helmut knew he shouldn't have given a name. 'Who knows,' he replied.

Missing the significance of the name "Mailler", having got what he came for, Martin left Helmut the rest of the pie.

'Are you telling me you never had a delay with limestone and petrol and steel and labour being dropped off at Ebensee?' queried Martin.

'Oh! I never count those,' said Helmut, 'outside my control.'

A "Muller" was on "the list", and Martin wondered if he could possibly relate to the Muller from Menzenschwand who was ambushed at Pont Celere. Helmut was to be guard on the train Travers ordered to be ready for the next day, armed with a packed lunch and a tin of cheroots, Martin boarded, sitting in state in the empty carriage, as clean as a pin. A cheroot picked out of the tin, and another piece of pie, Helmut was eager to answer questions. He agreed it was "most unusual" for the train to be used as a "daylight flit". Two different carts brought the furniture to Dachstein, he thought they came from different houses.

He remembered there was a piano, a large Rocking Horse, something they called a "what-not", he wouldn't recognise them separately but might if they were grouped together. He never understood why they loaded on at Dachstein when

Muller had brought them unnecessary miles from Colonel General's Strasser's farm near Bad Aussee, moving household goods in such a closed community was difficult to keep quiet when the move was in broad daylight, Gert had kept the two carts contents separate all the way through.

Happy to talk and gossip about Bad Schwartzel, he concentrated chuckling on the Royal Grand Imperial Crown Hotel Spa and Resort at Kleine Bad Schwartzel. It was built to be the gambling Monte Carlo of Austria, outdoing Carlsbad or Baden-Baden; when the water at Schwartzel was found to be poisoned, despite spending a fortune to clear it up, they ran out of money and the hotel was abandoned.

Ahead of the hotel opening, the Imperial Railway Company had built station offices, had extended the platform, built a coach park, widened the road up to the hotel, all for nothing. No one had lived up there since, because of the dodgy water, it had fallen into ruin so far as he knew, though he hadn't been up for many years, why should Muller, why should anyone, take beds, table and chairs up to Kleine Bad Schwartzel?

Helmut liked a good scandal, he warmed to his subject. When it was being built every Austrian knew about the hotel; the Banks, the Railway and the Steamship Companies, the Salt Mines, all the big companies, bought shares, the Royal Family let it be known they intended to take part of their holiday there as well as Bad Ischl. It was rumoured the Crown Prince had booked "a honeymoon apartment" to be available throughout the year under a false name; the duchess found out and was furious, thus the Grand Imperial Crown Hotel was again in the papers; then the construction company ran out of money, the Zurich financiers jibbed and made the Levis, who owned it, raise capital by bringing the grand opening forward from a July to early June, before the hotel was properly finished. They'd invited opera stars, Max Baer, politicians, Charlie Chaplin, everyone to the opening, but the word had gone out, Hitler frowned, and the opening didn't get the publicity it needed, as many stars didn't come and those that did didn't stay.

Even so It was a huge event for an isolated valley and a huge disaster for the owners, because not only were the facilities not up to scratch, many of the guests went home ill, the service was poor because nearly all the staff were untrained and fell ill. The disaster continued into the following week; it was the same the next week, and the next. They brought experts in from Evian, who finally decided that the water was poisonous, but they went home before they came up with a solution.

The water was poisonous and no one could find out the how, or the why, or the source. Some thought a landowner higher up the valley seeded it with chlorine or something, the mystery and the misery dragged on over the winter, they stopped all work and closed it over the winter. There was, a modest re-opening the following year but guests still fell ill, they hadn't solved the problem, and the hotel was abandoned, never to reopen. Locals took out what they wanted and it became a ruin.' Helmut puffed contentedly on his second cheroot.

'How do you know so much?' puzzled Martin.

'My father was a plasterer there, my mother was a chambermaid, and when I said some went home ill, three didn't, altogether five died.'

'What do you think it was, Helmut?'

Helmut stepped out onto the Hallstatt platform, two women had walked up the steep path from the ferry. The ferry boat had an outboard motor, it ran across the lake from the village to meet the trains, bringing and taking passengers, checking no one was on the path Helmut waved his flag, blew his whistle, and stepped back up.

'Poison, some thought it was Count Rublein, it could well have been him, he owned the hunting estate higher up the valley and was afraid the hotel would affect his shooting and his hunting, but he only hunted four weeks in the year. I myself unloaded from this very van. glass carboys at Unterval, next station along; who I ask needs carboys at Unterval, perhaps one broke, chemicals ran into a pool, if the chemicals were heavier than water they would sink to the bottom, then when it rains heavily, the poison chemicals might get syphoned higher up the valley and get into the water that feeds down to the hotel. Water syphoning has happened in Italy I'm told, but I don't myself know how it works.'

'Helmut, that's quite a theory, whose carboys, were they?' Martin asked. 'That's railway confidential sir, anyway it was a name I'm afraid I've forgotten. There wasn't anything on the glass, but look, the previous year Herr Simmern, mayor of Bad Goisern, opened his own Alpine Spa Hotel and Gardens. The Royal Grand would have hurt his business.'

Martin thoroughly enjoyed his trip out, he'd made a friend in Helmut who was a hive of information, but he was no nearer finding Colonel Strasser. Convinced that whatever remained of Kleine Bad Schwartzel was a probable home for wanted, hunted men, he spoke to Travers then phoned the US Gmund Airfield.

Although the RAF wouldn't let him fly, the USAF raised no objection and Martin flew Trapper in a Lysander over the Royal Grand Imperial Crown Hotel Spa and Resort. The air was calm they made four passes, nowhere to land, even with such a light plane, there were wheel tracks in front of the frontage of the main house, a trace of smoke came from a chimney, but no other sign of life.

Chapter 8
Flight to the Berlin Bunker

Our story goes back several weeks in time:

SS Lieutenant Colonel General Strasser picked up papers from his desk and without so much as a glance dumped them in his out tray, never to be seen by him again. Glancing at his watch, he went over to switch on the radio to hear the News. The Russians were bombarding Seelowe Heights; Seelowe Heights, the last natural but weak obstacle before the Russians entered a shattered Berlin… Had the moment arrived, would he dare? Need he dare? Should he leave it to the Russians to exact the vengeance the Strasser family had yearned for over many years? But Hitler might elude the Russians!

After the failed assassination attempt the previous autumn, where Hitler escaped the main force of the blast at Rastenburg Forest, OKH war control, he had discussed the Strasser family's determination for revenge on Hitler for the tribulations he had brought upon the close-knit family in 1934. 'Looks as if we nearly missed our chance,' he had said.

In the preceding months Strasser had attended several Internal Weapon Production Meetings with albert Speer at Hitler's bunker under the Reichstag Gardens, now the rat-riddled home to the Fuhrer. Broadly familiar with its security arrangements, he held earlier documents of certification which he hoped would give him access to the bunker. He, as well as anybody, knew that Authority was breaking down… could those old passes gain access to wreck the family's vengeance for the killing of their brother Gregor?

'It's now or never,' his insistent inner voice, 'Do it. Do it now!' He listened on to the news, newsreaders no longer breezy optimistic young broadcasters reporting the capture of Warsaw, Paris, Dunkirk, Kiev, even announcing the capture of Stalingrad and its tens of thousands of prisoners; now for months on end the nation listened without belief at the daily strain of solemn voices of older men relaying optimistic news of successful withdrawals and planned retreats as fighting drew nearer and nearer to the German border. Every day they read reports of day and night bombing raids on German cities, raids their listeners knew only too well as they listened at the entrance of their air-raid shelters. Inflated scores of shot down Allied bombers, lifted morale, then as they emerged in the morning out of fetid shelters, the new and the higher piles of debris led them to doubt.

Strasser switched it off, he'd heard enough, Berlin could only have days left, Hitler might have even less, everything he knew, everything he heard made a break-out, or an army break-in to Berlin impossible. He made his decision, he called in his immediate staff to tell them what it was.

Before they arrived, he ran things over in his mind; Walserval was set up, running well, Muller and his wife coping, having got over the difficulties with the department for food over bulk food supply to the apartments. Repairs to the dilapidated Black Forest Mansion near Fredenstadt were on hold. Thanks to his sister the house embedded into the walls at Dilsberg, with its five bedrooms was ear-marked, Charles Edward, Duke of Saxe-Coburg-Gotha, English grandson of Queen Victoria, President of the German Red Cross, his long-time associate over prison camps, was installed, bedded down with his wife and servant. He must keep a room for himself and Anna. Two rooms yet to fill with important wealthy Nazi fugitives.

His staff shuffled in, subdued, standing awkwardly around the cabinets lining the walls, he came straight to the point. 'I must and am going to Berlin,' he announced. His best uniform, brushed and ironed, same with his boots. His revolver must be checked and clipped into the holster on his belt, extra bullets kept separate The Transport Officer must arrange a vehicle and driver to get him to Anaheim Airfield, this still operational airfield was south of Marshall Konev's Army sweep south of Berlin, it was the nearest functioning airfield to Berlin. 'The transport officer must arrange with Anaheim for a Fiesler Storch plane to be ready and fuelled up with kerosene, ready to depart at midnight, if that's still the fuel they're burning?' he added.

His secretary was to prepare passes, the most impressive passes; it didn't particularly matter what the passes were for. Specific bunker passes for the right time for the right day in the precise format were simply not available. Just any imposing pass, backed up with passes from months earlier, were required. Expecting to be away for five days, the kitchen was to provide him with food and drink for 24 hours, Kohler was to take command in his absence. Were there any questions? The transport officer said he hadn't authority under Regional Orders to requisition a plane at Anaheim, never mind claim aviation spirit. 'Your Promotion depends on it,' was the brusque reply. 'Use my title as colonel general acting on the wishes of the Fuhrer, and instruct Anaheim to inform Berlin of my flight plan, which is to fly over Koniev army and land by the Brandenburg Gate just before daybreak. I depart my HQ in two hours. If Anheim says it can't be done, I'll speak to the airport commander myself.' With a confidence he didn't feel, Strasser strode out, to uncertain "oohs" and clapping from his staff.

He relished the drive to Anheim, half expecting it to be his last ever car journey. Car hot, he didn't open a window, enjoying drowsy dreams of family vengeance on Hitler for the death of Brother Gregor. Darker memories, two nights of fear, under arrest at SS HQ in the cellars of the Bendlerstrasse. Hours of intensive prying into his brother, his parents, his friends and his acquaintances. 'Why did you go to brother Gregor's political meetings, who else was there? Removal of his belt throughout the questioning was sinister. The nights were worst, not knowing whether he was under proper arrest prior to charges being laid?' 'Why am I down in the lab?'

The Lab, or Laboratory was a complex of cells in the basement of the building where systematic questioning of undesirables was carried out to the point of death. You aren't under arrest, your cell won't be locked, you are free to explore the Lab and it's workings, you're merely helping our enquiries. The last thing he did in his nights down in the Lab was to see what was happening; screams, whether teeth extractions, wooden splints, chip-cutters, pliers to body parts and body functions were more than enough.

The change on the third morning was sudden, unsuspected and astonishing. Belt back on, shaven, showered and groomed, he was taken to the office of a Colonel Heydrich. Without apology Heydrich announced that the testimony of Gauleighter Wasserburg, Party Member Rondel, and others had succeeded beyond the efforts of well-meaning Party Members to undermine his efforts on behalf of the 3rd Reich. Major Strasser was to be re-instated and such were the reports received that he had been placed on the list for rapid promotion and should plan on receiving promotion to colonel within six months.

Strasser was asleep when the car arrived at Anheim. No flights in were expected, so no lights were shown, in the dark the airfield more resembled a farm than a remaining artery of the Reich. Guards manned the gate, but neither the night or the airfield commander appeared. Directed to a blacked-out hut, the NCO and a couple of fitters came out as the car headlights flashed. 'Everything's ready, all checked, your plane's been refuelled, the right tyre loses pressure; you'll need to have it re-pumped up before you return.' He raised his voice 'you are going to fly it back aren't you? It's the only undamaged plane we have left.'

'Of course,' the only words Strasser spoke. 'You've a full tank, enough to get you to Berlin but not enough to get back here, so you'll have to top up in Berlin,' the NCO laughed without mirth, producing a pad of forms, Strasser's driver signed, 'Right, lads.' Two fitters moved over to a grey shape 60 yards away, drew the camouflage net backwards off the Storch, the one with a limp pulled chocks away from the two front wheels. 'It runs well, I had it started an hour ago.'

Strasser climbed in and sat motionless behind the controls. Not allowed to fly a Luftwaffe plane since losing his hand, he had however 'kept his hand in' on civilian aircraft and flying the Storch would not be a problem. 'Take off down the left side, less holes,' shouted the fitter. Strasser waited a full minute, strapped on a flying helmet, before giving the signal, the fitter swung the prop. The engine stuttered into life; taxiing to the left side of the runway, he looked ahead, gritted his teeth and concentrated hard. Even with full tanks less than 100 metres was needed for the Storch to lift off.

Flying over Koniev's southern army into Berlin was a surreal experience, expecting to be cold he'd changed his cap for a flying helmet, thick leather gloves and a blanket over his knees, but surprisingly he was warm. He flew at 300 feet, no one shot at him, but occasional up-draughts from invisible fires below him swung the Storch around. He had timed his take-off so as to land by the Brandenburg Gate by the light of early dawn. The river Elbe was too far to his left to be seen, and he was relying on recognising the shape of the lakes he was overflying, to prevent him becoming lost, but these shapes were no longer fresh in his memory and intense anxiety set in as he realised he was both lost and lost over Russian lines. He jerked his head from side to side, went into a gentle glide to escape the light cloud and see better, then wondered whether to fly higher to see further.

Fear turned to a panic which lasted seven minutes, before St Christopher, Patron Saint of Travelers, came to his aid in the shape of the St Christopher Power Station, now a shell of its former self, a cooling tower silhouetted against smouldering houses. Greatly relieved, he picked out the reflection of the moon from the concrete of the Great South autobahn and followed it, soon railway lines narrowed in to Berlin's Central Stations, still no bullets flying, he overflew the Brandenburg Avenue north of the gate itself, trying to see if there was anything to block his landing, he banked a full circle, straightening out before landing down the tree lined avenue, pulling up 10 metres short of a disastrous crater, 100 metres short of the Brandenburg Gate itself. Switching off the engine, he climbed out of the cockpit, pulled off his helmet and replaced his cap, three men wearing Luftwaffe overalls, saluted this immaculate General in full fig, gesturing where he should park the Storch. Stiff, he climbed back up, restarted and taxied 80 metres under the shadow of trees. Then, folding the blanket, taking off his gloves, he resumed high ranking hauteur and climbed out of the cockpit for a second time.

He had to wait 15 minutes for transport to take him the mile to the bunker, with the men telling him how desperate the situation, with Russian artillery a mile to the east, 2 miles to the north and patrols all over the place. With so many rapes it was surprising the Russians had strength left for fighting. Food was short, but with so many casualties, surplus rations sometimes became available, bullets were in shorter supply than food. It was a dismal story. They could not refuel the Storch until the ordered spirit arrived. He was glad when the back seat of a motor bike became available to take him to the Fuhrer bunker.

Arriving unannounced and unexpected at Fuhrer Command HQ, is a nerve-wracking experience, more so since Colonel Stauffenburg had tried to blow up the Fuhrer in the Rastenburg Forest eight months earlier. Strasser drew himself up to his full height. He didn't speak, thrusting a wedge of passes and imposing travel documents to an armed unspeaking sergeant, pointed at by soldiers with sub-machine guns. The sergeant passed the papers back to a corporal asking him if he had any news, Strasser said he'd landed at Brandenburg gate flown in from Anheim, he'd not been attacked but the suburbs were in flames, although he couldn't see them, he imagined the Russian southern army stretched many miles around the south of Berlin. What?' he asked, 'Was it like in Berlin? Had Steiner, had Wenk, had anyone, fought through with reinforcements?' He anxiously explained that his pass for the bunker hadn't arrived at Anheim in time for his take-off, if he was to arrive by dawn. A captain came forward from the back, 'Colonel General, do you have anything else, the proper pass isn't here.'

'No, Captain, as I told your Sergeant, I have just flown in to the Brandenburg Gate from Anheim, and the pass hadn't been received prior to my departure, I'm afraid time didn't allow me to wait any longer.'

'That's two passes not in place since last night, stamp "approved", Sergeant,' thus spoke a weary officer. He initialled the stamp. Once inside the bunker, Strasser passed the body search, his revolver sticking out of its holster ignored, visitors had been allowed to wear small arms since the final withdrawal into Berlin; he was inside unfettered and armed.

A large wood cross blocked off the entrance to the lift, alone he walked slowly down two bleak empty flights of stairs, till he was facing a window in a door leading into a large office. At a table behind the door sat another sergeant. Strasser offered the top copy of his wedge of papers, the Sergeant saw the stamp with the time of entry and thrust them back into his hand. 'Eaten? Frihstuck!' he questioned, 'The canteen is down the corridor,' pointing.

'Herr Bormann's office?' Strasser asked for the man he knew to have stayed at Hitler's side.

'Number 3, two levels down,' replied the Sergeant, 'take the fire escape,' again he gestured, laughing bitterly at his own joke.

Strasser passed the wad of redundant passes over, 'I shan't need these again, would you put them in your Security Waste bin please,' the top stamp was all he needed to get down even to the Fuhrer level. Music could be heard and remembering his whereabouts from his previous visit he piloted his way into a dining room. The room was hot and smelled of fish, clearly the air extraction fans were not working properly, it was not till that moment that he realised how hungry he was. The food put up for him, he'd left on the plane, feeling conspicuous, he took beans, two bockwurst and mushrooms to a corner table, it was 24 hours a day standard food. A neat waitress brought over a mug of coffee.

He was joined by two of majors from outside units on the lookout for information, by way of introduction they told him they were "Company Runners" whose job was to liaise with the units fighting within the Berlin perimeter, so that the Bunker knew exactly how far the Russian forces had advanced and could then judge how many days they had left before the bunker would be over run. Totally frank, they reported unit estimates of how many hours before they ran out of ammunition, how long before the Russians broke through, how many dead, how many injured, how many remain fit to fight. 'All they're interested downstairs is yardage, how many yards the Russians are away, they no longer believe how long commanders think it will take, they want to know how long it will be before they're given the order to leave the bunker. How long before they can flee? How long before "the man" takes his last and final decision and issues his last and final order?'

'I've only just flown in from Munich with a report, is it as bad as you say, is there really no chance of Steiner, Wenk or any reinforcements getting here?' Strasser asked.

'Reinforcements,' said one under his breath, 'as far as I can make out, every unit is fighting to get as far away from Berlin as they possible can, who puts their head in a noose,' even more quietly he added, 'we've had it, my friend, our only horse, and it's an outsider without a pfennig on the saddle, is for the Yanks to get here first. We're just waiting till the boss says we can leave then I'm heading west. But he'll not say leave while,' he nodded his head, 'he's here.' There was silence.

'What do you think he'll do, he's in between a rock and a hard place, go out to the streets with a machine gun, or make a run for it, or just kill himself?' The other Major joined in, 'have you heard they've hung Mussolini, from a lamppost in Milan. Hitler won't risk that, he can't risk going outside and being wounded or taken prisoner, no one wants that, we won't let that happen here someone would shoot him first. Whatever happens, we can't let that happen. Hitler hasn't come this far to be hung by his ankles from a lamppost with his trousers down. It mustn't happen.'

Surprised, although the Major had voiced his own feelings, he had not expected such frankness to be spoken aloud, to him an unknown General in uniform, 30 metres above the Fuhrer's Head. Beans finished, thirst quenched, he spent 15 fulfilling minutes in the washroom, taking time to recheck his revolver, before walking through to Bormann's Office, stepping aside for a pastor leaving in a hurry, Bormann came out into his Secretary's office to greet his unexpected visitor:

'Good news I hope, Jed.' Only for Strasser to disappoint him.

'Well, at least that's consistent with everything else that's happened in the past 24 hours, Goering then Himmler showing why the 3rd Reich has come to be in the state we're in. Both are negotiating with the Allies, but the Fuhrer has dealt with them for what they are: scoundrels; then Wenk, Steiner, Kettelring, none with the fuel or the shells or the spirit. Well Jed, we appreciate you coming here to be with us in beleaguered Berlin. How did you break through the Russian ring, why have you come here to share our misery? Speer dropped in a couple of days ago but he's the exception.'

'Yes, I know, Speer rang me, he flew out by Brandenburg, the way he told me to fly in, well, I felt I had to, we've been through so much, I just had to.' Bormann took his hand, patting his wrist,

'It won't be a long wait now, the Fuhrer has signed his political testament, Doenitz has been chosen, Eva Braun is now Frau Hitler, and the Fuhrer is composing himself before the final decision is played out, but you must excuse me, I've an urgent message for Goebbels which only I can deliver; Magda is threatening to poison her children, stupid having them here in the first place. I should never have allowed it.' Putting on his belt, he hurried out leaving Strasser behind together with a weeping secretary asking what's going to happen.

'Where is Frau Bormann?' he asked, 'Is she with the children?' Wiping her eyes, she told that Bormann had kept them all at Altaussee, not like Frau Goebbels who's brought her children into the bunker, Bormann hadn't seen wife or kids for over three months. She was sure all would be finished before the end of the day, she didn't know what she was going to do, except leave the bunker.'

'You mean…' Strasser flicked his head in the direction of the Fuhrer's quarters. He rolled his eyes and put his thumbs down 'Yes,' the Secretary brought her handkerchief up to her eyes again.

The bunker's lower levels were carpeted and sound proofed, and few men were about. No one around, doors opened onto empty offices, Strasser peered in, *They must be at the party upstairs,* he thought having earlier been brief witness to men without ties, girls with blouses undone, drinking from the necks of bottles. He peered into offices, one in particular appeared to have been ransacked. He pocketed a map of Greater Berlin lying abandoned on a table. He perched his bum for a minute on corner of an empty desk,

'Revenge, we've waited 12 years, brother Gregor, it's now not never,' he murmured, steeling himself and checking his revolver was safely in his holster.

Strasser walked purposefully down the last flight of stairs, seeking to give the impression of one he knew exactly where he was going, and that he was not to be deflected from his important mission. Wasted acting, no one saw him because no one was about, he looked around, 'Where was the guard?'

The background hum of the generators could be barely heard, he had reached the lowest habitable level of the bunker, the Fuhrer's corridor, 'where was the guard? Without a pause, he walked past unmarked doors to the end of the corridor, pushing open the last door. As expected it was the bathroom, not as expected marble and chrome, narrow pine planks panelled from floor to ceiling, bands of colour change as the sap had oozed out, not a tile to be seen, only a floor to ceiling mirror.

He shivered, turning on the hot tap he waited till the water ran hot filling the sink, waited till the white face-cloth was so saturated and so hot he could hardly pick it up. He rubbed the cloth all over his face, instantly feeling much better and more alert; pulling out his revolver for the first time, as if expecting rats to appear, cautiously he put his head around the door checking the corridor was empty before he stepped out. Shrugging his shoulders releasing nervous tension, he walked up to the door of Hitler's private apartment, paused, revolver in his left hand, he grasped the handle firmly and thrust the door open.

A woman, he guessed was Eva Braun, was lying as if asleep on the couch. Hitler, dark suit, white shirt, dark tie, was sitting quietly at the side of an antique desk, a gun before him; he said nothing to the intruder, raising his head sideways without great interest to see who had entered. Without a word Strasser brought his revolver out from behind his back, pointed it directly at Hitler's head and fired once. The Fuhrer fell back, Strasser stared at the blood staining the dark hair, stared looking for the certainty that he had killed; it wasn't until he was convinced that a motionless Hitler was dead that he looked around the room:

Eva Braun, on the couch had not moved, her mouth had fallen open, pallid cheeks. *Dead, poison,* he thought. He looked around the room to see more. *Will anyone notice that*

Hitler's own gun hasn't been fired, should I change over the gun? No sooner had the thought occurred than he jerked and without knowing why, knocked Hitler's gun onto the floor. *Get out* was the next thought, he turned, took the few steps to the door and without look or pause closed it behind him. Out in the corridor he shivered, slid his gun under the flap of his tunic and pushed it inside his belt.

Still no one had appeared, no one had reacted to the sound of the gun, he looked down the corridor towards the bathroom, turned and walked quickly away, climbed to the top of the stairs as Bormann came out of his office, nodded and walked past away from him. The Secretary was still sat behind her typewriter, still weeping, Strasser made a beeline for the stairs to be with people he didn't know and wouldn't have to talk to. The boozy party. Grabbing a bottle and a glass he sat quietly in a corner, ignored by man and woman, until a smartly dressed woman, favourite to be the superintendent of the typing pool, came and asked if she could sit next to the General. Not drunk she opened the conversation by saying how disgusted she was with everybody, but her skirt rose far above her knee, as she sat too close against him. Strasser wanted to tell her what he had just done, he wanted to punch the air shouting, but the instinct for self-preservation shut off the triumph beginning to well up. He took hold of the woman's hand, put it on his knee, leant over and with the back of his fingers stroked her stocking till his knuckles disappeared from sight.

Minutes later commotion at the door, men rushed in excited. 'It's over, he's dead. The Fuhrer's dead.'

'Shot himself.' Those sitting, stood up, some even clapped aimlessly, some wept, 'Shot in the head, he's dead all right.' Several rushed out to get to phones to pass on the news, no one cheered, some women hugged and cried. Some wanted to know if they could leave.' 'Everybody can go, we can all go, Blucher said so,' words that echoed around the room. The two Majors he'd spoken to earlier, came up: 'We're off, you can come with us if you like.' Strasser told them he preferred to wait until it was dark.

The party broke up, several sought to take the release of tension to a quick conclusion in situ, but most kissed or shook hands before leaving in groups of mixed men and girls, all anxious to get out and as far away as quickly as possible from the bunker.

Leaving the refined lady to her own devices, Strasser returned to Bormann's office. SS NCOs, officers and the men given their orders earlier had gathered in the corridor outside his office and were forming up into separate parties to carry out the plans issued in advance and in anticipation of the Fuhrer's death. Not least the draping of black sheets to double as shrouds over two stretchers. There was delay until the SS Major had checked and double-checked they had enough petrol. Avoiding the crush, Colonel General Strasser slipped into Bormann's office, avoiding any tie up to the burial party.

Present in Bormann's office were two young Lieutenants in the uniform of the 9th Tanks Division, they were folding and marking a series of maps earnestly discussing the details of the route they should take out of Berlin, having already been ordered by Bormann to map out a route and lead his small party away from the Fuhrer bunker and break out of Berlin, aiming to escape north west towards the British forces.'

'You must join our escape group, Colonel General, there'll be just me, Axmann, Bruckner, Reinhardt and Max. I would greatly appreciate your presence,' he gestured to the Lieutenants, 'our tank commanders are planning a route taking us towards then through the British lines.' Strasser nodded a "yes", surprised Bormann asked him, until he realised his attraction was that he was wearing a general's full uniform, whereas the others were in civilian clothes, perhaps Bormann thought the Germans still fighting were less likely to shoot them as traitors.

Bormann straightened his tie, 'I must see to the burning,' he stopped, 'the disposal of the bodies, the last rites,' he hurried out into the corridor where the burial party was waiting. A wave was all that was needed, and the two stretchers covered by the two shrouds were picked up by the SS, and the party moved towards the stairs.

Quiet returned, Bormann's escape party was now gathered in his office, but Bormann was no longer in charge, his authority had disappeared at the moment the knowledge of Hitler's death became known. Strasser was sitting in his chair, sitting behind Bormann's desk, ready to spell out his credentials 'I came into Berlin alone, I'm ready to go out alone, but you are welcome to come with me and Bormann so long as you are prepared to follow my orders. Can any of you contribute anything towards a successful escape?'

Bruckner jumped in immediately, 'I know everything that's known to the High Command about the Russians' troop dispositions; I've worked night and day on Russian dispositions, ever since they reached the River Vistula.'

Heinz the young tank commander outlined their plan, 'We should follow the blue commuter line for nine miles then take the diversion north to Halbe.'

Bruckner stopped him, 'Young man, let me warn you, Halbe is nothing but a death trap, OKW call it the "Halbe kessel" there's a 13 km circular kettle around Halbe, it's a nightmare. The outer ring is defended with what remains of our tanks, they have ammunition, but without fuel they can't lead a break out. The Russians can't break in because of our tanks and because they know they've won, they're already celebrating and neither their soldiers nor ours want to risk being killed. We must avoid Halbe at all costs, we're best to follow the south fork where the line splits towards Kolkerheim; if we're lucky, we'll find gaps when their units withdraw to form their night encirclement camps, like the apaches used to do.

Artur Axmann, German youth leader, who had been silent said he was no help so far as getting out Berlin was concerned, but in open country, he knew every youth hostel, walking-hut, every footpath and shelter between Bremen and Heidelberg. 'If we ever get out of Berlin.' he added. Strasser glowered.

'When we get out?' he reproved.

Strasberg asked about weapons, food, clothes and fitness. 'I'm not taking any invalids, can you walk a shift?' he addressed Axmann, who though aged, looked as fit as a fiddle and who shook his fist, nodding vigorously.

The bodies of Herr and Frau Hitler had gone, the SS party had carried them upstairs to the dark garden, petrol from dark green jerrycans was poured, drenching the sheets, tucked tight beneath the corpses. Goebbels arrived his narrow bony cheekbones resembling a skeleton, with Bormann he stood separate from the soldiers, without birdsong, with light trembling in from far away, the Chancellery Gardens looked as low key and dispirited as the occasion. Goebbels nudged Bormann, Bormann nodded to the SS officer commanding the burial party, who lit a rag and threw it into the shallow open grave. A roar as the flames took hold, but no light, no words spoken as 15 men watched the end of an Empire, hearing only the lick of flames and the rumble of distant cannon. The principals stayed silent, keeping their thought to themselves.

Artur Axmann, Hitler Youth Leader had stayed below nurturing his own thoughts had no appetite to watch the cremation muttered, 'they'll be lighting the fire now. 'No one answered, he went on.

'What chance do you think we have if we're caught?' Axmann answered his own question. 'The Russians haven't shot the Generals they captured even in the Ukraine, they seem to have treated Paulus quite well since Stalingrad, but they shoot the SS out of hand, so I'm told.'

'I'm not wearing my army SS uniform and have the Luftwaffe version for that very reason,' Strasser explained, 'I think SS who fall into the hands of Ukraine soldiers will be killed out of hand, Baba Yar has become a totem for them I fear.'

'It's not just Russians who'll kill me,' said Axmann spewing up his own ghost, 'German mothers will kill me for making 16-year-old boys fight to save Berlin. (Axmann could never bring himself to say the actual age of 13) I made a dreadful mistake, they'll never forgive me for that and I'll never forgive myself, but the Fuhrer insisted. They blame me, and I don't blame them.' Axmann was a haunted man. Strasser offered consolation,

'We were all under orders. How about going downstairs to see where he died?' Axmann agreed, wondering if there was anything they might pick up. About eight people were already in the Fuhrer's drawing room, the desk and the tables had been cleared and the drawers had been wrenched out, and were now lying on the floor. Rather than join in a scrum for souvenirs, they took in the scene before returning upstairs to rejoin Bruckner and the Tank Lieutenants, it was clear that former political power no longer rated highly with commanders of tiger tanks only days returned from fighting on the Selowe Heights. They didn't want to hang about the bunker waiting for Bormann a minute longer than necessary and were wondering aloud whether to just leave unless he was back very soon. Fortunately, Bormann returned at that moment, saying nothing. Changing clothes, in less than five minutes the six were climbing the stairs to the bunker entrance, pausing where the barriers had been abandoned with only a drunken soldier lying, snoring, propped up. His head against a sandbag.

'We did have enough petrol, after all. At least Russian hordes can't mistreat the body like the bloody communists treated fat Mussolini.' Bormann now wanted all to know that with his attendance at the burning he had faithfully carried out his final duty to his master of so many years.

Personal survival, everything else had been excluded.

From the mouth of the bunker not a soul could be seen across the wasted Chancellery Gardens. 'Can you see anything?' the question was everyone's lips, a couple of looters lugging heavy bags slipped past and disappeared into the dark.

Army training to the fore, despite their earlier anxiety "to get going", the lieutenants insisted on standing in the open for over a minute for their eyes to get accustomed to the dark, 'stand still till we can smell the smoke.' The young Tankers in the vanguard, Strasser bringing up the rear, in single file, stooping, the six jogged out of the gardens into a foreign broken world of smashed rubble and masonry. Within minutes a panting Martin Bormann, yards behind the tankers, had fallen and gashed open his knee. Bruckner fished out a bandage, Axmann put his boy scout expertise into use, cut away the trouser leg and roughly fixed it over the knee. 'We've got to keep going,' the tankers had target times they planned to reach landmarks only they could recognise; unhappy as the injured overweight unfit panting Bormann slowed them and the party down.

The tankers first target was to find and identify the "Green Line", the suburban train line running directly north west away from Berlin's centre, not easy in the dark, flares a kilometre away were little help, if Strasser's information from the two majors was correct, this western area was still under German control, but the tankmen were concerned that German troops were just as likely to fire on them as deserters, the fighting troops on the ground didn't know that Hitler was dead and that the war effectively over.

They came up to what they identified as the "Green Line" where a high bank overlooked this branch line, running on the left alongside a wide expanse of commuter lines and a marshalling yard. Broken engines, carriages and trucks tossed about like jetsam on a sand bank made crossing such a jumbled area a perilous risk, the tank men conferred, deciding not to walk alongside the Green Line itself, but use it as a marker and aim to keep parallel with it, 300 metres to the west. Compass in hand, they moved along the shadows of bombed out houses, progressing steadily before bullets ricocheting, made them dive into the nearest empty doorway, its door having been used for cooking weeks ago. Whoever had done the shooting didn't show themselves or pursue them, they spread around the room in a defensive formation, hands clutching their means of defence—hand guns and a single light machine gun, which a tank man carried with panache, Bormann cursing all the while, rubbing at his gashed leg and a sprained ankle.

Not moving, after 10 minutes the tankmen, who had previously explained that soldiers, Russian or German, fighting hand to hand in towns during the day, at night normally withdrew to heavily guarded circles, leaving big gaps between the circles, fanning out again in daylight to continue the fight from the previously held positions. The tankmen talked to each other, then said they would recce ahead and plan the next part of the route. With Bruckner at the door on watch, the others settled down with Bormann taking the moment to ask Strasser about his rumoured safehouses. Given an outline, he said because of his position he had not been able to plan for a life after Hitler in a defeated Germany, could a safehouse be placed at his disposal, assuming they all escaped from Berlin alive. Martin agreed, but would Bormann be prepared to share limited high-class accommodation near Dilsberg, 'perhaps Axmann would be interested in sharing too?'

Before long it was clear that the young tank commanders weren't coming back, killed or fled, 'who knows,' realising they were down to four and notwithstanding the presence of two ex-Ministers of the Reich, without so much as a word, Colonel General Jed Strasser was doubly confirmed as their commander-in-chief. His next decision… the plan to follow the line of the Green Line was sound and he would continue to follow it. his second decision he kept to himself, having Bormann at Dilsberg along with the Duke of Saxe-Coburg-Gotha or in any of his safehouses was a very bad idea, so notorious was Bormann that with Himmler there was bound to be a large price on his head, a large bounty coupled to this national hatred made it inevitable that informers would give Bormann away and whoever gave Bormann away, gave Dilsberg and his whole set up away as well. This and a limping Bormann's gash and sprain made him too large a liability.

They entered an area with little noise and less damage, paths between broken houses were relatively clear and progress cheered them up. The end of the road brought them back to the rail line, climbing the wall Bormann fell again and needed help to get back on his feet. Strasser seized the opportunity, he took out his revolver and before Bormann had taken another step forward, shot him in the head, pushing the body down towards the rail track 'Too much of a liability,' he announced.

To his surprise, Axmann agreed, 'We're better off without him, Bormann was right about the survival of the fittest, he'd have got us all killed. You did right.'

Bruckner just said, 'Let's crack on.'

An hour later dawn approaching, they sheltered in another abandoned house, to their surprise they found company, upstairs were half a dozen nurses, their hospital destroyed and occupied by "The Rapists", six girls with whom to share food and board for the coming daylight hours.

Inevitably, they recognised Youth Leader Artur Axmann, 'Is the Fuhrer really dead?' they asked, 'How did he die? Does it mean the war's over?' Axmann comforted the two most troubled women whilst answering honestly and firmly. The hours passed in a mix of waking and sleep, with Bruckner excelling himself telling the girls "Tales from the Bunker", stressing how Hitler shared the fate of his people with steadfastness, as did, Bormann and the staff. Not a word about Eva Braun, who till the day he died, Axmann could never bring himself to call Frau Hitler.They shared their food, those who couldn't sleep, were forever peering out from the shadows, back from behind unbroken windows.

Almost dark, preparing to leave, like a conjurer Axmann pulled out three boxes and six straws, offering the straws to the girls, mystified the girls drew lots, the three with the long straws were each handed a black jewellery box printed with the word "Glory"; opening them, a medal against a silk ribbon, sitting snugly on black velvet were silver figures of girl and boy climbing the Zugspitz, (Germany's Highest Mountain) topped by an enamelled swastika, underneath lay the word "Honour". The girls admired them, Strasser and Bruckner examined them.

'Let the three of us decorate you.' Strasser never even explained to himself why the pinning ceremony became embedded in his memory, after all, he had presented hundreds of medals himself, it was part of his job, perhaps it was because it was so unexpected and Axmann's speech and that Axmann was still regarded as something of a hero by the girls.

Axmann told the girls 'this is the highest youth decoration ever presented by the Reich, only 12 solid silver medals were struck, only three holders remain alive, von Shirach, myself and Hermann Goering, three dead youths lie in the rubble and destruction of Berlin, these are the remaining three medals. He lay them on their ribbons on their velvet, on the table. With his single arm (the other buried in the mud of Kharkov), he pinned the medal to the first girl's chest, saluted, and presented the box and the velvet to a girl unsuccessful in the draw. Both girls were given the full Nazi salute by the three men, no handshakes.

Axmann stood aside and Bruckner repeated the ceremony, as did Strasser, keeping the metal hand behind his back, so all three men and all six girls played a part. Axmann spoke the closing words:

'Your fathers served the Fatherland with honour, their service is now ended, you, in turn, must serve the better Fatherland that is to come.'

'We must go.' They kissed the girls, fastened their coats and left the ruined building for a darkness brightened by distant fires. Strasser was always to regret his parting words: 'In 50 years, the Jews of Wall St will pay 10,000 dollars for each of those medals, double if you keep the ribbon and the box together, with a note of the people who presented it and the circumstances in which you received it.' Strasser never asked Axmann what had happened to the final three medals, suspecting the old rascal still had them hidden in his pocket.

Stormviks no longer roared overhead, engines screaming, unopposed strafing everything that moved, gunfire was now far away, single rounds, not the ear-shattering repetition of a Stalin organ, a distance away eerie surges of music blew along in the wind, fading no sooner than begun, a fusillade of tracer fired into the heavens in celebration, all helped them avoid concentrations of Cossacks. About 20 T34 tanks were spotted together with a bonfire and a huge party going on around it. Looking down from the top of a ridge, over 20 fires could be seen, all seeming to mark celebrations rather than destruction.

Uncle Joe had kicked off his shoes, undone his tie, unfastened his belt and unbuttoned his flies and opened the vodka.

In open country, in the silence of no man's land between Russian and English forces, their talk concentrated on how to cross the Elbe. Strasser said nothing, Bruckner knew the roads, knew where the villages lay, knew every bridge, he even knew the narrowest and the shallowest stretches of the Elbe river, he knew the stretches where the remnants of the 9th army had defended over the longest time, what he didn't know was where the British had crossed in boats. Strasser took him to one side, they looked at their map for the umpteenth time. They drew a sketch, they chose a spot and their combined expertise was so good that even walking cross-country, they hit it directly.

Langhorn, the spot chosen, was away from any bridge, away from any village, Langhorn, the widest and shallowest the most open stretch of river was where the Green Howard's had paddled across at 2 am, on Wednesday the 3rd, ditching their PB's on the east bank.

Patrolling four hundred yards of bank, Private Richard Fletcher of the Pioneer Corp was on watch: the lookout between midnight and 2 am. He wasn't the brightest, he wasn't as alert as he might have been, but he wasn't under the influence and he wasn't asleep. When a half-empty PB was pushed out into the water 200 yards away from where he lay relaxed against a grass bank and a rower crooning his unique rendering of Lily Marlene in a mixture of English and terrible German, he wondered where on earth have they had come from; what's so splendid on the other side, but he felt no need to stand up, challenge or fire in its direction; raising the alarm, calling out the guard never entered his mind. Watch on the Elbe was a joy compared with the previous three weeks when the Pioneer Corps had been feverishly involved in checking latrines; curiously he watched as the boat drifted out into the main stream and disappeared from view. Only ½ an hour to go before he could get back to his wanking pit.

The men were over, they had crossed the Elbe, they had sidled through the encirclement of Berlin, they had crossed its perimeter, picked a route avoiding all the kessels and all the death traps; they had crossed through the Russian lines and the forward British line and now they had crossed the Elbe, safe and dry in one of the British army's own boats, first used as practice to cross the River Tyne.

Strasser led them singing, out onto open fields, through copses where living trees bore leaves, and singing birds no longer held their breath; holding open his map they gathered around as he pin-pointed their location, 'Hamburg's that way, Koln's over there, we're heading for Dusseldorf,' he swept his arm in the general direction, proudly repeating his earlier claim that unscathed, they had not had to swim across a river or creep across a guarded bridge.

Not a road block, not a burning house, not a detour was henceforth to delay them and apart from a burst of fire from a trigger-happy distant patrol they avoided confrontation with every British soldier, who were now only interested in food, amusement, loot and getting home, now that the war was over.

Over to you Axmann, Strasser had shot Bormann, he had led his group to relative safety, he had done this by an inner authority, he had nudged rather than issued orders, time for him to give up the reins, Axmann was now entrusted with finding routes along the by-ways, friendly Naturfreunde houses, youth hostels and sympathisers which would take them south to Heidelberg and beyond.

They were in open country, Artur Axmann was in his element, Germany's youth leader had walked every path, knew youth leaders in every District, in every town, he knew where every youth hostel and Naturfreunde House was located, often knowing where the keys were kept. He knew the songs he led the singing.

The next days were the most enjoyable of Strasser's life: spring sunshine lightening the constantly changing path in their trek to their goal, the sparsely occupied, little fight over middle and Southern Germany, the sunshine was accompanied by the exhilaration of having tweaked the noses of both the Russians and the British.

From the first Naturfreunde refuge they "borrowed" a billycan, spoons and most importantly salt and pepper. At first, every patch they crossed, every field they skirted, was scanned for vegetables. Days end having reached a gem from Axmann's collection of remote houses, they prepared their one solid meal of the day: potatoes, carrots, onions, swede, pea pods all went into the pot, the baby rabbit, stunned from getting Bruckner's boot under its belly, provided the meat, the fire crackled, far too much seasoning was added, but it resulted in the hottest tastiest stew ever brought to the boil.

Axman beamed as the compliments headed his way. During the day, he had unburdened his soul, emptied his conscience like a Whitechapel chamber pot over Hitler's head. 'Hitler made me enlist 15-year-old boys (he was slowly creeping towards the actual age) to defend Berlin. God knows I didn't want to, I knew I shouldn't, but he gave me no choice.'

Axmann had gossip at his fingertips, 'That farm over there, the farmer had three wives, he hung them up side by side in that barn,' he pointed. Next day, they passed another farm, 'I was 13, I went to Suki's birthday party, older than me, the barn was full of hay. She gobbled me up.' There hardly passed a village where no seed was sown.

Bruckner fed in his own contribution; for over two years he'd been "map man" to the high command, he lived maps, had listened in on every tactical discussion and argument from Kursk to the Ardennes. He had a view on every general, surprising Strasser by having a high opinion of the Fuhrer, it was Bruckner who reading maps had suggested how the banks of the Vistula near Krakov could be best defended by withdrawing and positioning the German artillery behind Hill 17, from where the broad Russian advance positions could be shelled in two directions; it was his suggestion that the code word "Watch on the Rhine", what the Allies called "The Battle of the Bulge", had been adopted. He'd been in the room when Stauffenberg had planted his bomb, escaping injury by being at the far end.

He testified to Hitler's personal bravery, believing that the attempt gave him additional strength to carry on. Giving his view of the generals, he blamed Von Manstein for not rescuing Von Paulus and the 6th Army from Stalingrad, wondering whether it was jealousy and rivalry that contributed to the failure to raise the siege and rescue the 6th army earlier in the winter. Von Manstein had later failed to grasp control of the Russian front and make a huge orderly withdrawal whilst he had the chance, Jodl, Keital, von Rundstedt, even Model might have backed him.

In his opinion Hitler was a military competent, if he hadn't been, the generals would have rebelled; he was way better than any other on the general staff, even if he was only kept going by Dr Morell with pills and injections; but Hitler couldn't accept that Germany had bitten off more than it could chew, and that the Russians were more resilient and more determined than he gave them credit. Odds of 100 men against 30 can only lead to one final result The Fuhrer needed someone to force that fact home, particularly as Goering had drugged himself out of contention.

The next day they all sang; Axmann led the singing just as he had done on so many Hitler youth rallies:

I'll sing you one Oh
Green grow the rushes oh
What is your one oh?
Adolf Hitler is his name and evermore shall be so,
Bruckner took up the tune
I'll sing you two oh…
…Herman Goering is his name and flying is his game oh.
The song petered out when they reached number 13.
Focke Wolfe is the plane…

Despite Bruckner's skill with maps, Axmann took over the selection of routes to his safehouses, Strasser handing him the key map. 'If we walk till 4 am, we'll reach Sterntal.' Dawn had broken before they walked up the path and knocked on the door of a well-appointed corner house. Axmann's embrace with Frau Kobel was protracted, they were clearly more than acquaintances, be that as it may, by late afternoon three bicycles had been acquired, three boys riding on the handlebars, they were safely on the route which would eventually take them out of the wake of military advances into southern Germany.

The boys stayed perched on the handlebars until they reached a marshalling yard alongside a tributary of the river Ruhr, they lowered the seats, turned the bikes around and said goodbye and thank you to the boys; a paper was handed to the gateman. 'RUN!' the gateman urged, pointing to where an engine was being force fed with the last of the coal slack from a giant hopper. Showing the paper again to the engine driver, they were pushed under the dirty tarpaulin covering the tender. Within an hour, they had shovelled out for themselves quite a nice living space inside the coal, inside the tender; black faced, the goods train was by this time jerking its way south and west to meet the river Rhine.

The Rhine still in spate from melted Alpine snows, the train stopped by a bridge over the River Lahn, a tributary of the Rhine to take on water and give the crew a break. The stoker gave a shout, a dozen shovel loads brought them out from their burrow, he pointed to the quay, 'There's your barge,' picking out a coal barge riding high in the water, they walked the three hundred metres, talking animatedly as if it was the most natural walk in the world, they walked up the narrow gangplank, a whistle, a hand from the wheelhouse summoned them aft, where a loud whisper told them urgently to get below deck, they hid not moving until the barge had pushed off the bank, out into the river, 'OK now.' On deck, a pipe lifted vertically to a perforated can, one after the other they stripped and showered until the black coal dust had washed from their bodies down into the scuppers, then it was the turn of their clothes, first their top garments. The three men watched the cold water swirling away into the fast-flowing Rhine. Shivering, one towel between three, they dried themselves and huddled around the stove in the wheelhouse. Bruckner promised he would connect hot water to the shower, if they could provide welding equipment.

Against the current yet the barge was soon through the Rhine Gorge, past Rudesheim, town of wine women and song, invisible, dark as death where the river was wider and slower. Sailing down the middle without a light in sight, Strasser felt safe and relaxed standing next to the skipper, warm now in the tiny wheelhouse. He wasn't safe, suddenly the front of the barge was struck by the bright beam of a searchlight mounted on an invisible craft coming up behind. The beam swept back down the barge to shine directly into the wheelhouse, the captain gestured—hide, he stuck his head out of the window, against the wind. 'Heave to, we're coming aboard, military,' was the message from the loud hailer.

Travelling against the current it was easy to bring the barge to a halt and easy for the dark cutter to pull alongside and for three armed men to jump on board. 'Papers, skipper,' hardly bothering to look, 'Cargo skipper.'

'We should be so lucky,' he replied, 'no coal to be had anywhere, we've hardly got anything; we're light hoping to pick up timber at Mannheim.' The soldiers pointed torches at the empty holds, 'anything you want to sell us?' They laughed at the skipper.

'We've got 20 boxes of carburetors for Tiger Tanks.' Everybody laughed.

The lights of a bigger barge travelling swiftly with the current, appeared to starboard. A soldier nudged the officer and pointed: 'Yeah I feel vulnerable too, stopped in midstream, let's get going.'

'Have a good trip, fella,' he thrust the papers back and jumped back onto the dark cutter. Panic over.

'At Wiesbaden, they were down to two, the silent escaper Bruckner, taking his leave, planning to lie low at his sister's flat in Frankfurt, which next to a small brewery he understood was still habitable. He didn't leave before they held a post mortem on Germany's defeat, sitting close in the tiny cabin; fascinating, were four men each holding different points of view. Axmann, influenced by losing his arm on the road to Leningrad, blamed their failure on the 'Russian Adventure, biting off more than we could chew.' Colonel Strasser, whilst agreeing that Russia was the key, blamed the Hungarians, Roumanians and Latvians. 'Until Stalingrad we had never lost, after Stalingrad we never won, if it hadn't been for our "friends" running away, Stalingrad would have been the victory to convince Russia she no option but to sue for peace, and this would have secured us all the oil and raw materials we needed—the Allies would never have dared to put a toe across the English Channel against our army, fully armed and equipped, fully prepared and fully rested.

Bruckner had served in Army HQ throughout the war and had experienced every advance every withdrawal against a background of logistics at army conferences, with their rows and detailed plans plotted on paper, maps poured over, a thousand miles from the battle front, such was the scale on which Germany was fighting, hundreds of maps were needed, many having to be changed and updated every single day, ready for the Fuhrer to make and change his plans for the generals.

He had a different take on the defeat, political decisions not military defeats lost Germany the war, before Stalingrad Germany was in an impregnable position, Sweden was prepared to act as broker for a peace with Russia which would have given Germany Hitler's main strategic objectives, we could then have bided our time, waited until our V weapons were ready, then finished off England without needing to cross the channel or suffer a single casualty.

Hitler's other political error was to declare was on America the day after Pearl Harbour,

'What do you think, Captain?' Axmann asked the barge owner to give a civilian point of view. 'I've always thought it was the Jews,' he began, three men groaned, the captain felt squashed and knew he was out of his league, he didn't utter another word, except to ask who would have become Fuhrer if the bomb had killed Hitler. Axmann was vocal, the Generals versus the Party, any successor must be and look Aryan, the Party was sensitive, Himmler and Goebbels didn't look right, looking more Jewish than Nordic, Goering had got fat and got other things, Racial features put von Shirach, persona non grata to Hitler, had been held in reserve in Vienna, and might have been acceptable to the Generals, who had no candidate of their own except Goering.

Warm in the small cabin, half a dozen empty bottles behind them, Strasser asked about Eva Braun. Bruckner claimed to know all about Eva, but she never came into the map room and Hitler never spoke about her, but Axmann knew.

'She was nice, she dressed my arm several times, she was natural, but no one, even herself knew exactly where she stood with Hitler. Weeks, she hardly saw him. He was never openly affectionate. She was nice, she deserved to be married, but she never influenced him. I think better of Hitler because finally he married her. It was a decent thing, she'd have enjoyed a week as a wife, but I'm sure she died happy, and perhaps for a few minutes Hitler was happy as well.'

Bruckner was to make it on his own, rather than risk tying up to a berth, he skiffed over to the Weisbaden east shore, his departing words ' von Manstein should have shortened the defensive line by 1,000 miles in 1944.'

Mannheim, where the captain hoped to fill his barge with wood was journey end, saying goodbye to the bargee and his wife, food in pockets, they jumped onto the bank, again Axmann took charge, milking his contacts to the full, the pair slept on clean sheets in different beds, changing Hostels every night, passing slowly south in a succession of milk carts, bread and mail vans, cycles and farm carts, fed with fried, boiled, steamed potatoes and swede at every stopping point. Five days later Strasser and Axmann, arrived in Salzburg as friends.

Killing Hitler, an objective that had festered for 10 years, had released Strasser's demons, and revenge whether on Cockburn or Hitler passed out of his mind, his full attention returned to running his safehouses, earning a profit and outwitting the Allies.

Salzburg, dangerous to be on the streets, US jeeps patrolling randomly, Strasser led to the apartment of one of his former deputies. Delay but finally the wife, Alice opened the door, beckoning them quickly inside. 'Johan's under arrest, the Palace has been occupied by the Allies if you're seen you'll be arrested.

This was all they needed to know, waiting till it was dark, Strasser took Axmann to his flat, an annex to a house owned by his sister. Cooking Alice's vegetables, they listened to a radio Berlin with a Russian accent before switching over to the American Forces Network, which they found more informative. Early next morning Strasser found a working public phone and resumed contact with Muller who reported that all the "clients" had arrived, Walserval was full and there had not been any visits by the Americans. Back at his flat:

Unmentioned throughout their flight south, was the unresolved question of a safehouse for Axmann, who daren't raise the subject fearing a rejection, Strasser was still pondering,

'It would too dangerous to have Axmann living as part of a large group, he would be recognised and as a main target for the Allies would have a price on is head.' It was time to say something to Axmann, at last he came out of the long grass.

Axmann could stay in an "historic house" on the Neckar with several other fugitives. Chief among them, English born, Charles George Grand Duke of Saxe-Coburg and Gotha; Axmann knew of the Grand Duke, knew he was a grandson of Queen Victoria, had become a naturalised German when accepting the Dukedom and knew he had been stripped of his English title, the prestigious "Duke of Albany", he knew the Duke personally as he had headed up the German arm of the Red Cross.

It wasn't until Axmann accepted the proposition blind, that Strasser told him the refuge was a house built into the wall of Dilsberg, a medieval walled village high on the escarpment above the River Neckar.

'You've put joy in my heart,' he told Strasser, 'I love Dilsberg, it has, had,' he corrected himself, 'our leading Hitler Youth Group in the entire Neckar valley.' Axmann, the Dilsberg address safely committed to memory, put himself back into his own transport system, travelling north in under an hour.

Strasser had still to decide on where he was going to live, where was the most secure long-term living arrangement, what better than the comfort and prestige as owner, captain and head passenger on the steamer Queen of St Gilgen, hidden up a creek on the Wolfgangsee; or incognito in a discrete flat in Munich; or his girlfriend's flat; he discounted sharing the safehouse at Dilsberg with the wobbly elderly Duke of Saxe-Coburg and his wife and wobbly servant; certainly not in the apartments at Walserval, whilst his farmhouse in Aussee was so well known to be associated with him, it was much too risky, especially with distant family already living there, that would make him a sitting duck for his enemies. Black Forest houses were death traps, the forest already swarming with a hatful of fugitives. He briefly considered and as quickly rejected Ritter's formula, a hide on the Dachstein massif… much too inhospitable and too far away for him to be able to look after business.

Chapter 9
Cleansing the Stables

Weeks upon weeks of interrogation of thousands of suspects loomed, Martin was unenthusiastic, of course he wanted to catch war criminals, but most of all he wanted to find and catch Strasser, everything else paled into insignificance, and he planned carefully; there were four season ticket "hotspots" in the area south of Ebensee, stations at Hallstatt, Goisern, Bad Aussee, whilst Bad Ischl Station was in sight, down the hill below the hunting lodge. The whole area was littered with the fine chalets of wealthy people.

'Bormann,' deputy to Hitler. Two jeeps dropped Martin and support in the drive of Number 5, a commanding house in Altaussee. Speaking German, Martin pushed back the woman at the door, his men filed past into the kitchen.

'Your husband, Frau Bormann?' he asked, ignoring the children. Frau Bormann was the wife of Martin Bormann, Hitler's factotum and 2nd in command.

'He's not here… he stayed true and stayed with the Fuhrer,' Frau Bormann was proud and matter-of-fact, she made no attempt to hide her identity, or her pride in her husband. The photographs of family groups and of her husband with Hitler displayed throughout the house would have made denial pointless.

'We don't know Hitler is dead, do we. No dead bodies, no photos, I'm doubting Thomas, me,' said Partridge from the kitchen.

The children sent upstairs, Hillary and Partridge in the lounge, Martin began the questions. He picked up one photograph after the other, some were taken at the Berghaus Hitler's Alpine home at Berchesgarden, but most were taken at official party functions. Frau Bormann answered easily and believably, giving dates, locations and names without being asked twice. As a rule, the people photographed next to her husband were politicos from Italy, Roumania and satellite Axis countries, so far as he knew none were linked to Death Camps except Reinhardt Heydrich, assassinated by the Resistance in Prague, Frau Bormann appeared infrequently, it appeared that like Magda Goebbels, she regarded the task of looking after a clutch of children was a full-time task.

Martin noted one exception, appearing several times was a fat priest, always with one or other of the children, at a christening ceremony, festivities, or at a meal.

'Father John, our parish priest,' she said, 'he lives in the presbytery over there,' she pointed towards a house surrounded by trees, on the far side of the open field away from the lake.' Martin nodded. He and Partridge went into the kitchen to confer.

Partridge took a jeep, knocking vigorously on the Presbytery door.

'Inside,' Partridge pushed the fat elderly priest back into the hall. No sooner had he closed the door than he rammed his fist into the fat paunch. The priest doubled up, Partridge slammed the side of his hand into the priest's shoulder, and without waiting for Father John to recover, walked down the hall. When he had recovered somewhat, Father John followed Partridge, limping into the kitchen.

'Father John, I'm here so that you can help me and also help Frau Bormann—understand,' said Partridge. Wiping blood from a swollen lip which had hit the hat stand in his fall, Father John mumbled something.

'You and me, we're going over to see Frau Bormann, she needs your help. You know where I'll hit you next if she doesn't get it.' Father John knew.

Back in the Bormann lounge, a jug of coffee was transferred from a trolley to stand steaming on pot stand on a side table. Hillary poured, 'this will help soothe your mouth and loosen your tongue,' said Partridge unnecessarily, passing a cup to Father John.

In the months recovering from his stomach wounds, Martin propped up in bed, read many detective novels and thought he had mastered the techniques of interrogation. He pushed his chair away, slowly and deliberately, slowly he got up from his chair and walked slowly and deliberately to the window. He pointed, wincing at the spasm of pain hitting below his shoulder.

'There's a woman on the field with an easel, painting up on the knoll, a friend of yours Frau Bormann?'

'That'll be Molly, she's good. She paints in 360 degrees, do you know what I mean?'

'Obviously no,' he said.

'From that knoll she paints all points of the compass, so her paintings show a completely round view, as if she is sitting in the centre of what she paints.'

(In September 1965, Bloomingdales in New York were to enjoy a bumper sales month, the reason was the success of an exhibition of 360 degree art a technique mastered by an unknown German painter called Molly Vintner.)

'A round view, what a splendid start for our questioning,' Martin began, 'I am sure you both regret the violent events at Berlin, what I most regret and what I'm here to investigate are earlier more violent and more evil events that happened at Ebensee so near to here, what I need from you both is a round view of the people who live in your exclusive estate here at Altaussee. Here, he pointed, we have listed every house, however as your most recent electoral register appears to have disappeared, we need you to fill in the names and detail of the people who live in each house, I'm sure your husband had each and every new arrival vetted, to ensure your children never mixed or played with Yiddish swine.'

Martin still at the window, motioned to Partridge, wheelie truck in front of him, the postie halted at the kerb.

'Get him.'

Opposite Frau Bormann's gate, Partridge pulled out his handgun and stuck it firmly in the postie's ribs.

'Bring your truck, follow me.' Eyes wide open, mouth firmly shut, the postie entered the drawing room, he bowed slightly to Frau Bormann, who inclined her head.

Martin repeated his instruction, they must list who lived in each house.

'I'm not allowed to pass out such information, the Bureau won't allow it.'

'But my Government allows it, postie, and my friend's gun positively insists on it. Postie shrugged his shoulders.

We will do this in separate rooms, and if we find discrepancies between the lists, we will have to find out why.'

Frau Bormann and the postie moved through the addresses, Father John was painfully slow, and as Partridge said, 'Wasn't doing his best.' Martin and Partridge both held low opinions of Catholic priests, they called them "Galileos" between themselves.

'This is a direct threat Father, I merely seek neutral information, bland, non-incriminatory information, but should I not get it, my friend Partridge who only ever acts with my complete authority, will take you to your own quiet confessional, draw the curtains, where he can confess or scream out his sins at the very same moment as he commits them. Should he not get absolution I will take his place and you can hear my confession between you screams as we start afresh. From your own confessional, you might even be induced to confessing the secrets of the Catholic ratline that speeds Nazis across your altars, down to the pope in Rome bound for Rio de Janeiro.'

Father John speeded up.

Martin left with a comprehensive list for every house in Altaussee. who lived where and who did what, Frau Bormann's children were told they had a brave mother they should look after and be proud, 'If I hear anything about your father, a brave man to put himself in harm's way in Berlin, I'll let your mother know,' were his parting words.

As they left the chalet Martin still wincing from his shoulder, changed his mind, 'Hillary, I'm suffering; I'm going to have a word with the doctor.' The doctor's home and surgery was 700 metres down the steep hill. So steep that, with Dr Heidi Frohm being a vinegary 60-year-old spinster, her surgery was rarely full. Hillary told Dr Fromm who Martin was, Martin told the doctor what he wanted.

'I've no questions for you doctor, I'm not here to challenge the Hippocratic Oath; I'm in pain and I want you to examine my back and my ankles whilst my colleague Hillary Cowperthwaite plucks out some addresses from your records.'

Taken aback, a suspicious and sullen Heidi set up Hillary in her office motioning Martin to go into the treatment room. Clean to a fault, a bare couch, a single chair, although no one else was in the house Dr Frohm by habit, drew the curtains and closed the door. She turned to find Martin already half-undressed.

'You mustn't think that the British Army don't have good medical resources, doctor, but Salzburg is a journey, and I prefer to keep my difficulties to myself and my friend, and away from my colleagues; I'm sure you understand. Your Luftwaffe Hospital at Hamelin repaired me after I was shot down three years ago and very well they did it. You're highly recommended.'

Heidi Frohm was flattered, her shoulders rose. 'Let's have a look at you then, I've only limited resources here of course.'

'Of course, Doctor, just see what you can do.' Martin was naked, it was a private pleasure to strip off at every opportunity to Hillary's alarm, her years in the vicarage had not got her used to that, not allowed in the vicar's bedroom.

'Turn around,' Dr Frohm put on her glasses, she looked him up and down, 'you have been in the wars.' The word "have" being stressed.

'Up,' she slapped the couch, drawing a sheet across, Martin lay down, uncomfortable without a pillow. 'Let's start at the bottom,' she tugged, he winced, the plaster on his heel came off.

'How long has that been suppurating?' she asked. After squeezing the abscess, she wiped off the puss, concentrating down she squeezed, a yellow blob of horribleness ejected from the volcanic plug in his heel, oozing down to the sole of his foot, on to the couch, staining the sheet. Wiping it up, a bandage wrapped around two fingers, she used her foot to open a metal bin and plopped blob, bandage and everything in it. Wrapping gauze around a splint, she wiped off what remained of the disaster from his foot; this swab followed the yellow monsters into the bin.

'I'll just cover this up for now, get to your medicals and ask them to give you an American antibiotic I read about which I haven't any here, haven't had any ever.' She stuck on a plaster. 'And keep it clean. Don't leave it and don't forget. It's serious but it isn't embarrassing like some of the volcanoes our soldiers bring me. What's next?'

Martin lay on his back, he pointed to the angry area where Strasser's two bullets had entered and done such damage to his stomach. Without a word Dr Frohm opened another jar, yellow ointment was rubbed all over, thin plasters held fresh lint over the area.

'Same again, ask them for biotics, if it doesn't clear before weekend, show it to your own people, there's little I can do here.'

'Could you look at my shoulder blade? It's hurting. I got hit with shrapnel.' Before he could turn over, Heidi Fromm lovingly ran her fingers over his magenta coloured knees,

'You have been in the wars, did you know burning chemicals leave their own fingerprints, burns have distinguishing colours. Russian shells cause a deeper brown burn than burns from our explosives, yours are much more like a rainbow. I expect both TNT and petrol were involved; I was in Russia for months treating tank burns after Kursk.' Months since Martin wallowed in his injuries, it was therapy for him to talk.

'Mine are aviation spirit mostly. I was shot down near Benburg, drenched in shrapnel and fuel, two broken legs and a broken arm. Luftwaffe Hamelin fixed me up. It's a year since I took revolver shots in the stomach, but it was peritonitis that almost killed me. That was the Schaffhausen Clinic that was. I got peritonitis in a Swiss Clinic, can you believe that?'

'It happens!' Dr Frohm was philosophical.

Martin turned over. The doctor moved her hands to his shoulder.

'I know what's happened here: shrapnel has worked its way up out of spaces in your spine and is rubbing on a nerve by a muscle; it happens to our troops all the time. I can take it out without an X-Ray or you can go to your own hospital or to the main hospital in Salzburg, what do you want?'

'This is the second time a shrapnel has come out of me. Did you take much shrapnel out at Kursk?'

'Tons, tanks are notorious for shrapnel wounds.'

'Can you take mine out now, please?' Hillary must have been standing outside the door listening, she burst into the room.

'You're never going to have more shrapnel taken out surely!' she exclaimed.

'Dr Frohm says she's done it a thousand times.'

'It'll only take five minutes and five stitches, watch if you like.' Dr Heidi was preparing to give an injection.

'No fear, do it if you like,' she gave Martin a kiss and fled the treatment room.

A pethidine injection, German to cure-all pain, six stitches, six minutes, Martin held a minute piece of his Wellington's fuselage in his fingers.

Unaccountably, Dr Heidi was as pleased and as proud as a peacock, whilst Martin dressed, she made coffee using boiling water from a steamer designed to sterilise instruments and produced homemade biscuits given by a patient for her unexpected visitor, doctors are doctors, patients are patients the world over. They sat around her kitchen table as Martin asked:

'Do you know a friend of mine, Hans Strasser? He used to own a farm around here.'

'Colonel General Strasser, yes I know him, he has a false hand, the metal joint needed attention. He lost his hand in an accident, a colleague chopped his arm off slamming down a hatch cover or something. I haven't seen him for months.'

'Do you know where I can get in touch?' Dr Frohm shook her head. 'Nobody can find anybody these days and I wouldn't tell you even if I knew.' She turned towards Hillary, 'See you get your friend to a hospital where they can treat him with the latest bug killers or you won't have your friend with you for much longer.'

Hillary was first out of the door, jumped in the driver's seat; give her an hour, she had turned it into the US Medical Group centre near Gmunden. Penicillin works, sleep works, love, attention and loving care works. Within 24 hours, Martin felt fitter than he had for months.

At the breakfast table: 'Meet John Anderton, he's come to join us,' Travers introduced a tall lank newcomer, rising to shake hands,

'Don't we know each other,' it was Anderton who spoke, 'Menzenschwand, you're the Cohen who got away?'

'Yes, and aren't you the bugger who caught the spy from Harrow that the Germans had smuggled into Hut 2.' Anderton beamed 'my only claim to fame I fear.' Travis jumped in before a chin wag to which he wasn't privy, started.

'Catch up on all that later, guys, I want you to fill John in on everything that's happening, and tomorrow take him to Ebensee, take him inside, show him the camp, the town, the oil plant, the production line, everything, the thousands of hopeless hungry men the Yanks are trying to feed to recover from maltreatment and malnutrition.'

The drive to Ebensee, they talked of the missing years, released from Menzenschwand Prison Camp before war-end, Anderton returned to London only to find his wife Elsie living happily with a Peter Clarke and a new baby, she didn't want to know Anderton anymore. His wife's story as he heard it from a friend of his wife's:

Before I married John, I lived with Barry Saxon, it was great, we were at it all the time. It was like travelling on the Northern Line, we did Waterloo Station, the Strand, Trafalgar Square, Warren St, Goodge St, Euston Station, you've missed out Tottenham Court Rd said the friend.

Tottenham Court Rd, that was why I kicked him out and married John, he was changing onto the Piccadilly Line every week behind my back as, regular as clock work.

John was kind, but he was dull, we only took the tube on Saturday night, no good for me that, I need my wheels tapped regularly.

'I was devastated, Martin, I just wanted to forget and get as far away from her as I could, I went back to Hendon and asked them to help. They offered me this job, anywhere away from London I told them, so I took it and here I am, but what about you, you were the real hero. The camp heard you'd got to Switzerland, then we heard Jim had been caught and killed; shot by Strasser.' Martin did not want to talk about Jim, didn't even want to know about Jim, it was a scab which suppurated whenever Jim was mentioned, a blemish that would never heal.

'I was lucky John, I had trouble crossing the border and bumped into a couple of border-guards and we had a shoot-out, because of this I was stuck in our embassy in Berne as an illegal, translating, doing one thing after another. Hillary, worked there and we've been together now for over a year. We're expecting a baby and we'll be married as soon as we can get back to Sussex.

'Congratulations, nothing easy in war. Travers told me you'd been shot in the belly.'

'Yes, but that was much later, Jim wasn't the only escaped POW shot by Colonel General Hans Strasser, the bastard shot me in the stomach, and I've got the scars to prove it.' Anderton returned to the subject uppermost in his mind.

'Menzenschwand camp never understood why you and Jim split, you went south, and he went north, no one could understand you splitting, you such a good German speaker. Did he not want to travel with you?' Martin was silent, finally he spoke.

'We split because I'm a selfish sod John, I knew I'd have the best chance of getting away if I stayed by myself, let's leave it at that; it bothers me that he's dead, he might still be alive if we'd stayed together. I know that.' The awkward silence wasn't broken until Martin asked,

'Why did Digby choose you to winkle out the spy in the camp, John?'

'Digby knew I'd been a tax investigator before the war, I told him I was good at it. He didn't think much of the redcaps, "planks", he called them. You know Digby (Camp Senior Officer) told Strasser to pull the "Harrow Boy" out of Menzenschwand, it was after your sketch of the Duke of Windsor and the ghastly Archbishop.'

'I remember that,' Martin chuckled. John returned to the bee in his bonnet.

'Jim was caught on a train near Mainz, we heard the SS brought him back and Strasser shot him in the head, just like he had Tom and Dick, the airmen killed on the wire before you got away. The "Harrow Boy" was a Nazi plant; anyhow, after I told Digby of my suspicions, he decided that if the word got out the men would hang him. Digby decided that rather than risk letting this happen, he'd tell Strasser that we knew and Strasser arranged for him to be pulled out. Pity that.' Martin didn't say a word, John continued,

'There were consequences, shortly before the Yanks liberated Menzenschwand, Strasser came; he'd not been near for months, he had a long talk with Digby and wanted him to certify we'd all been treated well and according to Geneva conventions, he wanted a carte blanche.'

'Surely Digby didn't give him that?' Martin sounded incredulous.

'Digby did give him something, don't know exactly what; by the way, did I tell you who won the sweep?'

'What sweep?'

'The sweep of when Uncle Sam first came through the gate. Everybody bet a day's pay on the day and the hour we'd be liberated. It was mayhem, plenty of men got the day right, only John Whalley in Hut 4 had bet 2 am; Nigel Mackereth in Hut 1 bet 3 am, but nobody had ever said whose watch they would go by. John had promised a piss up to his hut if he won, so you know what they all said. Digby was asleep when it happened; the Yanks couldn't agree a time. In the end, the Huts couldn't agree, and in the end everybody got their money back, and the bets were cancelled.'

'I bet Nigel was livid at losing out on a wad of money,' said Martin. 'By the way, how did you rumble "Harrow Boy"?'

'Trade craft, old boy.'

'Tell me and I'll tell you how I nailed our spy in the Berne Embassy.'

No one spoke, the mood sombre, they'd arrived at the gates of the Ebensee Labour Camp, opened up to their Land Rover. They parked up, emaciated men still there to gather strength before returning home, gathered round, looking for food, but ready to help. After a minute Martin decided to drive up to the caverns, he'd had enough forced labour camps. 'I've not actually been in the caverns myself,' he said. Reversing, he drove up to the foot of the mountain, stopping in front of the houses built to hide the cavern and save it from RAF bombing.

'Bloody hell,' said John Anderton.

They drove through the mock house, into the huge cavern, only the lights from their vehicle, eerie, abandoned lines of machine tools, several men were caught in the head lights before they vanished in the darkness a single bird, heard but not seen, flapped towards the roof.

Martin turned right, against the cavern wall a row of prefab offices appeared. 'Let's see if there's anything worth taking.'

Taking flash lights from the glove compartment, skirting a line of machinery, they got out of the jeep and went into the offices, John returning a minute later with a typewriter he put on the back seat,

'We can do with that back in the office,' he said defensively. They poked about for another 10 minutes but with the flashlights fading they got back in the jeep. 'Let's see if we can find 42nd St,' said Martin, 'I think the Yanks have put a bar there.' He put the jeep back onto what looked like a road way rubbing alongside a cave wall, sure enough the headlights picked out an arrow and a sign saying 42nd St. Slowly they bumped and bounced their way along for a quarter of a mile hardly able to see what was on their right-hand side. They entered a tunnel driven through a large supporting rock face; as they emerged, the faint sound of dance music could be heard, the 300 yards ahead a bright pool of light.

Martin parked beside four other vehicles, getting out they sauntered up to a sort of counter; a voice from a man sitting at one of the tables asked them whether they wanted a burger or coke, fries or coffee, that was all there was. They both said, 'Yes.'

The voice said, 'Ilse, got that.' Ilse had and within a minute papers plates and cups were in front of them.

As their eyes had become accustomed to the gloom, they were able to make out the outline of a row of tanks like a rank of guardsmen in line down the huge cavern. Seeing where they were looking the voice told them, 'Yes, they were to hold the gas, they brought the lignite in far side and stored the gas here, dinky ain't it?'

Filled up coffee and drank it, it was time to go. 'Let's get out of here, curiosity had evaporated. Is there another way out?' asked Martin.

'Follow the signs to Mont Blanc, it's a climb, fella.'

So they did, finally reaching daylight and blue sky a thousand feet higher than where they started. On the slow road down the stone road's 'S' bends, Martin filled-in some back ground.

'After Hamburg and the RAF busting Peenemunde, Gerry decided to put key war manufacture underground, expanding natural caverns, blasting holes from out of the hill side. Ebensee was ideal, a mountain of solid limestone, already part hollow from limestone to make cement, situated in a narrow valley, at the limit of RAF's bombing range, an obvious choice with a railway already going along the valley connecting to a main line.

Not a word reached London.'

'That's strange,' ventured John, 'How come?'

'Don't get me started,' Martin began, but he started none the less 'Churchill was never in favour of hard pounding in Europe, with 50 million to feed and an Empire, Central

Europe didn't figure high, it wasn't in the Empire. Millions of £'s spent on equipment at Bletchley Park to tell the Navy that German submarines are operating in the Atlantic a statement of the bleeding obvious. Central Europe he largely ignored, but, spies, guns for the French Resistance, boy scout groups in Egypt and Burma, bugger-all for the Serbo-Croats who didn't go to Harrow. The huge number of potential resistance fighters, Jewish Slav or otherwise in Eastern Europe were ignored.'

'You miss out Churchill's good points, he supported the Jews up to a point,' Anderton interjected, uncomfortable at the attack on Winnie.

'Don't know that, but London didn't know of Ebensee till me and Hillary told them, and we discovered Ebensee entirely by accident, 10,000 foreign labour, 100 tanks a week, and we were sent to look for Hitler's Mountain Fortress a bolt-hole to hide when the war was over. Dilettante Stuff. Ebensee was never bombed no wonder I'm annoyed. Not bombed, no priority, but then Churchill wasn't facing 2,000 tanks at Kursk, and a million Mongolians never got entered on Eden's spreadsheet.' Martin became even more indignant:

'Can you believe it, the UK spending mega millions at Bletchley, reading off signals for German food requisitions, to tell convoys there are German submarines in your area and not a single British spy within 100 miles of Ebensee, with 10,000 informers anxious to speak already on site. Me and Hillary came past in a train over a year ago and Whitehall still did fuck all about it. Perhaps I'm too harsh, they've at least put mutton into the cabbage soup we're feeding the Polacks.'

John Anderton was feeling uncomfortable and didn't quite feel knowledgeable enough to defend Churchill's conduct of the Central European operations.

He changed the subject,

'It's a lovely railway line, how it follows that lovely river, I couldn't take my eyes off it as we drove along the valley, was the line always there?'

'The single-track was to take Austrian Emperors in comfort to holiday at our lodge at Bad Ischl, for hunting, shooting and fishing, there are thermal baths, and they surrounded themselves by musicians and beautiful women in beautiful clothes. Queen Victoria might have done much the same for Balmoral.

'What did they make here beside petrol, Ebensee's a long way from a large town, where did the German workers come from?'

'Over 10,000 prisoners hacked out the caverns, German specialists came from all over to install the machinery and escape the bombing of the Ruhr; prisoners operated the machinery, some quite skilled. Most came in via Mauthausen, an extermination camp, I've not been there.' They were out of the car, they'd reached the bottom of the hill...' Anderton kicked a stone,

'That's limestone, thousands of tons of it they turned into cement further north, but mostly they made components for tanks and rockets.'

On the journey back, Martin repeated that Ebensee wasn't an extermination camp, there weren't gas chambers, but thousands died of disease, starvation and mistreatment and the nine thousand remaining, were the survivors of nearer to 15,000 who had worked at the plant. The Americans had swept the town of the men who had worked at Ebensee, dumping them in the worst huts, these mass arrests made US statistics look good, which made Trackers results look puny indeed, but the Yanks had only arrested guards, operatives and office staff, the hierarchy did not live in the town, and they were still at large. Martin's s view was that the leaders had put miles between them and Ebensee, hiding up with relatives, staying hidden in the cellars and outhouses of their and their family's homes, a few had fled to the mountains, though one in particular, Ritter, the sadistic commander of the Ebensee labour force, is a fitness fanatic, was rumoured to have built a mountain hide on the Dachstein massif.

Mention of Ritter reminded Martin to tell John Anderton that every person interviewed at Ebensee, German to Pole claimed that Ritter proposed hiding the atrocities at Ebensee by forcing all the prisoners into a single cavern then collapsing it, burying men, equipment everything, so that the cavern, like the prisoners, no longer existed. Explosives were available, but technical and geological examinations were required, explosive technicians were needed, those consulted were very unhappy. Word got out, German's objected, and the labourers rebelled, the atrocity was buried, but not before Ritter's name had been carved on a thousand bullets. Just as every labourer reported Ritter as planning to kill them all, so the Americans reported that every Ebensee official, claimed they personally had stopped Ritter from collapsing the caverns on top of the workers.

'Let's concentrate, just go after the big beasts,' a long-standing theme of Martin, 'I know we've got to listen to the labour force, they deserve to be heard, but I've got tired of listening, I'm hoping to pass that job on to you and the others, John.'

'Did all the slave labour come to Ebensee from Mauthausen,' John Anderton didn't sound enthusiastic. Martin elaborated,

'Yes, mostly they brought them into Mauthausen by train from all over Europe, who selected the fittest and transferred them to Ebensee, killing the ones they didn't want, not many Jews made it as far as Ebensee. Back at the Hunting lodge, both John and Martin headed for a shower and change of clothes, before annoying Travers telling him the Americans had done at Ebensee precisely the same as they had done at the Augsburg Messerschmidt camp, sweeping up the small fry, and whisking the one good scientist that remained back to the States, "for evaluation". Travers promptly promised London and consoled himself that their imminent exercise against the "prominente", the powerful, the rich living in the idyllic towns and villages in the surrounding valleys, the St Wolfgangs, the St Gilgens, was nearly ready to go.

Next morning Martin came down to find Travers had left HQ, he had left a note attached to the Black Book, leaving him in charge for four days; Travers had accepted a last-minute invitation to tour Dracula's castles, Brasov and medieval towns on the lower Danube, with Generals Walker and Rosencrantz. 'We can't fall out with our cousins,' he had written.

Martin snorted, enjoying being annoyed and pleased at the same time, this was the first time Travers had let the Black Book out of his possession. The Black Book had been produced by London listing details and photographs of "persons of special interest", notably British traitors, prominent Nazis and known Rocket and Engine Scientists, included was the Duke of Saxe-Coburg-Gotha.

It was now the third week in the month, the week the Americans in southern Germany and Austria celebrated, and did they celebrate, it was a week of Victory Parties, excess and joyful sin. First, the US Signal Unit took over an hour to let off 100 cases of Very lights, many fired from the ramparts of Traunsee castle, a medieval castle gracing the hilly spit of land which jutted out into Lake Traunsee. It was these Very lights rather than the thousands of training thunder flashes, that set alight three medieval thatched cottages in the town, burning them to the ground. Later that evening a company of a Paratroop Regiment rioted, the Paras were competitive, notoriously undisciplined, a life force unto themselves. Nobody was going to out-do them, pushing their CO's newly acquired personal transport, a veteran Studebaker onto the town square, they stripped it down to its component parts, laying them out in line as if for inspection at the end of the line was a child's buggy and that was before they really started, leading to the Burgomaster of Gmund making a personal visit to General Eisenhower with pictures of the Elector's golden coach from the 14th century, desecrated but able to go at 40 mph.

The repercussions were awful, the CO was transferred, and despite three generations of his family having served lifetimes in the Army, he resigned before the month was out, but not before knocking cold Colour Sergeant Elton Turner, who he held to be the ringleader.

Next night, the Medics dispensed medicine early, before putting their patients to bed, joining the nurses aboard a paddle steamer sailing in circles around the Mondsee until it ran out of fuel, seven drifted onto a gravel bank. Upon boarding, all were presented with a present from the scarlet cupboard holding sachets designed to prevent early morning sickness… to the detriment of the lake's sewage disposal arrangements. There were gate-crashers. The gate crashers were seized, stripped and injected in the bum to prevent the onset of every disease known to Africa. They were however issued with the appropriate certificates and excused duty for three days.

Most spectacular; word spread like wildfire, even the Austrian towns folk turned out in force—at a discrete distance of course; an open mountain side south of Salzburg, later chosen as a setting for *The Sound of Music* was chosen as the stage for the "Danz of the Tanz", II was an event not to be missed; 60 tank engines rumbled, the PX stores had been emptied of all their amplifiers and loudspeakers which spewed out the "Ride of the Valkyries". Sixty tanks, including a couple of Tigers, Sherman's et al pirouetted around on open pasture in a macabre dance, in five minutes their tank tracks had completed the job of a hundred horses and ploughs; three Matilda and two Cromwell tanks about to make their final exit, packed full of everything except the kitchen sink, sat barely visible in early evening gloom, unmoving on the top of a low hill. At last Wagner whimpered to its death, to be replaced by Glen Miller's Orchestra and his *String of Pearls*, then *Rule Brittannia*, then *Cavalry of the Steppes.* The French were not to get a mention, with a resounding click from the loudspeakers, the music was switched off. Now only the rumble of engines echoed around the hills as the tanks lined up on the down slope of the shallow valley facing the hill.

They switched off their engines and as the echoes died just as slowly quiet settled into silence. It was uncanny.

Then from behind the hill came the sound of an Indian war drum mimicking a Western movie, and puffs of smoke rose above the skyline. Nothing moved until a red Very light soared into the sky. One after the other the tanks opened fire, pulverising the Matildas, blowing their parts high into the air as they "brewed up". The sound was deafening, the explosions frightening. When it was over General 'Robin' Hood turned and shook Tank major Cecil B de Mille's hand vigourously. 'We showed 'em.'

More sedate was a Pistol Darts Match which followed in the Officers Mess, or more precisely a Colts versus Luger Darts Match. Only a shortage of Dart Boards stopped the event dead at midnight.

'Help me, Help!' Travers implored his staff, he had not appreciated how big this celebration week was going to be. 'We've got to have a "do".' His small British Group isolated away from major British forces, couldn't compete with the Americans, his budget for the party barely covered NAAFI food for 30 visitors. He made stipulations; not one Military Policeman, no Airmen, no US Marines and no one from the Highland Division, Parachute Regiment or the Guards were to be invited… stories were rampant of the pitched battles in Osnabruck between the HLI, the Seaforths, the Coldstream and the Parachute Regiment.

"A quiet evening" was the promise to "friends" from the US Investigation Department, Signals, Medics, French, Polish Liaison Officers and four Russians including Major Irina, who Martin specially invited over from Vienna.

Drink and canapes were in place of a meal. Lump fish was not to be served until drink had been taken (no one could tell it from caviare after the vodka), nibbles, tit-bits, pretend canapes, dim sum, tapas, they were all to be there, the girls were to go into the parkland for bilberries, blue berries, raspberries, strawberries and blackberries, which under ripe weren't eaten, until everything else had left the plates. Grapes, lake shrimps, cheeses, mushrooms, snails everything was soaked in wine from bottles brought up from the cellar. The wine was king.

Maria Engels and her staff had kept the lodge spick and span for 25 years, her husband Thomas had kept the wine cellar likewise, hiding the "good stuff" away from philistines. The morning of the party Thomas and Travers went down to the cellar, 30 of the Tricorne Wedding Breakfast bottles each bearing the Archduke's Karnten seal, were opened and brought up to breathe, heaving a sigh of regret Thomas Engels drew back the cobweb curtain with a deep sigh, he had managed to save some of the "really good stuff", but Thomas never felt the same about his wine collection again.

'Sublime Haute Couture', 'Rubbish' were alternative verdicts on the food, but the cellars of the lodge, the cellar of the famous merchant in town had been raided, alcohol was exchanged for tins of span, corned beef, ovaltine tablets, capstan cigarettes and the drink, all passed the Plimsoll test (better than water), there were to be no complaints about wine, spirits or beer from anyone at all… except Thomas Engels, and he didn't count as he lay dead drunk, alone in his cellar.

Whilst Tracker was selecting and tasting wine, not in that order, Partridge, ignoring fraternisation regulations, 'These are Austrian not German girls.' (there is a difference), as well as the speed limit, promised the Austrian Hospital Matron (with the help of two pairs of Du Pont nylon stockings) and a Bedford Van to go shopping, to lend 20 of her nurses to the party bringing them home sometime after midnight. Pleased at this coup, returning from hospital, stopping at a crossing, Partridge heard music coming out from a rain-soaked bandstand. A carton of cigarettes guaranteed the attendance of 15 aspiring oompah musicians, without having to mention they would be required to escort 20 nurses home after midnight.

The attendance, after fearing no one would turn up, was solid, a visit to the hunting lodge, proving to be the main attraction. After the vodka, the canapes, with the wine came the toasts. Drink does not necessarily lead to an audience having tolerance for speeches, short or long, however three toasts received a less grotesque reception than the others:

'To the last, to the very last war!' that was US Colonel Earl Grey.

Host Tracker Travers recalled holidays hunting on his Grandfather's Country Estate: He jumped up on a table:

'To the ghillies, to the beaters, to the stags, to the grouse, the fish, to the rabbits, to the hunters, the fishermen, to the butchers, to the cooks, to our girlfriends, to us, may we all live forever.' Many of his listeners groaned at the first ghillie, few had the slightest idea what he was talking about, but as Travers said later, 'It's the accent, old boy, it's the way I tell 'em.'

Pride of place, the best toast, remembered till death by the sober, went to Russia. The Russians are good at toasts, getting more practice than most. Major Rokosovsky, collar unfastened, the dominant figure in the room, didn't begin until he had quiet and attention, no means an easy matter in ribald company: He finished,

'The British bought time, America brought money, Russia shed blood.'

Martin sitting between Irina and Hillary whispered, 'WHAT a fine toast, Irina.'

'Rokossovsky got it from Comrade Stalin,' she whispered back.

'Don't you mean Uncle Joe?' he squeezed her.

Major Eric Albright, Martin's oppo in the US team came up, fishing in his wallet he brought out the photo of a youngish women. 'This woman says Strasser's talking to Argentina.'

'Who is she?' Martin studied the picture, 'Name's on the back. Her boyfriend's left her and she wants revenge.' Martin said he'd look into it as soon as could, not wanting to sound too eager.

He joined the VIPs in an alcove, Partridge was pouring yet another bottle with the care a surgeon opens a vein, cobwebs, a bottle history being charged out to the English at a shilling a bottle, a shilling, Tomas's pride and joy for 25 years. Partridge made up a history of each bottle, where it came from, how many were left worldwide, how much they charged at the café with the flourish, the Café Rheinhardt in Berlin. The VIPs (and there were few true VIPs) treated each bottle with great and equal solemnity, keeping it away from the ensigns and the riff raff, trying to ensure no one drank quicker or with greater reverence than they did, such was the depth and quality. Like Partridge they knew they were drinking history.

Travers took briefly to the floor, thanking guests for coming and introducing Partridge, who without further ado announced:

'All vote for the best equipment the Allies have brought to Germany, Mike will demonstrate,

Boots: In came Mike wearing a pair of heavy black British army boots, toecaps gleaming throwing spirals of light up towards the ceiling, segs at heel and toe, 'leather laces, guaranteed to snap within 24 hours,' was all he said. 'Woollen socks complete with needle and matching wool for darning.'

Next, he brandished US boots: 'Light, synthetic, non-slip soles, elasticated, no laces and without holes, waterproof. Man-made synthetic nylon from Du Pont, indestructible socks.' All votes plumped for the US waterproofs. Major Rokosovsky spoke up:

'Gentlemen, last year the Manchurean Rifle Division received out of a Murmansk Convoy, 2,000 pairs of British Army grey socks. The number of invalid bad feet from Trench to Athletes to Gangrene fell from 30% to 2% in six weeks. I myself wear no other and my brother, Marshall Rokosovsky, is in contact to buy 100,000 pairs for our northern armies.' Applause was slow in coming. Partridge resumed control:

Rifles: Coming back in front of his audience, Mike presented arms with a standard British rifle:

'Five single shots, kills at 2,000 yards, four feet long, this 303 weighs five kilometres.' (The British had not yet grasped the metric system.)

Fifty rounds a minute, the shorter lighter semi-automatic infantry equivalent from the USA took the votes, with the cut and slash German bayonet preferred to the British pig-sticker bayonet, 'good for filing invoices,' someone muttered. 'No it's not, it rusts,' someone called out. On and on it went, from capes, mess tins to blanco, British equipment losing at every turn.

The final comparison: "Tommy's" rimmed helmet and the larger American helmet covering the ears.

'Let's have a "shoot out",' someone called, the audience was getting restive, they had had enough of army equipment to last a lifetime. They put a turnip inside and propped the helmets up in an old chair, volunteers took pot shots. The tin hat brought the highest price, as a colander.

News of this attack on British Infantry equipment found its way back to Army HQ, Hamburg. First a phone call to the office, 'was this story true?' An hour the Duty Officer was asked for confirmation of a report. Followed by 'who was there? And who was the SBO (Senior British Officer) present at the party? A Conference Call for Trapper Travers was booked for 10 am the next morning, who promptly cancelled a projected trip to traverse down the Swarz Klammer Gorge with US General Hood, it was that serious.

If the canapes hadn't been to your taste, if the hors d'oevres weren't fresh, if the tapas were off colour, and the fish less than fresh. If you were tea total, there were the Austrian girls, the nurses and the music. If the oompah band was too loud, and the tunes not to your taste, the night, the perfume, *the gardens and the grass were quiet and warm. The old hunting lodge had never had such a good time for years, never enjoyed itself so much since the Grand Duchess took off her girdle, threw her pumps on the fire and rode bareback on a young Hussar, down the grand staircase.

All told the party did Travers proud. They knew they hadn't attracted the "A" List. Giving young people access to a free bar from the beginning was risky, a tremendous error which worked out splendidly. The young musicians were a roaring success with a succession of girl and boy instrumentalists jostling to get to the front to perform their party pieces, the Inkspots, Al Jolson and surprisingly often, other US Hits. The girl echoing Marlene Dietrich singing "Underneath the Lamplight" was forced to sing it again and again, the non-existent sound system bounced raucously from pilaster to chandelier to hillside gardens. The party was remembered fondly, in Kiev, Texas, Maidenhead and even Vienna, but in Bad Ischl the fireworks on the hill and the early hour singing lorry, round and round the centre of Ischl provoked resentment and ire from Matron waiting at the door of the nurse's home for the return of her wards.

With an open bar, the nurses/waitresses had needed no persuasion to join in and dance, and they were fit, no wilting as midnight approached. For those who only wanted to watch or drink, frauleins, ATS and WAAFs were available, 'All in the best possible taste,' as Hillary said. The house and grounds had never looked so attractive in the moonlight, even the horseplay was decorous. 'Someone for everybody,' said Partridge and there really was something to everyone's taste, particularly as half of the dancers didn't understand a word, and as pats on the bottom and slaps on the cheek were par for the nurse, that is until the kegs of beer, cool in the conservatory, next to the newly christened "snuggery", didn't run out until lunch time next day.*

Maria Engels made an inventory of breakages, expecting trouble she had hidden the vulnerable, the rarest, the costliest glasses and ornaments beforehand. Without a tremor, Travers wrote out a personal cheque:

'Who shall I make it payable to?' he asked. As no answer was forthcoming he tore up the cheque, closed up his cheque book and put it back in the drawer.

'Barrack Room damages, Maria, we'll put it down to barrack room damages.'

When the "party week" was over; the "signals" very lights, provided most colour, "tanks" made the biggest bang, the "Paras" redefined mayhem, but pulchritude, the male/female balance of youth and lust and trouble-free piss-up, earned the Royal Hunting Lodge five stars, and with 90-year-old red wine racked out at one shilling a bottle, best value.

Major Irina loved her moments with Martin and wrote to tell Ambassador Morov how proud all were of Rokossovsky.

Tracker Travers luxuriated in the warm glow of success, the Conference Call was abandoned due to bad and crossed lines, plus a report having been received about the paras.

The hunting lodge was soon to receive its first VIP, General Urquhart fresh from military success east of the Rhine, side-lined and earmarked to head Britain's Hunt for Nazis, he was "not wanted"—surplus to requirements, at HQ by Field Marshall Montgomery, having mimicked Monty before American General Bradley, who detested Montgomery even more than General George Patton, echoing the eternal truth: 'Opponents in front, enemies behind.'

'When I took over the 8th Army it was a dog's dinner, afraid of Rommel, ready with plans to withdraw across the Nile. I soon put a stop to all that, I knocked it into shape and

hit Erwin Rommel for 6. Then the politicians, I wasn't having them interfering, telling me what to do, when to do it, what to drink, when to drink, water only served in my Mess, I sent them off with a bottle of brandy to swim in the Med.'

During the long campaign following Normandy, Urquhart had only eaten with fellow officers, all male, the lodge, without an officer's Mess, ate on the long tables favoured by Travers, surrounded, not by the hoi polloi you understand, but by lower ranking WAAFs and ATSs, all eating German sausages and mash; although he might not have, Urquhart loved it, and no one went to bed until he climbed the grand staircase, his ATS driver in tow.

General Urquhart, next morning, Travis had set up a recce to Kleine Schwarztal, north of Ischl, Yvonne in charge; four of the younger girls volunteered to dress as Wanderkind, kitted out with help from the German serving girls, they inspected each other's outfits, gathered in the lodge entrance hall, twirling their skirts to admiring men, enjoying the fuss and the spectacle. Singing *She'll be coming around the mountain when she comes*, squashed in a Land Rover, driven over the back col, they were to be dropped high up Poison Valley, above the abandoned hotel carrying baskets for mushrooms, berries, nuts, anything they could pick and eat. They were to walk down the valley, wander around the abandoned hotel buildings and report.

They entered into the spirit of the thing, this was better than the daily cross-referencing of unrecognisable German names, umlauts and all.

Before they left, newly acquired Czech cameras, with too many options for their newly acquired owners, appeared;

poses were struck with a famous and embarrassed General Urquhart, reluctant to forego such amiability, General Urquhart who had missed Arnhem, been rock-steady at the Battle of the Bulge, travelled with the girls into town, needing their help to search out climbing gear for his trip to the Dolomites. *War's over, I'm missing it already,* he thought, sorrowfully.

After lunch, he yawned as Travers went through the traps laid to catch real Nazis, dreaming of his next epic traverse in the Italian Dolomites.

'Must I go and see that Ebensee place Tracker, Belsen was more than enough for me—I made the town people go there to see what they'd done, it made them sick, it made me sick, bone men everybody. Anyhow the Americans are calling a Conference soon, us, the Russians to pool what we have found, compare the different camps, and agree how to proceed.'

Middle of the afternoon, the girls returned as bubbly as when they left, excited by their mushrooms, proud of their bilberries, impatient to get their flowers in water, thrilled at being spies, they'd taken tramping miles downhill through dense forest in their downhill stride.

'Nothing till we reached the hotel, in front of the house there it was—a hearse… Yes, a hearse, of course they saw us.'

'Yes, it was—yes, definitely a hearse, why, because my mum went to our church in one when she died, we went up to it and saw the bodies. Yes, yes, yes, two bodies, yes, we saw two corpses. Brought out of the building, yes.'

'Two men carried out two men and put them in the hearse, they must have been men; they seemed heavy. Well, Carol said they looked young. No, she didn't see their…' Yvonne burst out giggling.

'There was a doctor and a Priest there as well, well, Francis heard them call the woman, "doctor", and the man wore a dog collar, and they called him "Father". Don't you believe us?'

'The hearse went off down the valley, no, we didn't see which way they went.'

'I did…' nobody ever took much notice of Mildred, nobody had ever taken much notice of Mildred, 'I did, it turned right I saw it through the trees, it turned right towards Bad Ischl.'

'Why didn't you say so before?' Yvonne was annoyed.

'I did, but you didn't take a blind bit of notice of me, you never do, you fat cow!' There was no answer to that, this outburst was a "Road to Damascus" moment, nothing could ring truer or be more convincing than insignificant Mildred calling Yvonne a "fat cow", in front of Travers and the General.

'Did they suspect who you were?

'Of course not, look at us, we're wanderkind, she twirled, 'and only Carol actually spoke, we just giggled and kept quiet.'

'That's suspicious in itself.' Travers was pleased, General Urquhart thought the whole thing amusing, the girls must eat at his table, he decided to stay overnight and "help" on the next part of the plan. Sorry that the dirndl skirts would have to go back downstairs, taking off the blouses and the dirndl skirts, the girls reappeared later in stockings, heels and skirts to the knee, long before "the new look" hit clothing coupons.

Later the "team" gathered around what Urquhart called "the operations table", the General had his own planning method, 'I go quickly'—different to Monty— as he was at pains to tell everyone. Some sat around the table, some stood behind the General, it was not secure with the German girls appearing and disappearing with jugs of Vimto, Victory V gums which had come from some forlorn NAAFI consignment and packs of damp crisps, the damp salt, when it could be found, determined not to be shaken out of its screwed up blue wrapper. Hillary took notes.

Martin would ask Father John who was to conduct the funerals, the who, the where, the why and the when.

Fritz, the groom would be sent to the Ischl Funeral Parlour, to get the same information and confirm the deaths happened in Kleine Swartztal. Quickly the information was obtained, quickly decisions were taken.

Travers, would arrange with Barney, for 20 US Marines to be on standby, ready to take away suspects attending the funeral at the church. The mourners would be taken away and questioned separately.

General Urquhart rapped the table.

'That's it chaps: Intelligence... Recce... Plan... Resources... Action.

Let me know how you get on, I'm off first thing, don't forget a Conference in 10 days.' (Nothing would keep General Urquhart away from climbing in the Dolomites.)

If Martin made little contribution to the General's Meeting, by the following day he was back on form; the General gone, Travers had taken a couple of bottles of the MacCallan to the US base near Salzburg to fix the marine's attendance at the church,

'Guess what they've got over at Gmunden' he announced 'Hitler's private Mercedes, the one he used to parade about in. It's a magnificent beast.'

Martin wasn't interested in cars, he now had detail. Both funerals were to be held together in Ischl church, the names, the addresses weren't yet known, for some reason the natives were keeping that information very close to their chests.

He drew up detailed plans, outside, five minutes after the funeral service was due to begin, 20 US Marines would drive in and occupy the café tables on the opposite side of the church square. About 11.15 am, when the mourners were due to emerge, at a signal from Major Rheinlander, the Marines would surround the mourners, load them onto three tonners and take them away for questioning in the foul huts used to house the prisoners at Ebensee.

It was a bad plan, interfering three quarters through a two-body funeral service with mostly women attending, wasn't wise, but Trapper and Martin were too young to know and not wise enough to enquire, that after the church service there would be a "touching" of the coffins at the church gate, and further words at the graveside inside the church wall when the bodies were interred.

The early morning weather started calm. Wireless communication brought the lorries and Marines to the church square, on time, five minutes after the coffins and the mourners had entered the church, and its high and heavy doors closed.

The bell no longer tolled, the café proprietor, sighing at not being allowed to serve coffee and biscuits to 20 thirsty customers, wondering what was going on. Travers took his elbow telling him to stay inside out of the way, Martin was nowhere to be seen. Two late mourners walked onto the square, up to the church door, paused, looked up at the door, looked round, looked at the Marines, muttered to each other, hooked up their skirts, turned and walked back the way they had come.

Silence was broken by the bell resuming its mournful toll, the church door creaked slowly open, and solemn organ tones, percolated out to old grave stones, which higgledy piggledy dotted the lawns down to the wall lining the square.

Side by side, bearers brought out the two coffins, each bearing a wreath, one large, the other barely a spray, down the path, to a plinth in front of the gate. The Rondel mourners heavily outnumbered the Grunes, both families lined up behind the coffins, the mourners filed down the church steps, shaking hands, touching the coffins, some throwing a single flower, then standing awkwardly around the gravestones. Few noticed the Marines, but one woman did and she darted back into the church. Alerted, the mourners switched from reading gravestones, to staring across at the Marines.

Next, five women broke away past the coffins through the gate, heading for the main street, as Major Rheinlander said later, 'I had no alternative,' he barked an order, six marines sprang forward blocking the women, stopping them dead in their tracks.

At that moment shots echoed from the back of the church, Rheinlander signalled, two marines detached and ran around the side, machine pistols drawn, crouching low. Other marines moved to stop the body of the mourners splitting away. The tallest of the two priests, who had moved to wait by the open graveside, moved back towards the coffins, this mistake, caused a greater mistake, thinking to gain attention, emphasise who was in control, and for no one to leave, Major Rheinlander drew his pistol and fired two shots into the air.

One of the marines who had run down the side of the church moments earlier towards the shots, reappeared shouting:

'Doctor, doctor, we need a doctor.' A woman put her hand up, stepped forward and followed the marine around to the back of the church.

At the same moment, dead on cue, two army lorries drove into the square, screeching to a stop. Major Rheinlander shouted for everyone to board the lorries, when you've answered our questions, you'll be brought back.

Although a couple of women moved to board, the women who had earlier started to leave, were having none of it and sat down, within moments the churchyard was full of mourners sitting down on grass and gravestones. Marines stood silent, uncertain, shifting from one foot to the other. Although their report was to say "they conferred" Travers and Rheinlander were actually whispering in a near panic.

'Do we take the gravediggers?' a marine asked. Rheinlander looked at the two men with spades, he conferred, 'Nah,' he said. He didn't know what to do, in the end he decided, 'Force the men in the lorries, we'll just take the women's details for now.'

'You tell them, Tracker, your German's better than mine.'

Travers's words and rifle butts, the men, a small fraction of the mourners, more amenable than the women, got to their feet and prepared to board the lorries.

'You as well, Padre, particularly you,' Rheinlander wasn't in the mood to brook further opposition.

'Move out,' a lorry drove off the square.

It was now very awkward, the women were sitting next to the coffins, near two open empty graves, with a solitary small priest, so insignificant he had been overlooked, again Travis and Rheinlander conferred, 'better get them buried. We can't leave bodies in coffins lying about,'—awkward and unsatisfactory,

'Get on with it,' Father Julius, the priest had his instructions.

'One body after the other, the priest turning first to his left then to his right, one set of stammered words covering a dual situation, the bodies were interred, to the accompaniment of sobbing and angry looks from the women. Father Julius was already composing, his letter to the bishop, for transmission to the Cardinal, for transmission to the Popal See. He would be summoned to Rome, this was promising to be his finest hour. He drew himself up, his voice ringing with unsuspected authority. Whether he spoke in German or Latin Rheinlander neither knew nor cared.

One at a time the women, who refused to form a line, were led to café tables, not till the final woman was documented was anyone allowed to leave, together they walked into the town like a gaggle of angry strutting gesticulating turkeys, swarming into the elegant café where the Rondel family had laid-on cake and coffee. None ventured to tell Frau Grune, mother of the second dead man, who'd followed them to der Rosenkavalier's, that she hadn't been invited and shouldn't be there, her son being the reason there were two funerals.

The undertaker, an ignored cypher in all the turmoil, who had gone back into the church, was ready to slink away, Hillary came up behind him,

'I'll have that if you don't mind,' before the undertaker could stop her, Hillary pulled the broad leather wallet from under his arm.

'Hey, that's mine you can't have that, it's got all the details.'

'The details, that's exactly what I need, you'll get it back when I've finished.' Hillary wasn't for turning, and that was that.

Whilst this farce was taking place a makeshift stretcher had brought the wounded man to the square where Travers had a quick look at him; a Bedford took him to hospital under the watch of a single GI. Catching dodgers, had been part of Martin's plan, it had worked to a degree, but Martin was nowhere to be seen, and hadn't been seen that day, he climbed down from behind the organ pipes to Partridge waiting in the aisle, brushing cobwebs from his jacket,

'You were right, squire,' Partridge said, who had been guarding the side exit, 'one of the bastards made a run for it, but I got him in the leg. Get anything from the belfry?' Martin hadn't got much, a photo of the two people who had been beside the runner was the gist of it. He'd recognise them again. Partridge said 'you know the women all sat down outside and wouldn't move, they've taken the men to Ebensee but all we've got on the women are names and addresses.

'Jesus Christ,' said Martin, 'We've cocked this up.'

'You and Tracker cocked it up, keep me out of it,' quoted Partridge.

The sun in her eyes, Hillary was glad to get away from the square, down to the path following the inside bend of the river Traun, to where a tributary added cold pure sparkling water to a slower river, past the cascade rippling across both banks, crossing the bridge she carried the wallet with the names and addresses back to "Her Hunting Lodge".

She brewed herself a pot of tea, settling down with the wallet's contents; four separate coloured files for each body. The red files were marked "Accounts", she had a quick glance, who was paying, how much did funerals cost in Austria. *A quarter of Dad's stipend,* she thought. The green file was "Funeral Instructions", *Not much in there,* she thought. Yellow—Intimations—showed the contacts needing to be told, the newspaper, the family members, etc. Lastly the blue files—Attendance—held the messages and the cards the Undertaker had collected, left in pews for mourners to let the families know they'd attended the funeral. She flipped through the cards. *Not many Germans get this much attention in 1945,* she thought.

"Strasser" the name flashed off the A1 size card, 'Strasser…' Strasser hadn't been there, she was sure of it, she'd been lookout, she'd looked at every mourner, *He must have slipped in by a side door,* was her first thought, *I couldn't have missed him*. Could he have been disguised as a woman? She couldn't believe that the fat women were dressed in black, the attractive wore muted dirndl, a 6ft 2' blond haired airman with an artificial hand—no way.

In her mind's eye, few were tall enough certainly, perhaps three of these had fair hair, all wore suits or lederhosen type trousers buckling at the knee with thick green socks, no one had metal hands.

"Hans Strasser" was written. She went through the other cards, no "Ritter" no other name she recognised as being on the "wanted" list.

She went back to the Intimations files, and its separate lists, a very short list of four for Herr J Grune, a much longer list for Herr Heinrich Rondel. Neither listed a Strasser or a Muller.

Back to the red files, bills for grave digging, priest's attendance, organist, bell ringer. The bill for Rondel's undertaker services was made out 'Muller—just that!'

She placed the card in her handbag and waited for Martin. She skipped down the drive, in time to meet his jeep at the gates. Jumping in to drive back to the lodge, hugging his arm, she pulled him upstairs, Martin thought he was on a promise. 'Who's a bonny girl then?' he chirruped.

She wanted to know how hiding in church had gone on,' was it you who shot the fellow?'

'A disappointment really, and uncomfortable up in the gods, Partridge shot the fellow who ran out, so it wasn't a waste, we'll grill him as soon as the doctors allow. Major Rheinlander's holding the men at Ebensee overnight, for Travers to sort out in the morning. What have you been up to, you look pleased with yourself?'

'And are you going to be pleased with me,' Hillary was bubbling, 'Strasser was there in the church, right in front of

Your nose and you didn't see him.'

'Oh no, he wasn't,' Martin chuckled in the best pantomime tradition.

'Oh yes he was 'she responded, 'and I can prove it.'

'Prove it.'

Hillary opened the Undertaker's wallet before drawing the precious piece of paper out of her bag. 'This is the attendance ticket left in the pews to tell the families who had been to the funeral... look "Strasser"... Hans Strasser. Nearly all the tickets are for Rondel, only three for the other chap called Grune.'

'When one shot the other, why a joint funeral, very odd.'

Martin picked up the ticket, he held it before his eyes, 'The pencil's not very clear,' he turned the paper towards the window, 'there's something in front,' he peered again, 'It's got "pp" in front, that stands for post proxy or something like that, someone's given Strasser's regret at not being there himself.' Placing the ticket back on top of the pile of tickets, 'at least it means that someone at the service has been in touch with Strasser within the last 48 hours. Let's go through all the tickets and find out who, we should be able to get a match by comparing the handwriting.'

He spread the tickets into two piles, trying to match the pencil scrawls. They narrowed the search to three tickets, with one outright favourite. Now they needed to compare the lists of women who'd been arrested at the funeral service.

Travers had introduced a neat system to ensure they got verifiable names and addresses from the women. The women were put in pairs, each knowing the other, then separated. The two each wrote their own name and address and also her friend's, if they didn't match they were interrogated.

Within an hour Hillary was back with the three possible matches, but only one probable, this the favourite, had an address in Altaussee.

The hunt for Colonel General Jed Strasser had begun, soon it would turn into a stalk, later it became a chase; finally, it had its own file '**The Hunt for Colonel Strasser.**'

Travers, Anderton, Martin, Hillary and Partridge and the WAAF, gathered in Traver's office where Travers began:

'Gentlemen in Whitehall have been comparing our totals to the number of war criminals the Americans have bagged, apparently we're OK in the North, but they're asking why we in Austria have arrested so few in comparison. I told Quincy I'd been concentrating on top men, and that the Yanks were trawling with a close weave bottom net, what do you think?' the cheeky blighter said, 'make sure you aren't using drift nets. And yes, I told him they were separating out the scientists and the best engineers and shipping them to the States, but all I got was "we've got engineers coming out of our ears, just pull your finger out". Anyhow, we'll have to increase the number of our numbers quick, so I want to step things up and bring forward the raid on Altaussee, tomorrow. Any problems, Martin?'

'No, I don't think so, John and I are having a go at the women we hold, but we should be ready for a raid tomorrow. The girls in the office have collated the lists.'

'Another signal from London for us all to note and keep secret.' Travers started to read from the note in front of him: 'Member of Royal Family, Charles Edward Duke of Saxe-Coburg and Gotha, old Etonian formerly the Duke of Albany, a grandson of Queen Victoria Apparently, he was invited as a young man, early this century to accept the title and become Duke of Saxe-Coburg Gotha, this he did and stayed in Germany and fought alongside Kaiser Bill. It says here he later joined forces with Hitler and was sufficiently in favour as to introduce the Duke of Windsor to Hitler. During the war Hitler appointed him President of the German Red Cross (didn't know they had one), he muttered as an aside, as their President he led their investigation into the Russian massacre of Poles at Katyn.

Whitehall says this puts him high on Russia's list of most wanted Nazis.

In addition to his castles, the duke owns a hunting estate up the valley at Bad Goisern in our area. Intelligence has been received that the duke has fled to this estate called Huntingtower.

'Bad Goisern, in your neck of the woods I believe, Martin,' Martin joined in,

'Yes, but for God's sake, don't mention Katyn to the Russians or the Poles, I asked Irina about Katyn, she has been there and she went spare, she will not, repeat not, talk about it.'

Calling in Taffy their newly arrived signals expert, Travers issued precise instructions. Vehicles holding suspects—bugged. Rooms at the hunting lodge—bugged. Recording machines were to be planted in the apartments left empty at Altaussee.

Taffy was a worrier: 'By tomorrow, by myself,' he exclaimed, as if he was being asked to fly to the moon, 'I'll have to go to stores.' Martin was annoyed.

'Taffy, we're after the big guns here, I don't care how you do it, just do it, if everything isn't in place tomorrow afternoon you'll be trawling sandworms and samphire on Barry Island by Saturday, clear?' Taffy would do his best but if the equipment didn't work don't blame him.

'We fucking will,' Travers and Martin spoke with feeling and in unison,

As the meeting broke up Martin consoled Taffy, 'if you need anything see me, I'm OMSK, black arts, me and Partridge, we're dirty bastards.' Taffy took a jeep to Stuttgart, worked all night, Taffy borrowed a couple of Marines with know-how, and he wasn't fed leeks.

Now came the final preparations for the raid on Altaussee's chalets and apartment blocks, which would take all their resources.

Using contacts and goodwill, Travers "borrowed" 30 Marines and transport.

Hillary had copies made of the master list prepared from their files of information. Frau Bormann, Doctor Frohm's surgery records and Father John's information were key to placing the senior officials living in Altaussee. This master list, set out who was expected to be living at each address, Travers and Taffy, who had risen to the occasion, held a final briefing. Taffy, bubbling now with optimism, access to new American equipment had increased confidence and altered his mood.

'Good luck, set your alarms for 4 o'clock. Good night everyone.' At 5.30 am 30 Marines were slapping arms together trying to keep warm.

No need for the Glasgow boot, inside the apartments "Limehouse Arfur" took 15 seconds for an exterior door, five seconds to open an interior door. Travers isolated Blocks A and B, concentrating on Block A. In stocking feet "Arfur" had opened all significant doors before feet had touched bedroom floors.

Systematically, men found in Block A were taken to the reception hall, papers from their apartments labelled and bundled up into marked bags. Only after all apartments were searched were they shepherded into lorries and Taffy and his helpers got to work under the beds and behind the pictures.

The clearances in Block B didn't go smoothly, the man in room 3B hadn't slept well, screams, fires told of documents being destroyed. In the foyer of Block B, Hillary marked progress, four women were thought to have worked at Ebensee and were "of interest". These women and the men were not segregated in the lorries, and were not loaded until peace had returned to Block B, and peace did not come until a man trying to get out of a window had been shot, till every radio set at full volume, had been switched off, and the corridors cleared of running screaming women.

Eventually, Hillary ticked her lists, filing them under the black cover, the lorries revved up and drove away and Taffy was eventually left in peace with his drill and helpers to hide small US devices. 'I'm not staying here playing hide and seek,' said Tracker, walking to his Land Rover. Keep the women in the flats till Martin's finished with the chalets.

Agreed in advance, as Tracker hit the apartment blocks, Martin of OMSK, as he persisted in regarding himself, began searching the chalets, which stood as proud as the procession of the Grand Fleet at Spithead, sailing in line astern along Millionaire's Row. Houses occupied by pensioners, Martin had decided to leave until last the men marked down as over 80s. List in hand he issued the orders. With "Arfur" at the apartments, Martin decided on the muffled "Glasgow Boot", to reduce noise and awareness.

Two applications of the boot around the lock were enough for even the stoutest door. Inside, the chalets were spacious with large kitchens and reception rooms, never less than four bedrooms, all with ladders up to the spaces below the roof timbers. All the chalets had out-buildings, and searches took far longer than Martin's estimate. The first search, in the largest chalet, turned up a priest's hole built under the eaves. The hide was occupied by a powerfully built middle aged man, who was so reluctant to come out he had to be dragged downstairs claiming "he shouldn't be arrested as he'd done nothing wrong". Martin instructed. 'Keep him separate, I want to talk to that one, particularly if he really is the von Hipper he calls himself.'

Whereas men from the apartments had been taken away in what they were wearing, pyjamas mostly; Martin allowed his suspects to get dressed, and washed and watched. Every house Hillary had marked up as having a suspect held a man, two of the chalets marked "gone away", held men, one living in the garden shed, the other, a man with a waxed moustache matching the description of the chemist in charge of the synthetic oil plant, was sleeping contentedly by the side of his wife.

There were still three chalets to go, secrecy had been abandoned, the whole of Altaussee was live to the sound of vehicles, Tracker left the apartment blocks and drove along Millionaire's Row in his land Rover, tension gone.

'How's it going? Martin, the apartments went better than I expected.'

'Three to go, Tracker, Hillary's lists have been spot on.' Martin looked again at his list, 'Two to go, one house holds two 90-year-olds. Still they all have children or even grand-children.' Destructively the Glasgow Boot smashed another door made of the finest sapele.

Martin pointed back up the Row to the houses already searched, 'the top house, it's got good views and I've moved everyone out, if you agree I'll put Shirley, Yvonne (he winked) and Kathleen in with a radio for 24 hours to see if anything happens.' Travers nodded, unhappy at losing Yvonne for the night.

'One other thing Tracker, our men are nicking everything they can carry, what to do?'

'Same at the apartments, do like me, pretend you've not seen anything.'

'As long as I don't see it, and it can be carried in their pockets, I'm not bothered. I'd better tell you I got Margaret to sew me a poacher's pocket in my coat, and I know some of the men have done the same thing, and God knows what Hillary's found in the jewellery boxes, she can't keep her nose out.' Martin knew full well that Travers was a collector and was on the hunt for Nazi decorations and medals. 'What are the "redcaps" going to do when we all turn up at Zeebrugge with kitbags stuffed full of cameras, watches, jewellery and things I can't begin to imagine? Travers laughed. 'You know what I think: the military police are as bad as anybody, just as long as it's come from Germany and can be carried, it'll be ignored. Everybody's collecting stuff, the German's nicked it in the first place.' Martin turned towards the final chalet,

'I expect you're right, I'm OMSK of the dirty party, I'll pretend we never had this conversation.' A non-smoker, he pulled a gold lighter out of his pocket together with a gold cigarette case: 'Want a ciggy?'

End chalet, final house, although Martin assumed the occupants already knew they were being raided, in fact they weren't aware. On the kitchen unit stood three vacuum flasks, alongside 10 food containers, empty and clean, together with freshly baked bread. The message they gave out was as clear as the lovely fresh baking smell permeating the kitchen.

'Going out delivering?' he asked Frau Saunde, 'Or is someone collecting?'

Mouth shut as tight as a clam, she shook her head. Martin went to the window, although it had been light for several hours now, the blinds were down. He released the cord, the blind shot up. "Arfur" who had followed down from the apartments asked, 'Shall I take her to the truck?' Martin nodded. Taking his binoculars from the case he fiddled to adjusted the lenses, 'Bloody thing.' Try as he might he could never get the mountain beyond the lake in focus. He gave up. Had the closed blind been a signal that the coast was clear? He asked Hillary who had followed him in, but she was no help.

Pointing to the top house, Hillary got the three girls together, Yvonne knew how to operate the radio, she also knew how to use the Austrian phone system, all promised not to take risks, report hourly, and note everything they saw, Promising to stay awake and not eat too much food, Martin drove the Bedford up the path at the side of the chalet, silently the girls slipped out, entered by the back door, positioned their make up in pecking order in the bathroom, moved the chairs and took up observation behind the bedroom curtains. 'Make us a cup of tea, love,' said Yvonne.

John, back at the hunting lodge, Travers and Martin began the questioning as soon as Partridge was around to threaten punches to the nose or stomach as required. He quite enjoyed it.

As standard practice, they linked two men together, just as they'd done for the women at the funeral. Martin's questions inevitably focused on Strasser and Ritter, the identified sadistic commander of Ebensee labour, his role and behaviour was established beyond doubt, the remaining doubt on his death was who got to him first, not who would be first to kill him.

'What's happened to Major Strasser?' automatically brought a correction to his rank being either a "Colonel", or colonel general, who calls himself colonel. They all knew of him.

'Where did he go to after leaving his house on the Bad Aussee road, why did he move his furniture to Bad Schwarztal, what's being hidden in Poison valley?' Few had heard of Muller, less still of what he did.

He moved on to known relationships, 'Where's Halder? (a missing man), what was his role at Ebensee?' Will Halder be with Ritter?' Negative answers had a snarling Martin saying, 'You're lying, he lives on Millionaire's Row, your wives go to church together, children in the same class, you went to work together on the same train every day, do you want me to bring your family here, let's have some better answers this time. Halder's wife will certainly tell me everything I ask her about you.'

Usually this worked, if it didn't Partridge hit him, if that didn't work, Partridge hit him again, harder.

Chapter 10
Martin Misses a Trick

Martin missed a second "Strasser clue" Johan Schroder was anxious to claim that he had never wanted to live at Altaussee, he knew it was a den of Nazis, he had never been a supporter of Hitler, he just wanted to work for his country. When Schroder first enquired, the apartments were full of military pensioners, next time he asked, the pensioners had been moved along but were still in the care of the charity that was providing injured ex-service men a home, suddenly there were apartments available in Altaussee at a high price but in a splendid area and his wife had insisted they bought a flat and they moved in.

Von Hipper had been kept apart. Martin decided his questioning would be at a different level from the rest, he drew Hillary and Partridge aside and told them what he wanted. 'This von Hipper's on a higher level, best house, arrogant bastard, but most interesting of all, he's the only person who wasn't included on Frau Bormann's list.'

Von Hipper was stood in the middle of Martin's Office, facing two separate desks set in a 'V' formation. Hillary and Partridge sat quietly behind the desks. Partridge introduced himself as the sifter of prisoners who may be wanted for questioning at a senior level, weeding out the hoi polio as he put it,' did von Hipper put himself in that category? 'If he did, rather than routine questions, our Mr Cohen—we don't use military rank here—would seek strategic rather than tactical detail from him, "if you know what I mean". Hipper acknowledged he was in the upper echelon and would be prepared to answer questions on that basis.

OK, Mr Cohen then, would question him accordingly, but whilst fanatical SS werewolves were still operating, Jewish Mr Cohen, would be prepared to house Herr von Hipper in isolation in the Secure Block if he so wished.

'Perhaps Mr Hipper would prefer to sit,' Hillary beckoned the guard to bring up a chair, Hipper sat in the centre of the room. 'Before Mr Cohen sees you I need to clarify several points,' Hillary referred to the papers in front of her:

'I see from railway documents that a von Hipper travelled regularly to Munich on Monday, returning to Bad Aussee on Friday evening, were you that von Hipper, and were you part of the "Brain's Trust".

Von Hipper responded, he was a founder member of the Brain's Trust, in fact he provided most if not all the brain. When asked where in Munich he worked, he listed towns frequently visited, finishing with the address working out from 'Nazi Party HQ in Munich.' Hillary continued,

'I also see that rail compartments were reserved from time to time to take von Hipper and M Bormann to and from Berchesgarden.'

'I did visit Hitler at the Berghaus from time to time, but I usually went by chauffeur driven car.'

'Mr Cohen will want to question you on your role and what was discussed at the Berghaus, He will see you shortly,' Hillary gathered up her papers and swept out of the room.

Shortly, was after Martin had showered and changed into his best suit, Martin was sitting on a garden bench half way up the slope behind the lodge, as von Hipper climbed up alone to meet him. They shook hands. Von Hipper talked quickly, openly and frankly, not evading a single question. Martin remembered being in the Luftwaffe hospital, there he had exchanged RAF information for repair of the injuries to his body; here the situation was reversed, von Hipper was giving political information in exchange for his life.

Martin's father had impressed on him that notes of interviews are only worth the paper they were written on, nevertheless they must always be written before going to bed, timed, dated, and signed. His note was seized upon with glee by London, spelling out as it did the modus operandi of the inner circle, the set up at the Berghaus, the inter relationships between the Nazi Party, the Military and the power factions surrounding Hitler, and how Martin Bormann had established himself as the eminence grise. A rough command schemat was sketched with the promise of a detailed one later. Clouds appeared above the mountain peaks, rain threatened, they hurried down to Martin's office. A pot of coffee,

'Tell me about Colonel Strasser,' Martin opened.

'Jed Strasser, what do you want to know…?'

'Well, you can tell me why you called him "Jed" for a start. I always understood he was christened Hans.'

'Jez, Jed, short for Jesuit so I heard, but he'd shoot you if you called him Jesuit, he's a private fellow and he bears grudges.'

During long discussion, the positive fact on Strasser to emerge was that in the last weeks of the war he had sought customers for long term accommodation at safe-houses with the promise of providing new identities, particularly for married couples. He himself had not sought a safehouse and didn't know where any were, but he knew there were several, every castle owner had space to rent and Strasser had at least one reserved for senior party and army personnel, so he heard.

Being highly regarded within the establishment, Hipper believed that several colleagues had trusted Strasser, paid for security, and disappeared, the locations only being given after arrangements had been agreed. Strasser was also feared because he had a strong connection to Ritter, though he didn't know what their relationship was.

For the first time Martin now had a line to follow in his pursuit of Strasser—safehouses—he would no longer have to listen to tale after tale of German atrocities, listening to pleas from Germans "just doing their duty", now he had a strong line to follow. There was a knock on the door, Partridge appeared, 'Could he have a word?'

'Got an interesting answer from a guy called Holness, the fellow missing from Apartment 7B, has probably gone to live with Strasser.' Martin perked up: 'What does that mean?'

'It means that he's gone to stay at a safehouse, and the house was arranged by Strasser, and he has got an idea where it might be,' said Partridge.

'I'll see him in the cellar.' Von Hipper was left alone for the time being.

Without a word, rough hands stripped Holness of every stitch except his socks, Erich Holness naked, stood shivering, a frightened overweight bully of a man. Frog marched into a small room, Martin sitting behind a table. Without a word and without warning Partridge thumped him in the stomach, no sooner had he regained breath and standing upright than he was thumped again.

'Sit down' Martin waved towards a chair. 'When we asked you about Henry Hundertmark, you said he'd gone home to Colonel Strasser. Did you say that?'

'Ja.'

What did you mean?' Holness didn't hesitate.

'That Hundertmark paid the money and joined Strasser's scheme.' Martin didn't hesitate.

'Put your clothes back on Erich.' As soon as Holness was dressed, before he had time to sit down, he was handed a cigarette and a box of matches. Everyone settled down,

'Tell me about Strasser's scheme's then, Erich? I'm interested.'

'Strasser says he'll arrange long term safe secure accommodation for SS men or women at risk, no children though, anybody, at a price.'

'Who's anybody?' asked Partridge.

'Well, couples, he likes couple, he won't accept families SS Officers from Russia, Labour camp personnel, Officials, Nazis, Nazis have most money, so it's mainly Nazis, he charges high fees.'

'If he only takes couples he must have two room accommodation, mustn't he? Accommodation Erich, here in Austria? Up in the mountains? Abroad?' Martin had taken up the questioning.

'Here, not abroad.'

'Where's here Erich?'

'SE Germany, NW Austria, but he's got several safe places.'

'Names of these safe places?' Martin's questions came thick and fast.

'I heard Strasser had bought a steamer.'

'You mean a lake steamer?' Holness nodded. 'Here in the Salzkammergut, Floating or laid up?'

'Floating, I believe.'

'Which lake?'

'In the Salzkammergut.'

'Which lake? There are a lot.'

'Don't know, only big lakes have big boats. Wolfgangsee is the most likely, but I don't know for certain.'

'How do I find out Erich?' Erich didn't know, only that steamer registrations were kept at St Gilgen, in the Town Hall and that there were only four or five lakes with proper steamers.

'What big lakes have Steamers, Erich?' Martin opened his fountain pen, a Waterman, present from his father, he loved this pen like no other, it wrote first time, it didn't leak, it flowed free, just to unscrew the cap was to remind him fondly of his dad, he wrote down the names as Holness gave them. 'Wolfgangsee, Traunsee, Mondsee,' but smaller lakes had small passenger steamers, and there were lakes in Carinthia as well.

'They'll all be in the register you know, boats carrying passengers have to register.' Erich Holness was not holding back.

'A Steamer doesn't sound much like a safehouse to me, does it to you, Erich?' Holness shrugged his shoulders.

Holness didn't know who recruited customers beside Strasser, but said a "Muller" and Ritter had been mentioned. He knew all this because a friend had asked his advice.

'And where's your friend now?'

'He disappeared and I don't know where he went.'

'Erich, just write down his name please.' Erich did so.

Martin got up from his desk, in a change of voice

'Before you're back with the others, we will let it be known that although we stripped you and gave you a going over, you told us nothing.'

'Thanks for nothing,' Holness muttered, his cigarette butt crushed, soaking and alone in the ashtray.

Partridge took his motor bike. He reported from St Gilgen Town Hall, that the only steamer ownership transfer made in the past 12 months was the "Queen of St Gilgen", moored on the Wolfgangsee, to a nominee Company registered in Tubingen, bought with money transferred from the Geneva Branch of the BBBB. The BBBB stuck out a mile, Martin knew that Strasser had had extensive dealings with that Bank and its Director Gustav Holst. He took the information to Travers who jumped at his suggestion that they borrow a US spotter plane and reconnoiter Wolfgangsee.

Next morning, they drove to Fuschl where General Wesley Hood had placed an Oklahoma bi-plane at their disposal.

They walked twice around the Oklahoma, 'A bit old, the floor sheeting has gaps, Martin, you can see through down it,'

Martin nodded, 'It'll do.'

An air frame engineer showed Martin around "the kite". 'Have you flown these things before?' asked Tracker.

'One's like it,' was the gruff response, a voice telling Tracker not to ask any more questions. The bumpy runway had Tracker regretting agreeing to come on the trip even before they were airborne, heading into the wind taking off facing north, Martin banked 360 degrees to bring them back over the town of St Gilgen; in a gap between mountains the wind blew the plane sideways and Tracker felt sick. Turning east the Oklahoma flew low over the water, over several hangar type buildings, moored in front two boats laid at anchor, a smaller one pulled on the bank out of the water, only one of the two in the water could be classified as a steamer. Flying down the eastern bank they saw nothing of interest, not even by the piers and harbour at St Wolfgang.

Martin flew out past the lake for a mile following the river until it was no longer broad enough to shelter a steamer. Satisfied, turning he followed the river back to the lake, and flew over Strobl to follow the west shore to Wolfgangsee's sheltered islands and indentations, Martin circled the nearest island and spit of land close to it. Pointing to Tracker, he banked to get a better view. 'If that's not the Queen of St Gilgen I'll eat my hat,' he shouted. Tight by trees, in a creek, lay the Queen of St Gilgen.

'Go low, fly over it!' shouted Tracker.

'No fear, let them know we're on to them, I'm going back to Fuschl.' And he did.

'The engineer was waiting with coffee on the stove, 'remind me never to fly with you again,' said Tracker warming his hands.

'You ungrateful sod,' was all he got in reply.

Tracker and Martin remained on good terms, despite Tracker's historical visits, and despite Martin's obsession with Strasser. When relations were friendly, it was "Tracker", and Martin, other days it was Travers and Cohen.

This particular morning back on terra firma it was "Tracker" and "Omsk".

'Look Omsk, 10,000 inmates of Ebensee Camp are screaming why haven't we caught Ritter, most of them have never heard of Strasser, it's Ritter they want, he shot prisoners, he's the sadistic bastard. As well as shooting people, he set up a brothel, skilled technicians, German and Poles working the machines on the Production Line could earn tickets for more food and a sleep over. Get me Ritter, and I'll give you as much time as you want to go after Strasser.' Martin wanted a way of combining the pursuit of both Strasser and Ritter.

'From that fellow Holness, there's a fair chance Strasser is holed up on the Steamer we saw, we know where it's moored up on Wolfgangsee, there must be a chance that Ritter is there with him. Strasser only bought the "Queen of St Gilgen" two months ago, Ritter was close to Strasser, fair chance they'll both be hiding on that boat, let's raid it, it's in our area, if he's not there I'll take a party to hunt near the Oberhung Hut, up above Schwarztal I bet that's another of his safehouses where another community is being set up. If that still doesn't work, I'll take you climbing on the Dachstein; we know Ritter's a mountain man, and if that still doesn't work, we still have Huntingtower, the Duke of Saxe-Coburg's estate at Bad Goisern to have a look at.'

Tracker gave the nod, raiding "the Queen of St Gilgen" would be exciting, when he got home he could get out the family diary which went back to the 17th century, glue pictures of the Lysander, and the Queen and tell how he hunted Nazi war criminals, but he would need to call in the US Marines for back-up especially for an amphibious operation, Wesley Hood would just love it. He got on the phone and was put straight through to General Wesley Hood or "Robin" as he was widely known. After explaining the tip off, the possibility of Ritter being aboard the Queen of St Gilgen, the alternatives of attacking the ship by land, air or water, General Hood, marines and their equipment and helicopters at his disposal, quickly became enthusiastic, action, that was what he had left Ohio and come to Europe for. Action, with the possibility of bagging Ritter, 'Everybody wants that bastard,' he said. 'He's on all the black lists. Come on over we'll sort out the logistics over steak and a Bud.' Tracker had still to learn that logistics to the Americans were god, on a higher pedestal than food, drink and sex.

Tracker and Martin whizzed up to Gmunden without delay, over juicy thin wartime Texas steaks, they showed the notes, played the tracks, and the source of the finance when Colonel General Strasser acquired the Queen of St Gilgen and why they believed he intended to use it as a safehouse; from their aerial reconnaissance they pin-pointed on the map exactly where the "Queen" was moored, they sketched it all out in big, the configuration of the creek sheltering the "Queen", the proximity of Helicopter landing sites, and how near the road ran to the edge of the Wolfgangsee. The Brits did not want the raid to be launched from the water, afraid that doing so, they would lose all control to the Marines, against his better judgment "Robin" agreed that his Marines should move in through the woods, "with rubber cover" (fast rubber dinghies)to stop anything escaping by going down the lake.

'Bring the bible, Barney.' Wesley stood up, unlocked the door to the Ops Room; six men filed behind him into the Operations Room, maps and half the secrets of the US Marines were pinned up on boards lining the wall, the boards themselves covered by lined curtains. It was only then that Martin discovered the key to Tracker's popularity with General Robin Hood. 'St Jesus has got a plan and I want to run it past the book.' Barney laid the blue backed bible "Lake Operations" on the table.

'St Jesus,' Martin arched his eyebrows.

Tracker whispered, 'Middle name's St John, and he hasn't mastered it yet.'

'What's your Christian name then?' Martin whispered back.

'Paul,' came the reply.

'I'll be St Paul of the Ephesians if Robin gets to hear.'

Barney had the "bible" open, 'Lake Operations,' he said, holding the thick manual open. General Hood leafed through till he came to the section he was after.

'Can't do it at night,' he mused, 'Ain't got two camouflaged riggers, Ain't a single chopper landing spot in spitting distance of those woods, and choppers can't carry enough men. Can't go in by sea, not with only one bag of sails.'

'I'll go in by land, sea and air, combined operation, US and Brits together with Uncle Sam providing the kit and the manpower, OK by you, Jesus?' it was a question not requiring an answer.

'You're the boss and the brains,' said Paul Tracker St John Jesus. (Names were ranging queer and wide.)

'Those people will have their spies everywhere, we'll go in heavy and fast; that OK?' It was.

'We'll rendezvous here,' he pointed to a side-road three miles away, I'll have a chopper, and an air boat tanked up ready to go here, and here,' again he pointed to spots which Barney marked in blue crayon. '30 men should do it, small arms, nothing heavy, we don't want to sink the Queen, do we? If Wesley Hood was not decisive, he wasn't anything.

'That OK then, Jesus?'

'That's OK,' Tracker sought with his voice to register admiration and discipleship from an aristocratic aloofness, but it is doubtful if Robin appreciated it.

'Never be ashamed of your name Jesus, the name your parents gave you, they invested money in you.

'Not ashamed Wesley, just wish you'd use it, it's St John, pronounced "sinjun".'

'That's OK, so we're related, I'm a Cherokee myself. We'll circle and go in like Geronimo.' Before they left, Wesley called Barney to bring the Operations Book.

'Put this one down as a training exercise, Barney, that way if it goes ass up, no one loses any sleep and it's no skin off my nose.' A wise precaution as it turned out.

Before they left Wesley asked Barney to wise the limeys up on the evacuation of the abandoned workers still at Ebensee whose homes were in central and eastern Europe, all over a thousand miles away, they were preparing lorries and a couple of Dakotas, to disperse these thousands of ex-prisoners back to centres within their own countries beginning in two days' time, lorries were taking former prisoners to Rotterdam, Brussels, Copenhagen, Prague and Warsaw, no lorries were being sent to Russia itself, as there was a problem with Russians who had been forced to work for the Germans, these were regarded with great hostility, suspected of being traitors and most were afraid to return to Russia.

Barney was short of thousands of food packs needed to last out over these long journeys, could the Brits help. With more hope than confidence, Tracker said yes, showing his ignorance of the detail by adding, 'Will there still be anybody left to question about what happened at Ebensee?'

There was only one answer. 'There'll still be thousands left.'

Back at the hunting lodge, at his wit's end, Tracker called for help on food packs. Partridge came to his rescue.

'There's that NAFFI stuff,' remembering the RASC three tonner that had turned up last Friday afternoon with a consignment addressed "NAAFI, SIDI BARANI, LIBYA". Someone, an angel probably, had scribbled on it, "Gone away, try HL Bad Ischl, Austria". I told the driver "We've no NAAFI here," but he refused to take it away; he had an order to make a pick up back in Salzburg and for that he needed his lorry to be empty, I told him 'I'm not signing for anything, but you can store it in the Stables if you like.' The driver scribbled a signature, and though it's unheard of as drivers never ever unload their own lorries, he was in such hurry he even helped unload the cartons, and scarpered without so much as a cup of cha. The ration packs are still piled up in the stables where we dumped them.

Partridge thought the consignment mostly consisted of desert ration packs, he had thought of sending it down as charity into town but hadn't got around to it, he had opened a typical carton and they were all ration packs, but he was sure there were some six cases of Blanco, desert sand code 7B, no use in Europe. He thought the ration packs all comprised hard tack biscuits, dried dates, Bourneville plain chocolate doubling as a laxative, tins of spam, tins containing tablets of Horlicks and a tin opener though he didn't see any tins. Travers was delighted, and sent Hillary off to count and double-check.

As soon as she was back he rang Barney, 'Green pallets hold 192 cartons of Iron Rations, Desert Pack, each carton holds 12 packs, that enough for' he paused, somebody give me the figures he muttered, covering the mouthpiece, '2104 packs, I'll get them to you tomorrow am, no problem Barney. The yellow pallets hold exactly the same, but some are crushed, so that's 4208 packs.'

'Owe you pal.' An hour later Travis rang back, 'Mistake Barney lad we've double 8416.'

The briefing was done the evening before, a lift from the boredom that had come after the fighting. Early call for the cookhouse, then like greyhounds in the slips, straining upon the start, the helicopter, the airboat (a pneumatic tyre rather than a boat), and 30 men and their vehicles were all in the right place at the right time. Barney was there, Martin and Tracker were there, General 'Robin' Wesley Hood sent a message: 'Go get 'em, Jesus.'

'Let's go.' The men climbed into the lorries, engines started, coughing out clouds of smoke the lorries pulled out onto the St Gilgen road, and went at the standard convoy pace of 30 mph up the western side of the Wolfgangsee. Tracker in the lead vehicle studied his map, then as they got nearer, roared ahead to identify the drop point. 'There,' he pointed the driver swung over to the lake side of the road and stopped, the lorries pulled in behind him and 30 pairs of silent rubber soled boots hit the gravel.

No hedge, across a small field into the cover of trees, no sooner had they reached the trees than there was the sound of a petrol engine being started up ahead, increasing the urgency of their running. The engine started at the sound of the second pull, opening into a roar muffled only by the canopy of trees. Martin pistol in hand, ignoring the mud on the narrow path, was ahead, at last he could make out the outline of the "Queen of St Gilgen" between the bushes and the trunks of the trees, then he ran out onto five metres of clear quayside mud.

He heard the crack of a revolver, he paused waiting for back up, then marines at his back he chased up the rickety gangplank onto the deck, falling over the piece of rope securing it to the rail. Picking himself up he rushed to the far rail, the motor launch was 60 yards away down the creek, moving into the lake proper. He aimed and fired, but nobody fell into the water, and nobody appeared to take any notice; he looked around, nothing very much to see on the Queen herself. Two marines appeared at his side. 'Shoot them,' he said pointing, but by the time the marines had unslung their automatics, found a rail to steady their foresights, the launch was disappearing around the head of the creek, and their bullets counted for no more than had Martin's.

'Fire, fire at it, sink it,' Barney was shouting hoarsely but uselessly, in truth the distance was too far for rifles designed for close-quarter work clearing out buildings; only a 303 would have been really effective. 'Look,' the marine pointed, there was a man in the creek, thrashing water, trying to get purchase on the side of the St Gilgen Queen. 'He can't swim, throw him that rope, Andrew.'

Barney was shouting to his radio operator who had fallen behind on the run to the boat, 'the air boat, get our bloody airboat out,' he fired a red very light; in less than a minute, out from the yacht anchorage guarding the long route down the lake towards St Gilgen, roared the airboat, its prow, as wide as a fakir's grin, was hardly visible being of the same colour as the lake's surface, it's wake as high as a peacock's feathers and as frothy as the piss of an African elephant, it's tossing wake would have swamped Noah's Ark if it hadn't beached on Mount Ararat somewhat earlier.

Martin switched attention, the two boats were now well away from the creek and from each other, both, heading directly across the water towards St Wolfgang on the other side of the lake, too far away for detail to be made out. Quicker than the launch, but a long way behind, the airboat was running parallel to the launch, Barney flipped out the spent cartridge and pressed a new round into the very pistol, a green flare caused little disturbance in the mountainous scale of things, but the helicopter pilot, saw it, started his engines, lifted off, at 30 feet before he moved forward over the lake, banked and raced low across the water in the direction of the launch.

'How many bullets will it take George?' asked the pilot.

'Which fucking gun?' said the co-pilot.

'The 5.1, will blow every fucker to the bottom of the lake, they said not to sink the ship.'

'Better get permission then before we use Big Tom,' replied the pilot.

Back at the rail of the Queen of St Gilgen, originally white, now weather crackled grey, a life belt was thrown to the struggling man, who grabbed it with two hands and pushed with his feet away from the boat side, threshing his legs in a poor attempt to swim. 'I can't swim,' he called out.

'Tell me the bleeding obvious,' the marine who had fired at the launch was contemptuous. 'It's only nine yards to the bank.' Other marines were more caring, and the struggler, still wearing pyjamas, was pulled onto bank, then up on to the Queen. Martin moved over to look at him, he couldn't believe it would be Ritter or Strasser, *But one never knows,* he thought. It wasn't, but as Martin peered, the more certain he became that he'd seen the man before. Like a flash:

"Seydlitz", keeper of Goerings's art, curator to the stolen museum treasures of WW2, organiser of transport of paintings from Northern Germany to the salt mine at Hallstatt, where corpses of foreign labourers were used as carpet underlay. Seydlitz wasn't on the wanted list for Austria, but was a real capture in the wider picture of criminals of the third Reich.

'I know that guy,' he grabbed Barney's arm, 'it's Seydlitz.'

Clearly Barney didn't know a Seydlitz from a Rembrandt, but he acted instantly on Martin's prompting. 'Shackle that guy, Munro,' he called, 'Shackle him to your wrist, don't let him go whatever, we'll see to him later. Oh and find out who he is.' The name Helmut Seydlitz was heard.

By now the boats were specks. Martin urged Barney, 'Let's get over to the other side, see if your navy have grabbed them before they could get away. Orders shouted, 10 men followed Martin, as he ran back through the wood. The lorry drove at breakneck speed around the end of the lake towards St Wolfgang. By-passing Strobl, twisting through St

Wolfgang and taking a wrong turn in the village of White Horse Inn fame.

For years after the landlord of the White Horse Inn was to recount ad nauseum, how he sheltered the Austrian Bonny and Clyde, who in pyjamas, thumbed their noses at a US Marine division, a gunboat and a fleet of US Helicopters, escaping by train up the Silberhorn on the mountain railway.

The crew of the airboat did their best, they did well, but they had been positioned down the lake to cover a dash down the Wolfgangsee towards St Gilgen itself, they couldn't cover that as well as a launch sprinting away from them, straight across the lake. Although they drove a faster boat, they started nearly a mile behind the launch, too far for their assault rifles to be effective, particularly as the bucking prow led to fears that they might shoot holes into their own boat, and skipper John Brown wasn't going to risk that; when the fleeing launch hurled itself onto the shelving shingle of the far bank they still hadn't fired a shot, nor had the Helicopter pulsing up above the launch, which was proving to be just a noisy distraction.

The Silberhorne rises to a height of 6,000 feet direct from the east bank of the Wolfgangsee. The Austrian Emperor was instrumental in building the first ever steam driven mountain railway from St Wolfgang to the summit, the ascent taking over an hour. There the Austrians built their highest meteorological station, a seismic observatory, a telescope, and various other scientific bits and pieces, all around and about the summit of the Silberhorne. Come the war, radar and radio masts and dishes, and much later a TV mast were added, making the mountain look like a bedraggled hedgehog, a 19th century tourist experience had become a commercial and military site making the mountain so important, that throughout the war the train ran up to three times a week, replenishing men, victuals and materials as required. Coal made available, the steam engine ran as needed, wind and snow permitting.

'Barney, Tracker and Martin met up with the airboat crew busily painting resin where the prow of the boat had hit the shingle hard, and that is how it might have remained if Barney and Martin had not driven up breaking fast after their wild ride through Strobl and around the end of the lake.

'They got away on the train,' the boat commander pointed to the wreath of smoke appearing high above the top of the trees, 'They rammed their launch hard into the bank, ran up the rise to the station and jumped on the train just as it left to go up the mountain.'

'Got away on a train, got away on a train!' Barney repeated himself 'I do not believe it, got away on that thing,' he pointed to an old engine by the road as a tourist advert.

'What the fuck were you doing when they escaped, painting your bloody boat. Why didn't you go after them? Is there a road up there?' Barney wanted as many men to know he was most annoyed that the marines had failed to even start to give chase to a puffing, panting hundred year-old train, so he shouted and swore.

They all sat down on a wall, took breath, deciding what to do. They checked out that there were three men in the launch, they accepted that they'd escaped and were now up in the forest and although the helicopter had followed the train for 15 minutes, there was little to be done immediately.

Martin cursed, the targeted men had got away, the Brits, Barney, the crew of the boat had all lost face in the eyes of their men, and they were all irritated beyond belief. He was now anxious to get Seydlitz back to the hunting lodge and press him alone to find out about the still missing Strasser and Ritter, for that he needed to get him away from the Marines and take him back to Ischl. Back to HQ was also where Barney wanted to go, before the journey back he made a point of stressing that General Wesley Hood would be calling the operation an Amphibious Air Training Co-ordination Exercise, and they should all do the same repeating they must all "sing from the same hymn sheet". The men pushed the launch back off the shingle, Martin and Tracker got in to be sailed back across the lake to the Queen of St Gilgen, where Barney would drive around, pick them up.

'They got away on a train,' General Hood exploded, 'wearing pyjamas! At least we know someone wasn't asleep.' He burst out laughing. 'What was Henrietta Helicopter doing, don't she have guns?' He listened to the excuse that their only gun would have blown the launch out of the water, and they'd been told the boat wasn't to be sunk... but that was the Steamer, not the bloody rowing boat,' but General Hood was still laughing.

'Put this down in the book as a training exercise Barney.' Tracker mentioned he'd like to interview Seydlitz.

'Bring the list, Barney,' Barney brought the list, the guts of a vast punched card system, 'How'd you spell Seydlitz, Initial?' They tried different combinations without finding him. 'What do you say he is? A museum curator? You Brits want him, if he's not here, I don't want him; he's all yours, Jesus. Get the pad, Barney.' Barney brought the "Transfer of Prisoner" pad; thus did Tracker Paul St John Travers sign for H Seydlitz.

At US HQ, both Tracker Travis and Martin, anxious to have their first crack at a "prominenti", had not found it necessary to tell Barney that the paintings transferred from Northern Germany and hidden in Hallstatt Salt Mine had resulted in the workers brought in from Ebensee being shot and buried under the mine floor; they drove back to the hunting lodge. Seydlitz, handcuffed to a stanchion of the Bedford, his pyjamas still wet, making him especially vulnerable when Partridge helped him down from the pick-up, scared to death, he was a different man when seated at last in Travers's office, wearing dry, clothes.

Starting at the beginning, realising he had more to gain by "singing" than by remaining silent, Seydlitz affirmed he'd been taken to the "Queen of St Gilgen" a day earlier, still angry that Strasser hadn't turned the launch around to pick him out of the water; he had lost the slippers he was wearing when he tried to jump off the deck into the launch gripping his own secret tight, disregarding everyone else's secrets he spoke easily. Yes, there were men beside himself, Ritter, Strasser, an assistant called Muller, and a woman, Strasser's squeeze, called Anna, yes there was a woman, but the Marines said only three men had left in the launch, and a woman hadn't been mentioned. Strasser had offered to hide Seydlitz for six months, he was to be given the choice of two houses, one Strasser was charging five times the cost of the other, but he hadn't been shown them and he didn't know where either of them were, he was waiting to see them before deciding, he knew that the expensive house was in a remote village and that he would have to share this with a high-ranking official, meaning that the someone was a Nazi.

Yes, he knew that men were shot and left at the mine, it was not his doing, he didn't know the workers were to be shot and left under the floor of the salt mine. No there wasn't a proper burial Hillary wrote it all down, Seydlitz signed with a flourish, adding "Curator to the Reich". *Not a wise move,* thought Martin, *I'll question him further when I've got him alone.* 'What's happened to the woman, is she still on the boat or is she hiding in the launch, I wonder?' Martin rang Barney suggesting they search the boat.

Whist all this was happening, a note was put on Tracker's desk. 'Three prisoners from Bad Aussee request an interview with the Commandant.' Weeks later, Traver was to say they reminded him of Wilson Keppel and Betty, shifty lecherous slithery toads. The three came seeking a deal: they were adamant that they were not at all the sort of officials the Allies were after,

Wilson Keppel and Betty were a music hall act performing between the 1930s and '50s, their act was a sand dance, next to a voluptuous blonde, two lecherous old Arabs shuffled along a sand carpet to a thin tune. Every time a cymbal clashed, the dance stopped, the young woman took off a veil until the seventh veil was reached when the curtain fell. The troupe also performed a longer version in nightclubs. This act, largely unchanged, toured British Music Halls for over 20 years.

'I'm a Metallurgist, I was posted to Ebensee, I hold a degree in Metallurgy, I analysed and certified metal integrity, my operatives were given extra food. I was never involved with the labourers,' Gregor Strauss pointed to his left, 'Georg

Centrop was 'Safety Officer, he saved dozens of prisoners, he tried to keep them alive.' He pointed right, 'Nick Niklaus was an accountant, he really looked after the clerks working in his office. We led the protest when we heard that Ritter had proposed loading the labourers into the blue cavern and imploding it, that act of ours by itself saved thousands of lives. It's Ritter and Strasser you should be after, we hear you've been enquiring about General Strasser, we'll tell what we know about Strasser, where he lives and so on. Ritter, we all agree was a terrible man, we know his plans.' Tracker didn't say that after the morning's "Training Exercise", he also knew where Strasser and Ritter "might be"—hiding high on the Silberhorne. The three men didn't ask to be free, they all owned chalets, and they asked to be put on "House Arrest"… with assurances naturally.

Tracker wanted to have some cells free, parole for these pleaders wasn't a bad way of freeing up cells, 'I'll consider your request, when I've heard what you've got to tell me.' The gist was, Strasser lived on a steamer on the Wolfgangsee, Ritter, a mountain guide before the war, had a hide in a cave hidden in the mountain spur called the "Haute Peignoir" on the Dachstein Massif. *Tell me something I don't know,* he thought.

'I'll consider putting you on house arrest, I'll let you know what I've decided in the morning,' he waved them out, Tracker could see more deals being done along these lines. Martin put his head around the door,

'Should we go out to the "Queen" to see what Strasser's left behind?'

Tracker lifted his head, 'You go, I'm busy.'

Instead of the expected scene of quiet and tranquillity, with the Queen of St Gilgen bobbing gently in the sheltered creek, Marines were buzzing about, the reason was immediately clear, blood splashed the deck, where two marines lay dead; apparently whilst having a smoke, a burnt down cigarette lay in the ashtray; both had been shot dead. The sergeant, senior man there, recognised Martin and was all too eager to spell out what had happened. 'We followed you in the Bedford over to Wolfgangsee, leaving Clark and Schultz with the Queen. When we came back to pick them up, you had come over in the boat and had cleared off; we arrived just as a smasher was leaving the wood, we gave her a wave. When we got to the steamer, Clark and Schultz were lying on the deck. They were cold. They were dead, nothing to be done. We went back to get the woman but she had gone. My guess is she was hiding on the boat all the time, hiding down below. Come on I'll show you,' Martin and Hillary followed him down the steps forward to the partition.

It had all happened after Martin had dropped off earlier, as the marine said, the woman must have stayed hidden on the Queen all the time. Hillary rummaged through the clothes hung up in a cupboard, apart from saying the smasher had money there was nothing, the decks were clean, Strasser, although, leaving in a hurry had left no incriminating evidence. All agreed that the woman, presumably Anna, Strasser's girlfriend, had not escaped on the launch, and must have stayed hidden on the Queen all the time. Nothing else to be done, they carried the dead bodies back to the lorries and returned to Bad Ischl, to take up further questioning of Seydlitz.

The phone rang, it was Barney, 'I've got something, we got a track on a car, and know where that Anna woman went, hopefully we're bringing her in as I speak. She ain't got long to live pal. You'd better get that fella you mentioned, Albert Pierpoint lined up, she'll be dancing on her toes, war's over or not.'

'What's the woman's address?' Martin was desperate for the information delighted when the answer came,

'19A St Sirius Strasse, Mondsee, not far from you.'

'Can I get in if I go now?'

'Sure, just give them my name.'

'Barney, I owe you, you're great.' He grabbed a coat, Hillary and a car.

Like the "Queen of St Gilgen", 19A the flat at the back of the block was pleasant and clean, but the meat safe in the kitchen held cheese, "Heimval", Hillary picked it up, smelt it and read the label, next on the shelf were "philosopher's sausages", and a bottle of wine labelled "The Grand VAT". Both Martin and Hillary knew the significance, Martin lead the chorus 'Where do these come from?' Then in unison 'HEIDELBURG' and 'near to Heidelburg is …DILSBERG'. But of the woman there was no trace.

Wide awake at dawn, 4 am, Martin's mind in turmoil, he tried to stop it and collect his thoughts to concentrate on the funeral. Arm around Hillary, she wasn't sleeping either, he recounted the events on the Lake. 'Tell me what Barney said to the Marines who let then go,' but Martin wouldn't tell her.

'American swear words aren't the same as ours, worse somehow, I'm not going to repeat them.'

'You're funny about swear words, aren't you?' said Hillary, 'you never say,' her mouth configured the word,

Martin put his hand over her mouth. 'But Partridge uses it all the time.'

'Hillary, let me have another look, in the morning will you get out the Undertaker's papers again, and the doctor's death certificates, I'm betting they won't show poisoning.

'Say please,' she reproved him.

'Please,' he copied.

'Have you forgotten about Helga Hopper, the women who signed in for Strasser?' she replied.

'Damn, I've been so involved with Hipper, he was an Admiral you know— Admiral von Hipper, and chasing the Queen of St Gilgen, I'd forgotten all about her. I'd better see her in the morning as well.'

Two days later Hillary was to storm into Martin's office, she threw a sheet of paper onto his desk.

'What in the name of Mary is this?' Martin reddened, he knew immediately what it was, even as he was shaking his head denying it.

'It's your report on interviewing Helga Hopper, shall I read back to you.' Hillary picked up the paper.

'Helga Hopper, 24 grew up through the Hitler Youth. To say she is beautiful is an understatement, she is the epitome of what Hitler must have imagined as the summit of physical Aryan achievement. Above average height, with blue eyes, fair hair, a figure to sketch and burn. Shrewd, intelligent without conceit, passionate without coarseness, the revelations coming out of Belsen, Auschwitz, and the like, have horrified her, appalled at SS excesses she wants to make amends.

'What the hell were you thinking when you wrote that, Martin?'

'I was thinking of you, Hillary love. I was describing you,' it was the best Martin could do.

Helga's questioning had been carried out in the drawing room of the lodge, the chandeliers sparkling, the heavy drapes drawn. Martin rose as she entered, introduced himself, and pointed to a seat for her to join Hillary, John Anderton and Partridge around the table.

Anxious to show off, Martin put on his best German accent for his rehearsed speech. 'As you know we are here on a mission, a task, if you prefer, if like me you detest the term, our task is to catch German war criminals. John, he pointed, and I have both been held as Prisoners of War in German camps and we don't harbour major grievances, in fact your doctors and nurses in a Luftwaffe hospital in Hamelin saved my life after my bomber was shot down. You will not be mistreated here, will she Partridge?' he looked at Partridge who didn't move a muscle.

Helga Hopper knew that Englishmen were gentlemen, but she was young.

'Despite Hamburg and Dresden,' said Partridge, 'and despite London and Coventry.'

Martin moved on, 'our need is to identify criminal Gestapo and SS, who carried out the atrocities, but I am more anxious to find high-ranking officials who authorised them, the men in the Stationmaster's office as well as the men on the station platforms making the selections, the men who organised the transport, who emptied the Ghettos, the organisers of the gas-chambers in the camps, who set food limits and who neglected the workers so badly that thousands simply died... like at Ebensee, Martin looked up inviting a response.

'Ebensee I know now, but I didn't know then, I knew they made petrol and things for tanks, we never got patients from Ebensee, because I thought they were taken to Gmund, I'd no idea we,' she hesitated, 'when we were all forced to go and see Ebensee for ourselves it was horrible, and they say Mauthausen was worse.' There was a pause. Martin lowered his voice and looked straight at her: Helga Hopper knew that what was coming was serious.

'What I say now mustn't be repeated, then I will never need to deny it; I'm not interested in decent men and women doing a job, obeying orders, I'm after the men giving the orders, the big clever fish who have successfully hidden themselves away,' Helga nodded. 'In particular Strasser, and you know Strasser, and I want to know where he is.'

'I only know of him, I don't actually know him, I've never met him.'

Partridge jumped in, 'But you signed his name on the paper you left for the undertaker at Rondel's funeral.'

'But I've never met him, I don't know him personally.' Silence erupted. Gently Martin resumed the interrogation.

'Let's start with the funeral, was Rondel why you went there or was it the other fellow?' Helga gave a soft "Rondel".

'Did you know Rondel, Helga?'

'I knew him, he was quite old, so we weren't friends or anything like that. I knew Peter better, he was my age, but I never liked him and I'd never ever have gone to his funeral.'

'Then why did you go?'

'I was asked to go.' John Anderton took up the questioning, an older man he was automatically more authoritative.

'Who asked?'

'Gert Muller.'

'Who is?'

'My best friend Ingrid's brother.'

'Who is?' the questions were rattling out.

'Sergeant Tomas Muller.'

'Who is?'

'Married to Ingrid.'

'And lives where?'

'Walserval.'

'Where's that?'

'Southern Germany, Bavaria, near Rothstein on Ebbs, I've never been there.'

'What division did Tomas serve?'

'Central Civil Command, Prison Camps, at first, so Ingrid said.'

'Where?'

'Salzburg. The Grand Palace.'

'Did he work for Colonel Strasser?'

'I believe so.'

The answers had streamed so quickly that whilst Anderton paused to assimilate them, Martin resumed with a softer line of questioning.

'Can you explain to all of us, why your friend, Ingrid, the wife of the brother of Gert Muller should ask you, who didn't know Strasser, to attend the funeral of Rondel, an old man you hardly knew, and leave his condolences on a church attendance ticket?'

'I delivered a letter as well, Strasser sent a letter,' Helga replied, 'I gave the letter to his widow, Rondel's wife, Kathleen. I don't know why I filled in the attendance card, it wasn't necessary, the card was lying in the pew, the woman next to me offered her pencil, we were waiting for the service to start, so I filled the card in without thinking, silly really.'

'You must know why Strasser asked you to represent him?'

'Ingrid and Gert told me Rondel had saved Strasser's life, they didn't know how, but it went back to the 'Long Knife Night, and the SA man Rohm and Strasser's brothers Gregor and Otto.'

'Just tell me anything you heard, anything at all.' Martin used his most placatory tone of voice.

'Rohm was boss of the SA strike force against the Communists, the SA were powerful and were plotting against Hitler, Rohm was killed down the road at Bad Aussee, and the Strassers were arrested. Rondel had been in the Frei Corps before 1920 and knew Hitler, and he spoke up and saved Hans Strasser, Gregor, the eldest brother was executed, Hans was questioned then freed.

Strasser couldn't get to Rondel's funeral, and he asked Ingrid to ask me to deliver the letter on his behalf. I hadn't anything to do and as I was invited to the funeral wake, I stayed on.'

'Yeah, it would be difficult for Strasser to get here from…' he cocked his eyes, 'Walserval.' Martin was still in placatory mode. 'But why would he ask this Ingrid to ask you?'

'Tomas and Ingrid and Gert all work for Colonel Strasser, Gert's got one arm, same as the colonel.'

'Did they both work at the camps.'

'Tomas once did, Gert only does jobs for him.' John Anderton came back into the questioning.

'Tomas Muller's a Sergeant, what rank is Gert?'

'I never saw him in uniform, he'll only be a private.'

'Why did Private Gert arrange for Strasser's furniture to be specially moved from Dachstein to Klein Schwarzal, why didn't he use the nearest station at Bad Aussee?' Anderton switched the line of questioning.

'Oh, that wasn't his furniture, it was his mother's, his father had a stroke and died when he was mayor of Aussee. It was to go into houses being done up.'

'How do you know all this?' Anderton wanted to know. 'I just do.'

'What houses, Helga?'

'A house in Dilsberg, and another in the Black Forest, it wasn't just Schwarztal.'

'How did Muller get in touch?'

'It wasn't Gert it was Ingrid, Gert only came into it later.'

'How did she get in touch?'

'By phone… I think.' 'I think' gave her away. John Anderton pounced.

'You're lying, Helga, you're lying, it's too late for lies.' Helga gave a sob, she reached for her handkerchief.

'It's too late for lies,' he repeated.

'Gert came to see me.'

'Where is he now?'

'I don't know.'

'Is he at Kleine Schwarztal? How do you get in touch with him?' she looked earnestly into his eyes trying to regain lost ground replying:

'He could be, but more likely at Ulm with his friend, he contacts me. I never know when or where he is. He travels, rings from public phones, no one lets anyone know where they are these days.'

Tea was poured from a silver pot, through a tea strainer, the porcelain cups and saucers were shiny clean without a chip, the curtains now drawn wide.

After the questioning of Helga and Holness, Martin listed four places of interest; Walserval, a likely "safehouse" for SS officers, no big wigs there, but It was well outside the British area, 60 km north of Ischl; next Kleine Schwarztal or more likely somewhere hidden in that valley. After that, a property within the 10,000 square miles of the Black Forest, a needle in a haystack, and well outside their area; that left Dilsberg, a medieval village, surrounded by its own defensive wall, where was there a more likely location to hide "promenenti", Dilsberg isolated, undoubtedly with a loyal wealthy population, proud that it had never been conquered for a thousand years. A raid there must be planned with care, particularly as the river running east west through Heidelburg and Dilsburg was well in the US zone.

Martin swigged back his tea, he sprang into action, telling Partridge to get 10 men together and two Bedford trucks; they were going out to Kleine Schwarztal tooled up.

Martin had three hours of daylight remaining, he stationed two men, openly, above and behind the ruined string of buildings, parking the Bedfords in front of the once grand entrance on a shingled parking reception area covered in moss. No one about. They peered and poked around the out buildings, leaving the largest most habitable main building till last. Cooking, a faint smell.

'Hello, hello,' Hillary shouted.

'Hello,' an answering call and a woman appeared around the side of the building. 'What do you want?'

In his broad northern dialect, 'To see who chooses to live in Poison valley,' said Partridge.

'Well, now you've seen, bugger off,' said the woman, bursting out laughing.

'We'll have peek at that good smell from your kitchen if you don't mind,' Partridge hefted his sub machine gun from one shoulder to the other.

'Come in, the kettle's on,' the woman was unabashed. Martin and Hillary sat down at the table, the men walked through into other rooms, guns cocked. The draining board held 4 plates, 4 mugs, 4 of everything. Martin nodded them at Hillary, who had in fact already noticed.

'How do you four like living here?' she asked. The woman began stacking plates away but it was much too late. 'All right, once you get used to it,' she replied.

'Only four now, two deaths the other day I hear, tell us about it.'

'Ask the doctor, not me, nothing to do with me.'

'They tell me at the Town Hall that the death certificate had the deaths down as bodily trauma.'

The woman shrugged her shoulders.

'What's body trauma?' Hillary wanted to know. Silence, at last the woman replied, 'the doctor never told me what body bloody trauma was and I never asked.'

'What's your name?' didn't get a direct reply, but later in answer to this and a series of questions, she was Elsa Pfalz, Rondel's daughter, and lived there with one other woman, when the men were shot it was terrible, in contrast to her earlier silence she now wanted to talk, but as she began to elaborate there was a crash from the other side of the door, she stopped. Partridge pushed two men and a woman into the kitchen, his men pointing their guns at the ready. Annoyed at the interruption, just as Elsa was ready to unburden herself, Martin told Partridge to take them all outside until they'd finished.

Banging their way out when everything had settled down, Martin tried to return to easy conversation.

'I believe you were all guards at Ebensee, just staying here till everything blows over.' Elsa nodded: 'Well, unfortunately for you perhaps, you've been found, we're here, your best move now is to face the situation, and answer our questions. We're after the bosses, not the other ranks, first how did your friend come to be shot.' There was a long silence before Elsa began to speak and sob at the same time:

'Klock tried to rape me, my father heard and came and attacked him; Klock shot my father. As soon as Ernst heard, he dashed up here and shot Klock. That was all there was to it.'

There was a pause, Martin raised further questions. Yes, her father Henry Rondel, had been in the Frei Corps, no she didn't use the name Rondel, yes, he'd known Goering, Himmler and Hitler in the Munich days. He'd known all the Strasser's and had been their friend. He'd intervened when Major Strasser was arrested, no, she didn't know what he'd said in defence. Elsa had had enough, Hillary moved and sat beside Elsa, holding her hand.

'Klock and Rondel are names on all our lists,' Martin whispered. Hillary pulled a face, Martin shut up.

Partridge came in, he put a slip of paper on the table: "Gert Mullers outside". Partridge pointed outside. They sat in the Bedford deciding whether to question Muller now or take him back to the hunting lodge. In the Bedford, Elsa sat next to

Martin, 'Who did you say shot Klock?' Reluctantly, the name "Ernst" was spoken. 'Has Ernst another name to go alongside Gert?' She was quietly asked. Elsa didn't reply. The inference was clear Ernst and Gert Muller were one and the same person.

'Was Gert Muller a guard at Ebensee?' Martin asked.

Sobbing, Elsa said, 'No.'

'Listen carefully, Elsa, as long as Gert, or Ernst Muller wasn't a guard at Ebensee, I'm not interested in his shooting Klock, not interested in the slightest, do you understand, just not interested? You've no need to shelter him, he's not in danger from us, not in the slightest.' Elsa nodded, 'I'm not a policeman, you see.'

'Gert's never even been to Ebensee, he was protecting me.'

'Then he's nothing to be afraid of.'

Martin pulled open the file holding the undertaker's papers and death certificates, both certificates were in the same handwriting, dated the same and signed by the same hand "Doctor Freda Colbeck", death had been certified as "Bodily Trauma".

'What in God's name is bodily trauma?' he asked.

Hillary who wasn't at all sure, volunteering, 'Damage to the body.'

'Get Dr Colbeck for me,' he said. Dr Colbeck lived up the valley of the River Traun and it took two hours to bring her to the lodge.

Warm and sunny Martin decided that as previous talks in the gardens had been most productive he would take Dr Colbeck for a walk in the parkland, he would ask about his troubling shoulder, yes, just him and the doctor in the park, might be the best approach. They drank tea from porcelain cups and saucers poured from the samovar, in the conservatory, before going putting on hats to sit in the sun on the seat by the pond.

'Doctor, at Ebensee you must have signed many death certificates, I hear there were up to 9,000 worker deaths over the period it was operating, though other figures have been bandied about, such large numbers of deaths must have kept you very busy.'

'I wasn't the camp doctor, so I don't have figures, and I was never called to certify any deaths, my understanding is that individual certificates were not required as most deaths were the result of diseases brought in from the east. Batch certification was deemed acceptable with two independent signatures. I was never asked to sign. Many deaths were from an eastern form of typhus I understand.'

'So you never examined the bodies from Ebensee, and no deaths were attributed to starvation or brutality.'

'Of course not, that would not have been correct.'

'Or convenient,' added Martin, 'however, I want to focus on the two death certificates you signed for Rondel and Klock, the two deaths at Kleine Schwaztal, I can't remember the full names without my file, the certificates were identical and both said "bodily trauma", could you please tell me what "bodily trauma" means and tell me specifically how they died, they didn't die from poisoned water.'

'No, poisoned water in the valley happened many years ago, if indeed it ever happened, I used a common term in our profession "bodily trauma". It's a blanket statement, I used it to spare the feelings of the Rondel family.'

'And hide the truth?' questioned Martin.

'Certainly not, nothing was hidden I didn't give the specific reason, like our politicians,' said Dr Colbeck, 'and the detailed reason was?' Martin cocked his eyebrows as he cocked the question.

'Gunshot wounds, bullets killed both men.'

'Same bullets, same gun, same shooter, doctor?'

No, different bullets, different guns, different times, two shooters, I didn't examine the bullets, I'm not an arms expert, but I'm confident the bullets were fired from different guns, and the deaths occurred at different times.'

'Were they both killed at Schwarztal, did you see the bodies there?'

'Yes, I did, Klock's body hadn't been moved, and I performed my examination as he lay at the spot without actually moving the body, Rondel had been laid out for burial in a bedroom before I arrived.'

'But you didn't report the killings to the police?'

'No, Mr Cohen, and I'll tell you why. So many deaths over five years of war, the police in disarray, another enquiry is the last thing we need, we all have better things to do and what good would an enquiry have done. Like most doctors, for the war years I've had to act alone as investigator, judge and jury for all manner of things, in this instance, two linked killings, murders if you prefer, and I acted exactly as I have done in dozens of unexplained cases, every doctor does; Look, Mr Cohen, are you interested in my conclusions on these killings?'

'Of course I am, that's why we're here, Doctor.'

'Different groups seek shelter and eke out a living, some in the derelict Schwarztal hotel and some make refuges in the valley, most of them were connected with Ebensee, all with something to hide, why else would they be there. Klock, probably an army deserter not part of our community, was interfering with a young woman when Rondel disturbed them and threatened Klock, may be with a gun, I wouldn't be surprised, anyway, Klock shot him, he would probably say 'in self-defence' if he could. Soon, the girl's boyfriend heard, rushed up to Schwarztal and shot Klock. End of story.'

I took the view that with the police no longer functioning, this friend whose name I didn't record and have forgotten, acted in place of the law who would surely have hanged Klock. This friend has saved you British a trial and a hanging by that Albert Pierpoint everyone is talking about. You, all of us should be grateful to that young man.'

'And this hero's name, which you didn't record, will your Hypocritic Oath allow you to mention it to me.'

'NO,' Doctor Colbck's answer was decisive and quick.

'Then let me give it you, Doctor. Gert Ernst Muller. That's the name you can't give me.'

'How on earth do you know? You didn't get it from me.' Oath forgotten.

'Perhaps we both have a reason to protect Herr Muller, if he's not a war criminal, he's lucky that I'm on the case, in view of what you've told me, I've no intention of pursuing him further or taking the death of Klock a step further. Perhaps you would make that fact widely known.'

In a cellar at the hunting lodge, the questioning of Gert Muller began. Martin began by saying he would not be enquiring into the deaths of Herr Rondel or Klock, but he did want to contact his brother and his wife who seemed to have moved from Salzburg, and with the end of fighting had presumably stopped working for Colonel General Strasser.

Gert Muller couldn't help, he didn't know. Although Strasser had been made a colonel general, he only used his colonel rank. Yes, he'd done tasks for POW Camps for Colonel Strasser, but never directly at any of the Labour Camps. Both of them had one hand and that perhaps explained why he was given occasional jobs, he got his jobs by phone from his brother, at a regular time in a public phone box; no, he wouldn't say what specific jobs, but they were all connected with the black market.

Martin maintaining his friendly approach repeated he didn't want detail just a general indication of what these jobs entailed, just an indication, nothing incriminating, no names.

Muller began to talk, there were lots of Frei Corps veterans, people like Herr Rondel, who had finished up being given Party jobs like organising things to be done around Labour Camps. The big camps and Strasser's organisation farmed out work and small working groups to Construction and Engineer Companies making components and so on for the war effort, these veterans were used as "progress-chasers" for these components and things the army needed, things like "mess tins". I progressed the progress-chasers

When it became clear to everyone that we were losing, everybody at Ebensee became afraid of the Russians, even the Russian prisoners were afraid. Raw materials no longer came in and the lines stopped working. The single men and men without children decided it would be best to disappear until things had settled down, before re-appearing with a new identity; they all wanted time and space.

I helped the colonel, passing messages to potential tenants for his safehouses, then recommending them to a Black Forest Syndicate if Strasser decided not to accept them—he doesn't much like single men for instance, and won't consider families—sometimes he uses me a go-between, a sort of "cut-out".

'I've got a list here Gert, of people missing from their homes in Altaussee, just nod when you recognise a name who might have been in touch with Strasser. He read out the list, marking six nods.

'What happens after your brother Tomas, Sergeant Tomas Muller gives you a name,' Hillary, who had been quiet, asked. 'Tomas is your brother, isn't he?'

Gert nodded. 'That's all I'll say, I've told you too much already.'

'I understand, Gert, but don't forget we have still to decide what we are going to do, we still hold your girlfriend; Elsa was a guard at Ebensee, you've got to decide on your priorities—it's not just you alone, there's Elsa to think about.' Hillary swept up the papers and left the room.

Martin and Partridge applied their usual formula, they took Gert Muller for a stroll in the grounds; mist rising from the river was curling around the trees, in this haunting atmosphere Martin's next ploy was irregular, dangerous and wrong, but, overriding every consideration was his burning desire to get Strasser, and Muller was key to fulfilling that desire.

'I knew your brother Tomas at Menzenschwand Prison Camp, he was well regarded.' Pausing to let the point sink in.

'I know you killed Klock, I know why you killed Klock. I know Elsa and the people hiding up at Kleine Schwarztal were guards at Ebensee. We can all put the Klock's death behind us, these are not normal times. I've spoken to Doctor

Colbeck, we are not pursuing the matter, period.' He let the point sink in, before repeating:

'No one will suffer from Klock's death, no one. But anyone who continues to screen Ritter, a serial murderer or help Colonel Strasser, makes himself very vulnerable, very vulnerable indeed.' He paused for a minute.

'Let me be frank, I have all the information I need to arrest Ritter and Strasser, but you know where he might be hiding, for that information I'm going to offer you a deal so good you won't believe, like Ritter at Ebensee, I have the power of life or death, like Ritter what I say… will happen; do you understand?' No words were exchanged for over a minute. He went on.

'We're walking alone in the Park for one reason only, there aren't any listening devices here, no one to know what you say, no one to know what I say, that's because of what I am now going to promise,' he paused,

'I am going to make an outrageous offer of protection that will apply to you, Elsa your friend, your brother Tomas and to Tomas's wife, but I won't make that offer until I know it will be accepted and that you're interested in a deal where in exchange, you and brother Tomas tell me all you know about Ritter and Strasser.'

'Would a deal cover Tomas's wife as well?' Martin found this a surprising question, and took time to reply, 'yes, provided nothing exceptional about her past emerges.'

'Does the offer of protection cover the Americans and the Russians?'

'The Americans yes, nobody can speak for our friends the Russians, you mustn't get caught by them—stay outside their zone of occupation.'

'Mr Cohen, I must be sure that protection covers all four of us.'

Their walk had taken them to the bench by the ornamental ponds, despite five years of war there was no moss or decay, a rub with a handkerchief was all that was required to mop up the remaining raindrops and for them to sit down without getting damp trousers.

'I'll give you…' Martin started again, 'I'll issue all four of you with individual certificate V11, Certificate V11 exempts the holder from prosecution for war time misdemeanors because of assistance rendered to His Majesties Government in the Spring Regulations of 1945; certificate V11, is recognised by the British and the US forces, but not by the Russians. Although the V11 certificate grants immunity from prosecution, it does not state what sort of help you have given, and it doesn't cover any date after the date the V11 is signed. It's signed by authorised officers and counter-signed by both high-ranking American and British officers.' He waited for the magnitude of the offer to sink in.

'It's an amazing offer.'

It certainly is, 'Martin spoke with gravitas, particularly as Elsa Rondel will be 100 miles away in Sigma 13 by lunch time tomorrow, if you don't accept.' Martin waved his hand as if he had not really made such a threat.

'You've not told me what I have to do.' It was still up to Gert Muller to decide.

'You must answer honestly and fully all questions about Strasser and Ritter.'

'You mean Ritter, the security boss at Ebensee, since it expanded in fact, I don't know much about him, he's a loner and his idea of pleasure is killing people. I do know he has a den up on the Haute Peignoir it's part of the Dachstein massif and I could take you there, I know exactly where it is. He keeps himself fit, he can look after himself all right. He killed a lot of people in Ebensee. Strasser has some kind of a hold on him Do I get this V11 form straightaway, then I can tell you about Colonel Strasser?

'Not too fast, Gert, not in public, no not in public, but we'll want to know everything; where he lives, his safehouses, his tenants, his killer girlfriend, how he gets people out of Germany, where his brother, his mother and his sister lives, where he might go in a crisis. You give us all your information, information you don't have, you get from Tomas and Elsa and your friend's sister, anybody. Only when we find and arrest your brother, not till then do you tell him that you hold a V11 certificate for him, and that if he cooperates both him and his wife, Elsa's sister will be safe… I know you can only ask. If I get Strasser without his answering questions, that gets him a V11, If he answers questions that enable me to catch Strasser he gets Certificate V11 for both himself and his wife.' This isn't exactly what he'd said earlier but no matter.

'How can I be sure you'll give me the V11?'

'You've my word.'

'Not more than that?'

Martin appeared affronted. 'What do you want, jam on it?'

Gert Muller thought for a moment. As Martin stretched out his hand, he added, 'We know about the Queen of St Gilgen, but you said steamers, plural, is there more than one?'

Gert Muller stood up, 'If this gets out, I'm as good as dead, but I've no choice.' The men shook hands, Martin signalled towards the lodge. Partridge appeared.

'We've done the deal can you get me four blank V11s?'

'Four!' Partridge held out his hand. 'Congratulations,' was all he said.

'Yes, two steamers, Strasser bought "The Empress of Vienna" weeks ago, it's sea-worthy, he's going to have it patched up and refitted it's in a hangar at Strobl.'

'We didn't find anything about the sale of the Empress of Vienna at St Gilgen Register Office.' Said Partridge

'There's a war on,' Muller was gaining confidence.

'We'll go inside. This will take a long time.' Martin walked ahead, head down in worry, *Had he overreached himself, had he done the right thing*? Muller followed elated.

Partridge brought up the rear, *Why didn't he let me thump it out of the bastard?* he said to himself.

Martin needing to do something, sensing the net drawing tighter, rang the number of Albert Pierpoint's UK Hangman's assistant.

'Of course, I remember you,' he said, 'Yes, we're lined up for lots of jobs in Germany and Austria, Yes, we've signed an agreement with the Yanks, they don't use hangmen in the States. Yes, I'll keep you in mind, you can get hold of us at Osnabruck.' Martin took down the number,

'We've opened an office there. Don't pass it on mind, don't want any cold-callers,' he laughed.

Chapter 11
'Queen of St Gilgen.' Colonel Strasser Escapes

Strasser knew as soon as he bought the "Queen of St Gilgen", that he'd made a mistake, but the knock-down price for the "Queen" following the battle of Kursk, was so low that he had to have it, with Sedlitz money behind him the price was "peanuts" and steamers on the Wolfgangsee had made a profit ever since the turn of the century when the railways brought day trippers from Vienna and Munich to the Salzbergerland to sail from St Gilgen to St Wolfgang. All his decisions were now based on Germany losing the war, and thousands of SS, Gestapo and Nazi Officials being executed if not by the British then certainly by the Russians, Jewry would see to that.

The wealthy would pay for new identities and a safe haven, his control of officialdom in Southern Germany enabled him to provide new identities, 'the Queen' could accommodate at least 30 adults in reasonable comfort. Moored inconspicuously among the reeds and creeks at the southern end of Wolfgangsee, it should avoid scrutiny. Then when the sun at last shone on Germany "the Queen of St Gilgen" could resume its tourist trips and make money from

American soldiers wanting to send snaps back to their families. A large fortune lay in wait, particularly as he planned to have Ritter to blow up every other sea-worthy steamer on the Wolfgangsee.

As the end of the war approached, he realised that the "Queen" was too conspicuous, too high profile for rich, for frightened Nazis to choose to live there. They would not able to sit on deck before nightfall and they would vastly prefer the isolated country ambience of Walserval with its lawns and allotments, or the remoteness and charm of his sister's house in the medieval village of Dilsberg. He decided that the "Queen" should be best kept as an occasional safehouse for his own use, making money from it would have to wait till the tourists returned.

Using the last of its fuel he had the Queen moved from its base in St Gilgen and moored up a twisting creek near the far end of the Wolfgangsee, invisible to boats passing up and down the lake. Trees made it invisible from the main road to Bad Ischl and from the lakeside meadows. Only from the air was it clearly visible, the Silberhorne mountain was too far away, and the weather generally too hazy or cloudy for it to be easily spotted from the far side of the Wolfgangsee. The "Queen" was reached through a wood, a wet winding path leading onto a rotting wooden quay, a few hundred metres from the main road.

There was a cottage on the corner where the path met the road. This cottage was inhabited by a fierce retired couple who cherished the field telephone Strasser had installed which they were trained to use to warn the "Queen" when trespassers were about. To make air reconnaissance difficult Strasser had ropes tied to the trees alongside the Queen, fastened to mooring buoys in the creek to pull the trees over at an angle, obscuring the steamer from air observation; but he knew the "Queen" was vulnerable to gossip, and had a fast "getaway" launch moored alongside.

Strasser was at Walserval when he heard of Rondel's murder, taking his thoughts back 10 years, with his brother Gregor killed for treason, brother Otto denouncing Hitler from the safety of England and he himself imprisoned and questioned by the SS Air Division. Two people had spoken up on his behalf, Gauleighter Wasserberg, furious that one of his men, his protégé, should be arrested behind his back and held without him being informed. Wasserberg was an original Munich plotter, a founder member of the Frei Corps, a trusted follower of Hitler to such an extent as to be on Hitler's Christmas Card List, next only to Josef Goebbels who had had Hitler himself as best man at his wedding to Magda.

The other supporter to speak up for him was Rondel, an uncle who had come forward at great inconvenience and no little risk. Like Wasserberg he had been in the Frei Corps and like Wasserberg he knew the Fuhrer. News of Rondel's murder came from Rondel's wife, the detail was sketchy, and the news arrived when It was neither safe or convenient to undertake the journey and attend Rondel's funeral at Bad Ischl, but he felt obliged to do something; through Tomas Muller he arranged for a letter to be sent, and for him to be represented at the funeral.

Conscience clear, Strasser put it out of his mind, but that funeral attendance was to lead days later to the loud "brrp" of the field telephone as the observant cottagers buzzed the "Queen of St Gilgen". In the galley still in pyjamas and slippers waiting for the milk to boil, he picked it up, to hear

Frau Smoulder's shout of 'American Soldiers have just jumped out of a lorry with their guns.'

'Raus, raus, Yankees.' Shouting a warning through the bedroom door, Strasser flew up the ladder to the deck, jumped down into the launch, ropes securing it to the side of the "Queen", ripped off the engine cover and wound the starting handle. The engine didn't start, he waited seconds which seemed like hours, and wound again as hard as he could, the engine stuttered, still no ignition, he pumped the choke, then held it down, panicky he thrust again, the engine ticked over ever so slowly before quickening like any new-born baby finally it caught, bursting into life.'

There were four men and Anna sleeping on the "Queen", they had arrived the night before to review progress and discuss plans for the derelict Black Forest mansion he had bought. Anna had retired early and was sleeping away from the men in a hidden construction forward and didn't hear the warning shouts. Ritter and Tomas Muller had followed quickly up on deck, their training making them wide awake functioning adults, they followed his lead and jumped down onto the launch, but not before Ritter fired his pistol at the American troops who were moving with intent up the path towards the "Queen". Seydlitz was still nowhere to be seen as Muller cleared the ropes lashing the launch to the side of the Queen before pushing ii clear of the side.

'Seydlitz, Anna Raus,' he shouted, by this time they were clear of the "Queen", Seydlitz at last appeared on the high deck of the "Queen", facing a goodly drop, he hesitated looking for an easier alternative. Strasser already had the engine engaged and was steering the launch forward and away from the side of the "Queen", he gestured for Seydlitz to jump, but the Museum Curator kept hesitating and looked around for a safer option. The launch was pulling away by the time he had decided; from the lower deck, a shorter leap was required, but this didn't make up for the reduced height. Seydlitz had vacillated far too long, finally he jumped in the general direction of Ritter standing at the back of the launch, it wasn't a great effort if the truth were told, his leading foot hit the polished top of the awning at the rear of the launch, with Ritter unable to grab him he spun off and fell with a splash into the creek. Strasser did not turn back, he continued to gun the engine and the launch gained speed as it pulled out of the creek into open water.

Only when into open water did he look back at the soldiers now lining the deck of the Queen, 'How many of them?' he asked.

Ritter estimated about 20, only then did the colonel look towards Seydlitz floundering in the creek, 'We can't go back for him,' gesturing towards the figure threshing about.

'No way,' he certainly wasn't going to risk turning the launch around and putting his boat in easy range of a platoon of armed marines.

The next 30 minutes were to be the most dramatic and thrilling minutes of their lives.

The engine so reluctant to start, had now settled into a steady roar, shaking the hull certainly, but with a top tenor's voice of certainty. Strasser looked for the petrol gauge, its glass cover was grimy, the needle wobbled, and it was hard to make out. When did we last put petrol in?' A question to himself really, keeping the tank filled up in the last year was a luxury out of the question, with petrol in such short supply and with thieves about. The needle seemed to show two gallons remaining. 'We've enough to get us across to St Wolfgang,' he shouted above the shaking, an assurance more to himself than the others, but he reduced pressure nonetheless on the accelerator to conserve petrol, handing the controls to Sergeant Muller, he pointed, 'head for St Wolfgang harbour, its church spire dimly visible on the far shore. He looked back at the "Queen", he'd heard several shots fired without feeling threatened, Ritter had again pulled out the revolver he had shoved into his blue striped pyjamas, to reload, but the launch was no longer threatened; they were out of effective range.

'St Wolfgang, do we know anybody there who'll help us?' Ritter shook his head. 'The garage by the Silberhorne Station has a car, we could take that.'

'Sir,' a very flare had been fired from where they had just left, Muller pulled Strasser's sleeve pointing north down the lake, a bull nosed pneumatic boat had pulled out from the shore and was heading in their direction. *Christ, full speed Sergeant,* he thought for a moment, then he pointed. 'There, change course, head for the Mountain Railway Station, we'll take the car.' Muller turned the wheel, inching the launch 10 degrees left, not quite certain whether that was starboard or port.

'Is that the Silberhorne Station?' he pointed. Strasser put his thumb up. The other boat had followed the change of course, the angle edging them nearer to the launch. Fuel economy forgotten, their engine screaming, the timbers trembling, the launch had never been driven so hard, eyes never strained so much, at the ominous grey wall with its high white plume, its piercing scream became louder as it reduced the distance between them.

They were now more than halfway across the Wolfgangsee, the Queen no longer visible, suddenly a new noise competed with the clonking of their own engine, a shadow moved across the launch, a helicopter had crept up unawares, it was 20 yards above them. 'Christ, what's this?' Ritter pulled out his gun for the second time. Strasser lurched towards him, 'God's sake, don't fire, don't let them see it, fire and they'll blow us out of the water, they carry cannon.' Ritter packed the revolver. For a minute the helicopter backed off as if waiting to receive instruction, when it came back overhead a loudspeaker burst forth. Although the words were barely distinguishable, the meaning was clear, Strasser clapped his hand to his ear miming as if trying to make out was said, Muller continued to aim the launch straight at the Silberhorne mountain rail station; the station, set back 80 metres from the shore line, was now clearly visible. The helicopter banked away, Trees and telephone poles and shingle ran along the shelving beach, a beach without a landing stage.

'Ram straight at it,' Strasser ordered, straining his eyes to see if he could spot the car. He couldn't, no vehicle was in sight, only a couple of women on the road. The launch was 20 yards from the beach, the helicopter was shuttling between them and the pursuing airboat 350 yards back, when the Silberhorne Mountain Rail Engine blew its whistle signalling imminent departure. Strasser had a flash of inspiration, in pyjamas, hot, oblivious to the picture presented by three men in pyjamas, 'We'll catch the train.'

Muller aimed the launch straight at the beach, his eyes aimed at the sandiest shallowest bit of beach, not looking at the airboat closing up behind, screech, judder, the prow of the launch crossed the water line, no jetsam here, and grounded growling like as if it had run hard into a shingle beach. Strasser first, they jumped off over the prow, the launch so far up the beach they didn't get wet, they ran across the road, past a pensioner stationmaster refastening a chain across the slope to prevent pedestrian access to the platform. Ritter drew ahead and again he drew his revolver. 'No!' shouted Strasser. Ritter was first to run up the steep platform and leap onto the old-fashioned wooden running board of the single carriage as the train cleared the slope to start the third of it's three times a week ascent of the Silberhorne. He held out an arm to pull the others aboard, only then did they catch breath and look back towards the Marines.

Three marines had jumped off the airboat which had stayed off shore rather than ram the beach at speed and risk a repair job, hampered by their weapons, basic training decreed that they moored their boat, not till it was secured, did the marines run across the road towards the station.

'Get inside, take cover, they we won't shoot at us inside,' Ritter had retained his poise, in singlet, shorts, running-shoes he was more comfortable than his colleagues in their striped pyjamas, and woolly slippers He crouched down below the benches, then poked his head up and looked back. 'They're not following.' The leading marines had indeed come to a standstill, running at first but now standing at the high end of the platform, staring at the departing engine, wondering whether to run up the hill after the train, shoot at it, or wait for further orders.

The helicopter noisy and useless, its crew (also noisy and useless) throughout, as the train puffed from view into the enveloping forest, flew back over the lake and was never seen again.

Calmer now, still dressed in pyjamas and slippers, the men on the Silberhorne Flyer, stood up as the cutting gave way to a canopy of trees darkening the single carriage.

'What do we do now?' it was Strasser who asked the question, 'You're our mountain guide, Ritter.' Nothing but the rhymic grunt of the old locomotive could be heard, as it nonchalantly continued to puff its way uphill as if this sort thing happened every day, the combined driver/stoker having religiously ignored the wild events happening behind him to his carriage as he continued to tap the pressure gauge and shovel more coal into a glowing boiler.

'Dressed like this we can't walk far, and I'm not sure what reception we'll get up at the observatory.' Muller had been examining the various boxes, baskets and parcels stacked on two of the rows of seats. 'At least we won't starve,' he said, holding up a couple of tins of peas.

Ritter spoke, 'There's a woodcutter's hut above St Wolfgang, I think I could find it, we could hide and make something to go on our feet,' so it was decided, they would jump out, find the hut and lay up before going down to St Wolfgang at nightfall.

The train entered a clearing, they jumped, rolling softly down a grassy knoll, ignored by the bellwether cows tugging on long succulent grass. The sun had risen, warm on open fell, no helicopter, soon no sun as Ritter led them climbing over and around fallen tree trunks, protruding rocks and brush wood to Seigfried's Hut, where sacks, a rainwater butt, rope, warmth and shelter were companions till nightfall, They had tins of food, a stove and enough ingenuity to survive.

Only when they were safe inside did Ritter say 'Seydlitz,' not quite knowing what Seydlitz's relationship was to the colonel. 'Dozy bugger, you couldn't possibly turn the launch around we'd all have been killed,' no one was going to contradict that. Strasser added, 'he just wasn't fit,' adding, 'I told Anna beforehand to hide in the bottom of the boat if we had trouble we made a hidey there, I expect she heard the commotion and lay low, hope she's OK.' Both agreed she was a woman with nous who would probably be all right. It was left like that, there wasn't anything they could do. He muttered to Ritter, 'If Seydlitz talks, and he will, you'll know what to do.'

Hours drag but making pads for feet, and drapes for clothes, time passed reasonably enough, particularly for the colonel, shacked up with fellows he needed but didn't normally mix with socially. He was tempted to fill in time and boast of how he had single-handed flown a Storch into Berlin, entered the Fuhrer bunker, witnessed its final hours and the final disintegration of the command structure of the Reich, seen the body of Eva Braun carried out to be cremated. He could sketch out the self-preserving actions taken by Herman Goering, Heinrich Himmler, coupled with accusations of treachery. He had first-hand knowledge of Josef Goebbels and Magda, poisoning their six young children, and of how they had prevailed upon the SS to shoot them in the neck in the same place in the gardens where Hitler had been shot and his body cremated. A shooting many of the guards were quite willing to carry out, such was the revulsion at their poisoning six children.

He could bear witness to Eva Braun's stoic acceptance of her death at Hitler's side. He could embellish Hitler's noble yet somehow pathetic final gesture of marriage before his end. He could enthral with this graphic picture, what Hitler was wearing, all without giving away that it was him who had shot and killed their leader.

A fleeting thought came to him, *Why didn't I go up to the Chancellery Garden, Hitler, Martin Bormann, if I'd participated in the killing of Josef Goebbels, I could have claimed a full house,* he grinned, 'too late now,' he said to himself.

He had a further boy's own adventure tale he could tell. The escape from Berlin under the cover of darkness and rain from out of the Fuhrer bunker, across the silent gardens, through to the ghostly rail junction where wrecked trains lying on their sides resembled Pearl Harbour. Escape with Martin Bormann and Artur Axman, Axmann wearing shorts dressed as a German Youth Leader, of dodging the Russians, of having to shoot fat unfit Bormann because his injuries no longer allowed him to continue and rather than endanger his companions further, to shoot him and save him from the Russian soldiers.

Later, of how, after getting away from the centre of Berlin crossing the lines of both Russian and British troops, and of the day with six randy nurses and of his return to Salzburg by bike, coal tender, barge and milk cart, He would tantalise, he wouldn't say why he went and what he did, only if the bullets that shot Cockburn, killed the soldier in the forest pool, and the bullet pulled from Hitler's brain, were certified after forensic comparison, as being fired from the same revolver, would he be able to take up his proper place in history.

I mustn't say a word, not a word, he thought. *Just play dominoes.*

All hungry, they compared memorable meals of the past, chose where they would eat their ideal breakfast… one from the rim of a volcano, Strasser a yacht on the Mediterranean, Axmann in bed with a blonde. They vilified Seydlitz for falling in the creek. 'Like a maggot crawling out of cheese,' said Ritter, 'no going back for him, we'd all have been caught or shot or both. Anna was quicksilver though, I think I saw her go forward through one of the windows.'

Strasser hesitated, 'She'd be going to the hidey I had built down in the hull, not finished, we'd agreed that if we were raided we'd hide there.'

Axmann's starting to repeat everything, he's going senile, thought Strasser.

Whilst the others slept, Strasser was left to ponder how the Yanks had caught up about the "Queen of St Gilgen", whether Walserval and Dilsberg were included in the same leakage of information, and whether Anna had escaped.

By late afternoon they had all had a nap, all had a theory of how 'The Queen' had been discovered. Muller insisted that nothing had leaked from him; wife didn't even know about the steamer, and it had only been mentioned as an alternative safehouse to two customers, with Strasser's agreement; the ship registration had been done by Strasser's agent in Switzerland through St Gilgen Town Hall, and this could be the source of the leak, though the ship's caretaker, Willi Russi, a cantankerous old man who had resented losing his job, or the previous owner Willy Barnevelt of Herman Barnevelt and Son was a possibility.

Ritter, a man of few words and pointed silent thoughts, nevertheless came up with a simple plausible explanation: 'A hidden steamer in a lake spells comfortable accommodation. The Americans were bound to check it out and they've cars, boats and spotter planes for the job. Strasser should never have set it up as a safehouse, and now he shouldn't go around asking questions, they would only raise more questions. He showed he wasn't subservient to Strasser, and they still relied on him to get them down the hill, to the safety of St Wolfgang.

Strasser kept his thoughts to himself. He'd used Gustav Holst for the transfer, perhaps Martin Cohen still had Gustav's wife as a spy in the BBBB Bank.

Sacks wrapped around their slippers, it was more than an hour's walk down from Siegfried's hut to St Wolfgang. Confident they would find friends, clothes and food there, Muller would then make his way back to Walserval—he'd only been at the "Queen of St Gilgen" for a night. Ritter would go back to his own hilltop festung on the Dachstein, Strasser had "places" in Salzburg and Munich for emergencies. Sorted.

Sacks as warm clothes, sacks as footwear, sacks to keep spring rain off, three suspicious characters crept beneath high walls in the quiet streets of St Wolfgang, hours after good women missing their soldiers had bolted their doors and retreated to lonely beds; the St Wolfgang Regiment had suffered high losses, even the doors of the White Horse Inn itself, where there were 'joys the whole summer through' were bolted; the White Horse Inn, their destination, they threw grit at closed shutters; this had the desired effect, help came.

'You must be the men the marines are looking for, did you escape on the Silberhorn Express, the marines came here.' For an hour, they were the centre of admiring attention, even old Axmann had "pulled". The following morning saw the same three odd characters, albeit no longer wearing pyjamas, sitting in the back of the bread van, passing 200 metres below

Tracker Travers, asleep in the Emperor's Hunting Lodge, to the Bad Ischl rail station. Shaking hands, they split, Ritter a day's walk on mountain paths to the "Grand Peignoir", 'his own cave on the Dachstein Massif, Muller carts, foot and bus to Rothstein and Walserval, Strasser saying little, his Storch many miles away, returning the way he had come, past the mooring site where the "Queen" rested, to find Anna and "his place" in Salzburg.

Chapter 12
Hounds without Mercy

So much information coming in, so many people to question, everything buzzing around his head, Martin's preoccupation remained Strasser, but he knew Seydlitz knew what had happened at Psalm, where Martin had watched a dead body being dumped in a mountain bog, he knew, he was the supplier in chief for the Art Syndicate and knew what had happened after their gold was hijacked. Much later than intended, Martin finally sat face to face with Seydlitz.

'It was simple,' Seydlitz said. After the hijack, the syndicate melted away, the curators too scared to continue, their dreams of great wealth overtaken by their fear of the SS. Of the ringleaders, Wasserburg their political protector was dead, Strasser concocted an alibi which he "sold" to his masters and which covered them all; that the gold was to fund a festung, a fund to commission a fitting statue of the Fuhrer. To cover up dead Germans in Switzerland, he told his masters he'd "found" money which needed to be shared; would "so and so" accept a share? Nothing really to do with the trouble over in Switzerland of course. Bribery worked, the deaths, the whole Swiss episode, helped by a smile from Goering, instead of being investigated under a Board of Enquiry, had been classified "Top Secret" and the deaths, even the death of the important Wasserburg were buried deep within the system. Strasser emerged financially poorer, but smelling of roses, and vowing vengeance particularly on you, Herr Cockburn.

The gold losses at the hijack, added to the bribery, cost Strasser a fortune. Subsequently, when he came to set up his scheme for safehouses and false identities, it was Seydlitz who had provided much of the funding. I gave him the money and the bastard left me drowning in the creek.

Some of this was a year before Strasser let it be known that he could provide a safe haven and a new identity for political figures and SS personnel, to thwart Allied hunters of war criminals. The asking money was very large, but his command of bureaucracy from his post in the Palace in Salzburg, and his reputation, made him as Seydlitz said, 'Bankable.'

Muller and Ritter were his lieutenants, working as direct helpers, the meeting on the Queen of St Gilgen was a "one off". Seydlitz had been invited as a friend who had lent money, and to decide if he was happy to remain permanently on the ship for safe haven, he'd helped finance Strasser to purchase both the Queen and a house in the Black Forest south of Freudenstadt called the Alte Oak. 'Yes, he'd provided Swiss francs Swedish kroner in cash, no paperwork between them, if anything was ever anything, Strasser was a man of his word.'

Seydlitz had never wanted to go to Walserval, it was of a lower standard, it was an apartment complex with many inhabitants, but apart from knowing it was in Bavaria, not Austria, he'd never visited and Strasser hadn't given him a more precise location, but Seydlitz wouldn't have been going there in any event, if he didn't like the Queen of St Gilgen, he was to be offered a place at a special address, a house with other VIP families. This wasn't an apartment complex, no he didn't know any addresses, but trusted Strasser as to the "actualite". Strasser was to be trusted he never directly lied. He was sure Muller knew where it was, as he did most of the work, Ritter, "horrible man", was called upon from time to time as an enforcer. He knew nothing about Anna, not even her other name, except that she was Strasser's squeeze.

Seydlitz had held nothing back, openly accepting he was a saviour of art works, a looter, a pillager who played up to the foibles of his political masters, but he didn't regard himself as a war criminal. His own side were entitled to shoot him, but the British weren't entitled, stealing from Nazis wasn't punishable under British law, he'd done nothing wrong to them. Martin opened up a new subject.

'I want to know more about the move from the Zurich Bank, the boxes were stout and when we examined them even the Meissen figurines, were undamaged.'

'British airmen made those boxes in one of Strasser's camps, yes they were good, the artefacts I was most sorry to lose was the porcelain, the Dresden and the Meissen particularly, so delicate, such marvellous colours after over 200 years. The majority of the paintings were nondescript, I'd separated the good ones in advance, but there were excellent icons, and diamonds are jewels, and jewels are small and keep their value and gold is gold.

'I can tell you something about one of the icons,' said Martin, 'I expect Strasser has already told you that Russians were at the hijack, one of them, a trainee priest, recognised an icon that was famous, it came from the Gutaski monastery if

I have the name right, where Stalin had trained as a priest, consequently the Russian Ambassador sent it on to Moscow, and now that the war is just about over I don't mind telling you, Morov the Swiss Ambassador in Berne got promotion and more than a pat on the back from Joe Stalin himself.'

'You didn't let Russia have the Czech crown I hope.' Unprompted Seydlitz had raised the topic Martin next wanted to discuss.

'No, but I don't really know, what crown?' Martin lied, 'I don't know much about it, what can you tell me about the Crown?' Seydlitz could tell him quite a lot and for five minutes Martin didn't interrupt. Finally, Martin ended the discussion.

'I don't think the Russians got it, I'll ask. I'll see they make you as comfortable as possible,' at the door Seydlitz paused, 'Did I tell you what Strasser calls you?'

Martin cocked his head, 'What does he call me?'

'The German Iscariot.'

'I'm not German, I'm a Czech,' Martin flashed back angrily.

'Well, he thinks you are a German, and that's what he calls you.'

'Shall we go up the Dachstein after Ritter? Gert has told me where the grand peignoir is.' Tracker hadn't decided on his priorities. He said "we", but after the recce in the Oklahoma trainer, he hadn't the slightest intention of setting foot on the Dachstein, particularly as Yvonne was to drive him to Feltre and Venice on a fact-finding fucking visit.

Volunteers were sought, five men led by Martin would climb up to the Haute Peignoir in an attempt to flush out Ritter. A list of climbing equipment, food and weapons was drawn up, an army cheque was walked down to the mountaineer's shop in the centre of Bad Ischl, to the delight of the impoverished owner, 21 days hungry, now a full price sale in British Army Currency, based on swiftly altered price tickets, to impatient customers.

One excellent outcome of Hitler's National Socialism was the money, planning and attention given, not only to roads, but also to the maintenance and mapping of walking and climbing routes in the Black Forest, and throughout Germany. Unlike the Silberhorne, none of the lifts were still running on Dachstein massif, the four men had to climb following the distinctive red and white triangles painted on square metal discs, nailed to the fences, the trees, and the boulders as they climbed towards the Haute Peignoir, five hours had passed and the men were in shit shape as they picked a route along first the east side of sharp ridge peaks then the west. Near to the Haute Peignoir itself, their next pause became a stop. Before them, the shattered rocks opened up to a three bounce, thousand-foot drop on both sides of the ridge. The path itself, on to a windy col, ending in an open narrow ridge of shattered stone, a trial of nerve in still weather, ropes essential with rain, or with wind in the offing.

They shrugged their rucksacks to the ground, and prepared to rope up, the wind strengthening all the while, they were in a bad place. The wind was so loud they hardly heard the crack of the rifle, it was the ricochet of the bullet from the rock and the bursting of a rucksack that alerted them to danger. Bob who had endured mockery and little sympathy after his return from Normandy, a bullet in his backside from scrambling out of the turret as Littmann brewed his Sherman tank (it was a Matilda) near Caen, hit the deck first; the ensuing breathless conversation was between four heroes lying on their stomachs, flat on the ground.

A jerky frightened conversation it was, Martin summarised the collective decision, they'd wave a white handkerchief and if they were sharpish, and the sharpshooter allowed, they'd be back down off the mountain and back to their vehicle before dark. Advance across that shattered rock drop was impossible. Not negotiable.

With trepidation, he waved a handkerchief, and after three minutes as nothing had happened, they sat up, nothing happened, got up and feverishly backed away, dragging their ropes, not waiting to shoulder their rucksacks, bent double, they got back into the shelter of the trees as fast as they could. Then circling their ropes, draping them over their shoulders it was back along the path, retracing their steps. Safe at last, they stopped, recouped and sitting against droppings on white boulders, justified their failure to confront Ritter, 'Ritter with a rifle, us on the open ridge. We couldn't see him, I couldn't get to my weapon, we couldn't cross that steppe, the wind, without roping up, we'd no chance, he could easily have killed us, he's let us live, let's be thankful and leave it at that.' Bob thought he'd left them alive because if he didn't, the air force would have blown the top off his mountain. *Thank God, it's only Ritter,* thought Martin, *what would I have risked if it had been Strasser?*

During the night, Hillary suffered "an event", alternating between the bedroom and the bathroom; by noon the following day an anxious Hillary had decided British Medical Resources in England, were preferable to anything war torn Europe could offer and had made arrangements; parents were put on notice, Tracker and what passed as a Personnel

Department in Whitehall had been told explicitly of her new plans, Martin could forget about Strasser and Ritter, she had issued "marching orders".

Hillary danced through Foreign Office best practice. She got a letter from her own German Medical Adviser, her alcoholic MO being unavailable, that she needed nursing supervision for a return by train to London, she would compromise if this supervision was carried out by her "husband" who was due for leave. Reluctantly the Foreign Office agreed.

Still in its infancy, the "blue train", shuffling British personnel across Europe from Harwich via the Hook of Holland to the garrison in Trieste, by ship, train and coach, had left Villach on its return to the channel port. It was ordered to have an unscheduled stop at Badgastein. Travis drove them; keeping the engine running in a warm Land Rover until the blue train free-wheeled down the High Tauern to a cold Badgastein station, hours late. On perhaps the longest most interesting train route in the world, blinds down, the pair slept warm hours in each other's arms, before embarking at the Hook on the "Pass of Ballycastle", where Martin fought long and bitterly to secure a single cabin for Hillary…

'We've no booking for the lady, sir! We haven't any empty cabins.'

'She's pregnant for God's sake, she's got a doctor's certificate to prove it.'

'Will she share with a WAAF officer?' It was the best they could do.

Martin was so ill and tired he didn't even beat his hammock to the 'bloody heads' as he called them.

Met at Liverpool St Station by a London taxi and welcoming parents, four-way love and attention squeezed into the taxi, fatigue and anxiety banished.

With father a vicar, a special marriage license was not a problem; accommodation was not a problem, the large vicarage swallowing both them and a day later, Martin's happy parents down from the north. A joyous white wedding, with bells, and a sprinkling of the vicar's congregation, a school friend came down from London as bridesmaid, Hillary's young brother pressed into service as "best man". Bride and groom spent blissful days in Eastbourne, breezy walks on white cliffs, hands clasped from prom to pier.

Hillary's mother, in her role as vicar's wife, had her own take to friends on the pregnant bride.

'Oh yes they consummated the marriage months ago in Switzerland, we held the ceremony here at Giles St Giles to please Martin's parents.' So that was all right then!

Martin was away from Bad Ischl for 19 days, Hillary settled at home on tenterhooks to await an eagerly expected baby.

Martin returned to Bad Ischl, repaired rail tracks had shortened the journey time by three hours. His first words to Partridge over a pot of the Yorkshire tea he'd brought back specially for John Anderton:

'What have you done about Walserval?'

Partridge laid out a roll of negatives and half a dozen enlarged prints, 'That's the house,' he pushed across shiny prints, 'that's the barn, that woman's the Manageress, Muller's wife, and these are the allotments, by the way, it's not called Walserval by the locals, it's called Old Barn, or the barn door or something like that.'

'How do you know you went to the right place then, everyone's always called it Walserval?'

'No, Walserval's a small-holding nearby, it's signposted and we went down the lane to it, no the Brown Barn's where the OAP's live definitely, they're all old people living there,' Partridge pointed to his photos of groups of old folk.

'You went down a lane to Walserval, before going to the Black Barn?' John Anderton sounded as if he was on to something, and when Partridge nodded, continued,

'You've caught the Prince of Wales's influenza, you've been conned.'

'The what, what's the Prince of Wales influenza?' Martin asked.

John went on: 'The Prince of Wales cough, it's a Welsh Nationalist thing, the day after Edward was crowned Prince of Wales at Caernarvon Castle, he was scheduled to attend an Eisteddfod at a country estate at Bard y Clyydd on the River Elwy.

'Every Druid, every harp, every Liberal, every Methodist preacher in Wales was to be there. His Rolls Royce was late setting off from Lord Caernarvon's estate on Ynss Mon, his driver, a Cockney, not one Welsh speaker in the car. The Welsh Nationalists were up before the Princebright and early, they turned all the signposts round, or pulled them down, or put up false ones, the driver went over the Menai Bridge off Anglesey and soon followed the signs. It was some time before the false signs ran out, only then did he realise he was not only lost, he had no idea where he was. The folds on the map all came in the wrong place, and he couldn't read or get to grips with road signs in Welch or match to names on the map, all the time Prince Edward chatting away oblivious on the back seat, the further he drove the narrower the roads, the more difficult to steer the big car, and the further away he was from Bard y Clyydd. Eventually they arrived at a reservoir, with a house by the side of the dam and a woman in the garden. They stopped and the driver asked for directions, the woman only spoke Welsh. There was a garage two miles down the road, was all they could get out of her. It took two minutes ringing the bell before the owner came out to his pump, and another five minutes to understand that they should not have been there, and to turn the car round.

They arrived four hours late at the Eisteddfod, he was never forgiven, and there has never been a popular Prince or Princess of Wales in the Welsh speaking part of Wales.'

'Are you telling me the German's have made a fool of me, that they changed the signs and sent me down a lane to give them time so they could get ready for the visit?' Partridge was visibly annoyed.

'Probably not, probably all quite natural,' Anderton said what nobody believed.

'Let's have another look at the aerial photos,' said Martin, he bent over the table. The photo of the allotment garden convinced them that they were looking at healthy adults, and not 80-year-old doddery pensioners. The allotment had been methodically tilled, paths were laid out, dividing the oblong into 24 equal plots; two sheds were in course of construction, everything pointed to a recent event, nothing old whatsoever.

John pointed at what looked like a grave was set away from the oblong.

'Are there any fit men in this gaggle of oldies?' Martin pushed a different photo in front of Partridge, 'have we a resident list with ages?'

Partridge fished out a document, putting on his glasses, 'According to these recorded ages, most of the plots must be being dug by the over 85s.' He was now annoyed, convinced he had been duped and the alleged residents moving about the house were "forgeries", was his expression, suspicions had turned into certainties, Martin believed John Anderton was right, Partridge had caught the Prince of Wales's influenza, this realisation making Walserval a very unsafehouse; to get backing for a full-scale raid in the US area of authority, he must first prove it to Tracker and then convince the Americans, a raid of this magnitude required "the Marines", who were thirsting for revenge after the death of their men on the Queen of St Gilgen.

Martin was in favour of flying a plane over it. Partridge wanted to send the girls on a blackberry picking jaunt, John Anderton favoured a more sophisticated approach—send a letter in from a relative of a resident, or from Helga or Rondel's wife and agreed to keep thinking about what the letter should say.

Conscious that the raid on the "Queen of St Gilgen" had been an exciting failure, with two Marines killed, and as Walserval was outside their operational boundaries Martin wondered whether they bring in their own men from the north and mount a raid purely from their own resources. 'Tracker wouldn't see General Urquhart without conclusive evidence,' he concluded.

'Who needs evidence,' said Partridge, 'why not just go in and sort it out, pretend they're Poland.'

'Good point, well made!' said Martin scornfully. 'What I need to know is, how does Muller and his wife communicate with Strasser, we need to raid when we know that Strasser's on the premises? Let's go and talk to Tracker.'

Tracker was in two minds, netting 30 or 40 high ranking SS and their wives at one swoop would be the coup he needed to gladden his statistics, and polish his reputation with his bosses in London. Walserval was miles outside "his area", and he was reluctant to ask the Americans to lead, particularly after two marines had been killed on the "Queen of St Gilgen", but he had to do something. Pontius Pilate washed his hands, Neville Chamberlain flew to Munich and waved a piece of paper, doubting Thomas Travers needed a higher level of proof before he risked his neck.

Standing in the entrance hall, Martin and John Anderton conferred, for a successful fraud you have got to get rid of the paperwork, the proof lies in the paperwork. Strasser hadn't been able to quite do that, 24 hours later Anderton had linked the deaths from the bombing raid at the Old Folks Home near Augsburg, with the names shown on the ration lists for Walserval. Partridge had visited the village near to Walserval and had seen two locals who he remembered had been at the apartments days earlier. Tracker now had no excuse to delay, the proof was there and he determined to nail down backing for a raid.

He issued an invitation, six brown horses, two pony and traps carried a high-spirited party from the US Base on a tour of the Hunting Lodge Estate, The Meissen dinner service laid out in the grand dining room, was best Fortnum and Mason, which more than can be said for the food that graced it, but the Berncastel and the bottled beer from two Bamberg breweries (someone had found space in a NAAFI truck) was pulled out of the lodge's own mountain stream, and the

Macallan, poured hours earlier, sat gleaming in the sparkling cut glass. The bottom line, Barney and Martin would liaise and plan in detail an assault on Walserval, the Americans would process the prisoners, Tracker could have the first shot at the statistics before a spot of double counting transferred the prisoners to the American compound.

Then came the difficulty, they couldn't agree on a code word. All agreed the word should be memorable, all agreed it should have a purposeful insider hint, unrecognisable to the enemy, the difficulty was that Barney wanted the code word to carry a US identity, Travers for it to be recognisably British. The code word adopted was Tuba City. *{The reader is left to work that one out.}*

Martin, John and Partridge spent the morning at Gmunden, Barney would have bugs planted in the transport and the depot sending out the rations, aerial photos from 2,000 feet were unlikely to raise suspicion. Surveillance on vehicles moving out from Rothstein would be discrete, by the following Tuesday, the day pencilled in for the raid, they should know all they needed to know. There would be a helicopter as back-up, armed this time with different calibre weapons and orders to shoot if necessary. As Partridge remarked on the journey back, 'all we need now is for an armada to sail in down the river.'

Sunday was the day to draw up final plans, no way was Martin going to antagonise Barney by insisting on his preferred timetable, the main point of decision wrapped around what time of day. He started with the Partridge theorem 'hit 'em hard, hit 'em early, but this met US resistance… 'If we move at 6 am, that means we've got to get the armourers and the helicopter engineers up at 2 am, and we're going to be moving troops through towns and villages at a disturbingly early time when citizen's antennae will be tuned in, perhaps we'd be better to do it casually at midday. We'll hit 'em over lunch.'

It was an unusual Tuesday morning, the air was so sultry and still, Martin sat on the top of his bonnet, and his jeep sat on top of the hill. The kick off was sharp at 12.30, and as soon as he had watched the ration lorry drive past his old school in Rothstein, a lorry carrying a hidden radio recorder. Tracker Travers had cleared the British share of the operation, with a distant Urquhart, the intelligence, which was the entire British contribution, fingers crossed, just had to be right.

The death of two men from the earlier enterprise with the British, meant General "Robin" Hood had had to change his nomenclature of the previous operation from "Combined Training Exercise", to "exploratory recce", he was not going to treat this latest "rumble" as an exercise, and had ordered "overkill". Two columns he decreed, from north and south were to converge on Walserval, timed to arrive with parachutists dropped inside the bend of the river directly opposite the house; this was to prevent escape by boat. Barney would lead the attack from a "Sheriff", an armoured car complete with inside toilet, designed to ferry Generals in safety to their front lines. This "Sheriff" had seen action from Tunisia, through Sicily and Italy, it had been used by General Mark Clark and still had its original paint "sahara sand", and thought was given as to whether it should be repainted "German green".

Half an hour after he'd watched the ration truck disappear, the radio crackled, Martin jumped off the bonnet, and at 20 mph, he led five vehicles in the direction of Walserval. A mile from their target, 30 yards short of a white-washed cottage, they passed a man bestride a brown horse. A minute ahead of time they stopped and waited. The horse turned into the garden and the man with a false hand climbed down and disappeared.

The timing was perfect, the columns arrived together for the last hundred yards to the House, parachutists glided slowly down without a sound in the heavy air, men hidden in a circle half a mile away stood up, their task to spot and stop any escapers. The picture before Barney was unexpected, before his men had jumped down from the lorries, instead of tranquillity, men were running from the house towards the barn, up from behind the barn other men came running, entering through a side door. These men carried rifles and machine guns, belts of ammunition draped around their shoulders.

Orders are orders and Tuba City was swamped with instructions, the main contingent of Marines were under instruction to surround the house to prevent escapes. The assault force, would burst into the apartments and enforce a total lock-down. They turned abruptly as a burst of machine gun fire came from inside the barn, peppering the "Sheriff". Without waiting for an order, a marine pulled the cover off his bazooka and kneeling, pointed it down the side of the lorry, covering fire giving him the illusion of protection; the darkened barn gave the panting men inside the illusion of safety. The bazooka wrecked the machine gun position, setting fire to straw bales stacked in a corner. Automatic fire from the task force support group wiped out several defenders who were visible, who had forgotten about personal safety, and stood firing from the hip. The Americans were so well-armed and primed to attack that protracted resistance was futile and it quickly petered out, even so it was 15 minutes before marines moved forward towards the white handkerchief thrown minutes earlier out of the barn door.

'We've fucking missed out again,' parachutists strung out along the other side of the river bank, thirsty for action left their extended covering positions along the river Ebbs and converged opposite the barn, some firing bursts into the side of the barn on the run.

Barney had gone in mob handed, no one had expected resistance on this scale. Cautiously the marines called for the defenders to come outside and it wasn't till they had done so and thrown out their weapons that they approached the men, not till they were certain there was no further resistance to come from the barn, did they enter and herd all the survivors out into the open, lining them up at gun point against a wire fence bordering a field.

Barney stood on the top of the sheriff for the best view, and to show courage and determination for the photographer. Resistance over, the barn silent, smoke drifting from a damaged roof, he enquired about casualties, Corporal Chappel had burned his hand on the bazooka, and was deaf from the explosion, but apart from minor scratches and burns his men had escaped unscathed. The wounded Germans were made to lie on the ground and wait for attention. The first attention they received was from the film unit, who moved to them after shots of Barney standing on top of the Sheriff, the bazooka posed again by Corporal Chappel, arms and blood lying on the floor of the barn, were safely in the can.

'Get yourself in there,' muttered Partridge giving Martin a push, 'make it look as much like an UK operation as we can—we should have worn RAF uniforms.'

Martin was torn, he wanted to get inside and enquire about Strasser and Muller (Helga's message had been specific—Strasser and Ritter will be visiting Walserval on Tuesday). He managed to conjure up a photo opportunity by picking up the bazooka before popping a pain-killer into the mouth of one of the injured.

'Will that do?' preceded Partridge's profane 'Jesus Christ!' raising his arms in exasperation as the film crew ignored his propping up an injured German. His was the sole British Army Uniform on view.

The prisoners were made to stand with their hands behind their heads, until one by one, electrical cable clips were clipped around their wrists and their pockets emptied into a kit bag for scrutiny later. The main body of men could now turn their attention to what lay inside of the apartments, Martin following Barney.

The short stormy battle had been witnessed from the apartment windows, indeed several witnesses became widows even as they watched. The marines urged to be careful, 'Work in pairs, take no risks,' the search began, every room ransacked, every piece of jewellery not worn on a person, disappeared, every watch, every clock, every camera, every handbag was seized "for inspection", any woman protesting was slapped, screams brought further slaps to silence. It was the "Rape of the Sabines" without the rape, Partridge, who saw no reason to hold back, slapped more women than "soft mick" as he called it… a field day.

Barney ordered his men to get the women outside, where they were allowed to attend and talk to the wounded, go into the barn and attend to the dead. Two teams systematically began the re-inspection of the house, any "lurchers" were to be blindfolded, tied up, and brought to the reception area. Barney himself led inspection of the cellars running the length of Block A. At the end of it all, six trussed up bodies stood in the hall, waiting for the return of Barney and Martin. Five women, one man. It took no time at all for Martin to tell Barney, 'That's Muller, we want him.' Taking Muller by the arm, he led him into a side room where as the blindfold was removed he asked, 'Remember me?'

Blinking, 'I certainly do, you're Cohen,' Muller visibly breathed out as if a weight had fallen from his shoulders.

'Yes, I'm Cohen, we met at Menzenschwand; the last time we met, you were lying in a ditch at Pont Celere, covered in blood as I remember, how are you now?'

'OK.'

'When we find your wife, Ingrid, isn't it, we're all have a talk, in the meantime it will save time if you tell me where I can find Strasser and Ritter, they were supposed to be here.' Muller's answer had the immediacy of truth.

'Strasser didn't arrive. If we're all lucky, you'll find Ritter among the dead.'

'Well, we aren't lucky so far. I've checked.'

'He was here in the office with me less than an hour ago, he must have hidden or he's got away.'

'What about Colonel Strasser?' Muller shook his head, 'he never arrived.' The confirmation that Ritter had been there so recently made Strasser's no show all the more perplexing and annoying. Before starting a further search, Martin asked

Barney to identify Frau Ingrid Muller and keep her separated. With four men, he and Partridge began searching the Barn, then the part-built sheds over by the Allotments, where they brought back and handed over, two shivering men. Returning to the house, he was intercepted by Jon Anderton who'd overheard a woman say that Ritter had escaped in the skiff which was kept tied up on the River Bank; hurrying there, loose ropes showed that this was entirely probable.

'Where were the bloody paras, they were supposed to be guarding the river?' Martin was cross.

'They moved up opposite the barn,' a reply he knew to be fact.

'Let's eat,' they found the 'chuck wagon', sausages beans and fried tomatoes never tasted better as they discussed events. Following the plan for "Tuba City" Barney decided the women from Block 2 should go to a Holding Camp at Gmunden, coming back for the remainder later. Guards would be placed on the house and grounds, he'd had the para lieutenant brought across the river and he played hell with the young man who had regarded the fire fight and the move upstream as more important than blocking the river to catch escapers.

'Ritter's skulled away because you ignored orders.' But as Barney said later 'I could only pretend to get mad, he did it with the best of intentions, he wanted his men to be heroes.'

His engineer had traced that a phone call from a land line had been received minutes before their arrival. The wire traced back to the cottage up the road a mile away. 'That fellow on the horse,' said John Anderton.

'Afraid so,' they echoed.

'Strasser,' said Martin, 'we've missed both Strasser and Ritter.' Barney agreed that Tomas Muller and Ingrid Muller could go back with the British for one night, provided that any information was conveyed back to him in its entirety and they stayed on the American stats.

The return to Ischl took well over the hour, Partridge as expected favoured a heavy approach, Martin was acutely conscious that he had made a V11 commitment to Helga and Gert Muller, he needed to be able to justify that Tomas Muller wasn't involved in anything particularly nasty. Let's eat, it's going to be a long night, despite the beans earlier they wolfed the braised beef and potatoes. The night began acrimoniously, Martin assumed he would question Tomas Muller, one to one, 'I've got the background,' but the others had never seen Martin in such a manic state, and quietly between themselves they decided Martin needed to be saved from himself.

They objected, 'You're too close, too involved,' out faced and recovering somewhat, Martin drew back, he would have his turn later and show them how to get information from a suspect. He would listen in, with John Anderton having first crack at Muller, whilst Partridge frightened the life out of Ingrid,

'Don't forget, all I'm interested in is you getting me Strasser,' the other two shut their ears. Abandoning an interrogation, they decided to have a night's sleep instead.

Partridge didn't have to shout, Ingrid Muller answered every question, she didn't think she was a war criminal, she hadn't been a guard at Ebensee, and she had heard that a Form V11 would be available, hadn't she. Interview finished before 40 minutes were up. Partridge sidled into the questioning of Tomas Muller, much to the annoyance of Martin couped up uncomfortably listening in a cupboard in the corner of the room. John Anderton was a professional, always in control, he began at the beginning, gave Muller time to think, and time to contradict himself. Meticulous when met with a half-truth he approached the same point from a different angle, bringing the lie into the open. Muller quickly realised Anderton was clever and held the top cards.

By concentrating on the Ebensee duties, the transport arrangements for the labour camps, the requisition of food and supplies, he brought Muller to realise that proof of such participation threatened his very life, particularly when associated with the setting up and running of safehouses. Muller and his wife Ingrid's only chance of survival was for Mr Cohen to make out form V11, and persuade General Robin Hood to validate it. There was only one way to get that signature, Sergeant Muller must tell everything he knows about everything, but in particular what he knows about Colonel Strasser and his safe-houses.

'Can't Mr Cockburn just sign it himself?' Muller asked anxiously.

'Certainly, he can, but a V11 needs an American and a British countersignature and a Validation Seal in front of an Accredited Person, quite a process I can tell you, but let us leave that and go on first to consider Herr Ritter; dozens of people have told us that he proposed to explode half of Ebensee mountain down onto the caverns where all 10,000 of the foreign labourers were to be congregated and crushed to death... for one reason only so that your monstrosities would never be found. We know Ritter was with you when you escaped across Wolfgangsee in the launch with Colonel Strasser, we know he has a hide up on the Dachstein, Haute

Peignoir I hear it's called, you've confirmed he probably escaped in a skiff down the river Ebbs at Black Barn or Walserval as I call it, I know he's acted as enforcer for Strasser, and comes and goes on the Dachstein. Where will he have gone now is the question?'

Martin put his ear against the door.

'If I knew I'd tell you, he's a horrible man, he'd kill me if he so much as finds out I'm talking to you, I don't know where he is, but I can give you two possibilities.'

'Go on,' John Anderton knew they were approaching a crunch point, if Muller informed on Ritter, he would inform on Strasser.

'Ritter will stay close to Strasser.'

'Why should he, what's the link?' Anderton asked.

'Strasser saved his life. There's an umbilical cord between them, Ritter was to be disciplined by the SS for something he did to a woman, the daughter of general; it was serious. Strasser flew him out to an einsatzgruppen in the Ukraine overnight, out of the way, and the charge was never followed up. Then he had flew him flown back.' Anderton grunted. 'Staying close to Strasser means he will be either at Dilsberg, or in his hideaway on the Dachstein.'

Anderton pushed a map across the table, pointing with a pencil… 'Is that the Dilsberg?'

'There are others.' Muller confirmed it was Dilsberg on the River Neckar near Heidelberg. 'Strasser has control of a family house there, he only allows leaders there. Artur Axmann, youth party leader who came out of Berlin with him, has gone there to stay only recently, but there are others I know, he uses the address Waldteufel.'

'Axmann, the Hitler Youth Leader, we're certainly on the lookout for him, we've had a signal that he escaped with Bormann from Berlin. Do you know anything about that?' Anderton wondered whether he should have given this information.

'Yes, the other possibility is a house derelict in the Black Forest, just a name, no address. It's being repaired, Ritter bought building materials from a firm in Freudenstadt, they'll know the address, I wasn't involved.'

'I'll need you to remember that firm after we've had a break,' said Anderton. He looked at Partridge, who led Muller away. Martin stepped out of the cupboard, rippling his muscles, 'Well done, John, getting there, slow, but getting there,' turning towards Partridge who had returned, 'Get anything out of Ingrid?'

'Anything and everything she knows about all the SS and Nazis in the apartments, she'll tell the Yanks, but she knows very little about Strasser, she hates Ritter, but so does everybody; just one thing, Ritter prides himself as a cook and has a signature stew with an ingredient he gets from a farm shop in Goisern it's called Gentian balsam, he is never without a bottle of the stuff, and he's running low, if we have surveillance on that farm shop we might catch our man. It's a long shot.'

'Martin, now you've simmered down, you must ask the questions on Strasser,' Anderton said, a cup of tea in front of him, 'I don't fancy 24/7 hour surveillance on a country farm shop waiting for Gentian balsam.'

'At last, yes definitely,' Martin had returned to the land of rationality. 'But I want you both in on it.'

When Muller was brought back in, he was more relaxed than before, and appeared almost happy to be met by Martin as if his friendly relationship from Menzenschwand would continue. Martin brought him to earth by reminding Muller that his life depended on his catching Ritter and Strasser from the intelligence he Muller supplied.

'Let's recap we had a good relationship before I escaped from Menzenschwand Camp, we were on opposite sides of the road in the hijack at Pont Celere, Strasser helped you escape from hospital in Switzerland, I spoke to you in your Salzburg office, or was it Munich, I've forgotten, that was after Colonel Strasser shot me in the stomach. As Mr Anderton has explained, your life is now in my hands,' Martin spoke through clenched teeth.

'You were warned soldiers were coming to Walserval minutes before we arrived, who warned you?'

'Strasser.'

'How?'

'Land line telephone from Churn Cottage.'

'How did Strasser know?'

'He must have seen your lorries on his way.'

'Does he ride a brown horse?'

'Both he and his friend Anna have brown horses.'

'Why was he coming to Walserval?'

'A fortnight since he was last here, he was concerned at the suicides, and probably wanted to check on how me and Ingrid were running it.'

'How did you know he was coming?'

'He had arranged a message service through the village milkman and the milkman's customers, so that different telephones can be used. The cows depend on us selling their milk, you know,' a jaunty remark from one threatened with death.

Martin turned to the wider use of safe-houses, and the properties owned of controlled by Strasser. Muller confirmed that although the farm in Bad Aussee was regarded as his main home, he wouldn't likely go there because it was too obvious and his relations lived there and looked after the farm, furthermore the railway station was a long way away and, the trek up the hill arduous. Too many people knew it was his. He was sure Strasser hadn't used the farm as shelter—but it was there as a backstop if he needed it. The "Lady of St Gilgen" was intended to be Strasser's own safe haven, mainly because he really liked the idea of living dangerously on the lake, but the customers who had seen it thought it was too risky. Partridge corrected him to 'Queen of St Gilgen, is there a Lady as well?' Muller shook his head the customers were right, it was risky, the steamer had been betrayed and raided in no time at all.

Martin had questions covering the raid on the Queen, Muller confirmed that just like Walserval, the warning had come from an army landline from a house up the road, 'Seydlitz was slow getting out of bed, then he was afraid of the jump to the launch, leaving it so late he didn't make it and fell in the lake, Strasser wouldn't turn back to pick him up, the soldiers would have shot up the launch, after that the American's never got close enough to fire, we were headed for St Wolfgang, when Strasser had the idea of heading for the railway where Ritter thought there was a car to be hijacked, it was just lucky that the train was leaving, it certainly wasn't planned, after we jumped off it, Ritter led us to a woodcutter's hut .We hid till dark and then went down to

St Wolfgang, someone at the hotel there fixed us up with clothes and transport. After that we split.'

'Where did Strasser go?' Martin wanted to know.

'That's another mystery, he never said, but he went north from St Wolfgang, probably Salzburg, or Munich, he had an official apartment in the Palace, but by that time it would be too dangerous to go there.'

'How many were on the Queen when we raided?' an easy question Martin thought, there was hesitation…

'Four, me, Strasser, Ritter and Seydlitz.' Martin banged his pencil on the desk and looked at John Anderton.

'Then who killed the two Americans posted as guards an hour later?' Anderton asked. 'Seydlitz was under lock and key and you were half way up the Silberhorne.' There was an uncomfortable silence.

'I didn't know anyone had been killed, it must have been Anna, Anna Fitzweiler, Strasser's friend.'

'How did she get there?' Martin asked.

'Strasser was constructing a hide past the engine room, she must have hidden there,' came the hesitant reply. Partridge stood up, thrust his nose in Muller's face.

'How did she get there, that was the question? Was she on the boat all night?' Muller nodded.

'Then you lied to us, there were five on the Queen.'

'Where would she go when she left the boat?' shot John Anderton. Words now tumbled out as Muller tried to recover lost ground.

'She has her own apartment near the palace, I never went, I only know it's luxurious, Strasser doesn't do cheap.'

He explained Strasser had called them to a meeting on the Queen, to consider what to do about the ruined and abandoned

Black Forest Manor House, Seydlitz was there because he had provided Strasser with money for property and was anxious to be safe and accepted as still, important enough to be allowed to live at Dilsberg, Ritter was to take over the Black Forest renovation, by bringing in Germans willing to work to make the house habitable, in return for food and accommodation. The details were to be agreed that morning, after Strasser had spoken to his banker, yes, the banker is at a bank in Berne.'

'You spoke of the mysteries, what were the other second mysteries?' again John Anderton had picked up a point.

By this time Muller had regained confidence, the apprehension at fighting for his life had receded; he leant forward as if to draw them all into the mystery:

'This is a real mystery; it was near the end of last month, so much has happened it seems years ago, the war was lost, everybody knew that. Everybody wanted to get as far away from Berlin and as far away from the Russians as they could, when out of the blue Strasser calls us all into his office. 'Get this, do that,' he's going that night to Berlin, to the Fuhrer bunker. No one believed him at first, it was crazy, but he was, he got out his General's uniform, a uniform he never wore, preferring to be known as just a colonel—to keep a low profile—he told me. He had a single-seater plane fixed up for him at Anheim, the nearest airfield to Berlin, there weren't any fighting planes still there. Without genuine papers for entry to the bunker, his staff put together a batch of old passes and papers, his driver took the last of the petrol, drove him to Anheim and he flew himself into Berlin. Why? No one ever knew, and I still don't know, other than saying 'it's my duty', he never said a word, but it wasn't because he loved or was loyal to Hitler, because I can tell you for a fact, he didn't and wasn't.'

'How do you know?' asked Partridge.

Muller shrugged his shoulders as if to say "don't be ridiculous", 'In private, he never ever said a good word about Hitler, when he was with other SS people he just mouthed the right words as if he was a politician, even when the news was good and we were winning, why change when we all knew we'd lost the war,' he went on.

'Over 10 days later he re-appeared, unshaven, in peasants clothes with Artur Axmann, by then the Americans were here, any man on the streets were arrested, Axmann went off to Dilsberg, Strasser stayed in Salzburg finishing off arrangements staying with Anna I believe, but now without a hundred clerks at his beck and call.'

'Didn't he say anything at all about his trip to the bunker, did he actually get in?' Martin sounded incredulous.

'Oh, he said plenty, but he didn't say anything about why he went, he told us he saw Hitler and Eva Braun's body carried out to be burned, he told me about everybody dancing and drunk, how nauseated people were with Goebbels and Magda poisoning their children, making them outcasts. He was mad at a couple of tank commanders who left them. He told us that Bormann was in their escape group and was killed by a Russian bullet, but Axmann told Ritter that Strasser had shot Bormann because he was injured and couldn't keep up. Strasser led them out of Berlin, but it was Axmann who brought them south. Don't forget Strasser doesn't really tell lies, if he says Bormann's dead, Bormann's dead, whether it was a Russian bullet I don't know.'

'How did they manage to get out?' he was asked.

They wriggled and just walked through the Russian lines, then out through the British Zone. It was Axmann who got them back through Germany, apparently he's knows every youth group in the country. They passed them like a parcel down the Rhine and the Main. He's grateful to Axmann, and I'm sure his putting him into Dilsberg is the reward.'

'But what's the address in Dilsberg, surely you've some idea?'

'Sorry, I've never been and I've no idea except it might be called Waldteufel and that it's in the walls, but every house in Dilsberg's in the walls.' Martin switched tack, it should be easy to find Anna's apartment in Salzburg, it shouldn't be too difficult to locate a recently purchased mansion in the Black Forest, an urgent visit to the farm at Aussee was priority, but when even Muller didn't know many details Strassers security had been tight and effective.

'What are Strasser's habits, what is he fond of, does he go to the same doctor, the same hairdresser?

'He doesn't socialise, he loves riding his horse, he never shops; Anna does that for him and only buys the best. A bit of a dandy really. He's been to the Cascade Restaurant at Eberbach on the Neckar a few times; he likes the river and their grilled trout with turmeric and kirsch, he usually drinks Bernkastel white.'

'Where's Eberbach?'

'Near Dilsberg, that's why I mentioned it, he eats there at least once a month, certainly every time there's anything to celebrate, his birthday for instance.'

'Which is…?'

'The 17th of June.'

'What about family, I know that Hitler had his brother shot, and that the other older brother Otto, writes diatribes about Hitler, his cousin, his tax and money frauds and his sex life in the foreign press.'

'His parents are dead, they were a wealthy Prussian family who moved to Munich, probably from that he has a fondness for fine clothes, I know for a fact that he used to get all his sporting clothes from an island called Tweed, he has a sister, called Edda, she never visited the palace but he kept in regular touch—she lives in Munich. She could have taken him in, I'm sure.'

'Is she called Strasser?' Anderton wanted to know, but though Muller knew she didn't use the name Strasser, he couldn't remember what particular spelling of "Schmidt" was used. 'It was a name like that.'

Martin returned again to the house in Dilsberg, how long had he owned it, how big did he think it was, was it for pensioners or just the important. Muller didn't know and they ran out of questions. One final word before Muller was led away:

'Getting your V11s depend on my finding Strasser and Ritter, if you think of anything else that will help, tell me tomorrow.'

Chapter 13
Three Ways to Skin a Cat

Whilst Muller was coughing, Strasser had moved to stay with his sister, Edda, his only sister Edda, the only confidant Strasser had ever needed; she knew his plans, his weaknesses, shared his aspirations, his enemies and his thoughts. Each anniversary of brother Gregor's killing, their brother Otto, from the USA or London placed a covert advert in the Munich weekly paper, to let them know he was alive, not where he was living—that would have been much too dangerous, as through the 30s he had continued to mount press attacks on Hitler, chronicling the Fuhrer's sexual history, and his rabid hatred of the Jews. After each anniversary, Hans and Edda met to remember Gregor's death, bring each other up to speed with what had happened, before going on to talk about old times and rekindle their hatred of Hitler and the henchmen who had been his instruments in trying to destroy the entire family.

Brother Otto survived because he was overseas on the 'Night of the Long Knives' when Gregor, Rohm and over a hundred political opponents of Hitler were killed.

Strasser had always told Edda about other slights and injuries; the colleague who slammed down the hatch causing the amputation of his hand, escapees from his Camps, which he took as a personal affront endangering his status, he shot them "pour encourager les autres", he related in particular, how one, Cockburn, an Airman, an escaped Prisoner of War, had bugged a Syndicate meeting held up in the mountains at Psalm, penetrated German Security and co-ordinated the allied embassies in Berne to ambush the convoy transporting l the syndicate's treasure and make off with millions of marks worth of 'his pension' held in the form of gold, art and objects (Dresden and Meissen table tableaux being his favourites. 'I expected Cockburn to die after I shot him in the stomach at Schaufhausen, but I now know he survived and he's leading **The Hunt for Colonel Strasser** so I'm told, he had the cheek to ring Sergeant Muller and threaten me, this isn't the last of this business.'

Together they regretted the failure of the "Valkerie" plot to kill Hitler, Strasser telling how he'd been summoned to drag up the case against Rommel, 'He was guilty right enough,' but that still left the prime task of exacting revenge for the death of Gregor and the scattering of the Strasser family. Edda Sommer was in no doubt that her and her brother's desire for revenge still burned deep.

As spring is sprung so daylight hours lengthened, and the days remaining till the fall of the Reich lessened, Major Reisinger insisted that his wife move into his Walserval's pentlet to prepare for the day when it would be safe for him to slip quietly away from administration at the Munich HQ Offices without arousing the attention of the SS and join her at Walserval. This message passed along the chain to

FrauMuller at Walserval, a messaging system, via the phone, the milkman and the milkman's customers.

Ingrid had worked feverishly to have the empty apartments ready, now with time on her hands, just a handful of proper pensioners to look after, she was excited, hoping her first "guest" would be a "celebrity". Never far away from the entrance, she waited to welcome her first tenant, their pentlet clean, stove alight. A lorry, belching smoke from the mixture of odd chemicals poured into its fuel tank, brought the quota of personal belongings allowed, but "quelle disappointment": overweight, no make-up, heavy rimmed glasses, bossy, the only "celebrity quality" was the middle-aged fur coat, hat, scarf, gloves and shoes, everything was middle-class, the new arrival even accepted help to climb down from the passenger seat. 'My husband will be here in a few days,' were Frau Reisinger's first guttural words. She was however to prove to be a valuable tenant, her initial appearance being deceptive.

Radio broadcasts now stated clearly that the Russians had reached the outskirts of Berlin, stressing pride in the Fuhrer being personally engaged in the organisation of the defenses, no longer did the serious newsreaders report advances, or claim major successes, no longer did they forecast victory in any dimension, they concentrated on highlighting acts of individual bravery, and warnings of the horrors the Russians would bring if national solidarity and resistance failed.

Following one particular Friday evening broadcast when a hollow note was struck, couples throughout the land still able to communicate, talked long and hard without censorship, they spoke of undying love, of cruelty rape and hardship, and failure, those with freedom of movement, considered where to go, planning unwelcome steps into the unknown.

This protracted radio broadcast brought immediate repercussions. Horse driven vehicles splashed down the drive to Walserval, whipped by drivers as uncertain of the route as were the horses and the fearful wives. Relief was palpable as the strong Ukranians helped unload, relief as Frau Muller led then to a warm apartment, before they turned the horses round, driving the carts back to Rothstein's railway stables, then to walk the miles back to Walserval, where wives, warm in the kitchen, had potato soup and vegetable stew waiting.

Over the soup, the relieved tenants held their first inquests, 'It's warm here, and there's plenty of wood, the water's soft, the plumbing works, but not much space in the bathroom. You must get yourself an allotment.' Husbands were mostly silent.

'Frau Muller has given me our rations for next week.' Without doubt the pentlets met with relief and approval, Walserval was so deep in the countryside, not overlooked, there was no need to stay indoors, they could go outside in daytime and feel safe and free.

Ingrid Muller, always on hand was bombarded with questions and concerns about security, food, activities and some about "the better houses". None knew where they were, but all believed there was one. General Reichenau, Martin Bormann, Streicher, Frank, Seyss-Inquart were just some of the names rumoured to be going to live there. Ingrid couldn't tell them as she didn't know. Dilsberg was a puzzle wrapped in an enigma held close, not to be divulged even to the colonel himself.

Muller liked being in command, his wife and the Ukranians did the physical work, his main duties were attending to arrivals, security, allocation decisions and adjudicating on disputes. Wary and anxious to show Strasser they were doing a good job, away from the horrible Ritter, delighted at being left on his own, he showed his importance, by visiting the pentlets regularly to get to know the occupants, who had all had bigger jobs than his own, to answer the questions that had been directed at his wife. Following the arrival of still more "guests", he called a group meeting on his own initiative.

After breakfast, he visited each pentlet, he had procured a fitment for each bathroom. Like Father Christmas he handed over to the wife a packaged new towel rail for her bathroom. easy to install for some husbands, a nightmare for others; by evening all the towel rails had been installed, mutually accomplished by a mixture of borrowed tools, cooperation, competence, and unbelievable incompetence from men who could push a pen but not an awl. Two of the Ukranians became heroes.

New bonding and hatreds had been formed. At 8 pm, they gathered in the reception/entrance hall, Muller sat behind a table before the locked front door, flanked by Frau Ingrid Muller and the Ukranians, who waited on till everyone was seated, wearing printed name badges on blue and white caps, modelled on the spa hotels of Baden Baden.

Introductions over, Muller began by stressing that they were all in danger of capture by the Allies, their common enemies, but their biggest danger came from people who talked too much; just as a chain is as strong as its weakest link, so they were only as safe as the most careless security blunder.

In different ways all their families were risks, whether it was communications with parents, children or former colleagues. No written security instructions had yet been prepared, the meeting was to outline the written instructions which were soon to follow. In particular, he set out the security precautions, management (he was instructed that Strasser's name was never to be used) had taken on their behalf. He stressed security guidelines and obligations, Herr Ritter would later speak on this and the sanctions that would follow breaches of security, the least of which were fines. As he was finishing with the actions should the military visit, there was a sharp sequential patterned rap on the front door behind him, Ingrid moved around the desk to open it. Framed was Colonel Strasser. 'No one on guard,' he muttered, but everyone heard.

Blinking, he moved into the Hall as Muller got up to greet him, but Strasser had summed up the situation. 'Carry on' Muller,' he moved to the back of the Hall and leant silent against the wall. Expressionless, motionless, he did nothing whilst Muller brought his talk to a somewhat lame conclusion finishing with the limitations and the opportunities at Walserval, preparing them for trial security alerts, and that fines were the least of the punishments for security lapses. Questions were taken and answered, Muller saw the signal; Colonel Strasser wanted to speak to him.

Colonel Strasser went into the office Muller followed him, but before disappearing he made a brief announcement, stressing the importance of everyone sticking rigidly to the irksome restrictions placed on them and saying that three houses controlled by the entirely separate Black Forest Sports and Leisure Hotel Group, had already been raided by the Americans, and over 100 colleagues arrested. Walserval was more secure, security only came with vigilance and a cost in money.

Colonel Strasser's brown horse clattered off back down the lane on the stroke of midnight. A mile up the road a farm hand was sitting smoking a pipe of dried grass, invisible and silent by a gate, handing the horse over, going through the gate, sitting in the corner of the field was the Storch.

'I won't be using this much longer, a couple more flights and that'll be it, the tank will be empty,' the farm hand nodded. Strasser took off in the Storch—direction Dilsberg. It needed only 50 metres of rough pasture, so quiet the cows were not even bothered to climb to their feet out of the dewy grass.

'The colonel said we're going to be full, three more coming tomorrow,' Muller told Ingrid, 'that takes up all the empty rooms, he had dropped the expression "pentlets", Ritter is to see about freeing more accommodation, we've to arrange for three of the oldies to go down to Rothstein tomorrow.' The balance of moving proper pensioners out to make way for the fee-paying refugees was a tricky call, 'That'll leave only six original proper pensioners,' said Ingrid.

These three bachelor oldies never returned to Walserval, nor did news of where they had gone or what had happened. None one saw or asked what the Ukranians did with their belongings, certainly no one saw anyone come to collect them, Ritter never spoke of them, but Ingrid was troubled, she had been left out of the loop, and she didn't hesitate to hide her worries from her husband.

One instruction issued was that if officials came to Walserval, only the original pensioners should appear on view, everyone else must hide; it had been arranged that pensioners from the nearest village would be rushed in as "dressing". A trial run went off without a hitch, the villagers being brought in a hay cart—'Just like a wild west film,' said one old boy, and the ersatz coffee and biscuits sufficient reward for the "volunteers", who had time on their hands.

A routine throughout the complex was soon established, within days 12 plots had been allocated in the allotments, these were dug as a collective and the following day 24 hands were being treated for blisters. There was one sprained ankle, three adulterous couples were increasingly happy with their new circumstances, and were honing their channels of communication, and four card schools had been established, providing many hours of quiet rivalry.

Frans Holbein, Apartment 1, had always been a loner; with his wife, he had arrived on day five but was the first to obtain maps of the area, the first to appear in walking boots and lederhosen, the first to take the coldest morning shower, and the first to make ever lengthening walks around the surrounding countryside. Ten days on, Frans Holbein was unluckily picked-up and pulled in by an American patrol; news that quickly reached Walserval via the milk distribution network.

Muller alarmed at this arrest, told Frau Holbein, only after he had warned the colonel, who as a precaution, ordered the village pensioners to be brought into Walserval for the next two days. Two days was the time needed after Holbein's arrest for his throat to be cut. Holbein was found dead in the Concentration Camp Ablution, dead his throat cut, dead in a pool of blood, "Suicide with reservations" was documented by the harassed Chief Surgeon, who had neither the effort nor the desire to specify what his reservations were.

Prevented from attending her husband's funeral at the concentration camp, Frau Holbein refused to continue living at Walserval; promising that her lips would be forever sealed provided money was returned to her. She was bidden farewell, paid off in almost worthless deutchmarks (Walserval didn't issue cheques), driven to the autobahn slipway near Rothstein and with a single case, a single ticket and a tip for the driver, was helped by one of the Ukranians onto the bus for Munich. Another pentlet was now available, and by evening Muller had contacted the next name on the waiting list, who was ready packed waiting to move in.

As the Walserval routines settled, the barn was made water proof, two damaged cars had been brought in to be restored, old motor repair equipment was being renovated, an inspection pit dug, and an engineer group of "apprentices" had formed into a workforce devoting time and effort to improving their knowledge of car engine and body work. For others, the sheltered allotment area behind the wood, was pure joy; away from scrutiny, wives, spring weather, sharing more and more expanding war experiences from the Libyan Desert to the Russian steppes and the Russian winter.

These apprentice gardeners foraged in nearby woodland and quickly collected enough timber to construct huts, and enough to keep stoves fuelled till winter came. One hut was built for shelter and storage, a second as a lean-to animal shelter (they planned to rustle some goats) and a simple latrine. The early back-breaking digging of the top surface had been eased by "borrowing" a horse, paths had been laid, drainage dug, composting and protection to force early crops, constructed. Wives were involved, deciding what proportion of fruit and vegetables to be adopted, segregating organic kitchen waste, selecting and buying bushes and batches of seeds in Rothstein, on rationed visits, the men being embargoed from going into Rothstein.

As well as preparing meals, the women operated a "swop shop", one blob of butter would swop for two spoons of ersatz coffee and so on; as the apartments became ever cleaner, and the evening entertainments became more organised, square pegs emerged, to give the Mullers difficulties.

Prussian Major General von Steinbeck had commanded thousands of troops in the advance through the Ukraine, a lovely man, he wasn't a Nazi, he didn't hate Jews, but his men burned villages, shot fleeing peasants and torched locked churches full of folk seeking sanctuary; he figured high on Russian wanted lists, and he knew it. Superiority sat naturally on his wife's shoulders, she resented living cheek by jowl by Nazi spawn (not that she ever spoke that word out loud). Failing to browbeat her neighbour from playing music on the radio too loudly, failing to discourage her from hanging frilly silk underclothes in full view of the general, and from preventing her neighbour's cat (the only kind of pet allowed) from peeing on her lettuce patch, she took her complaints to Ingrid.

The very next night, the pentlets in Block 2 had their sleep disturbed by the sound of two revolver shots. In the morning Ingrid was traumatised as Frau Steinbeck rattled her door to inform that their enemy, Major Reizlern, had shot himself and his wife Mitzi. Frau Steinbeck handed her the note found on the kitchen table. Ingrid passed everything over to her husband, Tomas passed the details to Strasser who got in touch with Ritter for him to go and "sort it"; Ritter had the Ukranians dig out a single grave in a corner of the allotments, before repainting the pentlet. Tomas Muller consulted on how the deaths should be recorded, and decided to do nothing. SS Major Helmut Rosenstern and his Austrian wife Olga, moved into the pentlet the following day. Two days later a second grave was needed. It was never dug, not wanting to make a body count easy, Ritter had the Ukranians dig the first grave deeper and wider.

On the following Thursday, Walserval had its first security alert, Camberg, a village three km away rang that soldiers had passed and had gone down the dead-end road falsely sign-posted "Walserval". Warning bells, installed two days earlier, rang in the house, the barn and the allotment. Tomas Muller sent out an urgent call for the pensioners from the village to get in as quickly as possible, four minutes before they arrived on the hay cart, two Bedfords carrying GI's front and rear, with a car carrying a pair in civilian clothes pulled to a stop before the entrance. This wasn't a raid, it was a random visit.

Ingrid's mien was welcoming, nervousness hidden behind a façade, nothing was to be seen of Tomas or the four Ukranians, Ingrid herself didn't know where they were. The Inspectors behaved pleasantly. Introducing themselves as mere functionaries, tasked with ensuring Allied orders were being followed, particularly rationing procedures, Ingrid produced details of the charity inhabitants, the ration documents, and the invoices listing the rations received, explaining that because of their isolation they drew rations centrally and she, herself, distributed food stuffs around the pentlets, against signatures from each pensioner.

Rejecting a glass of cabbage wine in favour of a cup of mulled turnip juice, the Inspectors murmured general satisfaction that food ration documents tallied neatly and completely, but they needed to satisfy themselves, they must compare signatures and verify that the inhabitants had received the food entered on their card. They needed to go into the apartments. Ingrid's heart sank, if only she could guide the Inspectors to the genuine pensioners, all would be well.'

Following instructions, the imported village pensioners who had now arrived, were milling about the hall and corridors, all apartment doors locked. The Inspector first called out 5 names, 4 women and 1 man came forward, one signature didn't match, 'oh Magda signs for me,' she said, 'but I get my stuff all right.'

'Where's Magda?'

'Down in the village.' someone called out. It was left at that.

The Inspectors called a further three names, needing to see the kitchens, they said, keys were produced, kitchens inspected, women thanked without a check to see that the names called were documented as the tenants of the pentlets inspected. The Germans called this failure to check numbers scrupulously "the English disease".

Speaking to Ingrid, 'Before we go, I want to have a look at all the facilities, I understand you grow your own vegetables,' said an unusually pleasant Partridge. Ingrid took the keys from the cabinet, following as they opened the barn, sheets had been drawn over the cars being refurbished. Five men, holding their breath, froze immobile under the sheets. *No one was around. 'Would you like to see the allotment?' It was a five-minute walk around the rim of the wood. Two old men, hats drawn over their hidden faces were leaning against their spades, not much digging was being done, the Inspectors walked around, passing the fresh earth of the grave, glowering, the old men weren't welcoming and few words were exchanged. The Inspectors passed on, taking a photo of the grave and the patches of ground.

'Thank you again Frau Muller,' said Partridge as he climbed into the Bedford, pulling out his camera and through the back window took a last shot of the house.

Check position of next

Leaving Ritter and Muller to their own devices at Bad Ischl station, Strasser jumped in the back of an empty army lorry where he lay down pulling an old tarpaulin over him; the lorry drove past St Gilgen non-stop to Salzburg, peeping out from under the side canopy, Strasser recognised where he was, when the lorry stopped at a crossing he jumped off, his pockets full of cardboard packets of tea he had found at the back of the lorry. Anna wasn't at home in their "nest". Next morning he burnt the under-waiter clothes the White Horse Inn had provided and after digging in a bottom drawer, dressed like a shop assistant, he walked to his deputy's house. Standing under trees the light Salzburg rain added a sheen to his grey coat. A man of habit, he knew Manstein left at 8.20, but not today. At 9 am he knocked at the door, Frau Manstein opened, gasped and beckoned him in. She couldn't stop talking. He mustn't go to the Palace, they'd all been arrested, so glad to see him.

For the first time since the bunker Strasser felt on his own, not lonely you understand, on his own. No support staff, no guards, he'd let Ritter go to the solitude of the Grand Peignoire, Muller was miles away at Walserval, and an apartment with no Anna. It was not only the US marines who were looking for Anna.

Chapter 14
Dilsberg The First Thousand Years

Tracker, Martin, John Anderton and Partridge drinks at hand, sat in easy chairs around a glowing fire, the evening having turned cold; what could be more pleasant, than discussing an intellectual problem to arrive at a practical method of spending the UK Government's money, without a woman anywhere near to cosset or defer to a superior intelligence. All agreed, Dilsberg was the key to catching Strasser quickly, they were close and there was a good chance that with Strasser there was also a good chance of picking up both Axmann and Ritter, this was so important they couldn't risk another failure.

Martin had pulled out the Michelin, Baedeker, and Fodor guides, he summed the place up for the others; a walled village on a hilly rolling escarpment above woods reaching down to the river Neckar, a thousand years old before you sink a spade to find evidence of earlier occupations, a survivor of the 10 year's war, the Black Death, the 30 year's war, the Plague, the 100 year's war, the Great War, WW1, and it appeared, Hitler's war.

Most of the houses were built into the walls, with the defenders manning the roof tops, the communal well was in the centre of the Green, next to the Village Hall, a youngster at 400 years of age so the carved stone said. The one entry was through a gate built into the Watch Tower, a Tower converted by the original Hitler youth leader Baldur von Shirach and Hitler's decree into a Youth Hostel. Within the walls, at the river end, the church tower peered at, not over, a forest of deciduous trees towards the invisible river Neckar 800 feet below. The absence of a spire was easily explained, Dilsberg didn't advertise.

All recent demographic information had been removed from the Administration Building in Heidelberg, so we don't know who lives or owns property there, he told them. The Americans, it's in their zone, would contemplate a blitz census, with completion within eight hours, but I don't know. A 1929 rating document lists all the houses. The air photos he'd had taken allowed each house to be identified, some houses were too small to be a commercial proposition, but 10 houses along the east wall were the Hollywood area of Dilsberg, much larger and he estimated some might have as many as 12 bed rooms.

'How do we get into the village without attracting suspicion?' The conclusion was they couldn't unless…

Martin remembered, "the girls" had not only collected mushrooms in the recce on Schwarztal, they had unearthed Gert Muller; why couldn't they stay at the youth hostel pretending to be nurses on a day away, they needn't give a reason, say a rambling holiday, 'They'd love it, and it's hardly dangerous.'

Afternoon the following day, four girls in walking gear, hot and sweaty from walking up the long hill, presented themselves at the Watch Gate a wrought iron sign bore the single word "Jugundherbage", they finally found the warden, 'Full, Full.' This was a surprise, the Youth Hostel was indeed full, full, but not with Youth Hostellers, 20 healthy young Americans had decided the Dilsberg Youth Hostel was much more salubrious than their allocated quarters in a school basement in Heidelberg, such was Army Authorities relaxed attitude at war's end that they had got permission to take a lorry, provisions and live there, provided they checked into camp by 8 am each morning. Several GIs were hanging about, and they didn't want "good stuff" going to waste.

So with good will, some rearrangement, as it was for only one night, and as the girls were so tired that the thought of a trek to Eberbach was too formidable… the Americans would have taken them in their lorry, but after a degree of pleading and flickering eyebrows the marines decided to shuffle themselves around and provide the girls with a room to themselves. The bathroom rostered, the girls cooked, the boys walked them around the village, pumped water from the shelter of the ancient well on the green, stood them an evening's inebriation at the one room ale house bar to the annoyance of the regulars, and unbolting the portcullis at seven am on the dot left chastely for duty in Heidelberg. Hair still needing attention, the girls ate a late breakfast, leaving the kitchen stove and the kitchen sink cleaner than it had been since Easter. Locking up they left the key with the grumpy warden.

Before departing, the girls had a leisurely walk around the perimeter, looking for signs of a safe-house. They noted houses with curtains drawn, those that seemed empty. The church door open, they crossed the porch into the gloom where an old woman appeared as if from nowhere, glaring at them, before turning to dusting pews without ever taking her eyes off them; on a query she pointed to the ancient stone baptismal bowl, the altar said it was from 1604, on a faded wooden notice, there was an even older wooden pulpit, "15 metres tall, highest on the River Neckar". Shirley, who was teaching herself German, read from an even more decrepit sign.

'Which is the duke's pew?' The woman turned and pointed to a pew hung with faded curtains.

Turning back, 'I've finished, I'm closing up now,' following after the girls, she closed and locked the church door as the girls sauntered back to the gatehouse, no one to be seen, but with 71 eyes upon them from behind curtained windows.

Martin and Anderton took the girls out to lunch at the Grune Baren, a mock hunting lodge, built at the autobahn junction west of Heidelberg for Group Conferences of the National Socialist Party, he pointed at the antlers of the stag's heads on the wall,

'Stags have ears, assume we can be overheard and bugged here, anything sensitive, whisper it in my ear, or wait till we leave.'

This was a mistake, each girl bent over to kiss his ear. They had listed four "interesting" houses, and relayed such gossip as they had received from the US soldiers, saving the best till last. The marines told them that the "Grand Duke" had come to live in the village, but that was all they knew, it was a duke without a name, still a duke is a duke as the saying goes, and most of the marines had no idea what a duke was. But when Shirley asked the church caretaker, which was the duke's pew, she pointed right away to one at the side near the front, and to Shirley at least this was proof.

There were no house names, numbers were haphazard, the name Waldteufel wasn't seen, but Yvonne thought a woman in a maid outfit was at the door of number 33 when it opened for a few seconds. Yvonne also produced a brochure picked up from church porch, 'the churchwarden woman showed us the pulpit and the altar, but this leaflet says a secret escape tunnel goes out from behind the altar 100 metres under the walls into the woods, the churchwarden didn't show us that or mention anything about it.'

'An escape tunnel, and the woman didn't mention it, that's interesting,' Martin glanced at the brochure. 'Well done, Shirley, well done all of you,' he gave Yvonne a peck on the cheek receiving a bosom to his chest in return.

With John Anderton, Martin poured over the aerial map, the house numbers, the girl's list of houses. They highlighted six addresses including Number 33, but three other numbers were also of prime interest.

They rose to go, the meal was awful. 'Worse than the NAAFI,' was the verdict.

A climb up the hill, as there wasn't a stable in Dilsberg and as the nearest horse farm was three kilometres distant, Strasser had a walk before passing under the Youth Hostel in the gate house before sinking his tired bones into the upholstered banquettes at number 33. Number 33 Dilsberg, Artur Axmann, Ritter, Strasser and Anna Fitzweiler were reunited, planning a period of calm and stability after a hectic and perilous sequence of escapes from Berlin and the Queen of St Gilgen; they were not alone, they were sharing number

33 with the Grand Duke of Saxe-Coburg and Gotha, his wife and servant.

Martin couldn't hide his mounting excitement, 'We're nearly there, I can feel it,' his excitement transferred itself to Anderton, 'Do we ask Tracker to get US approval for a joint raid, or do we follow up on Axmann and the Grand Duke, ourselves, not easy for them to hide a Grand Duke especially with 20 US soldiers living in the gatehouse.' Before any answer came, John put forward his own idea:

'We could watch that Eberbach fish restaurant Muller mentioned, there's no gourmet dining in Dilsburg, in fact there's not even a grocer's shop, there's just a market once a month. Strasser can afford it, maybe he'll take the risk and take the trip into Eberbach. I've been successful a couple of times with tax fraud jonnies dining lavishly in restaurants, criminals can't stay away from restaurants, and for bad criminals, night clubs act like stinking fish in a lobster pot, could be third time lucky, but then Eberbach is a long way to walk for an evening meal.'

Martin wasn't enthusiastic about watching farm shops or fish restaurants, 'Logistics,' he murmured. He was interested in the secret tunnel, musing that if we find where it comes out, we could use it the wrong way round, use it to go up into the church and into the village rather than vice versa, it can't be so difficult to find especially if we borrow some of the Yanks detection equipment, worked an absolutely treat at Kiental, couldn't have done without it.' Anderton wanted to keep the Yanks out, they've already had two of their men killed.

'What about using Limey Arthur, the locksmith we used at Aussee, get him in to go and have a look at the houses on our list, I'll bet money that the house with the best locks is Strasser's, as Muller told us, Strasser only does best.'

They decided on an expedition to search for the tunnel exit in the woods, "can't be difficult to find!", infiltrate their locksmith into the village at night to recce the selected addresses, then after seeing the results, would decide what to do, before approaching Tracker with a plan.

Sunday, climbing the hill from the river, invisible from the village, and sight unseen,10 volunteers without a single army metal detector, searched in the forest below the church, they found the tunnel in less than half an hour, the opening, buried under a pile of loose stones,' It looked so obvious!,' was secured by a padlocked metal grill. Back at the lodge they called in Limehouse Arthur and spelt out the problem and told him what they wanted him to do.

'Do you think you'll be able to open the old church door?' Arthur grinned. 'The grilles at the entrances will be padlocked.' Arthur patted the tool belt around his waist, 'padlocked, kidlocked,' was his comment.

That night Martin and Partridge, Anderton staying with the transport, climbed the hill from the River Neckar, straight to the stones on a route they'd marked. Placing the stones aside, they pointed the torch as Arthur stepped forward.

'This hasn't been opened for ages.' Arthur picked the lock. From the depths of his trousers, he drew out an implement resembling a jimmy, hit the cock of the bolt before drawing it back, next he used the jimmy to free the grille from its moss-filled socket, prizing it open they were in. The tunnel was high enough for a Herefordshire cow and wide enough for two Sandringham pigs, wet moss lined the walls. A second grille, to gain entry to the church was hidden under a chair inside a confessional off the nave in the church it was awkward to move away, clearly designed to get out of the church not to get in.

Arthur needed the torch and four minutes to fathom the locks of the church door, 'Never seen these before, needs oil and a wrench,' he muttered to himself, then later, 'they don't make them like this anymore.'

Moonlight, from the church porch Martin pointed out the houses of interest. 'Don't forget we don't really want you breaking in, we want to know which houses have really good recent security locks, and how quickly you can pick them.' It was three o'clock in the morning, Arthur in stockinged feet walked to the first marked house, in less than 20 seconds he had moved on, another, then another 20 seconds. 'This is the one,' muttered Martin, sure enough it ticked six minutes on his watch, Arthur had disappeared before a shadowy movement and Arthur moved further along.

Arthur returned down the same side of the green, Partridge opened the door slowly to deaden the groaning noise, Arthur stepped inside. 'What you got?' Martin couldn't wait to hear.

'Number 33 was a swine, bars and fancy locks, took me five minutes to get inside. Inside the hall there's an antique wrought iron letter box sitting on an antique desk, with letters reading "Saxe-Coburg-Gotha", all the others houses have bog standard locks, no problem.'

'Good man,' Martin and Partridge patted him on the shoulder. Arthur relocked the church door, not one dog had barked, 'Let's fuck off, I'm freezing,' he said, wrestling to put his shoes back on.

'We should have given you a camera, then we could have shown Trapper,' offered Partridge.

'Never travel without,' Limey Arthur pulled a small camera out of his pocket, 'It's an Iloca 2A, my pride and joy, I'm never without it, I snapped the letter box and a couple of the tricky locks.' Martin fell about. 'Good man, good man,' he kept repeating it to himself.

Martin never really forgave Trapper. Gleefully he developed the negative, gleefully he took it to show Trapper's how clever they'd been, as the next step to planning the raid on Number 33, Dilsberg. Congratulating them, without so much as a word, they were hardly out of the office, before Trapper triumphantly relayed the information about the Grand Duke of Saxe-Coberg-Gotha to London; The hunting lodge received an unbelievably swift response, within minutes held the reply in his hand, it read:

GRAND DUKE SAXE COBURG GOTHA, DO NOTHING, REPEAT DO NOTHING: STAND BY FOR FURTHER INSTRUCTIONS,

Trapper sat on it for three hours before showing it to a Martin incandescent with rage.

'I'm not waiting for London to tell me what to do and risk losing Strasser.' For the first time in their amicable relationship Tracker pulled rank.

'We'll both do as we're told, get a plan ready, find out what's special about this duke, if we haven't got permission in 48 hours I'll tell them we can't wait.'

'I know what's special about the bloody duke, I'll tell you what's special about the duke, I saw him when he came to the POW camp at Menzenschwand, he's a pal of Strasser and he was the head of the German Red Cross, and we all know what bloody good they were at looking after the Polacks.'

In the event a second telegram arrived early the following day:

'G D S C G: take no immediate action with regard to the Grand Duke, repeat take no immediate action. The Honourable Sir Piers Henley is to arrive 1900 hours at Innsbruck Airport, he travels as John Carver and should be met appropriately, with secure accommodation available. He carries CD3 authority and instructions with regard to the treatment and questioning of the Duke and Duchess of Saxe-Coburg-Gotha and their servants.'

Apart from Travers nobody had heard of Sir Piers Henley, to everybody's faint surprise Tracker himself went into the detail of arranging transport. The transport fleet owned by the Bad Ischl municipality, had been appropriated on day two of their occupation. Cleaned inside and out, the mayor's car would collect Sir Piers, Yvonne would drive, Daisy would go as chaperone, and Lord Charles Manners would go as armed escort.

If three people seemed excessive, soon after their arrival, a supply lorry, just one-armed soldier up front, had its provisions thrown out of the back, onto the nearside of the road; renegades had jumped aboard at a traffic signal. The driver and his escort each suffered a deduction from their pay, and from then on Travers ordered two men to accompany the driver on every occasion, He himself marked out the route for Yvonne, stipulating she was not to drive more than two hours continuously.

The mayor's car waited three hours at Innsbruck Airfield before coming in low down the valley, veering from side to side, the Halifax of the King's flight touched down, John Carver the sole passenger, had arrived, he introduced himself as Piers Henley.

Back at Bad Ischl, although Travers was waiting, Sir Piers went straight to bed pleading cold from flying high over the Alps, headache from no pressurisation in the Halifax, and deprivation of sleep. Failing to emerge for 12 hours did little to ingratiate himself with his hosts; Tracker took late advantage of a second-invitation to a jaunt to explore Trieste, Grado and Gorizia, and took himself off, but not before handing welfare arrangements for the visitor over to John Anderton, who immediately upset Martin, by allocating Sir Piers the use of Travers's office.

In his planning to raid Number 33, Dilsberg, Martin's research revealed that the Grand Duke of Saxe-Coburg and Gotha, was one of the many English grandsons of Queen Victoria, but special. Related to the Kaiser, he had been adopted/elected after the turn of the century to fill the vacancy of Grand Duke of Saxe-Coburg-Gotha; from this new elevated position as duke, he supported Germany, first the Kaiser, then Adolf Hitler through two world wars against his native land, support that led to his being vindictively stripped of his English and Scottish titles.

This loyalty to Germany and his royal persona led to the duke being selected to act as escort to first King Edward VIII on his visits to Hitler, and later to Edward as the Duke of Windsor on his kite-flying visit to the 3rd Reich.

Tolerated at first, these later activities made him "persona non grata" to the English Court, the British Parliament and now unpopular with the people and he was quietly stripped of his English Titles, except one, "Steward of the Beacons", which he kept hidden but never used. The loss that rankled most with him was being stripped of the prestigious title of the "Duke of Albany", particularly as he had incorporated "Alban" as one of the Christian names of his illegitimate son.

The duke had enough popular support and presence that despite his English birth, Hitler appointed him commander in Germany of the Red Cross, responsible inter alia for the welfare of POWs and Concentration Camp inmates. Clearly the duke with dual nationality was borderline traitor and a prime target for British suspicion and retribution. By the end of the war Strasser had overall control of all camps in southern Germany, and maintained direct regular contact with the duke, President of the German Red Cross with whom he had had a long friendly relationship.

Martin asked the backroom to enquire about Sir Piers Henley; they produced a thumbnail: "Knighted for services to the BLA, Berkshire Landowners Association, pupil at Eton where his six wicket spell of fast bowling at Lords, won the game against Harrow. Brought up by his Grandmother, Lady Glossop at Norvern Abbey, no brothers, no sisters, no mother or father were named in the reference or in Paget." This threadbare information was the most they could come up with. 'Did Martin want them to do more digging?' Martin concluded that Sir Piers must be a royal bastard from the 1890s, available for delicate jobs and accredited by the Palace.

An early lunch, Martin finally met up with Sir Piers in Trapper's Office.

John Anderton set out the position, with Goering captured, Himmler dead, the next high value Nazis, Axmann, Strasser and Streicher, two were believed to be sheltering with the duke at Number 33, Dilsberg, together with "Butcher Ritter". This house, No 33, formed part of the wall of the 10th Century hilltop village of Dilsberg; the only entrance to the village was through a gate in the wall reached by one single track approach road, however, a secret underground passage led from the church down into the woods above the river Neckar.

Martin outlined the plan, the portcullis was brought down during the hours of darkness effectively sealing the village. In the middle of the night a small force of US and British personnel would enter the village through the secret passage, break into number 33, and take everyone prisoner. The prisoners, except Colonel Hans Strasser, would be taken to the US Interrogation Centre at Gmunden. Colonel Strasser would be brought to Bad Ischl for special interrogation.

Sir Piers asked how big a force, what time of night, what cover to stop escape over the walls and so on. When he seemed to have covered all operational detail he drew back in his chair and rapped gently on the table.

'Gentlemen, I'm afraid your plan cannot go ahead.'

'What do you mean "cannot go ahead"?' Martin, who had been speaking quietly, spoke rudely, 'Not go ahead,' his voice rising, 'Why ever not? These are major criminals, we've been hunting them expressly for weeks. That's why we're here in Bad Ischl.'

'I'm sorry, but I repeat, not possible, verboten, if I may speak in the local tongue.'

'Who're you to verboten it, for what reason, just saying "verboten" isn't good enough.' Martin was challenging Sir Piers's authority with his own, and he was the authority in situ and commanded men with bayonets who would carry out his orders.

'It would be contra to our government's interests.'

'What profit and loss account of interest are they in?' challenged Martin.

'It's not in our Government interest for me to tell you,' although he was wobbling, Sir Piers wasn't letting go.

'If you don't give a reason, you'll have to supply us in writing with a specific order and on whose authority, I repeat in writing.' John Anderton showed which side he was on, continuing:

'If that bastard Ritter gets away from us again, and we strongly believe he's at Dilsberg, you'll have to answer to 10,000 poor sods being nursed back to life at Ebensee, plus the 10,000 already dead, and you'll have to answer to the News of the World as we wouldn't be able to keep it quiet would we boys? Not with the scale of feeling about Ritter.'

'And answer to me, the bastard Ritter made me cut my hand, shooting at us on the Haute Peignoir,' Partridge made the opposition three to one.

Sir Piers didn't do "things in writing", for the last 10 years he'd been doing the bidding of the royals, and the royals never do anything directly, and certainly never ever did things in writing, even when there was no alternative, Ministers ensured this was never reported, as Partridge said, 'It's called democracy.'

Sir Piers had to do something, he knew his name was a red rag to at least one owner of Sunday paper.

'I don't respond to threats, and I don't want to appear pig-headed,' he began

'Then be pig-headed,' Partridge jumped in before Sir Piers had time to spell out his concession.

'Frankly, it's your mention of the American involvement,' Sir Piers quickened up. 'Our Government simply can't allow the Americans to question the Duke and Duchess of Saxe-Coburg-Gotha under duress or at all. The duke was born an Englishman, and technically probably still is, even though he's lived in Germany for 30 years and speaks German. He's been involved in delicate and important diplomatic matters spread back as far back as 1910, many events that are open to misinterpretation, which the Americans might not understand, and which might be leaked to their Wall St, to the detriment of the UK.'

'Barney's as sharp as a knife, he'll understand, he'll keep quiet.' said Anderton. Sir Piers was not to lose his smooth flow.

'I'm not caring whether Barney's as sharp as a bowie, there's even worse,' he went on. 'The duke will be accompanied by the duchess, his wife and servants. Between them they are a cauldron of steaming witches, a cauldron full of 30 years of scandal, royal secrets, English and German state secrets. God knows what they would say, what the Americans would pull out of them under interrogation, and what Uncle Sam knows today the world knows tomorrow, and that includes India, Canada and Australia. John Anderton pulled a half sheet of typescript from his folder and pushed it to Martin, it read:

'Sir Piers's full name is: Piers Edward Alban Maxmilian Charles Henley, the Duke of Saxe-Coburg was stripped of title "Duke of Albany".' Martin took seconds to see the significance of the underlining, then stored it in his memory.

'So, you don't want the Americans to know what the Duke of Windsor agreed when he talked with Adolf Hitler?' Sir Piers inclined his head as a "Yes".

'So ignoring what happened in 1910, you don't want the Americans to know how the special arrangements made for the Kaiser in 1919 happened? Again Sir Piers inclined his head as a "Yes".

'What else do you not want the Americans to know?' Again Sir Piers inclined his head. 'Yes,' adding after a second, 'we don't know what we don't want them to know.' He smiled at his own cleverness, *Wasted on these plebs,* he thought.

'The world knows Windsor treadled around Germany with the duke just before our own war started, I suppose you want to keep his mouth shut about that as well.' Once again Sir Piers inclined his head.

'So, you've no objection to him being arrested so long as the Americans don't take part in the questioning, no objection so long as the Americans don't get their hands on him?'

Sir Piers inclined his head, turning it into a nod.

'Don't just nod your head, man, say it, Yes or No.'

Sir Piers muttered, 'House arrest,' followed by, 'as long as I conduct any interrogation.' He corrected himself 'questioning.'

Martin waited until that had sunk in. 'Oh no, I'm happy for you to be present at all our questioning, of course I am, I'll try to keep the Yanks out of it one way or another, we can fly him out to Osnabruck easily, but if we act whilst the iron's hot, the duke can lead us to other wanted men, and finding them is both my job and in my government's interest.' This compromise: Arrest, questioning, no American involvement was bandied about and eventually Sir Piers agreed.

The atmosphere calmed down, after the failures at Walserval and the Queen of St Gilgen, neither Martin nor Anderton particularly wanted American involvement, their small UK unit operating by invitation within the American zone of Occupation, with the US having all the immediate resources, it was almost impossible to operate without them, particularly if they decided to surround Dilsberg with troops, right in the middle of the American zone, 'just like the 49th parallel,' said Partridge *(though it wasn't)*. It was agreed that on capture, the duke, his family and Strasser would be interviewed at Bad Ischl or at the duke's house on his bad Goisern Estate with Sir Piers present. The others would be taken and questioned by the US at Gmunden, who could claim the statistics. The US resources to be requested for the raid itself remained an open question.

'Let's have another look at the plan John,' Martin concluded. Whilst he was fiddling to get it out, making conversation Martin mentioned that landings at Innsbruck Airfield can be tricky, Sir Piers seized on that 'My God, scary's the only word for it, we were blown about like a a...'

'Bastard balloon,' said Partridge, 'By the way, is our duke still the bastard Duke of Albany.'

Sir Piers stiffened as if an icicle had fallen down the back of his shirt, it was Partridge using the word "bastard", Martin felt a cobweb, not an icicle being pulled away from his brain, he exchanged glances with John, the jigsaw was falling into place, Sir Alban Piers Henley was himself a corner piece in the jigsaw being taken out of the box before their very eyes.

Sir Piers wasn't in a hurry, even during the blitz he continued to enjoy full breakfasts, constitutional walks, three courses at lunch and dinner with wine, without the need to submit to rigid authority, this is what he had always been used to; the Duke of Saxe-Coburg-Gotha could wait until he was ready and he had checked out that the Bad Goisern Estate Manor was proper for the duke to be held and be questioned. He asked John Anderton to lay on transport to Goisern he wanted to see if the Manor House was suitable. Martin, curious, went with him. Albert unpicked the locks and on a balmy summer's day Sir Piers agreed the Manor was isolated and large enough, but it was too cold even in the spring sunshine, why couldn't they do the questioning at Bad Ischl, much more hospitable; before agreeing Martin had a good look round, but could find no evidence of it being recently inhabited.

The guts of the note Anderton prepared, which Martin sent on to Hillary, read:

1. *Churchill wants to know from Saxe-Coburg, who the uke of Windsor named as sympathisers in the UK. In particular he wants to know who financed the White Club, and whether Windsor agreed to take the title of king if Germany won the war.*
2. *Sir Alban Henley (Sir Piers) is the bastard son of the Duke of Saxe-Coburg and Gotha, one time the Duke of Albany, this accounts for one of his many names being Alban. Raised by a "grandmother", we cannot trace "a mother or a father", no reference anywhere, his mother is presumably "a royal". Sir Alban is here to interview (look after), his own father.*

3. *The Duchy of Saxe-Coburg is next door to the Duchy of Teck. Sir Alban Henley's main mission is to safeguard royal secrets and the purity of the House of Teck, which married into the royal family— George V. Churchill's wish list is the excuse, for Sir Alban coming here, not the real reason. He's been selected to best preserve royal bedroom secrets.*

He and John Anderton would watch Sir Piers like a hawk, Martin would continue to keep safe the Infant Crown of Stephen of Czechoslovakia, and the ever-growing bank balance in his Zurich account.

With nothing appetising on the menu, Martin suggested they went to scout the Fish Restaurant in Eberbach, at least we'll know where it is. Filling up the jeep with a couple of the girls, they sped along the empty road following the bank of the Neckar. No sooner had the sign "Eberbach" appeared on the edge of an apple orchard, than they came onto the inn, its sign pitched into a garden snuggling into the fold of river. Swinging the jeep into the empty car park, Partridge rattled the locked door of the restaurant till a woman appeared.

Apologetic, they weren't open, but she could take a booking: she brought out the book from a table behind the door next to a telephone, 'We only open on Friday, Saturday and Sunday at present.' She was apologetic.

Partridge put a deutschmark note into the pocket of the woman's apron, with the finesse of a cart horse.

'Could I just check whether General Hood, US Marines has booked a table for the weekend?

'I don't think so, would you like me to check?' The woman handed the book over, Partridge quickly turned the pages before handing it back.

'Could I book a table, dinner for four people, 8 pm next Saturday, the name's "Grouse", G R O U S E, Peregrine Grouse, shall I write it down for you.' John Anderton pulled out a pencil.

Strolling by the river before going into town to find somewhere to eat, 'What was all that about?' asked Sir Piers, John Anderton explained that when the colonel orders meals in restaurants, he never makes a reservation under his own name, we've been told he always books under names with the same initials as Nazi leaders. There was a Saturday night table for four booked under Heinrich Graff, so it's worth a sniff. A minute later,

'Oh Herman Goering,' said Sir Piers.

Although having served in the Eighth Army as transport manager, ('Transport Manager!—he managed frying eggs on the bonnet of his truck,' mocked Tracker), Partridge had missed the significance of a Friday booking under the name of Erna Rachmann.

Dressed quietly, but unmistakably English, the Grouse party arrived early at the Fish Restaurant. Martin sat in shadow where he could hardly be seen, never mind recognised. HG, a doddery Heinrich Graff was identified, but Hans Strasser never arrived, "Erwin Rommel" had dined on Friday night.

Partridge acting as paymaster was winding up to pay, including a tip, he asked the same woman, whether a tall fair-haired man with an artificial hand had been in, she said there were three in last night, one had a metal hand. Increasing the size of the tip he asked if he could have another look at the table bookings.

Anderton took it off him: 'It's showing an Erna Rachmann,' he pointed.

'Yes, he had a false hand,' the woman replied.

Outside the restaurant, Partridge wanted to know why Anderton had picked "Erna Rachmann" out.

'ER, Erwin Rommel,' he replied.

'Fancy missing that and him chasing you up and down Libya, you, Partridge, you who told us you were personally responsible for Rommel's downfall.'

Chapter 15
Safe House

Tracker back, he went with Martin and the plan to Gmunden to see Barney, they had listed who they expected to catch, that if they caught Bormann, Axmann, Ritter and any other high-ranking Nazis, they would all be handed straight over to the US, all they asked was that the UK be given first strike at Colonel Strasser and the Grand Duke of Saxe-Coburg-Gotha who, after all, was born an Englishman and might be tried as a traitor. After they had questioned, Strasser, he would be handed over and the USA could claim the stats, 'What could be fairer than that?'

Barney agreed to keep patrols out of the immediate area for 24 hours and that the GIs staying in the Dilsberg Gatehouse, would close the portcullis as normal but keep someone on duty to open when called upon.

Once Barney had double assurance that political Nazis would be handed over, and that the "stats are ours", he readily agreed to provide back-up, and take care of the prisoners agreeing to the British plan of a night raid through the secret underground tunnel.

Before they left Barney had unwelcome news, General Hood had called for an official enquiry into the death of two of his men o The Queen of St Gilgen, and wanted Martin to give evidence. 'Please try not to mention they were wearing pyjamas,' he pleaded.

"NOT TO BE DISTURBED", Tracker, Martin, Partridge and John Anderton began their meeting early in the morning long before Sir Piers had put his elegant shoes under the breakfast table. Not having the resources to surround the walls, a formidable obstacle to getting into Dilsburg, but only needing a ladder and a rope to get out, they concentrated solely on having a silent raiding party, after all, the duke was a bit old to be climbing walls.

They divided the operation into three parts:

Two armed men would be stationed hidden near the secret tunnel two hours before the raid, with orders to observe any activity. The road into Dilsburg would be secretly monitored.

The raiding force, led by Tracker, would enter Dilsberg by the tunnel, Limehouse Albert would pick the lock of number 33, on his signal the raiders would creep into the house, seize everybody before calling up the transport to take them to Gmunden or Ischl as appropriate. Start: midnight plus 20.

Tracker would keep the duke, wife and servants untethered and separate. Strasser would be both handcuffed and ankle clasped. The other prisoners handcuffed before being sent off to Gmunden.

Martin and Sir Piers would search the house for documents to be brought back to Ischl, prior to a thorough search the following day. The duke would then be taken separately to Huntingtower in the belief that familiar surroundings would make him more likely to talk freely. He would not be introduced to Partridge at that stage.

Lunch wasn't served that day, dry dinner being brought forward, dry in the sense that no alcohol was drunk before or after. Without uniforms, dark clothes, pockets full of bullets, and a motley selection of guns, and torches, this attacking force more resembled a training unit of a young Home Guard than a unit of the SAS, apart from Tracker.

Partridge led the advance party. Dropped by the side of the Neckar, unobserved they climbed through the woods up to the tunnel, leaving two camouflaged man outside, to guard the entrance.

The others knew Tracker had brought a large trunk with him from Blighty, now he judged, was the moment to bring out a smidgeon of what it contained. The Hunting Stewart in full fig is the tourist to Scotland's dream, particularly when swathed in a Bonnie Prince Charlie Cloak to prevent dirt and damage to the ensemble when walking through the tunnel.

'You're a Scot then,' remarked Partridge.

Travers drew himself to full height. 'Like a Yorkie, without the Yorkie's generous instincts,' he replied.

'A bare bum then,' Partridge always tried to have the last laugh.

Like the advance party, they were dropped off on the road running alongside the Neckar between Heidelberg and Eberbach, here they lay gently pissed on, unobserved for an hour, as the rain silently fell, before following a scout in the climb to the tunnel. A labouring Limehouse, his rifle and bullets carried by somebody else, was urged up the slope, around the tree roots, threatened and coaxed, panting he confronted the tunnel grille.

Well in advance of zero hour a restored Limehouse walked along the tunnel, next task opening the grid in the church, he still made heavy weather of opening the Italian locks on the old church door. In three deep stocking feet, he moved in shadow, to the door of Number 33, which took him nearly as long to open as it had on the first occasion. Returning he sat down breathing heavily in the pew nearest the door. Nothing had stirred.

12.20 precisely, Martin at the rear, 12 men and 5 women, holding their shoes in their left hand, crept behind Tracker in the shadow of the terraced houses, until they reached number 33. Pushing the door wide open, a current of air wafted across them, Tracker could not but notice the ornate letterbox, photo'd by Albert as he passed into a wide hall flanked by medieval armoires, tables and cupboards, hinting at old money and distant battles.

The raiding party were now in the hall, and they closed the outside door Tracker had not heard a sound from the rooms in front, behind him no one had sneezed, farted or knocked anything over, leaving two armed WAAFs mounting sentry by the door, Tracker shone his torch on his crooked his finger, for the men to follow him. Little noise, outside, no Dilsburg inhabitant had ventured onto the Green, no bedroom curtains had been drawn, no dog had barked, but behind an upstairs window curtain on the far side of the square four anxious troubled eyes peered out, wondering what was going on and what she should do.

Ever since the Marines had taken to living in the hostel 10 days earlier, rumour in the village was that the Americans were there in advance of a snatch. The only people not to privy to these rumours were the inhabitants of number 33.

Colonel Strasser had come to stay at number 33 two days earlier, the first thing he had done was to have a device installed in the Gatehouse to pick up gossip from the Marines. Not until he had settled down after supper, everyone else in bed, he pressed in the tape and switched it on. Drowsy, he listened to a lot of bawdy talk and was on the point of switching off and going to bed when he pricked up his ears. Imprecise detail, but enough to warn Strasser that something was going on, a raid could be imminent, a marine was to be posted to stay awake that night available to open the portcullis as required. He rewound and listened again, the evidence wasn't conclusive, but listening for a third time he decided to act, even though it was now after midnight.

Where he was to go could wait till they were away, deciding who was to go with him couldn't wait. The servants would be a hindrance, they must stay, he wasn't going on a midnight march with them in tow, not after his experience with an injured unfit Martin Bormann. Axmann would be useful if they got stranded in open country, but again he decided he would perhaps be better without him, particularly as they would leave by the underground passage.

Quietly he went upstairs, woke Anna and Ritter giving them 10 minutes to pack a bag and get dressed. Next he woke Axmann telling him that as a precaution he was leaving as there was a chance they would be raided, Axmann should explain his absence to the duke in the morning. Although he expected to be back within two days, he would be in touch if alternative arrangements became necessary. Axmann promptly turned over and appeared to go back to sleep, his appetite for running away having diminished.

All this took a little time and even as they gathered in the kitchen, Albert was picking the lock. Poised to move out, Axmann fully dressed came down the open spiral stairway, he had changed his mind, he wanted to come with them. 'We could sleep at the Naturfreunde House at Eberbach, its only eight kilometres away,' he said.

'Good thinking!' Strasser abandoned his own idea of an open night in the woods.

Strasser picked the keys to Huntingtower from the key cupboard. Minutes before he had looked over the village green from the bedroom and had seen nothing, nothing was moving, but then he heard a noise from the front of the house.

'There may be a guard on the portcullis, we'll take the tunnel,' he led Anna, Ritter and Axmann down to the cellar.

Ritter undid the bolts, the hinges moaned as he lifted the trapdoor and climbed down the 10 stairs into the tunnel itself, before helping Anna down the cold dark stairwell, the other two followed, Strasser drawing down the trapdoor behind them as quietly and exactly as he could. Strasser flashed his torch, Ritter led the way through 200 metres of fetid air to the first bend as the tunnel led down towards the graveyard, till he approached the false wall which blocked this spur to the main tunnel. Ten metres to go, a muffled sound ahead. Ritter stopped, flashing his torch backwards. Strasser the only one having to stoop, moved forwards and the two tip-toed up to the false wall and listened. Someone was walking up the tunnel from the wood towards the church, all four waited in tension and silence.

Waiting minutes until the walker had moved on, and silence reigned, Strasser squeezed his arm,

Ritter picked up the hammer which had leant unused against the passage wall for so many years and with five blows broke through the blocking wall, breathing fresher air, squeezing through the narrow gap, stepping over the debris, listening all the time, they walked quickly down the tunnel. Neither the grille nor the slab covering the entrance were back in place, Ritter and Strasser led the climb out into fresh air.

'You've been quick,' the solitary guard didn't even have hold of his machine gun. Strasser shot him in the head, the revolver shot making little noise in the trees, and no noise whatsoever went back up the tunnel.

'What's that?' said the second sentry emerging from a piss in the trees. Ritter literally threw himself at the sentry, knife in hand he buried it in the poor fellow's throat.

Nice man or not, barely pausing to look at the bodies, 'This way,' Axmann, compass in hand, pointed to the east. Strasser was confident that when it came to picking out a route cross-country, they couldn't be in better hands. As forecast, tired out, they slept the end of the night in the Eberbach Naturfreunde chalet.

The eight kilometres had been covered in two hours, over breakfast ersatz coffee Strasser reviewed the options: The steamer "Lady of Vienna" was laid up in a shed at Strobl, he held the keys to Huntingtower, the Duke of Saxe-Coburg's estate at Bad Goisern, its false wing was thought to give high security, though Huntingtower's association with Saxe-Coburg made it a likely target for looting and for hunting fugitives, and Anna had her own apartment. His own farm house was out of the question as a refuge for himself unless he lived in one of its barns, though the others might like to use it. Involving sister Edda wasn't an option.

Axmann had decided what he going to do and he was incisive, the safe-houses no longer safe he would make his own way now, knowing a house which hopefully would gave him the security he craved. 'No, he wasn't going to say where it was.' Anna wanted to join her son, being looked after by her sister on Strasser's farm at Aussee, Ritter thought a brief spell at Huntingtower to put together food before going onto "his place" on the Dachstein was safest, 'You'll know where you can find me, boss,' were his words, knowing that the end had come for Strasser's dreams of an illegal property empire.

Strasser said he would take time at Huntingtower to plan, 'Sorry, everybody, sorry, I've let you down, I did my best. I'm afraid my safehouses just aren't safe anymore.'

As they all had journey's south, they left it to Axmann to get them back into "his web", and a day later they were dropped off at Mondsee, jumping off point for all. Before they split Strasser asked where Axmann was headed 'in case the Bormann business ever blows up!' Axmann confided that he would be heading into Switzerland, to an upland valley, which was lovely, remote—nobody will ever come after me in Kiental.

In your dreams, thought Strasser.

The pair dropped off Anna in Bad Aussee before backtracking to Bad Goisern Estate. Huntingtower was the name of the old Shooting lodge, standing in the middle of the valley of this its wide estate, they walked around the building, tall and angular, brown stone blocks and sharp edges rather than graceful lines, a windowed rooms on the top of each side allowed the duke to spot where his deer were grazing, as Ritter prepared to break in, 'No need for force, I have the keys,' Strasser jangled a bunch of keys.

Huntingtower, built by the 15th Duke of Gotha, was modelled on a Scottish hunting lodge, home to the clan MacMillan also called Huntingtower, because the high tower, allowed the chieftain to see and take the shortest walk to find and shoot his deer. The tower overlooked low fir trees, which hid two small fishing lakes. Like the Estate Manor a mile away it had been constructed in the period when Catholics constructed Priest Holes, which was centuries before millionaires constructed viewing rooms for stolen masterpieces, or deep nuclear bunkers. Like a straw in a milkshake, part of the East Wing was enclosed and cut off from the rest of the lodge. It was secret set of rooms, the entry through a hidden panel set high in the east turret, from where small windowless rooms cascaded down to ground level like a Jacob's ladder. Suffering from mild claustrophobia Ritter left on day 2, but not before detecting that someone had broken the tell tales he had placed in the grounds around the tower as they arrived. Strasser moved immediately into the secret wing, a wise precaution as it proved.

In quiet and in safety, his new safety plan began to take shape: a plan just for himself. He had money; like Axmann, he needed to get out of Germany, outside South America, there weren't any safe countries, but Germany was really dangerous; he would be safest alone. Inwardly, he cursed not to have had false identity papers prepared when his Office could have prepared them with ease. He mapped out what he wanted his new identity to be:

Professor Raoul Helm, born Konisburg, now occupied by the Russian, orphaned at 19, 45 years old, studied chemistry and basic physics at Leipsig, a sportsman until an injury prevented his joining the Luftwaffe.

Leaving University, he worked in the research laboratories of IG Farben studying the molecular properties of molybdenum, later moving to zirconium and niobium, held in the ore, columbite.

Seconded to Peenamunde, he researched linings for V1 and V2 rocket motors. Injured once again when his apartment was destroyed in an air raid by the RAF. He was sent to BMW to work on engine combustion techniques with Messerschmidt in Augsburg. He had never married, his girlfriend killed when the apartment was bombed.

With a false passport, credentials that demonstrated his time and quality as a student at Leipsig University, letters with Messerchmidt and Peenamunde headings, he was confident that the Americans would accept him as a potential valuable military science expert, not least that with most of this background being in land now occupied by the Russians it would be difficult for the Americans to verify, and they seemed most anxious to clear "good men", and fly them back to America before the British intervened. He had visited the east coast of America in the 30s and was confident that before his lack of detailed scientific expertise was discovered, he could disappear, and even without a valid US passport could live safely and securely in Miami, Florida, before sending for Anna.

Without finesse, two jeeps rolled up and parked by the main door. Four men jumped out, the drivers remaining seated. From the turret Strasser watched, listening as the men clattered all over the house. The drivers spread a sheet on the ground and set out food and bottles of beer. No sooner was the food eaten than they were gone.

Leaving the shelter of Huntingtower, leaving with ½ a sack of potatoes and a bag of freshly gathered field mushrooms, former Colonel General Hans Strasser travelled by road and alone to Munich, then on to meet up again with Juliette Bader, former "fixer extra-ordinaire" to the Gestapo. They had done business since the beginning of the war.

'Juliette, let me sum up: I need a German passport, Leipsig University certificates, and supporting scientific and industrial documents, the outline is set out in the papers I've brought with me. Furthermore, I'll need an American passport for a woman and myself; these are the details,' he handed over a couple more sheets stapled together, he spoke these words to Juliette Kramer in the living room of her sumptuous apartment, on the fashionable shore of Chiemsee, forty kilometres south of Munich, 'Can you provide them?'

Similar age to Strasser, Juliette Bader studied the list before her, her business acumen, her business, trading as an agent, came from her father who had run a wholesale confectionery business in Munich for 50 years, "Always give something to your customer, always hide something for yourself". The extra she gave her exclusively male customers was the immediate and prominent attention of her breasts, what she looked to gain for herself was a hidden 2% percentage through the business they put her way. The early bodily skirmish with Strasser over, she sought to maximise the financial return; Strasser hadn't listed any personal details besides a false passport, would he buy a birth or a marriage certificate she wondered. How long would he be prepared to wait, why did he want this unusual combination of false papers? But Strasser was an attractive and compelling man, and her husband was long gone and most unlikely to return, a strong body at night would be welcome.

She spoke, knowing better than to ask questions as to who the woman might be.

'Normally most of what you need I could obtain quickly, but the war's over, and things are difficult. The American Passport requires special paper, special ink, a particular font, a stamp will have to be made, as well as time, these items cost money, a lot of money and I will have to pay my supplier in advance, in a currency I don't have.'

Strasser wanted an estimated delivery date, she quoted between 15 and 20 days not negotiable, He wanted a price, her estimate between 10 and 15 thousand US $ wasn't satisfactory, but it was negotiable and Strasser agreed the lower figure, with penalties if the 20 day time limit was exceeded and a 20 percent bonus for under 12 days.

'I will have to go away tomorrow to arrange matters, but I don't expect any insuperable problems.'

As Strasser was counting out the $7,000 US, she asked where he was staying, and when the answer was non-committal: 'You could stay here with me if you like, there's only me and wine.'

'Idiot,' Strasser spoke out loud, then silently to himself. If he threw himself to the mercy of the Americans, they were bound to strip search him. Finding on his person false US passports would be a giveaway of the first order.

'I want to change my mind, forget all about false US passports, I won't need them. If his story was believed the Americans would supply him with a passport.'

Ex Colonel Strasser was never going to get a better offer, he accepted the offer of a bed with alacrity. No false modesty, he followed upstairs to the bedroom and was left to unpack the few items in his rucksack, then a shower and a change into clothes picked out of a dusty wardrobe in a separate bedroom. Back downstairs he made himself useful in the kitchen as Juliette chatted cooking dinner, telling him her husband was "place unknown", assumed dead.

It was exactly 9 pm when ex Colonel General Strasser pulled his vest over his head, he was tired, yet it was half an hour later before he turned over to go to sleep.

Juliette left early in the morning, mid-afternoon she was back anxious to impart the "good news", she expected to collect the documents in 18 days, her contact had never let her down, even after several of his forgers had gone home.

From age 14 to 40 Juliette's Bader's breasts had been prominent assets, reaching age 40 Juliette decided to tuck these assets out of sight as best she could, they had served her well and had taught her all she needed to know about men and how to secure orders, maintain contacts and clinch contracts, making her a superb agent in the sub-culture lying between legitimate and marginal business whether it be state, military, entertainment, or legitimate business.

Nevertheless, Juliette's breasts remained a lasting asset she prized and looked after daily, an asset well supported by shapely legs, topped with a dress sense and an ever-changing hairstyle as she got older.

Without breathing a word, she added further sheets, in withdrawing the order for US passports she added an order for an American passport for herself and wrapped it into the price she charged Colonel Strasser.

Fishing in Lake Chiemsee had been strictly controlled for hundreds of years originally by the rulers of Bavaria for their own benefit, and latterly by the Bavarian State Assembly for the benefit of its voters. The patrolling launch had not turned its screw in clean clear water for the last six months of the war, and soon tired of briefing himself on the engineering projects covered by his CV Strasser spent the remaining waiting period catching fresh fish for Juliette to fry. On the banks of the Chiemsee he did not fish alone, catches were less and less day by day as more and more hungry men lined the shore. Came the day, the passports and the fish lay side by side on the kitchen table, Juliette filleted the fish, Strasser examined the papers with a fine toothcomb.

Keen and experienced eyes found no significant fault with them, but prudence demanded he didn't hand over the remaining Swiss francs till the following morning, which was when Juliette asked how he planned to get himself accepted by the Americans, and flown over the Atlantic.

A routine US night patrol trundling around Ludwigshafenstrasse near Munich Hautbahnhof, chanced on a back-street melee; by the time the MPs had jumped from their vehicle and drawn their batons, the men in uniform and those still standing had fled, leaving just one man, lying on the ground. Using batons rather than helping arms to get him to his feet, his suit, stinking of beer, sick and urine, the man was clutching, as if his life depended on it, a leather attaché case. The patrol's main task was to keep GIs out of trouble, but they were also tasked to bring in any likely Nazis, and though the stink was off putting, they threw Strasser, for it was him, into the back of their wagon, where he continued to act drunk and cling to the leather case.

The following morning Strasser was allowed to tidy himself up before being processed, cleaner and sweeter, the Lieutenant looked him over. Like the night's patrol he was tasked to identify "persons of interest" not likely from a sick drunk, but he went through the motions. German-speaking he first examined the name on the German Identity documents, and confirmed Raoul Helm wasn't on the "Wanted List", the Lieutenant got the man to unlock the case and he riffled through the papers, he examined the CV, for that in effect is what the papers were, and decided the drunk from the night before would need to be examined higher up the chain of command.

Having passed the first test, Strasser expected to be taken near to the Messerschmidt Factory at Augsburg where his papers said he had last worked, but he wasn't, he was taken to the US base at GMunden, and kept apart from the other prisoners.

Two days passed of spasmodic questioning before the crucial interview. Three officers formed the interview panel, the youngest being the sharpest, and the most deferential to Colonel Murphy who was just four weeks away from a return to Boston and pass through the cloudy curtain into civilian life. Boston was a commercial not a military centre. The fourth member behind the wide Interview table was there to record and put the panel's decisions into effect.

Strasser's mind was razor sharp, he paid more attention to his questioner's body language than the questions themselves. Three days held at the Bendlerstrasse in Berlin, three days of questioning by the SS Disciplinary Commission, many year's earlier when still Major Strasser, living in the shadow of being Otto and Gregor Strasser's brother, had taught him how to lie. He perceived that the colonel's first concern was to establish whether Raoul Helm was wanted by the Russians or the British as a Nazi, or as a war criminal, not necessarily the same. Consequently, he looked Colonel Murphy in the eye when questions on Hitler Youth, Party affiliations were asked. When asked who he worked with at Peenamunde, was he involved with foreign labour, what his attitude to Jews was, he turned his gaze to the questioner. Without hesitation, he said he didn't like the English, but had no hang-ups about Jews or eastern Europeans, and had no fear of being "outed" over a full dissection of his record, only infrequently being involved with Jews, he was a scientist working on technical and scientific questions for the Fatherland.

Major Harry Fowler who continued to ask most of the questions as the focus switched to where he had been, what he had done, who he knew, who he worked with, probing into the laboratories, the equipment, the pressures, the disruption from RAF bombing. Strasser, who by this time had adopted the persona of Karl Helm, the name he was called at work rather than Raoul, was skating on thin ice, He knew that if Major Fowler had detailed knowledge of the people he was lying about, discovery was inevitable, but Harry Fowler knew even less than Karl Helm, whilst Lieutenant Arnold Pearson, highly knowledgeable about engines, rockets, flight characteristics knew little or nothing about the German scientists involved apart from the name von Braun, which was already whispered as the father of the V2. Karl Helm was careful to say at the outset that he had never worked directly with von Braun who concentrated on the broader attributes of rockets whilst he worked closer to the engine room.

Lunch, to his surprise, Helm, as Strasser was increasingly thinking of himself, was taken in the officer's mess, where he dripped on a white starch table cloth with game soup, Maryland Chicken, California peaches and cream, with robust conversation of what was going on in the world, particularly how soon they would be returning to the USA, and how quickly stupid Russian attitudes were beginning to sour relationships.

Back in the Interview room, Major Fowler had almost finished off his review of Helm's career and came to what had happened to him after the Allies occupied Augsburg and the Messerschmidt Works was taken over.

'What happened to you in the period since we took Augsburg, you left Augsburg and we picked you up drunk in the back streets of Munich?' Strangely, Strasser had not prepared an answer to this question; playing for time, he reached for his handkerchief and blew his nose. 'I went to my sister, Hanna, in Munich, and drank for 24 hours, then I went to sleep for a week, then I went fishing, collected berries for a week and caught food for her family; a neighbour's house had been damaged in the bombing and I've been helping them with repairs.'

'That doesn't explain why we picked you up drunk near the station, do you have a woman problem?' Helm shook his head. 'Then why were you carrying personal documents late at night on the backstreets of Munich? Do you always go around the back streets of Munich carrying your university graduation certificates?' It was Lieutenant Arnold Pearson's turn to ask the questions and he still had serious questions to be addressed.

'I need a job, in the morning I went into Munich to see if BMW then Farben had any jobs going, in the afternoon I went out to the Porsche main factory, that's why I was carrying my qualifications about with me.'

'Did they offer you a job?' Pearson wanted to know.

'They all just took details, nobody is offering jobs, no one knows what's happening, they're all coming or going at the moment,'

'But that doesn't tell us, Mr Helm, why you were picked up pissed, and drenched in urine late at night.'

Helm held out both hands, revealing his metal hand, a handicap which had hardly featured till then. 'I'm not a drunkard, you can see my hands are steady, but with hours before any chance of a bus I did go to a bar, I did have a drink, I wasn't used to it and I was taken ill, but somebody must have thought I had money, and I was set on by a gang of louts, who in turn attracted some GIs, and I found myself in the middle of a fight. I was punched stupid and they pissed on me. That's all I can remember, I repeat I'm not a drunkard.' Up till then, every answer had been delivered in a flat monotone, the 'I'm not a drunkard, I might have stunk, I'm not a drunkard,' was forced out with conviction. He was believed.

In the pause that followed, Lieutenant Arnold Pearson opened his file, 'I'd like to skip over your chemistry qualification from Leipsig, one of the finest oldest Universities in the world, but more renowned for sport and classical learning than chemical insights as I'm sure you'll acknowledge; on leaving University what made you attractive to the Rocket Establishment at Peenamunde?'

'I didn't go straight onto rocket research.' Helm told how he'd worked for a small glue making chemical firm taken over by IG Farben, where he'd worked on the physical properties of molybdenum and graphite, at Peenamunde he'd moved onto materials to line the combustion chambers of rocket engines, he became an expert on the composition and properties of niobium a constituent of columbite, particularly, and on other constituents manganese and niobium, particularly niobium whose hardness and ability to withstand high temperature and pressure made it attractive as the lining for combustion cylinders. At great difficulty, he had gone out to Nigeria to help Germany obtain, then ship columbite ores from Kaduna, Nigeria, a British colony, where deposits of columbite left over at mines after the extraction of tin were simply waste spoil on a tip. Asked how he had done this he answered: 'Bribery.' German rocket technology was advancing at a great rate until the RAF bombed and destroyed Peenamunde, killing many of the experts working there. The death toll there, was a body blow for the country, injured himself, after recovering, with Peenamunde abandoned as indefensible, he was sent to the Messerschmidt factory outside Augsburg to work on the jet engine for the world first jet bomber, which would climb higher and faster than anything the world had ever seen, the Dorado.

Still working on aero engines, he worked on an advanced method for splitting fuels into fine droplets which when sprayed into the cylinder block gave a power boost with the potential for great economies. Pearson was interested and there followed a discussion on the geometry of spray within an engine cylinder which moved onto the injection of minute amounts of de ionised water into the fuel stream, how they had tested intermingling and surge cascaded (spurts) injection, which could lead to even greater fuel savings, an important consideration for a Germany without a single nodding donkey of its own. A test bed had been under preparation at Augsburg, but the war caught up with the project.

Lieutenant Pearson turned towards Colonel Murphy to say he had no further questions but that secret work on mixing streams into combustion chambers was an ongoing area of R and D in the States. Before closing the interview, Colonel Murphy thanked Herr Helm, smiled saying that John Gumm, the non-speaking member of the panel would take down more personal and business details should his committee recommend that he be invited to join a US program in California. They all left the room except Gumm, who stayed behind to gather personal and employment detail.

Shannon Airport on the west coast of Ireland, rather than Croydon near London, welcomed Karl (Raoul) Helm five days after the conclusion of the interview. Anna, happy with her sister at Bad Aussee, did not know what was happening, and waited. Juliette tucked her US passport inside scented lingerie, folded tissue paper over it, and placed it at the top of a bottom drawer, and waited.

The elderly Duke of Saxe-Coburg-Gotha was nobody's fool, he didn't have Parkinson's disease, he didn't have Alzheimer's disease, he could still walk, he was as fit and healthy as his wife, and when it was a question of money or safety he was as agile as a cat.

They had both enjoyed having Number 33 to themselves, and were disappointed when Artur Axmann arrived at number 33, followed later by Ritter and Strasser. The duke bored listened avidly to the three men telling of their escapes from the "Queen of St Gilgen" in their pyjamas, followed by the raid on Walserval. The whole of one night was spent yarning about the happenings in the bunker and the adventures as they wriggled through enemy lines.

He realised that the raid on Walserval heralded the destruction of "Strasser's Business Plan", and was a warning call for Dilsberg, so it wasn't a big surprise to be wakened that night by the sounds of hurried activity in the adjoining bedrooms.

At his bedroom door, his long nightshirt trailing on the floor, he asked Axmann, 'What's going on?' to be told there was a flap on, they were moving out for the night as a precaution, they expected to be back.

'No need to worry yourself or the duchess.' He knew he no longer had any appetite for a midnight flit, and not wanting to go through the rigmarole of explaining everything twice over to his wife, he went back to bed, curled up beside her and tried to get to sleep.

His wife and servant Molly sleeping peacefully, the duke wasn't discomforted at not being included in Strasser's escape party, realistically three pensioners were too big a burden to piggy-back on what was essentially a military operation, particularly if a final flight of the Storch back to the mountains was envisaged. He would have to plan what to say to the Allies and the British Royal Family, who, despite all the water that had flowed down the Rhine, he expected to come to his aid. He didn't have long to muse. Sharp voices, heavy hands thrust open the door and dragged the bed clothes onto the floor.

Upstairs, the small dark box room at the top of the stairs had been first to be entered, Molly, the servant/dresser/old retainer, call her what you will, had a large hand put over her mouth, she fainted and that was the end of questioning her till the following day.

The secondary bedrooms were broached, and though a thorough search was to follow, no one was sleeping in the beds and no one else was to be found. Tracker was alarmed so it was something of a relief for him to follow into the master bedroom and from the grunts to be sure they had at least captured someone. Sir Piers kept himself shadowed in the background. The sleeping couple, the duke and his wife were rousted from the large bed and asked rather than instructed to dress, Tracker having stressed from the outset that the potential prisoners were "gentry" and should be well treated.

'Where's Colonel Strasser?' The duke would have liked to know as much as anyone and didn't hold back. 'He was here with the others last night, aren't they in their rooms?' It was soon established that the others were Strasser, Anna, Ritter, and Artur Axmann. The duke's party were shepherded downstairs to wait for the transport.

The raiding party silent at first, became noisier and noisier as they searched the house, considerably hampered by the lack of lights, without power as all power was switched off to the village after 7 pm. They shone and poked with their torches around the eaves. They prodded and looked for a hidden exit out through the back wall, which doubled as the village wall, they checked and double checked every cupboard and niche, by the time they climbed down to the cellars they were hampered by the torch batteries running out. Cursing that the duke wasn't immediately on hand for questioning, they finally got a break. The girls guarding the door hadn't used their torches, better lights revealed the trapdoor in the cellar floor, opening up to a second chamber leading down to the tunnel proper. It was clear, the church wasn't the only building with a secret underground tunnel. Flashlights, were much too dim to give a sense as to whether the tunnel had been used recently, the men conferred.

'Follow me,' Martin drew his revolver, switched on his still flickering torch and crouched slowly and uncomfortably walked down the narrow tunnel; manoeuvring around a bend, after a hundred yards he came to a stop, a wall blocked him, a wall through which a man-size hole had been forced, a spread of soil and rubble trampled with footprints, lay on the floor. The passage was a track into the main tunnel leading to the church, the branching door had been hidden by darkness and by a spread of earth, sealing it. This earth and the darkness had made the branch tunnel invisible when they had climbed past it, up from the woods into the church.

'Bugger it, they must have come down on this tunnel and broken through after we came up on the main passage to the church,' Partridge expressed the feelings of them all. 'Run, they can't be far ahead.'

Quickly now they pressed on downwards towards the woods, the only question being whether Percy Haddow had stopped the escapers. He hadn't, Percy Haddow, camouflage or no camouflage, was dead, shot in the head from close range, Martin had seen such shooting before, Haddow's Sten gun was missing, his mate Nigel Faulkner lay dead in a dark pool of blood.

'Blisters,' said Martin, using his dad's preferred expletive. John Anderton and Partridge behind him, they ran wildly down through the trees to the road. They saw nothing, they heard nothing, their prey having followed Axmann and his compass to the east. Strasser had escaped again, and this time there were no Americans to take the blame. 'What in hell's name am I going to tell Barney?' Exasperated they hurled useless flashlights into a fast-flowing River Neckar, turned, crossed the road and trudged back up the hill.

Chapter 16
The Duchess of Saxe-Coburg-Gotha

Calling up the transport, the main actors travelled back to Band Ischl.

Sitting alone. 'Hello, Father, bet you never expected to see me,' Charles Edward, the Duke of Saxe-Coburg-Gotha lifted a tired head and blinked in surprise.

'Well, I never, hello, Alban, you're the last person I expected, what a surprise!' he cranked himself up from his chair and embraced a son he had not seen for seven years.

'I'm called Piers here, not Alban, Sir Piers actually, stick with that please. How's the duchess?' he asked.

'She's as well as can be expected, not walking much these days. How's Sybil?'

'Sybil died of cancer a year ago, I'm on my own again.'

It wasn't Martin's or Tracker's intention that Sir Piers should be first and alone to talk to the duke, but the visit to Gmunden had allowed Sir Piers to grab his chance, and if it hadn't been his weakness to take a leisurely breakfast, he would have had more than enough time to get the really private business which was the raison d'etre of his journey out of the way before Martin came back.

There was one good outcome however, it gave Tracker an excuse to separate the duchess and prevent Sir Piers having separate contact with her or Molly Bonn (the servant, chambermaid, dresser; he could never settle on a description) until the two women had been questioned by Martin.

Before breakfast, an exhausted and despondent Tracker, furious that his plan had partly failed and worried about losing yet more face with the Yanks, a Martin, furious that Strasser had again eluded his grasp, uncertain what to say to Barney, with whom he had struck up an affinity, and a John Anderton, furious at being bested. It was convenient to believe that asking the GIs to keep the Portcullis open had led to a leak, but they couldn't say this to Barney. Tracker decided they would all go to Gmunden, and say what had happened even before they had breakfast. Meanwhile he told Partridge keep everyone separated until he they got back and 'keep the stuff we've brought back under lock and key, if Sir Piers enquires you can tell Sir Piers to sod off.'

The drive to Gmunden along the lovely valley of the Traun and passing the Traunsee, soothing commiserations from Barney; on their return, eggs and bacon, a shower and a change of clothes left them in a better mood to question the duke. Martin came in upon Sir Piers and the duke before their conversation had reached a critical point, bringing the father to son discussion to an abrupt halt.

'Leave off now please, you can bring us up to date with what your father has told you after we've spoken to Molly Bonn and the duchess. Sir Piers didn't like it one bit, but Tracker Travers was at his most abrupt and demanding, brooking no argument.

The men started on the duchess's dresser Molly Bonn, treating her on the basis that you treat a tart like a duchess, not that Molly was a tart, far from it; she was the youngest daughter of a most respectable middle-class family. Yes, she thought an alarm might have been raised in the middle of the evening when a youth, came to the door, but she and the duchess had carried on talking and playing cards whilst the men "busied about". Neither she nor the duchess had any idea when she went to bed that the men planned to leave. Now that she knew, she assumed they had escaped through the tunnel in the cellar. "The escape hatch" the duke called it, "like in a submarine".

Yes, they'd talked about the tunnel earlier, but she'd never actually seen it. She thought it all rather exciting, and didn't appear to be really worried about might happen to her, being only a Nazi in the sense that she had voted for Hitler in 1932 because the duke told her to. She didn't know where the escapers might have gone, but she thought the duchess might know as she was very friendly with them, even that horrible Ritter. Leaving further questions till later, Trapper had the duchess brought into the library.

Like the others on the raid, Sir Piers hadn't gone to bed, his first moments with the Duchess of Saxe-Coburg-Gotha were stilted, nominally his mother it was immediately clear, that their previous relationship had been distant in both time and familiarity, however an embrace, a kiss and a murmured "mama", were negotiated before they sat down well apart. It took only a minute to establish the truth of Molly Bonn's account, the duchess had nothing to add, except that her husband had been betrayed, left behind, blaming Colonel Strasser rather than that nice Artur Axmann. 'How could they take that Anna with them and leave us, we are the ones who paid Swiss francs for all that accommodation you know.'

On the question of where had they might have gone she was forthcoming. Ritter owned nothing, Strasser owned a couple of Steamers, a farm near Aussee, a derelict something in the Black Forest, now that Walserval had gone, she thought he had plans of his own, if she remembered anything else she would tell them. Nice Artur Axmann was wedded to the Hitler Youth, he owned nothing, had no woman that I knew of, she added.

Martin lingered after the others left, asking if there was anything he could do to make her more comfortable, then he became serious, he had seen the film the duke had commissioned with Goebbels, showing how well the Germans treated foreign labourers, and in it her interview to camera showing how she tried to improve conditions for mothers carrying children, there was a problem however, the Russians reported that the mothers were all dead, and none of the babies could be found. We might want to come back to that. The duchess was silent, before adding:

'I might be able to help you find Colonel General Strasser.' Martin remained silent.

'It's only an idea, it may not have been him, it could just as easily be Ritter, but someone has taken the keys to Huntingtower, our place near Goisern.'

Travers decided four hours in bed were required before he saw the duke, consequently it was late in the afternoon before the duke had his afternoon nap disturbed. An hour earlier than Travers had told Sir Piers the questioning was to begin.

The duke was wakened from his nap and brought to the orangery, where a low table covered by a white linen cloth held porcelain, biscuits and a pot of tea. After the recent austerity, duke gave out a sigh of relief.

'Is Sir Piers not here?' the duke's first question as he sat facing Martin.

'Later, he'll be here later, he's already given us the gist of your discussion this morning, now we'd like to hear it from you.' The duke was on the back foot, without mentioning that Sir Piers was his son, his recap was received in unbelieving silence.

Martin switched to asking what part the duke played as leader of the Red Cross, and in particular his liaison with Strasser's role as overall commander of southern German Labour Camps. In summary Strasser had complete control, he, the duke, was a mere cipher without control of budgets or manpower. He emphasised how pleased the Red Cross HQ in Geneva were with his efforts, and the minimal contact he had with the forced labour camps, another department entirely he said, but he said this much too loudly and repeated it far too often. British prisoners were well-treated as a result of his efforts, complaints received attention, even in difficult times, and Red Cross parcels got through without much tampering. He didn't believe Martin when he said POWs at Menzenschwand had been simply shot. 'Never came across anything like that,' was his comment, Russian POWs were over in the east, not in Germany or Austria and he had no contact, anyway, they were always trying to escape and possibly some were incorrectly dealt with.'

Martin continued his offensive by asking about the duke's film, featuring the duchess, showing the false impression of the camps and the false impression of the way inmates were treated. The duke blustered that of course this was wartime propaganda, they only filmed the best of them, Martin responded by repeating the lie he had already told the duchess, that the woman who were filmed were all now dead and none of their children could be traced, 'what did you, the German Red Cross, do for them or the tens of thousands killed at Dachau and the thousands who simply perished at Ebensee.'

In the sentence the duke and the Germans was to repeat ad nauseam. 'It was nothing to do with me.' John Anderton switched the attack, asking questions as he always did, to which he knew the answer.

To the opening question: 'Why did London choose to send Sir Piers to question you? The duke spluttered, saying this was not something he could possibly know, nor did he know what information Sir Piers might be seeking, he speculated it was possibly gossip about King Edward VIII's visit to Germany after he became the Duke of Windsor.

'What is your relationship with Sir Piers?' The duke didn't know what to say, floundered around before finally coming to a halt as his interrogators said nothing, letting him sweat. A minute's silence as he arrived at knowing that they knew, then,

'Sir Piers is my son.'

'Legitimate?' asked John Anderton.

'Of course,' the duke answered that question far too quickly.

'Then who's his mother?' The duke fidgeted and said nothing.

'Why does his mother's name not appear in the records, then of course there is the question of dates?' Anderton was a dangerous antagonist, he tilted an ear so as to catch the answer and narrowed his stare to catch if it was true.

'Of course, it doesn't, dukes receive special treatment from the authorities. Family records of the nobility are not available to the public in Germany.' John Anderton had set him up nicely for the kill.

'But their names and their dates of birth are, and as the duchess turned 12 on the day your son was born, you're either a pervert or you're lying, I ask again for the name of the mother, the woman who gave birth to Sir Alban which I assume is why your son was picked out and sent here specially from London?' The Duke of Saxe-Coburg-Gotha sat stone-faced and silent.

'Perhaps we need to ask the duchess, Sir Alban or Molly on that point, think about it we'll come back to it later.'

With his usual skill and tact Partridge asked who would succeed to the dukedom if the coming trial decided that an execution was necessary, particularly as Albert Pierpoint the English Official Executioner, was scheduled to remain in Austria for several weeks. The duke said Conrad was his eldest son and was in line, but the people would decide, just as they had decided to pick him so many years ago. He sat up, took out his pen, taking the top off he scribbled to ensure a good flow of ink, and quickly wrote a name on the pad in front of him. He tore off the top sheet and pushed it towards Travers, who without so much as a glance folded it and pushed it in his pocket

'Friend of yours, was she?' said Partridge who had looked over Travers shoulder and had seen what was written.

At that moment Sir Piers entered the Orangery from the garden.

Travers got up and brought an extra chair over to the table. 'We were just about to ask your father what happened when

Edward VIII visited Germany with new wife Wallis Simpson.' Excluded from the loop and the meeting, Sir Piers knew he'd been double-crossed by his colleagues, but there was nothing he could do.

The next period was taken up with the duke reminiscing over the Windsor's, visit, who they'd met, the gifts business firms had lavished on the duchess and how tight they were, what the duke said, and was going on to recount what he did off-duty, when Martin broke in to say that as this was political he didn't see how it would help him to catch Strasser and begged to be excused. This acted as a key to Sir Piers suggesting a tete-a-tete with him, his father and Travers alone. Abandoning the large table, the three men grouped on easy chairs around the fireplace. After discussions going long into the night, Travers in tune with Sir Piers, summed up the situation:

'So when we scrutinise the books and papers your father brought away with him, we shall expect to find lists of Englishmen less than enthusiastic to George VI, royalist supporters of Edward VIII, particularly members of the White Club, active when Windsor was living at Fort Belvedere, with the amounts of money contributed. Unsigned, a fool script memo of the broad understandings Windsor agreed with Goering outlining Windsor's budget and powers, particularly in regard to India and Nigeria as "king returning".

In a heavily protected case are family documents to be sent to London unopened, documents of such sensitivity that…' Travers paused, 'national security, issues kept…' He stopped again. Sir Piers took up the narrative.

'Naturally, we shall seek no publicity of the duke's arrest and we shall recommend that he be given some form of house arrest where he can live quietly in retirement. If it transpires that the duke is guilty of culpable responsibility for other's acts of wickedness, he will have to be accountable of course, but in the meantime "masterly inactivity" will advise our actions.'

'I can see there's a lot in this for the duke, but what's in it for us? By us, I mean the Allies, or as Partridge would put it, "What's in it for the families of the millions of the poor dead bastards?"'

Sir Piers, his father who had long since lapsed into exhausted indifference, was at his most soothing, 'Nothing can atone for the dead, what the duke can do and is willing to do is give an unfettered account of what took place in the higher echelons of state for the whole time Hitler was in power. In addition, he will give all the information he has about Axmann and Strasser. In this regard, it may be useful to speak to the duchess who was particularly close to Axmann.

Even as these words were being spoken, Martin and Anderton were chatting amiably with the duchess in the intimacy of the sewing room, accompanied by a bottle of gin, tonic water and a bottle of Berncasteller 1933. Three green glasses on the table, John Anderton poured eloquent quantities of the three clear liquids up to their necks, the addition of ice cubes, brought from the bowels of the kitchen brought tears to the table top. Martin knocked down a third, belched with delicacy behind a curved palm, "Wonderbar". The duchess was no slouch and in no time at all the glasses were refilled, and the duchess pleasantly sloshed.

Reluctant to mention family matters, she had no qualms in talking about "the Nazis" leading on from her earlier disclosure that Strasser had taken away the keys to

Huntingtower, she told them that as soon as he arrived at Dilsberg than he sent a message to trawl bookshops in Heidelburg, for books on aero-engines and metallic elements, and had pounced on them the minute they arrived. Other than that she knew nothing, and less than nothing about Ritter who despite her being told he was a "horrible man", Ritter was attentive and the first to stand up when she entered a room, and always leapt forward to pull out a chair for her to sit at table and see that her glass was full.

Pausing only to drink deep of a further glass of gin and white wine, Axmann she called 'a lovely man' was still upset with his role in forming the "zoo brigade"; the Berlin Tiergarten had recruited boys to look after their animals in lieu of homework, since 1943, in March 1945 he told her he had formed these boys into an army unit he named the "zoo brigade" and they were given a street to defend. They had no sooner taken up position when a salvo of Russian shells from those frightening "Stalin Organs" killed and injured over half, without them being given the chance to live, they weren't even given the chance to fight.

Axmann had been in the Fuhrer bunker in the final weeks, he had told her of Hitler's marriage and suicide, of Goebbels and wife Magda killing their six children "infamy" he called it. Goebbels got one thing right, his last words before the SS shot him, or he died of poison, she couldn't remember which and being burnt said, 'We'll go down in history as the biggest criminals the world has ever known.' Axmann had joined a small group that escaped at night from the Bunker. Strasser had shot and killed Martin Bormann when he became a liability, too badly injured to carry on, they had walked, crawled and hid in getting out of Berlin, sheltering in a damaged house for a day along with six nurses and how the Rhine barge was challenged by a British MTB, then as the MTB was pushing off from the side of the barge, Strasser had flipped two timed grenades into the MTB and watched to see them explode 30 seconds later. 'Our final victory!' he called it.

'Artur Axmann was a lovely man,' she was beginning to slur her words, 'he was always going on about a lovely desolate valley in the Bernese Oberland, a hidden valley that the world had forgotten, called Spieztal. 'Spieztal do you mean Kiental?' asked Martin. 'Something like that,' she replied, as they moved onto gossip:

'How did you get on with HRH when he came to Germany?' the duchess was immediately wary, political antennae like a porcupine's back.

'You know Windsor's my husband's,' she hesitated, 'cousin or something; well, he's not a patch on his wife, the American woman has him by the short hairs,' she stopped and giggled. 'Ooh, I really shouldn't have said that, I meant nobbies no hobbid, but truly she can turn him in to do anything she wants. She stayed back with me at the castle when her husband and the duke were off talking to Goering and Ribbentrop, but don't ask me what they agreed, I don't know, and if I knew I shouldn't tell. What I do know is she knew how to handle servants, telling them when she arrived that the duke was a generous man who liked his wife to be well looked after, actually he was a very mean man and never tipped, both of them looked after their money and consulted each other about it.'

The duchess went to bed happily. Her husband followed her, unhappy but too tired to fully undress.

Two days later, much of Sir Piers work had been done, the duke's papers had been assembled and listed, they were bulky and heavy, Travers not having the time to go through everything himself had gone for overkill and had had his girls pack everything except the kitchen sink, including receipts for spit roasted pigs purchased for the royal visit. Sir Piers looked at the parcels with alarm.

'I can't possibly travel back to London with that lot,' Piers was conscious that more admirals had been sacked for leaving secret documents on admiring trains than had ever been sacked for running their ships aground, 'can't we send them in the diplomatic bag?' The nearest "diplomatic bag" being the embassy in Berne, Martin volunteered to take them to Berne himself, 'If you'll give me leave to be away for a long weekend,' announcing, 'I'm due,' thinking an extra day would allow a side visit to Kiental for him to recover King Stephen's crown. It was over three years since he had hidden the crown of the young king, buried deep in the woodpile at the side of the Naturfreunde Haus in Kiental. Travers took his offer up had a jeep checked over, loaded and provisioned. He cleared the arrangement with London.

John Anderton had changed, he was now more interested in the political and royal scandals than in finding Ritter and other wanted Nazis, before all the knots had been tied, he slipped into the locked office where the papers brought from the duke and duchess's rooms had been gathered. There were inventories, properties, tenancies and tenants going back Centuries, medals received, correspondence between the Crown and the Duke of Albany when he converted to the Duke of Saxe-Coburg, but no records about King Edward VLII, except!

In a bundle of invitations lay a "thank you letter" from Wallis Simpson, styling herself the Duchess of Windsor expressing the hope that she would soon be able to entertain the Duke and Duchess of Saxe-Coburg-Gotha fittingly in Castle Windsor. Anderton took it and locked the door behind him.

He had certified copies notarised within five hours, by Frau Gertrude Schiller a solicitor in her office by the Ischl Town Hall. No sooner had he returned than Yvonne entered the room, 'That American guy, Major Barney, is on the line for Martin, it's urgent.'

Barney was apologetic, could he ask for a favour, General "Robin" Hood originally from Sherwood Forest, was interested in having a "chin wag" with that English Duke of Saxe-Coburg-Gotha, about possible family connections with "The Hoods", particularly if the duke has ceremonial uniforms with him, because the General thinks a photograph of the two of them would have good publicity value in both Germany—to show how well we treat our enemies, and in the States, eager to maintain old cultural ties, and ethnic Germans own 66 service stations on the route running from California to Boston.'

Tracker, who had been at the other side of the desk following the conversation, nodded approvingly, so it became a matter of agreeing when and where. General Hood deciding the aura of the Emperor's Hunting Lodge was "just fine", agreed he would bring "his team" over that very night. The line went dead, no sooner dead, Tracker had a brainwave. 'Get him back,' he said.

Reconnected.

'Why doesn't General Hood come over early, we'll arrange a hunt up in the lodge parklands and hills.' So it was arranged.

How do we get the general, the duke and Sir Piers to play ball? But Tracker had made and liked the arrangement, no need for Sir Piers to agree, he would just have to grumble and lump it. As soon as the duchess realised that General Hood was coming in full Military Dress, that photos were needed, that the WAAF would dress and act as ladies in waiting, that American food would be served, the duke's attendance and compliance was a foregone conclusion. He was encouraged to remember or over-play possible ancestral connections to an early Robin Hood, even though a 19th century Nottinghamshire wheelwright was more appropriate. The nitty gritty questioning on the duke's wartime activities surrounding Red Cross surveillance of Labour Camps and his fronting a propaganda film was put on the back burner. It was all straightforward, the US $ was king.

Martin was mainly interested in documents left behind by Strasser. The one to interest him most was a hard-backed book of memoranda, although few pages had been written in—he saw his name: It looked to be on a kind of death list, the ink on his name looked as if it had been written some time earlier, there more recent entries, including 'Martin Bormann' where the ink was fresh. Looking at the page as a whole his attention was drawn to a doodle at the top and bottom of the page where the circles of the 8 on the page number 18 had been recently inked in. He riffled through the book, no other numbers had been treated in this way. He knew Hitler was sometimes referred to as "88" Herr Hitler, the eighth letter of the alphabet. Could 18 be shorthand for Adolf Hitler? What could be the significance of an inked in 18 be on a page listing death and revenge? He went and took it to show John Anderton.

Driven by a "Boston Broad", his words, General Hood travelled in the second of a convoy of three jeeps, to be welcomed at the wrought iron black, red and gold ancestral gates at the west of the river bridge, by Tracker himself in full Highland dress. Barney and a photographer jumped out, after a "take" Tracker maneuvered into the vacated seat, Barney and Martin in his pilot's uniform chatted walking together up the hill to the lodge, with Barney making clear that General Hood as well as wanting 'a swan' was also interested in good publicity photographs as the ambitious General intended to enter politics after the war and already had photos of himself with Glenn Miller, Ike, Winston Churchill, and Rooseveldt, with Hitler no longer available a resplendent fully uniformed Prussian duke, born English, was the next best thing, particularly as the duke was also the cousin of George VL, King of England.

German battlefield Kubelwagons, a kind of jeep taken from Bad Ischl Army Barracks, were fired up, the hunting, shooting and fishing party drove high into the hills. First stop, a mountain stream cascaded into three pools each deeper than the first, each yielded General Hood a rainbow trout each bigger than the last, everything was going well. Next stop, the Kubelwagons whisked them higher up the hillside, without organised beaters only a modest number of partridge took wing. 'I'm not good with these long two shooters,' said General Hood, firing off without success, gimme an automatic every time… only joking fellas.' Travers gave him the two dead birds he had brought in case of any disappointment.

Higher still, a herd of deer had spread themselves on the far side of the fell, but persuaded that approaching them in a vehicle would scare them off, the General had little enthusiasm to climb the mile needed to get into a lee side position for a successful kill.

Down at the lodge, four bows and four quivers were propped up in front of a makeshift straw target, even a Robin Hood Hat complete with feather was available. The General won the Will Scarlet competition, being well versed in Sherwood Forest folklore.

On entering the lodge, General Hood was met and was soon talking affably to a resplendent duke, one hand only cuffed to his chair. Cameras and lights already in position, Martin had the key and taking up his new role as warder and locksmith, unlocked the "Duke".

The duchess loved the attention, silk and lace, years younger than her husband, looking serene and lovely with the authority and graciousness, money health and power unfairly but inevitably bestow on well-born royal intelligentia, she joined in the conversation answering for the duke. Connections between Queen Victoria's family and the Nottinghamshire Hood's proved tenuous, but both agreed that a direct ancestor, one Robert le Hood, had either been at the side of William the Conqueror or been a groom to Prince Albert (which was never quite established) but there were other more risqué stories, and the duchess delighted in telling how Victoria's Prince Albert had once been caught in flagrente delicto with her Grandma Princess Catherine of… her words slurred and none caught the name, only that it was on Christmas Day.

The duke and duchess with General Hood, Tracker and photographers toured the lodge including the duke's lodgings for the night. Many photographs were taken, all hated by Sir Piers, on edge less the fact that he was the bastard son of the duke should be revealed to General Hood.

Sir Piers saw no need to mention the General's visit in his report to Number 10 and the Palace. Only later did the significance of the portfolio of photographs emerge, when the Poles mounted an enquiry into the massacre of Polish Officers at Katyn and it was discovered that the duke had led a German enquiry into the massacre. The Polish Government requested interviews with Sir Piers and the Duke of Saxe-Coburg-Gotha, This request was filed and is currently being eaten by the voracious ants feeding in the special store room at Bryn Argoed, Aberystwith.

No sooner had General Hood driven over the bridge than Travers heeded a summons to attend at General Urquhart's HQ in Koln, no sooner had the autobahns returned him a day later, than Martin's jeep roared down the drive, by 10 am he was in Berne, greeted everyone from the ambassador to Francois in the boiler room and soon got the signature required to free him of the duke's documents. Lunch in the fish restaurant by the river with Nigel Buonapart, he hit the road for Spiez, next came the slow ascent of the mountain wall lifting him up to the Naturfreunde Haus in the Upper Kiental valley.

Martin went to Kiental intending to retrieve Stephen's crown from the woodpile and return it to London possibly by way of the diplomatic bag from Berne, he hadn't decided, what he had decided was to stay the night at the Naturfreunde Haus, where it would be easy to disappear and work on the woodpile the following day without attracting attention. He booked in, picked at the bunch of bananas he'd bought in Berne, walked around the house, then down to where the avalanche had swept Lord Gael's chalet over the cliff.

Walking around the house, picking up the axe and splitting a number of trunk lengths Martin was satisfied there were no signs of the woodpile having been disturbed and that St Steve's crown slept safely. Sleepy and satisfied he went to bed.

Finishing off the last of the bananas with rolls and coffee, after breakfast he started on a constitutional walk up the valley, coming down the track he was met by a one-armed middle-aged man who stopped and stood aside to let him pass, greeting and touching his hat with his one good hand on his only arm. Martin stopped, he knew who it was, he held out his hand:

'Artur Axmann, I presume,' were his words, as they briefly shook hands, before he continued on his way. Twenty yards on he stopped and turned to see what Axmann had done; a shocked Axmann was staring up the path in disbelief, he hadn't moved. As Martin was to explain to John Anderton later:

'No, I wasn't surprised, it had always seemed obvious to me that a large number of Germans would seek refuge in Switzerland, particularly the German-speaking cantons, and a man with only one arm was conspicuous, it had to be Strasser or Axmann.'

The Polish Government in exile weren't the only rump busy in London, over a month earlier, Eduard Benes the Czech Leader in Buckinghamshire had received a cryptic letter from a Martin Cohen; he passed it in confidence to his

Intelligence officer, Milos Czerwiński, together they decided it meant that the Steven Crown had been recovered from the hands of the Germans and was safely held. They had placed the required advert in the Times and weeks and phone calls later Czerwiński and his wife arrived in Bad Ischl, where his wife waited behind the frothy top of a stein of beer under the sign of the Juicy Heifer, waiting for contact with the man with St Stevan's crown.

Contact established, Martin and Czerwiński walked then talked on a bench by the river. Czerwiński's concern was to establish that Martin did have the Crown, that it was undamaged, that it was safe; the answers Martin gave to describe the crown itself were not entirely convincing, particularly as he had only actually held the crown in his hands for about five minutes. Czerwiński, who had a force of six ready to form an armed guard for when the Crown was passed over, despite misgivings, he had little option but to accept Martin at his word.

The elaborate precautions that had been taken to ensure secrecy, and his own familiarity of the exiled Czech Government meant that Martin knew he was dealing with Benes's special adviser, his next concern was to retrieve the Crown from the woodpile at the Naturfreunde chalet, and ensure that provision had been made to keep the Crown safe from the moment it passed out of his hands for return to the Castle at Prague.

A time, a date, a rendezvous was set, Czerwiński and his men would be in the station café at Kandersteg when summoned, armed and complete with transport. Phone numbers were exchanged in case of difficulties. Martin did not divulge the whereabouts of the crown, deeming the requirement for sturdy vehicles sufficient clue.

Chapter 17
Close Encounters with the
Duke of Albany

Tracker was called to General Urquhart's HQ near Koln, leaving Martin in charge, tasked with taking part in the final questioning of Charles Edward Duke of Saxe-Coburg and Gotha. Wanting to fully brief himself, clearing his desk, bringing in John Anderton he had a bottle of wine still at 1/- a bottle, (not available to ORs) brought up from the cellars and together, they quizzed Sir Piers.

Sir Piers's father, the duke, had been stripped of his English titles by George V, but political sensitivity meant obscure Irish and Scottish titles were ignored and of course it didn't apply to German titles. His father insisted on the duchess being addressed as "Her Royal Highness", a title apparently still attached to an old German Principality. This royal address had apparently annoyed a sensitive Edward Windsor as Wallis, his wife, had not had the title of "Royal Highness" accorded to her. 'This titles business,' said Sir Piers, 'was messy and arcane.' And he wasn't interested; he expected his brother, whom he hadn't spoken to in years, to claim the titles on his father's death, if the Russians who held him prisoner, hadn't shot him by then, but he openly admitted that as a bastard son, he knew he wasn't in the running.

Being asked why Germany had plucked old Etonian Charles Edward to be a German Duke he replied, 'The most charismatic princeling candidate.'

Asked why the most intelligent grandson had been relinquished by Queen Victoria's family, he replied, 'Not tall enough.' Unspoken in all of this chat was the name the duke had written down and pushed across the table, the name of Sir Piers's mother, the mystery, the secret woman who had given anonymous birth to the duke's illegitimate son. Was it possible that Piers's mother's name, forced out of the duke, had even been hidden from the son himself, and that Sir Piers's hidden agenda was to find out who his real mother was. John Anderton didn't think this was possible, but he wanted confirmation from Sir Piers.

Keeping this question of royal parentage secret and as a side issue, the thrust of Sir Piers's enquiries on Churchill's behalf was knowing what commitments the Duke and Duchess of Windsor had made during their extended stay with the Saxe-Coburgs in 1937. Sir Piers said the art historian Blunt was scouring the Archives at Koblenz; with the Americans, Carinhall, Goering mansion was being strip-searched for documents, as was Ribbentrop's house. When John Anderton asked whether Churchill was seeking to destroy the duke, he was met with a withering smile.

'Not destroy, have him in the palm of his hand, same as with Windsor's supporters, Churchill wants to be able to control them as well, not destroy them, they're no use to him if they're destroyed. Enemies are best controlled, not destroyed.'

'Do you want us to scare the living daylights out of your father? Do we play him the Red Cross film with his wife on it?' Partridge's words entered the conversation, without Partridge himself being physically present.

'If the duke cooperates fully, we could probably offer house arrest in the American zone, the question of appearing before a tribunal being left for the time being. Cooperation is telling me everything he knows about Strasser, the party's modus operandi and its innermost structure. No cooperation, an early trial.' Martin wanted to close the discussion.

'What I need to send back to London, excluding any private family documents, are facts, and if no facts, rumours of Windsor's deals with the Nazis.' The exchanges were petering out when John Anderton threw a grenade on the table:

'I shall ask your father the detail of the military information he sent Churchill in the run-up to the war, Churchill was an extraordinary MP, extraordinarily well versed in the Nazi preparations. He got inside information from someone, he was the same age as the duke, they met on holidays, we've seen letters he sent, they were school friends, so why shouldn't they be friendly, and after the Great War, my guess is that your father passed and exchanged military and political gossip, why shouldn't they; perhaps your father Sir Piers, neither of them spies, acted as a kind of foreign news channel, each informing the other, mutual sounding boards for the period leading up to the war. I expect Winston really relished that kind of activity and returned the favour.' He sat back, waiting for the explosion.

Sir Piers's answer, before they all went to bed, never progressed beyond ridiculous, Sir Piers did not sleep that night, there was an intruder, instead of the constant wondering about who his mother was, he went over and over again the day in 1934 when he was sent from an address near Grosvenor Sq. in the West End, to deliver a large, unaddressed brown envelope with German lettering on the back, to an ugly manor house in Kent.

'Don't give him any breakfast in the morning. Record his conversations when we put him back in with the duchess.' Martin went to bed.

The duke looked ill and old, deprived of breakfast, deprived of the stimulus of his wife, fearful of what might befall, he held tightly to the arms of his chair. The energy summoned for his meeting with General Hood had evaporated, Partridge aimed a lamp into his eyes, and he couldn't see his questioners. The first wave of questions caused maximum anxiety, revolving around the inhuman treatment of the eastern nationals, the propaganda film and the failure of the German Red Cross to become involved.

The duke hardly helped himself by initially claiming he didn't really know anything about the camps.

'Liar, we've found files in your offices for each and every one of the labour camps, the extermination camps, as well as files for satellite component manufacturing firms using non-nationals.'

Shifting his answer as well as his position on his chair, the duke's Red Cross knew in theory but hadn't the manpower to follow anything through.

'You had plenty of manpower; there were over a hundred on your staff working in Munich alone, you knew thousands were dying and being killed every month.'

When asked why didn't he ensure these workers were fed adequately, he shuffled that he had never felt it was his responsibility.

'Of course, you were responsible; you can't pick and choose, just because you fed a few Red Cross loaves and fishes through to RAF camps, doesn't absolve you from ignoring the five thousand.'

'You did NOTHING,' Martin banged on the table.

'There wasn't enough food for everybody; nobody had enough food, you've no idea of how it was,' the Duke fought back.

Establishing that the duke had led the Red Cross since 1937, appointed by Hitler, because he had a good reputation abroad as well as in Germany. This was the signal for Sir Piers to come in and take over, the lamp was switched off, and a mug of coffee arrived, he asked about the Great War.

'The Great War almost destroyed our royal family,' he began, Martin shot up in his chair, did Charles Edward still really consider himself part of the English Royal Family.

'Alban, millions of soldiers killed, the Royal Family, Battenberg, Glücksburg to a man, with German names, the family had to change to mask their German genes, so they chose Windsor and made me a scapegoat because I kept my name and stood by the people of Saxe-Coburg-Gotha. They stripped me of the Dukedom of Albany, a title before Bonnie Prince Charlie.' This was clearly a sore point, and Sir Piers hurried to calmer waters.

'But they let you stay on as Duke of Saxe-Coburg-Gotha. Let's turn to Windsor's visit, that was quite a coup, Hitler asking you and the duchess to be hosts to the Duke of Windsor and his wife, how did that come about?'

The duke breathed more easily: 'I was popular and in good standing; Saxe-Coburg had contributed towards the Olympics, and when Ribbentrop told Hitler that as Windsor's cousin I was the most likely person to get the sort of cooperation from Windsor he wanted, I was appointed and given carte blanche.

Ribbentrop needed my help to get Windsor to agree to return to Britain as a puppet king, of course, we didn't say puppet, and we talked his role up. Edward was still popular in South Wales and in the parts of the Empire Hitler wanted to keep onside after a war, particularly India.'

Sir Piers followed this up, 'What else was Hitler after, names for a king's party, the White Club, scandal on Churchill and Baldwin, what did Canada and Australia think about George VI, or was it something else?' The duke lifted in his chair.

'Of course, it was something else, Hitler wanted to be regarded as "a man of peace", but those who knew him knew he was planning for war, though even his admirals hardly knew which war or when. A divided England made it easier for him to get his way.'

'We met at Carinhall, Goering's shooting estate, where most of the discussions took place; what we tried to establish, what Hitler wanted to know—how far and how soon would the Duke of Windsor move to our side and if he did move in with us, would the English accept him again as their king. Goering and Ribbentrop never agreed on this point, and I sided with Goering, against, remembering the fuss over the abdication and the unpopularity of the American third wife. Then if we backed him, and Hitler gave him back the throne, we had to nail down how Windsor would behave. Windsor wouldn't be trapped, he wanted to know how much money would be made available, what his titles would be, what would happen to the fleet and would he still be Emperor of India.'

'Did you reach conclusions, was anything written down?'

The duke's mind was clear, 'Cousin David regretted having abdicated, not a shadow of a doubt about that, both the duchess and I believed he was beginning to regret even being married; my wife has several stories. Simpson would have loved being Queen and hadn't given up on the idea, but she was no more in love with David than I love my gun dogs, I feed them, I rub their stomachs that's it, then David was afraid he would be assassinated if he returned as King to a defeated England, he'd had death threats, he's not a brave man, he wanted reassurances on protection which Goering, who is a brave man you know, looked at with disdain and simply ignored.'

Sir Piers wanted to know what the sticking points were to his agreeing to be returned as King.

'Money! Cousin David was preoccupied with money, he didn't have enough, and he couldn't get enough, he touched the rich after the abdication, living and eating free on their estates whenever he could. Goering offered titles and military support at first but wouldn't guarantee Hitler would allow him to take the title of Emperor of India, Germany would provide the finance to get him firmly installed; after that, the people and the Bank of England would have to provide the money to keep the Monarchy running.'

'Were there other sticking points, Father?'

'I know it sounds silly coming from me, the Duke of Saxe-Coburg-Gotha has many titles to choose from, but he was preoccupied with titles, the minutiae of uniform, medals and so on, but more than anything he was obsessed about the style and address for Wallis Simpson; he got mad when your stepmother inadvertently, when she wasn't there, called her Simpson and insisted that everyone addressed her as Her Royal Highness.'

'With all the unresolved points would he have taken the crown, if Hitler had offered it?'

'My instinct is he would have snatched it, given the chance, why else would he spend hours and hours negotiating; anyway, his wife would have insisted,' Sir Piers, who by this time was wandering around the room, threw out a time bomb:

'What happened to the memorandum of understanding?'

The duke, who until then had answered every question without hesitation, paused, 'Where did you get that from, not from me,' framed a reluctant answer, Sir Piers didn't speak, and for over a minute the room fell totally silent.

'There wasn't a formal memorandum; only Goering could have approved that, Ribbentrop was the same as me, an "errand boy",' not wanting to admit that Sir Piers knew more than he did, the duke followed the question with one of his own, 'Who was the memorandum between? Ribbentrop was the Foreign Minister, Goering led the discussions.'

'What about drafts, where are they?' Sir Piers was pressing, but his father wasn't minded to help further beyond saying that old files were held in Gotha and that some burned after an RAF air raid in 1944.

'Did I tell you I went with Ribbentrop on a couple of other visits, he didn't know, but I was there to report back if Ribbentrop did anything silly. I went with him to Spain and then to Turkey, but nobody liked him very much, and nothing resulted.'

More biscuits and mugs of coffee arrived, Martin took up the questioning.

'You met Colonel Strasser through the Red Cross, he was your boss, but why pay Strasser for sanctuary when you had Huntingtower empty on your estate at Bad Goisern?'

'For the same reason Strasser doesn't use his farm at Aussee. That would be the first place the Americans would come looking,' he paused, 'Strasser allows Anna's family to stay and look after the farm.'

The duke repeated his work as liaison with the Red Cross in Geneva, arranging their visits, admin, advice and so on, he was connected with the POW Camps but not work camps like Ebensee, stressing the "good work" he had done in overseeing POW Camps, getting Red Cross Parcels through; when Strasser offered safe accommodation at Dilsberg, he decided to take it up, paying for six months direct into a Zurich Bank.

Asked about the men who had arrived at Dilsberg with Strasser and escaped down the cellar tunnel, the duke thought Ritter had spoken about building a hideaway in some mountain retreat, 'He's a very practical man.' Axmann was the best equipped to look after himself, knowing hundreds of people throughout Switzerland and Austria, every Youth Leader, every Chairman of every Naturfreunde Society, all these organisations owned huts and houses in pleasant countryside, being a pleasant and popular injured soldier and politico, he would be all right, 'You know he led Strasser, Bormann and another chap from Berlin down to Austria after Strasser had passed them through the Russian lines. Axmann's trouble is that he is well known and will be recognised. He appeared in dozens of newsreels and made hundreds of personal appearances you know.'

What Martin most wanted, of course, was information about Strasser. The duke mentioned the sister, the Black Forest Mansion, Anna had a flat, Strasser owned a farm near Aussee, all things Martin knew. His next question:

'Who owns 33 Dilsberg?'

The duke began to answer, 'His sis…' he stopped. Martin waited. 'I'm not sure.'

'You started to say something,' Martin prompted.

'No, I don't know.'

Martin dashed the mug to the floor, thrust his face in an inch snarling, 'You started to say "his sister", who's his sister, what's her name, where does she live, or must I pull it out of your arse.' He sat back, aghast at himself, horrified at his own crude language. *What am I become,* he thought. *I'm getting worse than Partridge.*

'Her name's Edda, but I don't know for a fact that she owns it.'

Martin rang the bell, wrote down the name and address and gave it to the answering WAAF, 'Find out who's the owner. Do it now.'

Turning back to the duke, he asked what Ritter's relationship was with Strasser, surprised when the duke said that on instruction from Strasser, Ritter had increased food provisions at Ebensee, at odds with his earlier claim that he had no knowledge that Ritter had proposed killing the entire labour force by collapsing a cavern on their heads, like Samson, bringing down the temple, Martin ended on a quiet note, 'I've arranged a family party, dinner with your wife and Sir Piers, tonight in the state dining room.'

Alone with the duke, John Anderton took up the last lap of questions for the session, beginning with an apology.

'I'm sorry I have to tread in a hidden aspect of our history, when did you first meet Winston Churchill?' The duke was taken by surprise.

'I don't know, I met him as a boy, probably at Blenheim, but it might have been Sandringham.'

'And did you ever meet him on holiday, your Grace?'

'As a boy several times down at Osborne House, I believe.'

'Did you go to the same school?'

'Winston went to Harrow, I had more of a private education, but we were both at Sandhurst.'

'Your Grace, when did your correspondence with Churchill cease?'

'We exchanged Christmas cards till the war.' The duke was shuffling in his chair.

'When did your letters stop?'

'There are no letters.' Without American technology, it was impossible to decide whether the duke lied on this point, or in the answers that followed.

'So we'll have to wait till Winston Churchill sells his memoirs for a definitive answer to that question.' John Anderton smiled at his own effrontery, adding further wickedness: 'Does Sir Piers know you have already told us who his mother is?'

'No.'

'Does Sir Piers know who his real mother is?' This was a real back-hander, and the duke took his time.

'I'm not sure.' Anderton waited.

'He knows the duchess isn't his real mother, as a youth he was given a formula to latch on to, whether he accepted this as he got older I don't know, it was never discussed.'

Sir Piers wasn't informed that the state dining room was bugged.

Cocktails, an alcove set with bugged branches from bushes from the garden provided the first snippet of information. Three courses, a white tablecloth, a bottle of wine from the cellars, followed by a second, anchored the ambience, eventually, the family news and gossip petered out, the talk turned to Hitler, Bormann, Goebbels and political intrigue, much more interesting, both to Travers, Whitehall and the Palace, than to a Martin obsessed with Strasser.

The duke, well into his third gin and tonic, asked his son if he could "do anything for us". Sir Piers didn't think he should worry too greatly provided there was no proof that he'd been directly involved with the work camps, 'Always call them work camps, father, so unless there's something to be discovered, don't worry.' Saxe-Coburg leaned forward and whispered into his son's ear.

'Jesus, Father, if that comes out, you're as good as dead. The Jews will have a field day.' The equipment didn't pick up the whisper, 'Just keep quiet, deny everything, I can't promise a thing if that comes out.' To himself, Sir Piers just said, 'How stupid can one be.'

'That escape, the deaths of those US airmen, that's why I paid to disappear and come to live at Dilsberg.'

The duchess wanted to talk again about the days when her husband had power and influence and turned the conversation back to when the Windsors made their official visit to Germany, and she was the grand hostess in Coburg castle.

'Hitler never told Cousin David he intended to invade France, so, of course, it was never mentioned. Hitler despised weaklings, Josef Goebbels and that Czech singer. Goering told me that he'd said, "What sort of man gives up his throne for a woman?" I myself heard him say: "The strong lead the weak to the wall". He wanted our opinion on whether the English would again accept him as king, uncertain, I doubt he would have had him crowned, such was his private opinion of the man.'

The duke came back into the conversation: 'Crowning, we spent ages arguing whether he should be crowned, he was only king for a few months and had never been crowned, he couldn't decide whether Westminster Abbey was any longer the best place. St David's was mentioned.'

He went on, 'Windsor named his supporters and his enemies, Churchill was financially dependent on the paper proprietor, Beaverbrook, but Churchill was unpopular, and after the abdication, Windsor neither liked or trusted Churchill nor wanted Churchill's advice. He didn't want an impoverished Churchill, as leader of a "King's Party", he knew that Churchill had come to the opinion that he was a "wrong-un", both Churchill and Hitler were agreed on that.

They talked about the Empire, Hitler wanted total access to the empire's resources, he knew where the tin, the oil, the copper, the jute and the cotton came from, and he wanted access.

Sir Piers knew the Palace had sent him to Germany to hear what hopefully was coming next, 'How much a traitor was the Duke of Windsor?'

'You said earlier that there wasn't an agreement.'

'Well, there wasn't, but there was a memo.' The Duke of Saxe-Coburg and Gotha leant forward and pulled out a double wallet from his inside pocket. Putting the wallet open on the table, he unzipped the back compartment and carefully extracted folded foolscap which turned out to be two pieces tightly folded together.

The piece that lay on top was the second page, there weren't any signatures; Sir Piers scanned it, then went back and read each line:

'Northern Ireland, six provinces plus IOM to go to Eire,' Sir Piers took his glasses off: 'What's that about, Father?'

'Alban, Hitler wanted to weaken England, Eire under de Valera, had secretly agreed that they would attack Northern Ireland, upon the invasion of England, Northern Ireland would be forced into Ireland under a catholic de Valera; he believed England didn't like the Irish, protestant or catholic didn't matter.'

'England to cede the Channel Islands,' he read.

'Most certainly, not back to France, you understand, Hitler thought Jersey would make a good holiday camp for his troops. Cousin David wasn't going to fight over trifles.'

'Gibraltar? Promised to General Franco?' The duke nodded.

'Cyprus, Malta, Gozo, all to go as well?'

'Not to Spain, Hitler liked Mussolini, Benito almost looking on Hitler as his protégé, he wanted the islands much more than Cousin David was prepared to fight.'

Sir Piers read the next line twice before reading out, 'To use his best offices to smooth the transfer of good relations and trade with South Africa, Canada, Australia and New

Zealand. What the hell does that mean, Father?' The duke took another long drink, Sir Piers refilled his glass.

'Top me up, dear,' said the duchess.

'This all seems silly and such a long time ago,' said the duke, 'Cousin David knew in his bones the white Empire couldn't stomach him, but he couldn't admit it to Goering. Windsor was reconciled to losing the big lands across the seas, Canada, Australia, New Zealand and South Africa. None had helped him during the abdication and he believed they would assume independence on the day England was beaten, they all had plans to do just that, so his "kingsmen" in the colonies told him. Installation as Hitler's puppet wouldn't change that. But Windsor always thought he might secure a role in India.'

'Oil?' the question was put.

'If the Navy supported him, he thought the Middle Eastern sheiks, princes and kings might still accord him and Britain a role, we had invested a lot of money out there, but Goering refused to discuss that. Hitler had his own plans for oil, particularly as Germany hasn't got any.'

'Let's sum up father, does it mean that if Hitler agreed to put Edward VIII back on the throne, he would effectively turn the Empire over to Germany, for them to supply their raw materials for Germany to turn into finished product.'

'It doesn't say it, but yes that was about it, Windsor had no choice, in the formula discussed, India was left out, David thought that with cheering crowds he just might keep some control of Middle East oil and of India. We didn't tell him he didn't stand a chance.

Sir Piers still had questions, 'What about the royal navy?'

'If Hitler got the Fleet, overnight Germany became a world power. Windsor fancied himself as a sailor and for some reason believed the Admirals were more likely to fall behind him than were the Generals, we pretended to believe him and it was used as a negotiating chip, it was Windsor's only ace.'

'What did you make of the American woman?' Sir Piers wanted to know. Father sat up, 'Well, what do you think? You've read the English papers, and you know George VI's wife, Elizabeth,' he winked.

'I'm asking you, Father.' The Duchess of Saxe-Coburg, who had been following the conversation closely, but keeping quiet, leapt in:

'I'll answer that; I'll tell you what we think—it was me who entertained her, I spent a lot of time with her. Before they arrived and went to Carinhall, Ribbentrop had the Foreign Office send us a file as thick as a Mussolini. Our people at the New York Embassy had really gone to town and wrote she was ambitious, always short of money, dependent on relatives and others she met and that she manipulated the men who found her fascinating.'

'Goering wouldn't allow her in on meetings, so we'd walk and talk for hours, Windsor would talk to her as soon as they'd finished and they'd have their own little meeting.'

'Then Goering put Flight Lieutenant Gruber on as an escort, to woo her, to apply blackmail later, she fell for Gruber, but who wouldn't, even I fell for him,' she grinned, 'didn't I, dear?' she turned towards her husband.

' I liked her, didn't much like Windsor, but we all felt a bit sorry for him with his hangdog face, he overheard a subaltern say Hitler should make her Queen and appoint him as King Consort. It was if he had been hit by a polo stick, his face dropped, and never recovered, for the rest of the visit his face had sadness sprayed on, look at his eyes in all the photos. Although she was smart, she wasn't smart enough to make him ever look truly happy again.'

The duke finished off, 'When she was one to one she had the ability to make a man feel special, she'd say things like, 'how do you manage to keep in shape and keep on top of your dukedom. Do you like these stockings? Oscar Frank brought them from Paris, but the seams won't stay straight, aren't they naughty, just see if they're all right please,' and if you did she'd show you. She was a mix of Greta Garbo and Marlene Dietrich. I hate that woman, don't I, darling.' He looked at the duchess.

Sir Piers pulled the other sheet to the top, picked it up and read it. It outlined the division of authority and who should make appointments etc. 'Why was the draft never signed?' he asked his father.

'I shouldn't be telling you all this, too dangerous. He ticked it but it was never initialled, a copy is in a safe in Coburg, he knew if he signed it and it got out, it was as good as his death warrant, the English are good haters, even if they're not good killers, or is it the other way around.'

'Father, there's nothing here about what was to happen to George VI, I suppose that was a bit tricky.'

'Well, it was Alban, nothing was ever written down, but it was discussed. Goering simply said 'leave it to us, meaning we'd kill him, if George fled too early to Canada, he'd be labelled a coward and a deserter, we'd have him stripped of his titles, and Windsor would have what he never had and had always secretly wanted, a Coronation at Westminster Cathedral.'

Sir Piers mulled this over, 'But what about the succession, the Simpson woman had never had children, neither had Windsor and it wasn't likely that one would come along, at that stage of life.'

'That was looking too far ahead,' the duke chuckled, 'let me show you what sort of a man Windsor really was, and this'll tell you whether he wanted his crown back. He always made a big show of telling us that the two princesses really liked him; he had played with them at Balmoral; he taught them how to goose step; how to give a Nazi salute; how to salute like Hitler; his arm across his chest. He wondered if he could adopt them so as to provide a succession, Princess Elizabeth was first in line to the throne and was now being brought up in a fashion for her to accept that she would eventually become Queen, different from her sister. Elizabeth might have fallen in with the adoption idea, if for no other reason that if she didn't accept her uncle's offer, the same offer could be made to Sister Margaret Rose, and she didn't trust her sister to the extent that she could risk that. Sibling jealousy—you more than anyone should know about that, Sir Piers. Hitler quite liked the idea. "Fit for the Borgias," he said, and it became a strong argument in Windsor's favour.'

'Well, I never, just fancy, I never even thought of that,' Sir Piers was taken aback, perhaps his elder brother would stay in Siberia and he could become Duke of Saxe-Coburg-Gotha. He dismissed the thought.

The duke's glass was empty. His arm around his shoulders, Sir Piers led his father out of the room, returning to help the duchess up from her chair and give her a hug which she accepted coldly. His mother, still wide awake, muttering 'Courtesan,' went off to bed.

Martin didn't go to bed until, he had listened to the recordings. The snippet at the outset, the duke had warned his wife to say nothing about Strasser and Ritter, if they ever found we'd talked they'd kill us. Anyway, we don't know where they've gone.'

'But we do know where they've gone,' said the duchess.

'Do we?' the duke metaphorically scratched his head? 'How's that?

'Strasser took the keys to Huntingtower with him.'

Martin wrote it down again. H U N T I N G T O W E R. He went to bed with the single word in his mind, before breakfast, he was down in the engine room, everyone was put on to finding "Huntingtower". Only when he casually mentioned it to Sir Piers did he find the answer:

'Bad Goisern, yes, I know it, Huntingtower is a novel by John Buchan, and it's also a lodge on Father's Bad Goisern Estate,' Martin remembered he had done a recce with Sir Piers to check whether the duke should be kept at the Manor, but he didn't remember anything called Huntingtower. He would seek out Huntingtower himself, then it couldn't be leaked, but as a precaution, he took Partridge with him. 'Dark clothes, tool up,' he said.

The map didn't show the name Huntingtower, but within the Estate away from the main house, the map showed a small square, a symbol identified by the key to the map as a small building, Bad Goisern Town Hall Records did the rest; Huntingtower. He timed the visit for just after dark. They first looked at the Manor house from trees a hundred yards back.

Looking at their map, for there was no proper path, they turned towards Huntingtower.

Backed by trees, fronted by parkland, tall and narrow Huntingtower showed the merest glimmer of a light chinking through an upstairs shutter, no light in the tower, nothing else, but it was enough to show that someone was there. Knowing Strasser's attention to security, Martin stayed well back, curbing his curiosity until he had a plan. They didn't wait long, Partridge saw to that.

He had abandoned phoning home to wife Hillary, waiting hours for a connection didn't sit well with him, so he sat down and wrote another daily affectionate letter, ending before the kisses: 'At long last, I really believe I've now got Strasser in my sights,' writing with an optimism he didn't feel. In bed, he realised he hadn't got a plan, just a thousand ideas spinning around in his head, so the following morning, he perched his bum on John Anderton's desk.

Anderton was cool and analytical: 'We moved mob-handed too quickly against the Queen of St Gilgen and missed him, again with the Americans, you moved in force against Walserval, you used a big net, you had a good plan, you caught a lot of B list bastards, but again you missed Strasser, and Ritter proved himself to be a good opponent in a crisis, and he eluded us. Now Dilsberg was a different matter, we planned well, we had a good method not dependent on our friends, but Strasser still managed to escape. If the duke is to be believed, somehow in the hour before we went in, Strasser got a sniff of our raid and left taking Axmann and Ritter with him. The duchess gives us our only trace, he took the keys to Huntingtower with him, after these escapes you can be certain that Strasser's nose for survival is super twitchy, and we've now got little chance of capturing him off-guard. We've got to be either super cunning or lucky, let's face it, he's as clever as we are.'

Martin pulled a face, Anderton continued, 'For my money, Anna will have split off and gone to lie low with her sister or her parents; Ritter's a loner, he'll have gone off to some mountain or other, Dachstein's been mentioned several times. Axmann is apparently his own man, he'll be pissed off at having been hunted out of several safehouses, and he'll have vanished and cut himself apart from Strasser, he'll be all right, he's got money, contacts and nous, but he's recognisable, so my guess is he'll turn up again without our hunting him. Single, a Prussian, no ties with Austria, he'll have gone over the border into Switzerland and gone hiking for the summer, it's what he likes best. It's getting more and more like the Wild West, border crossings, hideaways, we're the posse against Butch Cassidy and Sundance, you're the sheriff, you're US Marshall Tex Ritter, after German Ritter, you're the guy with the star, always one step behind the outlaws.'

'Yes, but what's your bloody plan,' Martin had had enough analysis. 'Do you want me to surround Huntingtower and drive up and challenge him to come out and fight?'

Anderton told Martin straight, 'We can't have the Americans involved again, another failure would be too embarrassing, Strasser can't have many resources left, go quickly at Huntingtower, and if he's there shoot him out, he may be so tired of running that he gives up, but before you do, try to anticipate what he'll do if he gets out of Huntingtower alive.'

Sir Piers put his head around the door, 'I'm off, chaps, sorry we got off to a bad start; still, I got what I came for, thanks for the wine and all your help. Don't be hard on Father; he's really a good chap.' They all shook hands.

'Wasn't a bad chap,' Martin observed after he had gone, 'but his father knows all about the 50 escaped airmen the SS murdered.'

Martin slipped downstairs to speak to Muller; he didn't beat about the bush:

'We both know Strasser planned ahead for every single event. After the "Queen" was discovered, he had prepared a contingency plan, if Walserval was discovered, he still had a plan, after Dilsberg what had he planned to do next, he must have known a ruin in the Black Forest wasn't any good?' Muller was anxious to help.

'Well, he thought his sister's house was secure, even the Germans don't know where Dilsberg is, and very few are hiding there. With his attention to secrecy, he must have reckoned on it being secure; he had kept it from me, I only learned of it by accident. I'd never heard of Huntingtower until I saw the keys in the cabinet.' Muller was determined to give the impression that he had been totally frank.

'I thought he might run to the ruin in the Black Forest, but last night I remembered something else, about two months ago, I heard part of a phone call, he was enquiring about a US passport and he mentioned his false hand could be used as identification, that was all I heard.'

'Did you not hear anything else, anything you must have picked up your ears?'

'No, that was it, but the call must have been serious, he got up to shut his door, normally he would have shouted for someone to do it for him,' Martin tutted with annoyance,

'How can he possibly get to America,' Martin stopped to think 'only the Yanks can get him across the pond.' He spoke aloud, 'Could he get onto the gravy train where Uncle Sam picks the best scientists and whisks them to the US?' He decided to have a word with Barney.

Apart from saying that exporting scientists was nothing to do with him, Barney didn't want to discuss policy or detail on transferring scientist to America, the subject of moving German scientists was classified and off-limits, it was certainly not up for discussion with the Brits, 'Sorry, old boy.'

Martin had come to another dead end.

2 hours before nightfall, 3 vehicles and 10 armed men drove up to the edge of the duke's Bad Goisern estate. They skirted the main house and fanned out in pairs around Huntingtower. As soon as they were in position, leaving the locksmith, behind Partridge forced a door.

Huntingtower was plain wood floors, wood panelled walls and ceilings. Little furniture, few small rooms with cupboards, they searched diligently, weapons armed and cocked, they knew nothing about persecuted clergy but it was two hours before they gave it a clean bill of health, a Huntingtower empty of mice, if their bird had been there it had flown, but for Martin there remained a niggle, the day before he had seen a glimmer, he could smell onions, the kitchen was clean and didn't look to be recently used, but he could smell onions, and it wasn't Partridge's bad breath.

Despondent Martin took everyone back to Sisi's Restaurant; he had been so confident, he had the girls order the owner to keep it open. Famous, Lehar's ladies of talent and beauty sang its praises 80 years earlier, Sisi's by the ancient bridge over the Traun; the choice was noodles or potatoes, but although the food was war-weary, the décor and the ambience welcomed over a dozen rowdy cheerful foreigners, who saw no reason whatsoever to share Martin's disappointment and were happy to embrace the few locals still able to pay. Martin threw off his disappointment and paid the bill, weather fine they continued singing as they walked through the town, *Roll out the Barrel, Lily Marlene,* echoed along the empty streets. Past the graveyard, back over the Emperor Bridge to the lodge. Up the hill, around the bend, the entrance to the hunting lodge came into view. Waiting at the entrance stood Hillary. Martin rushed to her side, 'What are you doing here?' Hillary burst into tears. She had miscarried.

She wept on Martin's shoulder. Martin kicked the ornamental garden vase. Hundred years of history lay in four pieces. He threw them in the pond. Viciously.

Next day Martin had planned to drive to Kiental, recover the Crown of Steven, before handing it over to Czerwiński.

'Will you come?' he asked Hillary, 'I'll cancel or go alone if you prefer.' No way did Hillary want to leave his side, she had good memories of Kiental and wanted to go. We'll stay a couple of nights at the Naturfreunde House, dig into the woodpile in the morning then we'll take the crown down to Spiez (he'd forgotten about Kandersteg, Spiez having been his original intention for the handover) and hand it over to Czerwiński.

Hillary asked whether it was King Steven or King Stephen, Martin didn't know. She rang and booked accommodation at the Naturfreundehaus.

Martin took the best kübelwagen, he wanted no problems ascending the mountain wall. Before the hill climb with its hairpins, they got out, stretched their legs, walking to the bottom where the avalanche had swept the Scotsman's chalet over the cliff, the site remained as it had been left, huge caterpillar tracks breaking across pine trunks flung hither and thither and the remnants of Falcon's chalet.

'We'd never have found all the boxes if it hadn't been for the Yanks excavators and their magic box.' Martin answered in reply to Hillary's question of.

'How did you manage to half inch the box with St Steven's Crown without anyone seeing you?' Hillary had to explain the cockney slang.

Parking the kübelwagen off road where Falcon's chalet once stood, Martin carried the bag up the path to the door where the warden was standing to greet them. He had only one arm, but Martin knew immediately, dressed in a suit, completely different from the hiking clothes, he was about to shake hands and meet for the second time the former German Youth Minister, Artur Axmann. *What's the Romanisch for HELLO?* he wondered.

'This is where we eat, the sitting-room's through there,' Axmann pointed, 'here is our pride and joy,' he led into the kitchen where a gleaming black stove took most of the room, it had so many holes for cooking it could have been a draught board. 'I only took over a week ago, so your wife will have to work out how it functions.' Hillary made cooing noises. 'Let me show you to your bedroom.'

The bedroom door had no lock, it didn't even have catch to close it. The only one bed it was 20 feet long and had 2 tiers, weight: it could sleep 10 on the bottom and 10 on the top, even when the house was half empty—when the house was full in August and Christmas! Nowhere did it say "herren". Axmann left them to it and warden went to sit on covered veranda, one side glass panel to stop the prevailing wind back but not the view towards Griesalp, they chose the bottom bunk and the far end nearest the light, a torch attached to a separate pocket-sized battery taped to the wall.

Martin sat on the bed, his head in his hands, 'would you believe it… it's Artur Axmann again, what's more I dreamt that I would meet him here.

'Axmann, of course I'm sure,' getting angry when Hillary challenged him, 'he lost that arm in Russia four years ago,' he replaced Baldur von Shirach as Youth leader when von Shirach became the Minister for Austria.

'You go and talk to him, keep him occupied, I'll look in his room,' Hillary was always practical. That is exactly what they did. Like all the house there weren't any locked rooms, and it didn't take long for Hillary to join the two men with a hidden "thumbs up". After a supper cooked in unison on the vast wood-fired kitchen stove with its eight separate hobs.

Hand in hand they walked around the house and the roughhewn garden, Martin checked the tell-tales he had left, all were in place exactly as he'd left them. Satisfied the Crown was safe, he revised the hacked about hand-over plan, there was a telephone and he had a long conversation with Czerwiński who was asked to bring his men up the mountain by noon the following day.

Martin was moving wood by 6 o'clock in the morning. The tell tales, the following cloth strips were all in place and by 10 minutes past he had brought the box holding St Steven's Crown out from the inside of the woodpile, he left the wood pile in a bit of a mess, he was never a tidy man, clearing up he regarded as a waste of time.

Hillary put a chair under the bedroom door handle and watched as Martin opened the box, remembering the efforts put in by the prisoners in Hut 2 at Menzenschwand POW Camp. In the dim light, the small crown was something of a disappointment to Hillary, though she affected to be as thrilled as Martin. She perched it on her head 'Why didn't I bring the camera?' she said. Rubbing the gold with her handkerchief, she carefully tucked it back in the box, put the box in the bag, drawing the strings tight before putting the bag under the bed, back against the wall, breakfast, no rationing in Switzerland, was rolls brought up from the neighbouring hose, jam and butter and coffee. More cups of coffee as they waited for Czerwiński and his men.

Bag over his shoulder, Martin walked the hundred metres to the top of the very last hairpin, out of sight of Naturfreunde, to where the road appeared out of the trees. He could hear the lorry 20 minutes before it appeared, hear as it reversed to negotiate the most severe hairpins.

The simple hand-over took place in the centre of the road, without any checking of identities. Martin hadn't even taken the box from the bag, when Czerwiński finally held the Crown in his hands he kissed it, before walking down the line of men to show it off. His men clapped then surrounded Martin shaking hands. A bottle of slivovitch was emptied from the neck downwards.

'Now the other thing. Follow me,' said Martin.

'We grab him, handcuffs on, he tells me what I want to know, then he goes between the seats in the back of the kubelwagon. Czerwiński posted men around the chalet, then followed Martin inside. Axmann was sitting in a dilapidated easy chair looking out over the valley, sun warmed inside the enclosed veranda, perfectly at ease, his cardigan unbuttoned in stockinged feet, his shoes lying beside him.

Few words, little roughness, the Czechs frog-marched Axmann out of the house, down the road to the edge looking down from the top onto the cliff, polished smooth where the avalanche had swept all before it.

'Let me introduce myself, Martin Cohen, I'm sure Colonel General Strasser has mentioned me. You're going to tell me where I can find the colonel or you're going over the cliff.' The silence was broken by light spats of rain on the road, Czerwiński signalled, the guards seized his arms again and pushed him towards the very edge.

'Wait, I'll tell you what I know, what more can I do.'

'Where did Strasser go when you left Huntingtower?' Martin, speaking through gritted teeth.

'Did he leave? My guess is he'll still be there working on his plans, he holed up in the secret wing of the tower.' A sinking feeling hit the base of Martin's stomach, the smell of onions returned. Axmann was a witness of truth. 'That's all I know.'

They took him back to the warm kitchen, Axmann was anxious to talk, from leaving the Fuehrer bunker, through the death of Bormann, the journey south, the escape from the Queen of St Gilgen, the flight through the tunnel, to Huntingtower by way of Eberbach.

One detail remained, Martin wanted to know why Strasser stayed at Huntingtower, what was he planning? 'His ambition is to get to the USA where he thinks he'll be safe, that's all he ever said. He's fully accepted that his days of running safehouses is finished.'

A Czech guard put his head around the door: 'There's a police car just climbed the hill.'

'We're going!' Czerwiński grabbed the bag and rushed out through the back door, gesticulating to all the men he could see 'get out of sight. The police car pulled up in front of the chalet. Through the door came Chief Inspector Tonneau.

'Good of you to give your details to our Zurich Border Post when you came into Switzerland this time, Mr Cockburn.' Turning to the caretaker.

'May I see your passport, Herr Axmann?' he asked politely.

Martin had willingly handed over St Steven's Crown to Czerwiński, he had no option but to hand a trussed up Axmann into the hands of Chief Inspector Tonneau. The only thought in his mind was to race back to Ischl and get together another search party to take Huntingtower apart to find this hidden wing.

'How will Strasser go about getting to the States?' he asked John Anderton as they raced towards the Bad Goisern estate and Huntingtower.

'Imitate a scientist, or stow away in the hold of a Douglas, don't ask me,' was all he got in reply.

Huntingtower was indeed deserted, not a mouse or a squatter or a hunted man to be seen, the entrance to the secret wing was concealed in a false wall under the eaves. Partridge called for Martin, revolvers at the ready the pair climbed over the partition and entered the hidden wing, through pygmy rooms, down twisting narrow iron staircases, hopes receding as they descended, only the faint smell of onions to remind them of who was missing and that they were too late. A miserable Martin arrived back at Ischl just in time to pick up a phone call from Barney.

'Thought I had the one you're looking for, a tall blond with an artificial hand, but it turns out he was a professor at Tubingen and worked on rocket engines.'

'What was he called?' Martin asked.

'Raoul Helm.' Barney was asked to spell it. Martin mulled the name over as he did every name knowing Strasser loved to use the initials of Nazi leaders. *R H*, he wondered, *what about Rudolph Hess, deputy fuhrer? But a longshot after seeking a peace treaty with his flight to Scotland, but he had been important once.* 'Did this Helm scratch the back of his head with his opposite hand?' he asked Barney.

'Don't know, I didn't see him myself I'll ask, won't take a second.' True enough he was back in a second, 'Yes, Sergeant Phibbs tells me Helm scratched the back of his head all the time.'

'Hold him, I'm coming over right away. Hold on to him Barney, whatever you do. That's our man.'

'I will if I can, but I think he's left.'

Martin shouted for John Anderton, Partridge and a couple of men, he drove recklessly, his foot pressed down on the accelerator all of the 20 miles to Gmunden. Getting through the security at the gate seemed to take an age, his brakes threw up loose stones from the front of Barney's office, Barney stood standing by the door:

'Afraid he's gone, probably in the air on his way to Shannon by now. I've put out a "Stop", but I don't think it'll work.'

Barney was busy; Martin was kicking the wall, it was left to John Anderton to thank Barney for his efforts, before driving off in the jeep back down the Traunsee. Martin asked him to stop by the Castle, getting out he walked to the shingle beach, still rubbish strewn from the weaponry discharged on Party Night. Under the Castle shadow he threw stones ever further into the dark water, then he searched out weighted flatties to see how many times he could skim them along the surface of calm water.

He threw himself into the back of the kübelwagen, 'Bastard, he's done me again.'

Back at the lodge he made a beeline for Hillary, they went straight to the bedroom, no dinner, not even a cup of tea.

His next appearance was in the dining room, half way through his meal Partridge came and interrupted,

'Message came in from Barney,' he held out a slip of paper.

Chapter 18
I Said We Were Close

'More delay, what's happening, what's the matter?' the American colonel had the seat nearest to the cockpit, and being senior and nearest to the aircrew was the best place to prise out information and ask what was happening. All the passengers could tell was that the engines had been throttled back, and the loud roar prior to take-off which had assailed their eardrums diminished quicker than it started, just as clearly those that followed every bump on the runway before take-off could tell that the Douglas DC7 was being turned off the runway and was heading back to the hangar.

'What's it this time? Two hours late already, what the hell's up now? I'm Colonel Sam L Short, and my schedule's already been screwed up. We must press on.' The colonel pushed his head into the cockpit space reserved for the crew, 'What's up?' he repeated.

'If you don't take your footwear out of my cockpit, you won't be Sam L anymore; it'll be Colonel Short, period.' The pilot wasn't standing any nonsense, particularly in front of his crew.

'Sorry,' the colonel retreated.

It wasn't till the plane came to a halt that the pilot pulled back the curtain that separated him from the passengers to announce there would be a delay, nothing to do with the condition of the Douglas you understand, but there had been an event in the air near Munich, would they all go back to the canteen.

Strasser, don't forget you're R Helm, he said to himself, seated near the back, had begun to relax as the chocks were pulled away, the engines started and the plane trundled towards the runway, turning back from the runway was a body-blow, return to the hangar launched the anxiety of the past 10 days. He peered out of the window, unfastened his safety belt, not for a second did he believe the fiction of "something in the air near Munich".

The passengers waited for the steps to be brought out humping their bags, before straggling back to the hangar, their questions of 'How long will we have to wait?' met with a shrug; the "something" became a freak storm, a wild cat Messerschmitt, a bomb on their plane—except no one seemed to be doing any searching. The pilot headed off to the control tower, coming back to tell his crew, 'Nobody knows, they've simply been told to stop our flight and await instructions.'

Between meals, the canteen was cold and unfriendly, but at least there were tables and chairs, and Strasser watched four sergeants in a game of poker, cigarettes as chips, trying to work out what was happening. The colonel had disappeared, to appease him, the ground staff had taken him where "hard stuff" was available, the flight crew chatted for a few minutes, then they too disappeared, paying not the slightest interest to the passengers. Over an hour passed before a cook appeared, he threw a few switches announcing coffee shortly.

Losing interest in the poker, Strasberg watched anxiously as two cars pulled up outside, soldiers jumped out, fell-in in two ranks, before filling into the canteen and lining up along a wall.

'Herr Helm, Raoul Helm,' the officer called out his new name. Strasser didn't stand up immediately, deciding what to do; no one there knew who Helm was or what Helm looked like. If he was going to run for it, the time was now, he could choose not to stand up, wait, then go the washroom and escape through an open window. Slowly, he raised his hand and got to his feet; he would bide his time.

'Follow me, please.' A soldier before and behind; soon two other men fell in so he now had four soldiers by his side, he followed the officer along a corridor.

'What's all this about?' The officer denied all knowledge; he was just carrying out an order.

'Wait in there, please.' There being an untidy small room with three chairs, two soldiers had to stand.

Partridge, who had been in the office when the message arrived, took it immediately to Martin, Travers being away again on a jaunt to the library at the ancient Admont Monastery.

Martin took the note, pausing before punching the air.

'We've got him, good old Barney,' he read the note out loud to Partridge, 'There was a delay, got a message to the airfield as Douglas was taxiing for take-off to Shannon, they told the pilot his plane had a bomb aboard, so the pilot turned back. Barney's on his way to pick up Helm; he wants me to get to the airfield, make the identification, and then—believe it or not, I can bring him back here.' He did a jig around the orangery.

'Get your gloves, Partridge; you're driving me to Tölz, do you know where the airstrip is?'

They raced up the Munich road to Tölz Airfield like bats out of hell, the canopy pulled back, conversation impossible. Barney was at the side of their jeep before they could jump out, he wanted urgency saying there was a colonel creating hell at the delay, that he'd observed the so-called Helm—he'd a false hand, he scratched the back of his head, he was sweating and he'd little fear they had their man. No doubt whatsoever, he did his party trick of scratching his ear around the back of his head time after time.

A day later, Martin told Hillary the story of what happened at Bad Tölz airfield:

'I followed Barney into the office where Strasser was being held, the moment he saw me he stood up, clicked his heels, bowed.

'"Pilot Officer Martin Cockburn, I presume," he choked out the words. I ignored him; now I wish I hadn't, I just nodded to Barney "that's him all right" and went out.

'Barney decided to have him taken back to his HQ at Gmunden in the lorry, there they would make out all the paperwork, and I would arrange to take him on from there to Ischl. He gave firm instructions, Strasser was never to be left unattended and must be handcuffed to a marine and to a stanchion, in the back of the lorry.

'Then I went to speak to the pilot and the airfield control staff to say thanks and apologise for holding them up. I went back to our kübelwagen ready to escort the lorry when I heard two shots from the offices. I jumped out and ran into the offices; in the corridor, the marines had got a woman spread-eagled on the floor, further down the corridor was another man lying on the floor, I could see it was Strasser, two marines were bending over him. The nearest of them straightened up before I could ask.

'"He's dead, fella," he said, "nothing we can do".

'"Are you sure?" He nodded. "Are you certain?"

'The marine still by the body, "Certain, see for yourself." I waved my hand away; I'd not the slightest wish to see for myself. The marine got up and dropped a handkerchief over Strasser's face.

'I went outside, shocked, then I was sick, after that I walked and walked around the block until I had settled down.'

Partridge acted as a proxy in Martin's temporary absence, a glass of bourbon, waiting for his return.

The canopy restored, the return journey to Ischl a blur, Martin furious with himself for not staying close to Strasser, all he could do now was ask Partridge repeated questions for third-hand answers to be filed in the regret cortex of his brain.

'Yes, the woman had appeared from nowhere.'

'No, nobody knew who she was.'

'No, nobody had seen her before, she came on the airfield with the other cleaners.'

'Yes, she had been on her knees in the corridor with a brush, a bucket, and as we know now, a revolver.'

'No, German cleaners weren't searched coming on to the airfield.'

'Yes, Strasser was escorted by four guards. They were going out through the corridor to the waiting lorry.'

'No, they didn't suspect anything, as they passed, the woman leaned back and looked up, pointed her revolver and fired two shots up at Strasser's head. He screamed, reeled back and fell.'

'Yes, she shot from a foot away.'

'Was he dead?' Travers returned from Admont, anxious to catch up with events, asked the question.
'Of course, he was bloody dead; he'd taken two bullets in his head from close range.' Partridge didn't mince words.

Back to the jeep, Martin wanted to know what more Partridge had been able to find out about the woman.

'At the moment no one has any idea, they're working on it, they know her name is Annelise, that her husband was called Karl, some German name or other and that he was killed in Russia soon after Strasser had had him posted to Russia; she holds Strasser responsible for everything that happened. She was vindictive because her husband was involved in the accident when Strasser lost his hand and Strasser sent him to Russia as revenge.

'The escorts said she shouted "Iscariot, Iscariot" when she fired the bullets into Strasser, repeating Iscariot until she began to weep, then wept and wept, going on and on saying "vengeance at last".

'Hitler killed her husband, he didn't take on board that the war could never be won after he lost the 6th army at Stalingrad; she's got her revenge, but she's cheated me of mine.

'Do you all know why I've been so determined to get Strasser? It wasn't the bullet in the gut; it was him killing two men with bullets to the head at Menzenschwand POW camp, killing me by proxy. By rights one of those men was me.

'Eventually, between us, I tracked him down, but a German woman's beaten me to it and killed him. What did you say her name was?'

'Annelise.'

For the first and only time, Partridge saw Martin drink a bottle empty in the kübelwagen. 'I must tell Hillary I love her,' he said over and over again. It was Saturday; he was reeling as he disappeared with Hillary shouting back over his shoulder for Partridge to ask Annelise for tea as he'd like a word.

It was 36 hours before Martin re-emerged, Travers sat him down to give him the message.

'Barney sends his apologies, the German woman fired from low down, the bullets tracked two separate furrows up the side of Strasser's skull, which knocked him out. When the doctors got to him, he regained consciousness and they sent him to the hospital. This morning he wasn't there, tell Martin.'

Martin didn't say a word, getting up just as Hillary walked in through the double doors leading to the garden. 'Hillary!' he shouted, 'Hillary, **The Hunt for Colonel Strasser's back on!**'